Rebecca Chance is the pseudonym under which Lauren Henderson writes bonkbusters. Under her own name, she has written seven detective novels in her Sam Jones mystery series and three romantic comedies. Her non-fiction book *Jane Austen's Guide to Dating* has been optioned as a feature film, and her four-book young adult mystery series, published in the US, is Anthony-nominated. As Rebecca Chance, she has written the *Sunday Times* bestselling bonkbusters *Divas*, *Bad Girls*, *Bad Sisters*, *Killer Heels*, *Bad Angels*, *Killer Queens*, *Bad Brides*, *Mile High* and now *Killer Diamonds*, which feature her signature mix of social satire, racy sex and roller-coaster thriller plots. Rebecca also writes for many major publications, including the *Telegraph*, the *Guardian*, *Cosmopolitan* and *Grazia*.

Born in London, she has lived in Tuscany and New York, and she travels extensively to research glamorous locations for the books. She is now settled in London, where she lives with her husband. Her website is www.rebeccachance.co.uk. She has a devoted following on social media: you can find her on Facebook as Rebecca.Chance.Author, and on Twitter and Instagram as @MsRebeccaChance. Her interests include cocktail-drinking, men's gymnastics and the *Real Housewives* series.

By Rebecca Chance

Killer Diamonds

REBECCA CHANCE

PAN BOOKS

First published 2016 by Pan Books
an imprint of Pan Macmillan
20 New Wharf Road, London N1 9RR
Associated companies throughout the world
www.panmacmillan.com

ISBN 978-1-4472-8287-7

1 3 5 7 9 8 6 4 2

A CIP catalogue record for this book is available from the British Library.

Typeset in Minion Pro 11.5/15 pt by Palimpsest Book Production Limited, Falkirk, Stirlingshire
Printed and bound by CPI Group (UK) Ltd, Croydon, CR0 4YY

Visit **www.panmacmillan.com** to read more about all our books
and to buy them. You will also find features, author interviews and
news of any author events, and you can sign up for e-newsletters
so that you're always first to hear about our new releases.

This book is for two people, without whom it simply wouldn't have been authentic: Sally Morrison, whose information on how celebrity jewellery auctions work was invaluable. And David Rudlin, who knowledge about fine jewellery is encyclo-paedic, and whose willingness to have his brains picked was hugely generous. David is also the author of a very entertaining and original mystery series, which I thoroughly recommend!

Prologue

It was her own fault. She was forcing him to do this.

It was completely her own fault that he was about to murder her.

Even though she was sitting quite still, her hands folded in her lap, the four-carat diamonds in her ears were glittering, so large and impressive that they threw off prismatic shards of light with the slow rise and fall of her magnificent bosom. Her make-up was immaculate, her posture perfect. Vivienne Winter had been a film star since she was fourteen years old, and she was as used to being the cynosure of all eyes as a member of the royal family; she might be American, but her bearing was positively queenly. More diamonds glistened on her fingers, but as always, Vivienne's eyes drew more attention than any of her jewels. Larger and more extraordinary than any precious gem, instantly recognizable by most people on the planet: those almond-shaped, violet eyes.

Vivienne was seventy-three years old now, but her mere presence was still capable of making grown men babble and stammer as if they were star-struck, love-smitten teenagers. The man kneeling in front of her, however, was the only one in the world guaranteed not to succumb to her charms: her grandson, Angel, whom Vivienne had brought up since she had forced his mother, her daughter Pearl, to hand over custody of her son when he was just seven years old.

Angel had fully inherited the Winter beauty. At seven, he had been a positive Little Lord Fauntleroy, all golden curls, porcelain skin, full red lips, and features as angelic as his name. But although he had grown into an equally beautiful man, at this moment he was almost unrecognizable as the gorgeous playboy who was a staple of the gossip columns. His nose had been broken just an hour ago in a violent attack and the wound had barely clotted; gobs of bright red blood were smeared over his cheeks, and bruising was starting to form. There were rips in his clothes, and his eyes, the same extraordinary amethyst colour as his grandmother's, were wild above the smashed, gory mess that had until recently been a perfectly straight nose.

Angel's face was so damaged that only his eyes expressed the frenzy of his emotions: they looked almost demented, the pupils dilated. Vivienne had been his last hope. Angel had just burst into her apartment high above Hyde Park, pursued by the police forces of two separate countries. Throwing himself on his grandmother's mercy, Angel had begged her to save him. To his fury, Vivienne had remained reclining on the chaise longue in her boudoir, not even standing up to give him a hug, surveying him with a cool, wary gaze. And once he had blurted out the size and scale of the trouble he was in, she had categorically refused to throw him a lifeline.

Angel blamed his grandmother for absolutely every factor that had brought him to this crisis. Vivienne had callously snatched him from his doting mother, breaking her daughter's heart, positively forcing Pearl into the drug addiction that had taken her life. Vivienne had neglected Pearl as a child, choosing her career and her love affairs over her daughter's needs, and she had done exactly the same with her grandson. He was the product of her upbringing. If he had turned out spoilt, venal and selfish, so utterly self-obsessed that he was willing to commit murder in order to protect himself, surely – considered in the correct light – that was entirely Vivienne's doing?

She had made Angel into what he was, and now she was refusing to take responsibility for having ruined his life. He had been simultaneously overindulged and overlooked, given no moral compass at all, taught to assume he could have anything he wanted. Now she had pulled the rug out from under his feet in one terrible swoop, abandoning him when he needed her help, literally, to survive. She was forcing him to choose between saving himself and her, and that was not even a choice at all.

Angel would make it quick. He would show more mercy than she was doing – condemning him to a slow, horrible death, rotting away in a third-world jail. But killing her was now his only option. If Vivienne dropped dead – if people assumed that an old woman had suffered a heart attack at the sight of her grandson storming into her apartment, his nose smashed, the police hard on his heels, an unbelievable story of theft and murder pouring from his lips – then he would be her heir. The promise of a vast inheritance would give him access to the most expensive lawyers available to fight the charges against him, block any extradition attempts, maybe

even keep him out of jail completely . . . access that his grandmother had just refused to offer him, which meant that it was
all her fault that he was forced to murder her now . . . all her
bloody fault . . .

She's making me do this.

It was those words that were ringing in his head as he
leaned forward, grabbed one of the leopard velvet pillows
from the chaise longue and, gritting his teeth, shoved it into
his grandmother's face and held it there with grim determin-
ation, pressing it down as she struggled frantically for breath.

Chapter One

Rome, 1966

'Vivienne! Vivienne!'
 'Signorina Winter! *Di quu, ti prego!*'
 '*O, bella! Bellissima!*'
Vivienne Winter – Hermès scarf wrapped around her head, huge diamond earrings glittering in her lobes, a pastel mink stole slung over her shoulders and a shantung silk dress swinging around her hips as she moved down the Via Veneto, sashaying in the four inch Ferragamo heels that Fiamma, Salvatore's daughter, had designed for her just this year – smiled dazzlingly at all the waiting photographers who had followed her Cadillac on their Vespas from Cinecittà, the famous Roman film studios. Rolleiflex cameras were pointed at her in ranks, their flashes noisy and blinding against the dark Roman night.

What was it they were nicknamed now, these guys? Oh yes, *paparazzi*, after the Fellini film that had come out last year, *La Dolce Vita*, with the news photographer called Paparazzo who dashed around this very city snatching pictures of celebrities.

Vivienne had loved that film – apart from the part featuring that whore Anita Ekberg. Ugh, Anita had had no talent beyond getting her tits out and messing around in a fountain. And she'd known it. Anita had, to Vivienne's certain knowledge, staged a publicity stunt in the lobby of the Berkeley Hotel in London where her dress, already straining at the seams, split open very revealingly just as a photographer was set up and ready to capture the moment.

She's such a bloody tart. And I'm not just saying that because she cut me out with Tyrone Power. God, he was a gorgeous hunk of a man. If it hadn't been for Anita, that self-obsessed slut, I might have got to sample the goods before he died young . . . damn her . . .

Velvet ropes cordoned off the entrance to Gianni's, the nightclub where Vivienne was heading. Security guards hired by the production staff of *Nefertiti: Lady of Grace*, the film she was shooting at Cinecittà, were holding back the crowds that had clustered in the hope of catching a glimpse of the film star. Vivienne cast glorious smiles from side to side as she processed down the street.

She had deliberately had her chauffeured Cadillac drop her off a little way away so that she could make the most effective entrance possible. *Nefertiti* was a blockbuster Hollywood production with a gargantuan budget, and its publicists were determined to build up as much excitement as they could during its filming so that eager fans would swarm the box offices of cinemas round the world on its eventual release.

Their main strategy, of course, was to focus on the physical presence of Vivienne, its star. The film had been written specifically for her around the planned tagline: 'The Most Beautiful Woman on Earth Plays the Most Beautiful Woman of Ancient Times!'. Vivienne had not become the biggest star in the world by shunning press attention, and she had arrived fully prepared to dress gorgeously off set, to be photographed around Rome, visiting the Colosseum and the Vatican, posing on the Spanish Steps, visiting boutiques on the Via Condotti, wearing boldly patterned Pucci-print frocks and carrying Prada bags in tribute to the country in which she was temporarily residing. Her make-up was stylized to resemble an updated version of the bust of Nefertiti in the Berlin museum: high-arched, pencilled eyebrows, black eyeliner and strong red lips, hair drawn up and back. Revlon was planning an entire cosmetic collection to coincide with the release of the film.

However, Vivienne was not the only star in the cast. The writers had plotted the film around a completely invented love triangle. Nefertiti's husband, Akhenaten, was scripted as so obsessed by his quest – to abandon the Egyptian religious practice of worshipping multiple gods, and concentrate instead on a single deity, Aten, the sun god – that he neglected the needs of his wife. Despite having a raft of romantic titles bestowed on her – Lady of Grace, Sweet of Love, Great King's Wife, His Beloved – it would gradually become clear that although her husband might love Nefertiti romantically, he had no sexual interest in her.

Viewers, especially female ones, were meant to sympathize with her plight. What was she supposed to do, a wife who had to bear children to her husband to ensure the succession of the royal family, if her husband wouldn't make love to her? And naturally, a woman who looked like Vivienne couldn't be expected to remain celibate! The producers' hope was that by the time Nefertiti finally yielded to her passion and allowed herself to be literally swept off her feet by the dashing and muscular Commander-in-Chief of the Egyptian army, Horemheb, the entire cinema audience would exhale a loud, collective sigh of ecstatic relief.

Akhenaten was played by Alec Guinness, who was doing an excellent job of conveying the discreet suggestion of concealed homosexuality that was supposed to explain his lack of interest in his gorgeous bride. And as Horemheb, the love interest who would be assassinated by a jealous priest after having fathered several children with Nefertiti, the producers had cast Randon Cliffe, British stage star and heartthrob.

'*Dov'è Randon?*' the paparazzi called. '*Vivienne, dov'è il signor Cliffe?*'

Vivienne's smile didn't flicker for a moment. She threw her arms wide, palms up, pantomiming 'Who knows? I certainly don't!' as she reached the entrance to Gianni's. Swivelling on one heel, she posed for the press, one hand up on her mink throw, fingers splayed to show off the diamonds on the rings she wore over her satin gloves, the other blowing kisses to her fans.

'*Ti amo, Vivienne!*'

'*Vivienne, mi fai morire!*'

'*Vivienne, guardami un attimo, ti prego!*'

Fans and paparazzi alike screamed compliments at her, told her they loved her, begged her to look in their direction; Vivienne, with a last wave at them all, turned away, the bouncer already waiting on her pleasure, holding the door of the nightclub open. She swept inside, her manager following closely behind her. Gianni himself was there to greet her, kissing both her hands in the Italian style, immaculate as always in his tux. Behind him, the club was already full, cigarette smoke as dense as incense, the dance floor crammed with couples dancing to the jazz band, which was knocking out a vivid version of 'Stomping at the Savoy'. The women's jewellery, the cut-glass chandeliers, the gold lamé hangings that draped the bandstand, all gleamed through the smoke in the artfully dim lighting. Cutlery clinked against plates, glasses were raised in toasts, champagne corks popped; the laughter and chatter of Gianni's customers, the pounding of their heels on the sprung dance floor, was almost as loud as the busy din of the band.

But Gianni did not gesture to his most celebrated client of the evening to follow him through the crowds to the best table in the house. Instead, he took her arm and escorted her through the red-painted vestibule to a side passage, her manager on their heels, pushing open a door that led to a room in such complete contrast to the dark nightclub that Vivienne blinked, momentarily dazzled by the bright fluorescent light strips and the white surfaces. A swift murmur rose among the cooks and waiters at the sight of Vivienne Winter; it was like a wave of awareness as the news swept through the large group, heads turning, jaws dropping. Italian men are never slow to show their appreciation of a beautiful woman, and her appearance was swiftly greeted by loud sighs of '*Bellissima!*' and kissing noises as the men bunched their fingertips together and raised them to their lips, theatrically casting the kisses out towards Vivienne.

'*Zitti tutti!*' Gianni commanded, telling them all to be quiet as he guided Vivienne across the kitchen, white-jacketed chefs and black-jacketed waiters falling to each side, forming a human passageway through which Vivienne walked, casting those enchanting glances from side to side, the men pressing their hands to their hearts, pretending to faint at the sight of her beauty – which she, naturally, enjoyed tremendously. Pans of bubbling, basil-scented tomato sauce, clams steaming in white wine, garlic frying in olive oil, scented the kitchen deliciously; boiling pasta in salted water was overcooked, would have to be redone, but at that moment nothing was more important than paying this tribute to beauty.

At the far end, by the double loading doors, Vivienne's personal publicist waited, dapper in a sharkskin suit, checking his watch. He looked up as Vivienne walked regally towards him, his smile appreciative of how her presence managed to turn every occasion into a near-royal procession.

'Your chauffeur's waiting,' he said, backing up to one of the doors, holding it ajar with his body. The dark Italian night outside twinkled with neon lights; above, a yellow, three-quarter moon hung low in the sky. He held out a coat to her, a beige Burberry trench, but she brushed past him, ignoring it, turning instead to blow a kiss goodbye to the restaurant staff before she ran out into the alleyway.

Two waiters propped the doors open to watch, unreproved by Gianni, the nightclub owner. The rest of the kitchen staff crowded towards the doors, and there was a collective sigh of pleasure, a supremely Italian appreciation of romance, at the sight of Vivienne running towards a man sitting on a Vespa at the end of the narrow little back street. As he turned, hearing her footsteps on the cobbles, the light from a street lamp illuminated his face, and the watchers sighed again in recognition.

None of the Italians would have had the faintest idea who Randon Cliffe was until a month ago; his casting as Horemheb had precipitated him onto the world stage. Those craggy features and piercing blue eyes, that wild head of dark curls, were now intimately familiar to every casual reader of Italian newspapers and weekly gossip magazines. Wild speculation about an affair between him and Vivienne had been rife from their first day of shooting together, when reports had started to leak out from the set that their chemistry was off the charts.

'*É lui! Il Cliffe!*' breathed one of the cooks.

'*Madonna, quant'é fortunato!*' said another, and a general murmur of agreement concurred that Randon Cliffe was indeed a very, very lucky man.

Vivienne hitched up her skirt, swung one leg over the Vespa and wrapped her arms around Randon's waist, riding pillion. He revved the motor and the scooter roared off into the night, the staff of Gianni's, together with Vivienne's publicist and manager, watching until the Vespa disappeared round the corner. Moments later shouts rose from the Via Veneto, loud enough to be heard at the back of the building. Vivienne's distinctive appearance – the Hermès scarf wound around her head, the pale pink fur tippet over the black shantung silk dress – had been spotted, and the shouts were swiftly followed by more revving of Vespa and car engines as the paparazzi took off in hot pursuit.

'She wouldn't put on the coat,' the publicist said to the manager, shrugging. 'Typical.'

'Movie stars – they can never get enough attention,' the manager said, pulling a face. 'But he's had a head start, and the villa gatekeeper's waiting up for them. With luck, Randon'll make it back there before the paps catch up with them.'

He grinned.

'Anyway, both of them will have the time of their lives pretending they're in one of their own movies. It's pretty much the way they live the whole time – as if cameras were always on them.'

The manager was absolutely right. Randon was gunning the Vespa across the heart of Rome as if he were filming an action sequence, tearing around the Piazza di Porta San Giovanni, the scooter's engine buzzing so loudly and insistently that one understood why it was named after a wasp. Vivienne clung on tight and let herself be tilted from side to side, following Randon's lead, leaning into the curves where he did. He was driving like a maniac – the wind would have whipped her carefully set hairstyle to pieces if she hadn't tied her scarf so tightly – and she was loving every moment. His leather bomber jacket smelt wonderfully masculine; she was snuggled closely into him, her nose pressed into the knit collar that held the scent of his aftershave and of his body, so enticing that she felt her body responding.

Not long now, she thought, and shivered deliciously.

'Steady on!' Randon called back over his shoulder, even as he gunned the bike down Via Britannica. She heard the rumble of his laugh, knew that he was thinking just what she was; if the paps hadn't been chasing them, she would have reached round to stroke his penis through his jeans. She was willing to bet he was half-hard, at least; risk and danger were a huge turn-on for him, as she knew very well, and speed added to the mix was bound to increase his excitement.

They had been sneaking around on set for a fortnight. Their attraction to each other had been obvious from the moment they met, but Randon was married, and the producers of

Nefertiti were paranoid about any scandal on set, worried that it would cause Vivienne to be seen as a scarlet woman. She had never been America's sweetheart: her looks were too sultry, her figure too curvaceous, her gaze too come-hither. However, she had grown up in the public eye, and thus was beloved all over the world. Her fans felt that they knew her almost as well as if she were a member of their family.

This had enabled her to successfully surmount a potentially career-destroying scandal when she became pregnant out of wedlock a few years ago. Controversially, she had refused to get an abortion, conceal her pregnancy and give the baby up for adoption, or contract an arranged marriage and pretend the new husband was the father. Her publicists had wanted Vivienne to issue a public apology for her immoral behaviour, but she had categorically refused, declaring that she was a modern woman, would raise her daughter on her own like many other mothers, and that the public would understand and support her. To everyone's amazement but her own, she had emerged triumphant, far from the box-office poison her team had feared; the takings for her next film broke records.

But her notoriety had instantly put the *Nefertiti* producers on high alert once it became clear how violently she and Randon were attracted to each other. It could not have been more obvious: the Ancient Egyptian costumes were as authentic as possible, and one of the reasons for hiring Randon had been his muscular physique, which would be shown to great effect in the white linen kilt-style skirt that, together with big gold armlets and collar, he was required to wear for most of the film. The folds of the skirt, however, were not up to concealing Randon's instant reaction to Vivienne in her equally clinging white linen dress, and a production assistant had been specifically tasked (on what was instantly nicknamed 'Dick Watch' by the crew) to ensure that scenes weren't ruined by Randon sporting an erection.

Both stars had been taken aside by the producers and lectured severely about not yielding to temptation. The production was costing a fortune, and if Vivienne were to be perceived as not just an unwed mother but a homewrecker to boot – a Jezebel who had tempted a married man away from his wife – it might finally cause film fans to stay away in droves, refusing to reward her for bad behaviour. Publicists were assigned to each of them, dogging their heels to make sure they weren't in each other's dressing rooms or spending time together after work.

Vivienne and Randon had managed to sneak the occasional kiss and fumble so far, but today they had rendezvous'd in a prop cupboard for a few brief moments, during which Vivienne had fully realized how aroused Randon was by danger, the possibility of getting caught. He had been hard as a rock instantly, urgent and pressing, dragging up her skirt and almost inside her before she realized what was happening; it had taken more willpower than she had known she possessed to push him off, hissing desperately that they were bound to be heard fucking in a cupboard. God help her, she wanted him more than she'd ever wanted anyone; just thinking about that hot, stiff dick butting between her legs was making her wet now.

She shivered again, her hands clasping tightly together to stop them straying down below his waist. Her mouth found his neck, and she licked his skin, feeling his body jump at the caress.

'Stop it, woman,' he yelled, and his voice was wonderfully mellifluous even when it was whipped back through the night air. 'Do you want to get us killed?'

Behind them, she heard the paparazzi's scooters gaining ground, the sound of their engines ever nearer. Wildly as Randon was driving, the native Romans knew their city better than he did, and had chased their targets many times down these roads.

'Look back!' Randon called. 'How close are they?'

Still clinging on for dear life, Vivienne turned her head as much as she could. The headlights of the scooters were a dazzling mass of brightness, as if the cameras slung around their drivers' necks were flashing in unison. And then she heard something else, a deeper roar, a single light moving faster than the others, and she turned back and yelled in his ear:

'Close – and there's a motorbike!'

Randon swore, a long poetic stream of words, many of which Vivienne didn't even recognize. It was mostly Shakespearean in origin, but with some Christopher Marlowe and Ben Jonson in there too. Randon had made his name playing the major Elizabethan dramatic roles on stage, and he had absorbed a great deal of the vocabulary in the process.

'Hang on!' he yelled, even as the scooter rounded a sharp corner and shot down a short stretch of road. Vivienne screamed: Randon was racing so fast that it looked as if he were going to crash straight into the stone wall ahead of them that bordered the Parco degli Scipioni. They were very close to her rented villa on the Appian Way now, but with the motorbike gaining on them so fast she didn't think they would make it. Its lights hadn't yet shown behind them, but it was only seconds, surely, before it was right on their tail—

And then she knew why he'd told her to hang on, because the scooter tilted crazily; but not, as she'd expected, because Randon was dragging the handlebars round to the left, towards the historic gate of Porta San Sebastiano. Instead he was skewing a ninety-degree turn sharply to the right, almost scraping the wall: their elbows missed it by inches. The scooter skidded sideways, brakes screeching, tyres burning rubber so fiercely that Vivienne choked on its acrid smell as Randon gunned the accelerator again. Just seconds later, the brakes squealed again and the bike ripped into another sharp turn, left into a side lane that was an access track to the park. The Vespa shuddered to a halt, churning up gravel, barely a foot from the gate at the end. Randon cut the lights even before the wheels were completely still.

Vivienne felt as if she had been through a tumble wash cycle, bounced violently up and down and side to side; she was amazed that she was still in one piece. Her breath was coming in loud pants, her body draped like a limp rag against Randon's back, as if every one of her bones had been pounded into jelly. To the left, across the Parco degli Scipioni, they could hear the engines of their pursuers' bikes screeching around the sharp corners, heading to the villa, aiming to catch up with Randon and Vivienne in time to snatch some pictures of the couple as they waited for the groundskeeper to open the entrance gate.

And then the noise of the pursuit receded, silence fell,

and all she could hear was her own breathing and the night breeze stirring the leaves of the trees in the park.

'It worked, eh?' Randon said in delight, his deep voice rumbling through his ribcage; Vivienne could feel the reverberations. Her hands were still entwined in a death grip around him. 'I checked this out earlier, driving around waiting to pick you up. Recced the whole route, just in case. Impressed by my Roman driving skills?'

'I nearly fainted three times,' she managed to say; she didn't have the energy to lift her head. 'You're a maniac.'

'I drive like one, and I fuck like one,' he said, and he let go of the handlebars, kicked down the bike stand and grabbed her hands, pulling them down to his waist and below it, to the zip of his jeans, distended by his erection pushing up against it.

'I knew you'd be hard,' she said, laughing as he rubbed her palms over the hump. 'I just knew it.'

'I've never been so fucking hard,' he said.

She reached out, tried to unzip his jeans, but he was already doing it, ripping open his belt buckle, unpopping his waist button, tearing down the zip. As her gloved hands found him, she realized instantly that he wasn't wearing underwear.

'Oh my *God*,' she said as her satin-covered fingers closed around his big, smooth dick, its tip already moist with pre-come, and started to pump it. He *was* like rock. Her words had issued in a moan of delight, and he laughed again, deep and low.

'I can't believe it's taken us so long,' he said, groaning as she worked him. 'I've been wanking off so much I'm starting to grow hairs on my palms. Getting so close to you in that cupboard today and not being able to shove it up you was bloody murder.'

'Shove it up me? How elegant,' she said, executing a clever little double-handed twist to her palm action that sent all her lovers crazy.

'*Fuck . . .*' was all he could manage; that double twist had had its usual brain-paralysing effect.

And then he groaned, because she had let go, was climbing off the Vespa and onto the gravel path. She looked back down the little access drive, but it was pitch dark, no street-lights at all, and no cars passing; even if they did, the scooter was far enough down the drive to be invisible to traffic. Another vehicle would have to make the turn itself to spot them here. And she was as desperate as he was, as wet as he was hard. It was worth the risk.

She hitched her skirt around her waist with one hand and pushed his chest with the other.

'Scooch back,' she said, and he understood at once, shifting back on the saddle, shoving his legs forwards to brace himself, grabbing the saddle with his hands as she swung one leg up and over, managing to climb onto the bike, feet on the base plate. Like him, she had been prepared: she wasn't wearing any underwear, just her garter belt and stockings, which made it very easy indeed.

'Help me,' she said even more urgently, and his hands clamped round her waist, lifting her up with those big muscles that he'd told her airily he must have inherited from his docker ancestors, because he'd never exercised a day in his life. The air was cold on her wet crotch. One hand was clamped in the folds of her skirt, holding it up; the other reached down to find him, positioning herself, directing the tip just where she needed it so badly. With a push of her hips she drove herself right down onto him, all the way.

She had never done this before, especially on so big a dick. And though she'd known it would be intense, it hurt like hell even as she welcomed it in. It took everything she had, every inch of physical self-control she'd learned as an actor, to stop her from screaming her head off as it ploughed deep in her. Although she couldn't see his face, she heard the breath shoot out of him as if she'd punched him in the stomach.

'*God*, woman—' he managed.

She took a long breath, her inner muscles beginning to relax after the shock of impaling herself on him as she started to rock back and forth. She didn't have the traction to lift and lower herself; her feet were dangling on each side of the Vespa, her hands gripping his shoulders, and if she moved too much the scooter tipped and wobbled, even with his feet braced on the ground. But it was enough, it was so much more than enough. She needed to get used to the sheer size of him, the way he filled her so completely, and the rocking action felt extraordinary.

This time had to be fast and furious; the risk they were taking was gigantic. She leaned over, found his mouth, whispered against it:

'Do it quick and dirty, come on . . .'

Randon surged up immediately, his hips rising, his thighs slamming up and pushing that huge cock even further up her; she did scream now in mingled pain and pleasure as it smashed against her cervix. But he clamped his mouth on hers, drinking in her involuntary shriek even as she felt his cock swell inside her, impossibly large, as it started to judder with its release. The warmth of his sperm flooding her, so hot . . . and his tongue in her mouth was just as wet and hot. He was kissing her all the way through his orgasm, one hand behind the back of her head, holding her close to him. It was back to front, the fuck first and the kiss later, and it was simply amazing.

He was the first man ever to do that, keep on kissing her even after he'd got what he came for. In Vivienne's experience, men kissed you till they got to fuck you, and then they took you for granted, stopped bothering. She adored to kiss, could do it for hours, and even as his still-hard cock filled her, stretched her to her limit, he kept on kissing and kissing her, as urgent and passionate as if he hadn't just come. He tasted strongly of Italian brandy – Stravecchio, a cheap brand he'd found at a Roman bar and promptly insisted be stocked in his dressing room on set. It had been on his breath that afternoon when they had been fumbling in the prop cupboard; she was already coming to associate the taste with him. For the rest of her life, cheap Italian brandy would instantly evoke bittersweet memories of Randon kissing her.

His hands tangled in her hair, pushing back the scarf, his lips traced down to her neck; she tilted her head back, unable to believe the sensations that were flooding through her. His curls tickled her skin, and she wound her fingers through his hair, exulting at how springy it was, how thick. Everything about him delighted her. His mouth, his voice, his eyes, his cock, God, his *cock* . . .

Finally, he began to subside, detumescing, and Vivienne felt liquid seeping out where their bodies were joined.

'Do you have a hankie?' she managed to say into his curly hair. His head was at her bosom, kissing her décolletage, his hands cupping her breasts, and he burst out laughing against her bare skin.

'Do I *look* like a man who has a hankie?' he demanded, raising his head.

He put his hands to her throat, unfastening the tightly knotted silk scarf. Even as she began to object, he pulled off the scarf, shoved it down to where their crotches were joined, and started to blot his sperm up with it.

'What are you *doing*? That's Hermès!' she protested, though she undermined herself a little by starting to giggle at his sheer audacity.

'So what?' he said nonchalantly. 'You can afford another one! We can both afford a whole shopful! I'll take you out tomorrow and buy you whatever you want. There's bound to be a Hermès in Rome. We'll empty out the shop, and every single time I come inside you I'll wipe it up with one of 'em.'

His penis slid out of her, more sperm flooding onto the leather seat.

'Here, give that to me,' she said, taking the scarf.

Happiness welled up in her at the way he was assuming this wasn't just a one-night stand. She might be Vivienne Winter, sex symbol that every straight man and every gay woman wanted to sleep with, but it didn't stop her from having the normal, human insecurities. Rita Hayworth had said, at the height of her fame, 'They go to bed with Gilda but they wake up with me,' a poignant comment on the fact that men expected her to be exactly like the femme fatale she had famously played.

But Rita, despite her sex-symbol looks, was shy and intro-verted in person, while Vivienne was just as earthy and uninhibited as the lusty, seductive heroines she played. She wasn't afraid that men would be disappointed in her without the glamorous costumes, elaborate make-up and clever lines she was given on screen. No, her concern was that having had sex with her would be a supreme feather in the cap of any playboy, something he would be able to boast about for the rest of his life. She was wary of trophy hunters who were simply after a one-night stand and bragging rights.

She found herself raising the scarf to her nose to smell him. It was intoxicating; everything about him was intoxi-cating. She had to fight a sudden, powerful impulse to rub the scarf all over herself.

Oh my God, she thought. *Just one fuck and some funny banter and I'm really far gone. What the hell is this man doing to me?*

'We should be using condoms,' she said, shifting back to wipe herself, keeping her tone as matter-of-fact as she could, hopefully to disguise how fast and hard she was falling for him.

'I've got loads,' he said, still nonchalant. 'I'm going to be fucking you a lot. I came prepared. Wipe up as much as you can and then wad the scarf up where your knickers would be if you were ladylike enough to be wearing any.'

'You're a fine one to talk,' she said as he tilted his hips up, tucked his semen-wet penis into his jeans and zipped himself up again. 'My God, you can't wear those jeans again tomorrow, they'll be all crusty! We'll have to wash them tonight.'

'Just like a woman, fussing about the washing,' he said,

putting his hands around her waist and heaving her up, helping her climb off the bike. 'Stuff that rag up you so you don't leak all over the place and get back on behind me. Oh, and take that fur off and give it to me. I'll put it under the bike seat. Without that and the scarf, you just look like a bog-standard Italian girl out for a ride with her handsome stud.'

'*Bog-standard?*'

She slapped him across the cheek, not lightly. He didn't even flinch, just grinned at her. But then she followed instructions, unfastening the hooks of the tippet. He was quite right: without the distinctive scarf and the pale pink fur, her black dress was neutral enough not to draw attention, and her black hair made her look like a local.

'I'm going to ride around for twenty minutes or so,' he said, standing up to stow the mink away under the seat. 'Then we'll do a pass by the villa to check. They should all be gone by then – they'll think that we made it in before them, and they'll know I'll be too busy fucking your brains out to leave for hours. But we'll buzz by at a normal speed, just in case. If there's no one there we can loop back, nip into the villa and I can start fucking your brains out again.'

'God, you have a filthy mouth,' she said as she slid into place behind him on the Vespa. 'And I'll be fucking you too, you know. It goes both ways.'

'No,' he said, revving up the engine. 'I fuck you. I have the cock. That's how it works. And you haven't got the least idea of how filthy my mouth is yet.'

A while later, she had a better idea of what he'd meant. His arms were wrapped around her legs, strong muscles wedging them inexorably apart despite her struggles to break free; his face was buried between her thighs, his mouth working her to orgasm after orgasm. She needed, desperately, to stop, at least to have a break; her senses were completely overwhelmed, her clitoris so over-stimulated that it felt like a huge exposed nerve. She would have thought he would come up for air at some stage, but it must have been a quarter of an hour and he hadn't stopped. She had screamed so hard that her throat was hoarse. Shooting tomorrow would be murder; she would have to drink honey and lemon nonstop. He was absolutely relentless. Kicking and squirming was having no effect; he just tightened his grip and made her come yet again.

There was nothing for it. He had begged her to keep on the satin gloves, and now she reached down and buried her fingers in his hair. The fabric was slippery, but his curls were so springy that she managed to get a good grip on them even in the gloves, enough to drag his head away from her by force. He tried to shake her off, but she held on for dear life, her knuckles digging into his scalp, shrieking:

'Stop, stop! I can't take any more!'

His eyes were such a dazzling blue with triumph that they looked like the summer sky lit up by the noonday sun.

'I like to hear you scream,' he said complacently, finally loosing his clamp on her thighs and wiping his mouth on his forearm. Her muscles were aching, her hips sore from being held open for so long.

'You're a bastard,' she said as he climbed up the bed and pulled her into his arms. 'There isn't a part of me that doesn't hurt. My throat's wrecked and I must be bruised all over. And my pussy feels like you've burned it with a red-hot poker.'

'Excellent,' he said into her hair. 'So we'll have a bit of a sleep and do it all over again tomorrow morning, bright and early.'

'I *can't*,' Vivienne said. 'I have major internal bruising. That cock of yours isn't coming anywhere near me for twenty-four hours.'

'Oh, come on, at least give me a dawn blow job?' Randon said, sliding his thumb into her mouth. 'God knows you owe it to me after what I just did to you.'

She sucked his stubby thumb, running her tongue around the flat nail, tracing its outline, then clamping her lips down, exerting enough pressure to hear his breath catch.

'Yes, like that,' he said, his voice less than usually steady as he pulled his thumb out again. 'I have to admit, you fuck really well for an actress. They usually just lie there and think you should do all the work.'

'I fuck well for an actress! That's so sweet of you to say! You're such a gentleman,' she added with a considerable amount of irony, which, unsurprisingly, he completely ignored, exclaiming instead:

'Oh! Just remembered something.'

He let go of her, rolled over the wide bed, jumped to his feet and strode naked across the room to the pile of clothes they had literally torn off each other several hours ago. His penis bounced jauntily on its thick bed of curly dark hair; detumescent, it wasn't particularly large. He was definitely a grower, not a shower.

'Your jeans!' she said, suddenly remembering. 'I'm not having you walk out of here tomorrow looking like you came in your trousers. That would be mortifying.'

'I'll have a production assistant swing by my hotel and pick me up another pair,' he said casually. 'Actually, I'll have them pick up all my stuff and bring it here.'

Vivienne sat up, putting her hands on her bare hips.

'How dare you take me for granted?' she said indignantly.

'God knows how you won an Oscar,' Randon said, grimacing. 'That was the worst acting I've seen in a *long* time.'

'How *dare* you!' Vivienne grabbed one of the pillows and threw it at him.

'You could do with some new dialogue, too,' he said, catching the pillow with one hand; his other was rummaging in his jacket pocket. 'You're starting to repeat yourself. Here, I'll feed you the line. It's "thank you". Catch.'

He extracted a velvet-covered jewellery box and threw it onto the bed. It landed in a tangled knot of sweaty sheets. Vivienne leaned over to fish it out.

'Could you throw another pillow first?' he suggested hopefully. 'I liked the way your boobs wobbled when you did that.'

But she was flipping open the lid of the case and staring at its contents, mouth open.

'Still waiting for the thank you,' Randon said, jumping onto the bed again and sitting there cross-legged, watching her. He was solid and muscular, black hair dappling his forearms and shins, which he had refused to let them shave for *Nefertiti*.

It was decades before the fashion for men being visibly ripped and cut, or for being waxed; male actors' bodies were much more real. Neither Robert Mitchum, who had been a boxer, nor Burt Lancaster, an acrobat who had worked as a trapeze catcher in a circus, had six-packs or chiselled pectorals; their bodies had been honed through physical effort, not targeted gym work and the consumption of protein shakes. Randon would have roared with laughter at the idea that he should do sit-ups or cut down on his drinking during production of a film to tone up his physique; he had been reluctant enough to agree to let the make-up team darken his skin with brown-tinted oil every day, saying that if they'd wanted someone who looked like an Egyptian, they should have avoided casting the son of Irish-origin Liverpudlians.

'I don't know what to say,' Vivienne eventually managed. '*Randon* –'

She tore her eyes eventually, reluctantly, from the contents of the box. It was no secret that Vivienne adored fine jewellery, collected it as men did vintage cars or rare vinyl. Film producers knew to greet her, on her first day on set, with a present waiting in her dressing room, both a tribute to her diva status and an investment in her future good behaviour on set. There was no question that having been a film star for almost her entire life had made her spoilt and demanding, and the best way to handle her was to parcel out treats to her much as if she were still the child star she had once been.

A producer had once commented about Vivienne that he'd been told in rehab that addicts got stuck at the age they were when they had first become addicted; a thirty-five-year-old who had become addicted to heroin or booze at eighteen would never grow emotionally beyond the latter age unless they got clean and worked hard on themselves. As long as they stayed on the drug or the drink, they would only possess the impulse control and immaturity of an eighteen-year-old.

The producer had said drily that one could see, dealing with Vivienne, that some actors also seemed to remain at the same stage of emotional development as when they had hit the big time. For Vivienne, that was in her early teens, and she could certainly be as capricious and impulse-driven as a teenager whose brain had not yet fully developed. Her love for pretty, shiny things was certainly childish; as she stared in wonder at the diamond and emerald earrings glittering up at her from the blue velvet bed on which they lay, her magnificent eyes were as wide and enchanted as a little girl who had been given exactly what she wanted for Christmas.

'They're *incredible*,' she breathed, stroking one of the earrings with as much devout worship as if she had been a Catholic allowed to touch a holy relic. 'Oh my God, they must have cost an absolute *fortune!*'

'They bloody did!' Randon said cheerfully. 'Put them on, then – let me see what my money's bought me.'

The earrings were so big and heavy they needed a clip fastening, rather than being set for pierced ears. They looked like pendant drops taken from a chandelier, costume jewellery made for a theatre production. Each consisted of just three stones: from two cushion-cut three-carat collet-set diamonds, set above each other, depended drop-set six-carat diamonds. They were as big as pebbles and their weight, as Vivienne affixed them to her lobes, was equally heavy, but she did not flinch as the clips snapped tightly shut. Instead she lifted her chin for balance, looking positively regal.

'You look like a queen,' Randon said, his normal joking tone quite absent as he took in the spectacle of Vivienne, naked but for her gloves and earrings, sitting in the centre of the canopied Empire bed, her posture superb. She studied herself in the huge, gilt-framed mirror on the opposite wall, the earrings so large that they were clearly visible even across the room.

'The bottom stones come from an Indian Maharajah's turban,' he said. 'They were set on either side of the Timur Ruby.'

Vivienne turned to look at him with a smile as dazzling as the diamonds themselves.

'Maybe you'll buy me that next,' she said, her eyes alight with pleasure.

'If the Queen ever puts it up for sale, I'll be first in line!' he said, grinning.

'I didn't know you knew so much about fine gems,' she said, looking back at herself in the mirror again, hypnotized by the sight of herself in all her splendour. She raised her arms to lift her thick black hair up and back, coiling it on top of her head with her gloved hands, the movement lifting her breasts in a way that she knew was extremely flattering.

'I don't,' Randon said, shrugging. 'But I wanted to get you something really special to celebrate our first time. That's where I was last weekend – in London, going round jewellers.'

'I honestly don't know what to say,' she murmured, as he crawled across the bed towards her and wrapped his arms around her from behind, propping his head on her shoulder and staring at the mirror with an intensity equal to hers; two actors both as famous for their extreme good looks as for their acting skills, both at the height of their beauty, unashamedly relishing how good they looked together.

'I'm going to photograph you like this,' Randon said. 'That pose, with your hands on your head. I did an interview earlier this year where I talked about how much I love taking photos – God knows why, I must have been on the lash – and Kodak sent me its latest camera. It's amazing. I'm going to take a lot of nude shots of you so I can have plenty of wank material when you're not around.'

'God, you're so romantic! You want to do porn shots of me with my tits out?' Vivienne said, laughing, but secretly relishing the idea that Randon would be masturbating to her image.

'Of course! They'll never look better!' he pointed out. 'Don't you want to have them immortalized for posterity? That way, when you're old and droopy, you'll be able to look at my photos of you and say to yourself, "Okay, I'm a sad old bag now, but by God, I used to have the best tits in the world."'

'I am *never* going to be a sad old bag,' Vivienne said with hauteur.

'Still, these won't always be this firm,' Randon said, reaching around to cup one of her breasts, his chunky, spatulate fingers closing round it with great appreciation. 'Don't get many of these to the pound.'

'Jesus, you're vulgar,' she observed even as her body responded to his touch, her nipples hardening.

'You love every second,' he said, bending over to kiss her shoulder. 'No one's ever talked to you like this before, have they? It's bloody good for you, woman. You need it. You need to be shagged and insulted on a regular basis. It's a tough job, but someone's got to do it. Marry me. I'm brave enough to take it on.'

Vivienne's jaw dropped, her mouth sagging open. Seeing how unflattering this looked in the mirror, she snapped it shut again, turning to look at Randon directly; for something this important, simply talking to each other's reflections wasn't enough.

'I do *not* believe you just asked me to marry you after one fuck. You're a drunken madman,' she said with absolute conviction.

'Always have been,' he said, his eyes bright. 'Always will be. But by God, I don't lack for courage.'

'All right,' she said, and saw his eyes widen, his perpetual cocky attitude momentarily dropped.

'All right what?' he asked, and her full lips curved with delight at having successfully caught him off guard.

'All right, I'll marry you!' she said with superbly feigned nonchalance. 'If you're fool enough to offer, you might as well take your punishment. I'll make your life a living hell. Oh,' she added. 'And I expect an engagement ring that makes these –' she flicked the earrings – 'look like cheap trinkets.'

'Hold on!'

Randon unwrapped his arms from her, jumped from the bed and dashed from the room, his stocky body moving with the speed of a sprinter, his round buttocks rising and falling hypnotically. Five minutes later he returned, just as fast, with a bottle of champagne in one hand and two flutes in the other. Taking a running leap, he landed squarely in the middle of the bed, making the ancient frame rattle with the impact, chucking the champagne bottle at Vivienne.

'Who needs to sleep!' he said. 'Let's drink until we pass out, wake up and fuck our brains out to celebrate getting engaged!'

And that was precisely what they did.

Chapter Two

Seville, 1970

'Not like that! Jesus, woman, anyone would think you'd never fired a gun before!'

Randon Cliffe grabbed the derringer from his wife.

'Oh my God, you're such a bully!'

Vivienne Winter put her hands on her hips and glared at him. She was a little drunk, but only someone who knew her well would have realized it; her speech was barely slurred, her movements only fractionally impaired, and if the glint in her eyes was partly a result of the bottle of champagne she had drunk over dinner, it merely added to the sheer magnificence of her physical presence.

'Men and guns!' she continued, as Randon checked the safety on the derringer. 'It's just all penises with you, isn't it?'

'It's all penises with *you,*' Randon said, looking up and winking at her. Vivienne refused to be distracted.

'Give me back my gun!' she insisted. 'I need to practise! This is such a crucial scene – it opens the play—'

'Don't hold it like it's a separate thing,' Randon said, handing it back to her. 'Feel as if it's an extension of your own body.'

'But she hasn't used it before,' Vivienne said. 'I wanted to show that.'

'How do you know? She might have been taking pot-shots at mongooses in Malaya for years!'

Randon paused, his blue eyes opening owlishly wide as a thought hit him; he had been nipping at Spanish brandy all day even before cocktails and wine with dinner, and although his tolerance was by now legendary through the length and breadth of the film and theatre worlds, that meant that he was rarely – if ever – completely sober.

'Is it mongooses?' he mused, momentarily derailed, his previous thundering tone dropped as he moved effortlessly into his best university professor impression. 'Or *mongeese*? Surely the laws of grammar should suggest the latter? What would the collective noun for them be, I wonder? A killing of mongeese? A *bite* of mongeese?'

'Oh, shut up,' Vivienne said. 'You're drunk. And you're making no sense. No one would want to take a shot at one! People *like* mongooses, because they kill snakes.'

Although she was making a good point, her voice had wavered, just faintly, over the word 'mongooses', and Randon pounced on it.

'You don't know either!' he said triumphantly. 'It *should* be mongeese, don't you think? Logically, it definitely makes the most sense!'

Vivienne turned on her heel, tossing her hair to make it clear that she was ignoring him completely, and swept from the room. Randon threw himself onto the sofa behind him and waited. They were staying in a rented mansion in Seville for the duration of their latest film shoot, a romance set during the Napoleonic Wars: Vivienne was playing a Spanish peasant girl called Conchita who fell in love with Randon, a British rifleman seconded to the guerrillas trying to harry Napoleon out of their country.

However, immediately after *In Love and War* wrapped, she was headed to New York and a tight rehearsal schedule for her Broadway debut as the anti-heroine of Somerset Maugham's play *The Letter*. Set in Malaya in the 1920s, it opened with a very dramatic scene: as the curtain rises on the veranda of a colonial house on a rubber plantation in the jungle, a gunshot rings out. A wounded man staggers out of the house onto the veranda, followed by a woman with a revolver in her hand. As he tries to escape, she fires again and again, advancing mercilessly; he collapses to the ground and she stands over him, emptying the gun into his body.

It had to capture the audience's attention from the first moment. They had, absolutely, to believe that they were watching a murder.

The click of a gun signalled that Vivienne had started the scene. She timed it perfectly, allowing her invisible target to react and stumble into the room, clutching his stomach, before she appeared. Although she was wearing jeans and a silk blouse, her thick black hair loose and tumbling around her shoulders, she walked now as if she were wearing a 1920s evening dress, tightly fitted in the fashion of the period, forcing her steps to be short and clipped. She held the derringer in both hands, much less tightly now, with a flexibility to her wrists, and Randon nodded in approval; that was what he had meant by telling her to think of it as part of her body.

She fired again, twice, and her eyes narrowed as she watched the invisible man fall to the ground, close to her feet. She made a gesture, as if sweeping something away from her legs, and then she raised both hands again, holding the gun, and fired down, three more times, a pause between each one, her expression icy, making it crystal clear that her intent was to kill him. And then slowly, a look of horror filled her eyes, as she realized the full impact of what she had just done.

Randon left several beats before rewarding her performance with loud and enthusiastic applause. She threw back her hair, flashing a smile, Vivienne again.

'*Much* better, wasn't it?' she demanded. 'I gave myself the shivers!'

'Apart from that thingywhatsit you did with your hand,' Randon said, imitating the gesture. 'What the fuck was that about?'

'My skirt! I wanted to show how disgusted I am with him. I can't bear anything I'm wearing to touch him.'

'Much too busy,' Randon said dismissively. 'Cut it out.'

'I shall see what my director says,' she snapped. 'I rather like it. I think it's very feminine.'

'He'll tell you to cut it out too,' Randon said, reclining back on the sofa and propping a pillow behind his head. 'You might as well listen to me and save yourself the humiliation. Take some advice from someone who's actually trodden the boards.'

'Oh, shut up! If I have to hear one more time about you *playing Macbeth at the National Theatre . . .*'

Vivienne mimicked Randon's British accent perfectly, sticking her nose in the air as she did so.

'You Brits are the worst snobs about the *theer-ter*!' she continued, nailing the 1920s pronunciation she would be using for *The Letter*. 'You think you *own* it! It's not like we don't have tons of good playwrights in the States—'

It was Randon's turn to ignore what she was saying.

'That accent isn't half bad,' he observed. 'Much better than the Spanish one you're currently hawking up from the back of your throat. You sound like you're about to gob up phlegm most of the time. I think you're actually getting worse the longer you do it.'

'It's really hard to use my diaphragm properly with that corset! And at least it's not as bad as that fake Texas drawl you did for *Rattlesnake Ridge*!' Vivienne snapped, putting the derringer down on a side table. 'You sounded ridiculous! "Sheriff, Ah'm bound to tell yah, stand aside or Ah'll have to let mah trusty Colt do the talkin' for me . . ."'

Her imitation of Randon in one of his rare failures was unfortunately much too accurate. *Rattlesnake Ridge*, his recent Western, had been a total flop, the dialogue just as cheesy as Vivienne's parody, and Randon's accent had been widely mocked. Everyone had advised him against it; that genre of film was considered old-fashioned, and the script was weak. But Randon had always wanted to play a cowboy, and had refused to be dissuaded.

'*I did not sound like that!*' Flicked to the raw, Randon sat up straight, his blue eyes blazing with fury, grabbing for the brandy bottle on the floor by the sofa and refilling the glass beside it.

'Just because your Spanish accent sounds like you have six angry dwarfs trapped in your windpipe arguing with each other,' he continued, after a long slug of his spirit of choice, 'there's no need to be so vicious! And you need the corset, woman, with all that paella you stuff down every night! They're keeping your waist the same size for the costume, but there's more of you coming out top and bottom every day!'

'Fuck you!' Vivienne screamed. 'It's so unfair! I hate how men can eat whatever they want! You're stuffing your face too, but you get to wear a uniform, which is the most flattering thing of all – you don't have to show off a twenty-six-inch waist in every bloody shot—'

'Oh, don't worry, darling,' Randon said with a syrupy tone of fake reassurance, setting down the glass. 'The twenty-six-inch waist may be a lost cause, but no one will be looking anywhere but at those increasingly huge tits ballooning out of the top of your blouse. I can't believe your character's supposed to be seventeen, by the way. Great boobs for your age, but—'

'*Fuck you!* My God, I need to get actual bullets for this gun!'

She grabbed it and pointed it at Randon; he immediately reacted, jumping up from the sofa, throwing his arms wide in surrender. Vivienne pressed the trigger anyway, the empty chamber clicking, and he clutched his chest with an expression of horrified surprise on his face, his blue eyes wide. Vivienne fired again, and he staggered back, the imaginary impact taking him into the arm of the sofa; another shot, and he was thrown right over the arm, his legs flying up, his body crumpling behind the sofa.

'Ow,' came his voice. 'Tiled floors. Bloody Spain. Forgot there wasn't a rug back there.'

'Serves you right for being such a show-off,' Vivienne said, putting down the gun again. 'No one made you do anything so scene-stealing. You could just have died on the sofa like a normal person.'

'I'm not a normal person,' Randon said, unmoving. 'Come and help me up, woman. It's the least you can do after having shot me down like a dog.'

Vivienne's heels clicked across the terracotta floor as she strode briskly around the sofa; her husband was lying there, rubbing the shoulder on which he had landed in his twisting back somersault fall.

'You're going to need to kiss this better,' he said.

'Kiss my ass,' she retorted.

'Language!'

Randon reached out, grabbed her ankle, and pulled her ruthlessly downwards; she screamed, tried to clutch the edge of the sofa, but ended up sprawling on top of him, his legs coming round hers to hold her down.

'I may have been a bit harsh about your tits,' he said, starting to unbutton her blouse. 'Let's have another look.'

'Randon, for God's sake – we're in the middle of the living room, anyone might come in – you're too drunk to realize.'

'Oh, come on, give me a quick look! We're married, for fuck's sake. If I can't grope my wife's tits when I want to, why the hell did I bother to put a ring the size of a tangerine on your finger?'

He had her blouse open, was squeezing her breasts now in just the way he knew she loved, his thumbs circling her nipples through the lace of her bra.

'Just a quick feel . . .' he crooned in the deep, sexy tones that had legions of women around the world swooning. 'Mmm, so good . . . real proper handfuls, ripe and juicy . . .'

Vivienne's eyes were rolling up into her head with pleasure. Randon had been doing all his own stunts for the film, dragging ox carts, packing rifles with gunpowder, and his palms were deliciously callused. Previous lovers had made the mistake of treating Vivienne Winter as if she were made of porcelain as delicate as her skin. She had been so famous for so long that it was hard for them to believe they were truly having sex with her, and most of them had consequently felt the need to comment on it repeatedly in near-worshipful tones. Unfortunately for them, Vivienne had no interest in soft caresses or endless compliments, and even less in men telling her over and over again how lucky they felt to have her in their arms.

There had been a few types who had tried the opposite approach, coming on too rough once they were alone with her to show that they weren't intimidated by her fame. Vivienne had once had to break a vase over the head of a fellow actor who had seemed to think that it was okay to grip her arms hard enough to leave bruises when they were just kissing. God knew what he would have done in bed! So, as soon as he'd let her go so he could undo his jeans – apparently he considered that he'd performed sufficient foreplay by shoving his tongue down her throat and marking her arms so badly they would have to use heavy body make-up on her for days – she had writhed away, snatched the vase and crowned him with it.

And he hadn't been the only one. There was something about the prospect of fucking Vivienne Winter, the film star who had been a sex symbol since her mid-teens, that drove men literally crazy; alone with her, they seemed to turn into completely different people, slavering beasts or humble slaves.

Randon, blissfully, was a rare exception. He was always himself, vulgar and unrestrained, intimidated by not a single person in the world, and in bed he treated Vivienne with happy, uninhibited lust. Right now, the way he was groping her breasts was perfect, his touch just rough enough without manhandling her as if she were a piece of meat.

Like Goldilocks with the porridge, she thought unexpectedly, her head swimming with the champagne she had drunk earlier. *Not too cold, not too hot, just right . . .*

She started to giggle tipsily.

'What? Why the hell are you *laughing*?'

Randon sat up, wrapped his arms around her waist and flipped the two of them over so that she was underneath, the tile chilly on her back. He propped himself on his elbows, frowning at her comically.

'Why is it *funny* suddenly when I'm touching your tits?' he demanded.

'I was thinking that you're like the porridge,' she said, still giggling. 'Goldilocks' porridge.'

'*What?*' Randon's frown of confusion deepened.

'Mummy?' a plaintive, piping voice cut in. 'Mummy, why doesn't the gun go bang? Mummy, where are you?'

Staring into each other's eyes, caught up as they were in their very intimate and particular world, it took Randon and Vivienne a long drawn-out moment to realize that Vivienne's daughter, seven-year-old Pearl, was in the room. To their horror, in the silence that followed, they heard the clicking sound of the derringer's trigger being pulled again and again.

'Pearl! Put that down!'

Vivienne wriggled frantically from under Randon, dragged her blouse closed and climbed to her feet, running around the sofa to her daughter. With her blonde mop of curls and angelic face, dressed in a white embroidered nightdress that tied with big bows at her shoulders, Pearl looked like Shirley Temple, which made the pearl-handled revolver in her small hands even more incongruous. She was diligently pressing the trigger with her forefingers, presumably trying to make it go bang.

'Put the gun *down*!' Vivienne screamed. 'Jesus, what are you *doing*? You're supposed to be in bed by now!'

Pearl dropped the derringer and burst into tears, the big purple eyes filling up immediately. However, Vivienne too could cry on demand, and, knowing that, she always took the sight of her daughter in tears with a pinch of salt.

'Maria!' she bellowed into the hallway. 'Get down here and take my daughter back to bed, *now*!'

Almost immediately the local maid who was tasked with looking after Pearl could be heard running down the central staircase of the villa and into the living room.

'What the *hell* is she doing up?' Vivienne demanded, as Pearl bawled even harder. 'She was playing with my gun, for God's sake! She could have killed herself!'

'I'm so sorry, Mees Winter . . .' Maria babbled. 'I theenk she is in bed with her dolls . . .'

Randon, who had been waiting for his erection to subside, was on his feet now, striding towards the little group, bending down to pick Pearl up.

'Come on, little Pearl, stop crying,' he said, bouncing her

up and down. 'You mustn't play with guns, you know! Mummy's quite right about that.'

'I just wanted to make it go bang!' Pearl sobbed.

'It's *way* past your bedtime!' Vivienne said furiously. 'You shouldn't be down here!'

'But I just wanted to see you, Mummy!' Pearl said, opening her eyes wide and putting on her best cute expression.

'Sneaking to the kitchen for some more cake, more like,' Vivienne said, with a total lack of sympathy. Pearl's eyes flashed as she shot daggers at her mother, so cross she completely forgot that she was supposed to be upset.

'Ooh, she got you!' Randon crowed cheerfully. 'And you look just like your mummy when you get angry, Pearl – it's very funny. Here, off you go to Maria like a good girl. Children should be neither seen nor heard after seven o'clock.'

'I never see Mummy at *all*,' Pearl said sulkily. 'It doesn't matter what time it is.'

Randon grimaced at the truth of this.

'After this film, Mummy will be in a play and you'll see her much more,' he said consolingly. 'She'll be at work in the evening and free to play with you all day.'

It was Vivienne's turn to pull a face.

'With two matinees and six evening shows?' she said. 'I'm going to need a *lot* of rest, you know.'

'Well, you'll have more time with Mummy than you do now,' Randon said to Pearl. 'You can wake her up every morning to say hello!'

Pearl brightened visibly; Vivienne shot Randon a dagger-look of fury. She was famous for sleeping in late whenever she could, to the point that filming schedules were adjusted to fit her requirements for as few early starts as possible.

He plopped Pearl back on the ground and nodded at Maria.

'I'll kiss you goodnight now,' Vivienne said.

'No! Mummy, I want you to kiss me in bed!' Pearl wailed.

'Then you should have waited there like a good girl!' her mother said, conveniently ignoring the fact that she had completely forgotten to go upstairs and kiss her daughter goodnight. 'You're lucky you're getting a kiss at all! Here.'

She bent down and dropped a brief kiss on the top of her daughter's head.

'Off you go,' she said, nodding at Maria.

'No! No! I want a proper kiss in my own bed! *No!*'

Pearl started sobbing again as Maria obediently took her hand and pulled her from the room, big hopeless cries that echoed all the way around the hallway, bouncing off the tiled floors, the terracotta staircase, the white-painted stone walls of the villa.

'Mummy! Mummy! *Mummy!*' she wailed. 'Mummy, I want you!'

'God, she's such a little drama queen!' Vivienne said, turning back to Randon, who was picking up the brandy bottle and refilling his glass.

'God knows where she gets it from,' he observed, straight-faced, tossing down the brandy and setting down the glass.

Vivienne executed a big, stage-fighting slap on the side of his face; he pretended to take it with a flinch, then doubled back to grab her round the waist.

'Where were we before we were interrupted?' he said, his hands sliding up to her breasts.

'Mmm, there,' she said, closing her eyes in pleasure. 'Exactly there. God, yes . . .'

'Here's the thing,' Randon said, kissing her shoulder, his brandy breath hot against her skin. 'I don't want to take my hands away. It's like they're glued here now. But we can't go upstairs with me groping your tits, not with Pearl on the loose . . . and we can't fuck in here either, as you boringly pointed out . . . So I'm thinking, what about a quickie in the study? That's only got one door. I can shove the desk or something in front of it. And then I can get your tits out and apologize to them.'

'What, with your penis?'

This was supposed to be sarcastic, but Randon chose to take it completely seriously.

'Great idea!' he said, still kissing her neck. 'I'll come on your tits. They always love that. It's the highest compliment a man can give . . .'

'God, you talk such rubbish, such absolute drunken *bullshit*—'

'You love it,' Randon said complacently. 'You love my drunken bullshit, and you love me. And I'll love you till the day I die, you colossal drama queen. Right, first I'm going to bend you over the study desk and fuck your champagne-soaked brains out. And then you can tell me why the hell you said I was like *porridge*, you crazy bitch!'

Chapter Three

Paris, 1990

It was an unusually warm spring morning, and both the beautiful young mother and her lovely little son were damp with sweat after a long walk across the Luxembourg Gardens and through the sixth arrondissement to the *hôtel particulier* whose doorbell, framed by elaborate metal curlicues, the former had just rung. The little boy's small hand was slick with perspiration, slipping from his mother's. She gathered it up in a firmer grip as a security camera attached to the high stone wall swivelled, fixing them with its lens, and a voice issued from the intercom beside the bell she had just pushed, discreetly labelled on a polished plaque: *Hôtel Delancourt de Saint-André*.

'Miss Pearl?' a male voice said tinnily.

'Yes! Baxter, I'm here with Angel!' the young woman said eagerly. 'We've come to see Mummy!'

There was a pause, lasting several seconds, before the male voice responded.

'Madame said nothing to me about a visit, Miss Pearl.'

'Well, she must have forgotten,' her daughter said sharply.

'I'm afraid that Madame is not at home at the moment, Miss Pearl,' the voice replied. 'She had a costume fitting this morning with Monsieur Lacroix and is not expected back till after lunchtime.'

This news seemed to come as no surprise at all to Madame's daughter.

'Well, buzz us in and we'll wait for her!' she instructed. 'We just flew in from London – we got the bus from the airport, but we've been walking *forever* from the stop, Angel's exhausted and thirsty and he needs a wee—'

'*Mummy!*' the boy objected in embarrassment.

It sounded as if Baxter had heaved a sigh, but possibly that was the hinge of the automated iron gate beginning to swing open. Pearl heaved a sigh of her own, but hers was of sheer relief. Clutching her son's hand, she darted into the entrance courtyard even before the gate was fully open, as if worried that Baxter would change his mind and start to close it again. She was making for the entrance across the courtyard, framed imposingly by double stone columns, but the little boy called Angel stopped, looking around him, his amethyst eyes wide with wonder.

'Does Granny Viv live in a hotel all by herself, Mummy?' he said in awe. 'When I grow up, I want a hotel all to myself as well. And then I can stay in all the rooms till I pick the one I like best.'

'*Hôtel*'s just what the posh houses are called in France,' Pearl said airily, dragging him into movement again.

Pearl's mother had done her best to secure her daughter the best of educations at a variety of very expensive schools – and then private tutors, when each school in turn had regretfully declined, despite her mother's celebrity and Pearl's considerable intelligence, the continued privilege of having

Pearl as a student. While Pearl might not have passed any exams, she had learned everything she considered necessary, including the ability to speak French and Italian – or at least, all the words relating to the high life.

'Wow,' Angel said in awe, swivelling around the *cour d'honneur* to take in the golden stone walls and soaring windows. The Hôtel Delancourt de Saint-André, which his grandmother was renting as her private residence while she shot a film in France, had been built in the eighteenth century for the Marquise de Delancourt, a famous society hostess whose weekly salons had hosted the wits and writers Madame de Sévigné, Corneille, Richelieu and La Rochefoucauld.

As Pearl had told her son, in French a *hôtel particulier* was the town house of an aristocrat, an imposing detached building that was always constructed *entre cour et jardin*, between the entrance court and the garden behind. Two high storeys rose around Pearl and Angel, topped by a mansard roof; the entrance door, which was now swinging open, was a good nine feet tall, carved elaborately with the crest of the Delancourts.

'Hello, Baxter,' Pearl said, pegging her chin high and sailing past the butler, who was holding the door open with a hand gloved in perfectly pristine white. The accent in which Pearl had been talking to her son had been more London-inflected, but when addressing Baxter, she sounded like a visiting English duchess about to socialize with the Marquise de Delancourt at one of her salons.

'Miss Pearl, Master Angel,' Baxter said, greeting them with a deferential nod even as he closed the heavy door. 'Welcome to Paris. I wasn't aware that you were planning to visit the city . . .'

He let this observation tail off enough to hint at a question, which Pearl completely ignored.

'Well, we are,' she said briskly. 'And it's hotter than we expected.'

She raised her free hand to push her hair back from her damp forehead. Grunge might be the current rage in London, where Pearl and Angel lived, but Pearl affected a 1970s boho princess throwback style. Her shoulder-length fair hair tumbled in loose tangles around her pretty face, which was nearly bare of make-up; all she wore was mascara, eyebrow pencil and pink-tinted Carmex lip balm. Her long-sleeved vintage blouse was white-on-white embroidered voile, falling off one skinny pale shoulder, and her jeans were faded and ripped.

Little Angel was dressed in a stripy T-shirt and cargo trousers, his tousled white-blond curls and big violet eyes making him a miniature version of his mother; they were an enchanting pair, and had turned many heads on their journey from London. The butler, in fact, was the first person they had encountered who seemed entirely unaffected by their picture-perfect good looks.

'Master Angel would like to use the facilities, I understand,' Baxter said politely. 'If you would like to follow me into the Gold Salon? And maybe you would both like some freshly squeezed juice? An *orange* or *citron pressé*? You always used to like *citron pressé* as a little girl, Miss Pearl.'

'What's that, Mummy?' Angel began, but Pearl was already pulling him across the black and white tiled grand hall towards the gilt-balustraded central staircase.

'Thank you, Baxter. Please set drinks up for us in the Gold Salon while we wait for Mummy to come back,' she said airily. 'White wine for me, and something to eat. Angel is terribly fussy about where he goes, though, so I'll take him up to Mummy's private loo. He'll be much more comfortable there.'

'*Mummy!*'

Angel writhed in embarrassment, but Pearl's grip on his small sweaty fingers was like a vice now, and even as he tried to say 'I want a juice, I'm thirsty! I don't need to—' she was squeezing his hand painfully to indicate that he had no choice but to follow her up the stairs, and hissing 'Sssh!' at him.

Baxter, a meticulously dressed man in his fifties, watched his employer's daughter and grandson trip lightly up the red-carpeted stairs, his forehead creasing. This was the maximum facial expression he ever allowed himself when on duty.

Turning on the heels of his immaculately polished black shoes, the butler walked across the hall, under the soaring sweep of the staircase. He was heading for the kitchen, where he would instruct the chef to prepare a selection of freshly squeezed juice, chilled Sancerre for Miss Pearl, which he knew to be her preferred white wine, and a selection of pastries, sandwiches, fruit and macaroons light enough to appeal to Pearl but substantial enough to satisfy a hungry seven-year-old who had doubtless worked up a considerable appetite.

But he paused before he reached the baize doors that led to the servants' area, stopping by the exquisite Chippendale side table. On it sat a Sèvres porcelain vase containing an arrangement of fragrant white and pink hyacinths, and a console phone with enough buttons running down the side of the keypad to be suitable for a company with at least twenty employees.

Raising the handset, Baxter touched one of the pre-programmed buttons with the tip of a white-gloved finger, waited for the person he was dialling to answer, and then began to speak in low, swift-paced tones.

Although Angel had not yet visited the Delancourt *hôtel particulier*, Pearl had been here a fortnight ago, on a visit to her mother that had not gone according to plan. Hence the return trip, with her adorable son in tow. And now that she had recced the mansion thoroughly, she knew how to find her mother's suite of rooms with no delay.

She was almost running as she reached the top of the staircase. The landing debouched onto a corridor on one side and, on the other, a long gallery spanning the entire length of the central wing, its tall windows looking over the elegant square of the *cour d'honneur* below. The back wall of the gallery was hung with dark red brocade, almost completely covered by gold-framed paintings. This was the Delancourt art collection, amassed over centuries: a mixture of landscapes, still lifes and family portraits, such beautiful images that the precocious Angel immediately said:

'Mummy, I don't need to wee! I want to look at the pictures.'

'Lovely, darling,' Pearl said without a break in her stride as she relentlessly swept the two of them along the landing to the corridor that led to the right-hand wing of the mansion. 'You can look at the art all you want later and say clever things about it. Granny Viv will *adore* that.'

'But I want to—'

'Angel, *be quiet* and do what Mummy tells you!' Pearl snapped. 'Don't make me angry! You know you don't like it when I get angry!'

There was enough harshness in her voice to silence Angel instantly. His big eyes widened and he pressed his lips together so tightly that the skin around them went white.

Unerringly, Pearl headed for the door that led to her mother's suite of rooms, pulling Angel through and shutting it behind them, moving fast across a sitting room tastefully appointed with silk-covered sofas and armchairs, occasional tables with vases of hyacinths and narcissi, and coffee tables laden with the latest issues of every glossy magazine imaginable.

Off the sitting room lay a corner bedroom, its windows facing south and east to give a view of the carefully tended back garden, an example of what the cleverest landscape artist could achieve in a small city space with its decorative topiary, low hedge-lined paths and central fountain. The bedroom itself was fit for a queen – or a major movie star – with its magnificent bed framed by pale pink silk curtains that tumbled dramatically from a carved and painted wooden tester fixed to the high ceiling, held back on either side by thick silk cords looped around the large posts at the head of the bed.

'Ooh!'

Unable to resist, Angel pulled his hand free from his mother's and raced across the room, throwing himself face down onto the velvet coverlet. His small body landed on deliciously yielding layers, and he exhaled in pure happiness at the sheer comfort, relishing the texture of the soft velvet against his even softer, more velvety cheek.

'Take your shoes off and don't jump on the mattress,' Pearl said over her shoulder even as she dashed across the Persian rug, hand-tied in shades of pale blue and pink silk; the window shutters were only half open to protect the priceless carpet from fading with the sunshine, just as the upper blinds in the art gallery were lowered to protect the paintings.

Angel was exhausted from having gone to bed way past his bedtime the night before. That was not unusual. Pearl's household was so chaotic that the whole concept of a regular bedtime for her small son had never been enforced apart from by the occasional boyfriend who had more of a conscience than Angel's own mother. This had happened only very occasionally: none of Pearl's boyfriends lasted long, but the ones who cared about the welfare of Pearl's son, and thus embarrassed her by showing up her lack of maternal instinct, were of particularly short duration.

Pearl was a classic narcissist who viewed her child not as a separate human being but an extension of herself. Any suggestion that Angel's needs were not only different from her own, but should be privileged above hers, was met with so much resentment and hostility that anyone trying to convince her of it was promptly ejected from her life.

That morning, heedless of the fact that her son had been running wild around her house until late into the evening, and had finally fallen asleep curled up on one of the living room rugs at eleven before waking up a couple of hours later and groggily staggering upstairs to his bed, Pearl had shaken him awake at six, telling him brusquely to get up and dressed.

Angel knew better than to complain or protest. It only made Pearl even meaner.

He had managed to grab a bowlful of Cheerios, and there had even been some milk in the fridge to pour over them. That was quite a luxury, so the day hadn't actually started *that* terribly, and he'd had more luck when Pearl kept changing her top, so he'd had enough time to almost finish his food, which was never guaranteed when she was in a hurry. By the time she'd come tearing downstairs and yelled at him to get his shoes on, his tummy had stopped grumbling too loudly, and he had enough sugar energy to keep up as she dragged him across London to Heathrow.

Mummy refused to get him anything to eat at the airport, saying she'd spent everything on the plane tickets, but at least there was free food on the plane. The stewardesses fussed over him, bringing him extra croissants and jam with lots of cold milk, and he'd gone for a wee all by himself when the pilot said it was the last chance before landing, while Mummy was sleeping. She'd been very pleased with him when she woke up and he told her he'd gone to the loo already, and promised him that he would have lots to eat and drink at Granny Viv's, plus a nap too if he wanted. Angel had said crossly that he was seven now, and naps were for babies; but actually, now he was happily collapsed on the cosy bed in Granny Viv's pretty shaded room, a nap sounded perfect . . .

His stomach was rumbling again, but his mother's word was law: he wouldn't be able to go downstairs and have the orange *pressé* juice drink or anything to eat until Mummy said they could. He thought that later on, he would use a loo on the ground floor in front of the man, to show him that Mummy had just been joking when she said he was fussy. He was a big boy now. He wasn't scared about being in a strange bathroom by himself *and* he knew not to wee on the seat, although he did have to be reminded to wash his hands.

But right now, he had to be with Mummy up here for some reason, and there was no point asking why because she'd just get cross again. So Angel's golden eyelashes flickered down to his cheeks, and a sigh of relaxation turned almost immediately into a muffled little snore.

Pearl was oblivious to the fact that her son had passed out on the tester bed with his little trainers still laced snugly on his feet, contrary to her command. She was in the adjoining dressing room, desperately trying out possible combinations on the large built-in safe. Especially for Vivienne's tenancy, the current Marquis de Delancourt had installed a floor-to-ceiling metal one, so huge that the only way to bring it into the mansion had been to take off one of the high bedroom windows, winch the solid steel safe over the back garden wall and then hoist it up through the window gap onto a reinforced dolly so that it could be wheeled into the dressing room.

It had been hired: the Marquis had commented wryly that the Delancourts' own collection of family heirlooms was scarcely valuable enough to justify purchasing a safe of that size. Vivienne Winter, on the other hand, had already accumulated a queen's ransom in her forty-eight years, enough to fill a pirate's treasure chest. And Vivienne always insisted on having her jewels with her, disliking the idea that a bank vault might be closed when, on a whim, she decided to load herself up with gems, pin her diamond and sapphire brooch into one of her signature turbans, and sweep her entourage out to a nightclub.

The safe's black-velvet-lined drawers contained all her major pieces: the ruby and diamond parure bought from an Indian Rani; the famous opals that Vivienne always declared, counter to the superstition, brought her good luck; the tiara set with emeralds and yellow sapphires around a central diamond that was regarded by experts as rivalling the Koh-i-Noor for cut, clarity and colour, if not carat size. Clearly Vivienne had either been advised – or been sensible enough – not to use an obvious code for the lock, as Pearl was failing with every combination she tried.

She had already gone through all the birthday dates she could think of: her mother's, her own and Angel's – and that of Randon Cliffe, the husband Vivienne had divorced last year but who remained not only the love of Vivienne's life, but the principal supplier of her superb jewel collection. Pearl's shoulders sagged as the heavy door failed yet again to swing open after she'd turned the dial to Randon's birthday digits; she'd had high hopes for that one. In swift succession she ran through the other dates scribbled on the yellow Post-it she had brought with her and stuck just above the dials.

She tried the dates of Vivienne's first and second Oscar wins, the statuettes displayed on the marble mantelpiece of the bedroom. Vivienne had no truck with her fellow actors who said modestly in interviews that they kept their Oscars in the downstairs toilet (which, in any case, was just a way of making sure your guests got a good look at them). No, Vivienne wanted those two shiny golden trophies to be the first thing she saw when she woke up and the last thing before closing her eyes at night. Nonetheless, neither of the dates on which she'd received them were the combination to her jewellery safe, and Pearl was rapidly running out of ideas.

She was running out of time, too. Pretty soon Baxter would manifest, politely but insistently ushering her and Angel downstairs, away from her only opportunity of getting her hands on some of Vivienne's hugely valuable jewellery – the jewellery that Pearl's dealer had assured her he could pawn for enough money to not only settle what she owed, but ensure her credit with him for months to come.

Pearl turned away from the safe, consoling herself with the knowledge that Vivienne's major pieces would have been very hard to pawn. She would have been given only a fraction of their value, disproportionate to the wrath that would have been called down on her head if – or *when* – Vivienne found out what she had done. She'd go to Plan B now: grab some of the minor jewellery not valuable enough to be kept in the safe – minor by Vivienne's standards only, of course – and get out of there fast.

But she'd been up here for long enough that she needed a watch placed on the door so she didn't get caught in the act.

'Angel!' she called, and when she didn't get an answer straight away she went swiftly into the bedroom, leaned over the bed and grabbed her son's shoulders, brusquely shaking him awake.

'Get up!' she hissed. 'Go and stand in the sitting room by the door to the main corridor and call to me as soon as it starts to open! Go on, run!'

Sleepy, stumbling, rubbing his eyes, Angel obeyed, his trainers catching on the rug as he went, disappearing into the living room. Back in the dressing room, Pearl started opening jewellery boxes, looking for daytime trinkets that her mother might not be likely to miss. She found a tangle of diamond tennis bracelets, and pulled out two: Vivienne wore those in stacks up her tanned arms, and probably wouldn't notice if there were eighteen now, rather than twenty. And it was the same with the hoop earrings – Vivienne adored them, they were a signature look for her, and had so very many set with diamonds. She wouldn't miss a few of those, or a handful of brooches, when she literally had boxes full of them . . .

In the sitting room, Angel had dutifully stationed himself by the main door. But presently, when he realized his mother wouldn't be appearing any time soon, he started to look around the room. Almost immediately, his attention was caught by a marvellous vase on a pedestal by the window. It was huge, as tall as he was and made of white china heavily painted in blue ink with all sorts of things on it, but what fascinated him was the huge tiger that seemed to be prowling towards him, as if it were about to step right off the vase and into the room. The tiger looked as if it were in a forest of bamboo, and wasn't very happy about it, in Angel's opinion: its thick furry tail was curved, looking just like cats' tails did when they got angry and lashed them back and forth. Dogs wagged their tails when they were happy, but Angel knew that when cats did it you shouldn't pet them, because they could bite or scratch you.

Angel decided it was a boy tiger. And it wasn't in a bamboo forest after all, he realized, but on a river bank. Maybe the tiger had just had a drink. But then why was it grumpy and lashing its tail? Maybe it had been fishing, but it hadn't managed to get anything for its dinner, and it was hungry.

He pictured a cat that lived with his mummy's friend Talisa. It didn't have a name – Talisa just called it Cat – and it was always trying to climb on Talisa's big fish tank and hook out the fish with one of its paws so it could eat them. Once the cat had managed it, and Mummy and Talisa, who were smoking their funny cigarettes, had laughed and laughed till Mummy said she was going to be sick, though she wasn't. The poor little fish had flapped around frantically for a second or two, and then it was gone, just a flash of yellow and blue disappearing into the cat's mouth. The cat was looking really pleased with itself, no tail-lashing at all.

Talisa had stopped laughing then and started wailing because she said the fish had been majorly expensive and her boyfriend would be really cross, but Mummy had said something about blowing him to say sorry, and Talisa had started laughing again, and Angel had asked why her boyfriend would want Talisa blowing on him, and then Mummy had snapped at him to go away and find something else to do. So he had gone into the kitchen to find something to eat, and the cat had followed him, padding on its velvet feet and winding itself around his legs, and he had sat down on the kitchen floor and stroked the cat for ages as it purred and rubbed its head against him, so it had been a very nice evening in the end.

Angel had pestered Mummy for ages after that to get a cat, but she just kept saying that it was too much responsibility. Now, however, looking into the tiger's blue-painted eyes, he decided that what he truly wanted was a tiger. He could ride on it when he was tired, and curl up and sleep next to it, and it would bite anyone who was mean to him. He sat down, cross-legged, and reached a hand out to stroke the tiger's head, wondering what name he would give it if it did, suddenly, step out of the vase and onto the carpet, just like animals in pictures sometimes did in films. He was so absorbed in deciding the best possible name for a pet tiger that he entirely failed to notice when, behind him, the sitting room door opened soundlessly on its well-oiled hinges.

Pearl had assumed Baxter would come up to check on her, but it was actually a younger, slimmer, elegant man, with smooth blond hair, enviably narrow hips, and a pair of black glasses perched on his nose, so angular and imposing that they might have been designed by a fashionable architect. He cast a quick look around the sitting room, noted Angel sitting with his back turned to the door, and proceeded into the bedroom, walking so softly that neither Angel nor Pearl heard his tread.

The sound of Pearl opening and closing drawers and jewellery boxes in the dressing room beyond was clearly audible. She was so absorbed in the pile of jewellery that she was accumulating on the glass-topped shelf in front of her that she completely failed to notice the presence of the young man standing watching her in the doorway. Only when she was stuffing the jewels in greedy handfuls into the small leather bag she wore slung across her slender torso did she turn towards the door.

Pearl gasped in horror. Crimson and vermilion lights sparkled from the ruby bracelet clutched between her fingers:

she had literally been caught red-handed. The bracelet tumbled to the floor, but Pearl didn't stoop to retrieve it. Instead, she fixed her eyes plaintively on the young man's, which were impassive behind the lenses of his glasses.

'It's Thierry, isn't it?' she said in a breathless, seductive voice. 'I remember you from when I came to see Mummy before.'

'Yes, Mademoiselle Pearl,' the young man said. 'I am Madame's personal assistant and secretary.'

'Well, Thierry, I know this looks bad, but please don't jump to conclusions . . .'

Pearl stepped towards the young man, over the bracelet, her big eyes fixed hypnotically on his face, depositing the rest of the jewellery she was carrying on a shelf without ever taking her gaze off him.

'. . . but honestly, it isn't what it looks like,' she continued, launching smoothly into self-justification; this was by no means the first time that Pearl had had to talk herself out of a compromising situation. 'I can explain. You see—'

'Mademoiselle Pearl,' Thierry said gravely, 'I am afraid that I will have to inform Madame about this incident.'

'Oh *no*! No, you don't have to! Honestly!' Pearl widened those magical amethyst eyes. 'Seriously, let me explain! You see, Grandma left me an awful lot of jewellery in her will, which Mummy was keeping for me. Only then Mummy and I fought, because she's been very unfair by not giving me the things that Grandma left me. Which is actually,' she added, warming to her theme, '*illegal*, but of course I would never dream of taking Mummy to court, because of the publicity! Can you imagine! So I thought I'd just pop up and see if they were here—'

'But those are Madame's own jewels,' Thierry commented, glancing at the heap Pearl had put on the shelf, and the bracelet lying on the carpet behind her, glittering alizarin crimson under the bright lights of the dressing room. 'I myself supervised the most recent catalogue list of all Madame's collection. I recognize them very well.'

'Well, yes,' Pearl agreed smoothly, 'yes, they are, but you see, I couldn't find Grandma's jewels . . .'

This, of course, was because they didn't exist. Pearl, an accomplished liar, had made the entire story up on the spot. But as a narcissist she could convince herself, as soon as she told a lie, that on some level it was true. Additionally, she instantly became offended if the person to whom she was lying didn't believe her.

'. . . and these looked about the same sort of value,' she continued, and then swiftly corrected herself. 'Um, I mean the same kind of style. And I thought that it would balance things out if I took these, and then I wouldn't have to take Mummy to court, or tell the papers about her not giving me Grandma's things . . .'

She tailed off, tilting her head in a way that men usually found endearing, as if she were asking them a question to which only they had the answer. Her rosebud lips were parted, her lashes fluttering.

'You will put everything back together there,' Thierry instructed, indicating the shelf. 'Everything that is in your bag must be taken out.'

'Oh, of course. I do understand. That's fine, you're just doing your job. But – can this be our little secret?'

Pearl touched the tip of her tongue to her lips, very briefly.

'You won't tell Mummy, will you?' she asked softly.

And she reached out to stroke Thierry's pristine shirtfront with one soft fingertip.

'Please say you won't?' she continued, her voice cooing now. 'Be an angel? No one really needs to know but you and me, do they? It can be our little secret . . . our naughty little secret . . .'

The finger slipped between the seams of the shirt, into one of the gaps between the buttons, finding Thierry's smooth bare chest.

'I can be awfully nice when people are nice to me,' she said softly, persuasively. 'And you're *very* handsome. I noticed you when I came to visit Mummy before.'

The finger emerged from the shirt gap and started tracing its way down his torso.

'We could have a little fun right now to celebrate our secret,' she suggested, watching the path of her finger as it landed on the waistband of his flat-fronted charcoal trousers. 'Couldn't we?'

Thierry cleared his throat.

'Mademoiselle, your son, you are aware, is outside in Madame's *salon privé*?' he inquired, his tone still studiedly neutral.

'Oh, just close the dressing room door!' Pearl said lightly. 'Trust me, Angel knows *very* well never to come into a room when the door's closed! It was one of the first things I taught him!'

Her fingers were now touching his waistband, but just as she started to slide them further down, Thierry's hand grasped her wrist and removed it firmly, replacing it at her side.

'You will return all the jewellery to the shelf while I observe you, Mademoiselle, *s'il vous plaît*,' he informed her politely. 'And then we will all go downstairs together.'

'But you won't tell Mummy?' Pearl asked eagerly. She was quite unaffected by the rejection of her offer of sexual services, just as long as she got what she wanted.

'Mademoiselle, I regret,' Thierry said, looking not regretful in the slightest, 'but I am employed by Madame Winter, and I must report to Madame what has occurred here today.'

White teeth sunk into her lower lip in frustration, Pearl dug her hands into her bag and emptied it out onto the shelf. She did not duck down to retrieve the bracelet, leaving it on the carpet. Thierry did not insist on that, but with a polite 'You permit?' he reached out to glance into Pearl's bag, checking that nothing still sparkled inside it. Pearl bristled at this humiliation, but said nothing, snapping the flap of the bag closed and stalking past him through the doorway.

Thierry bent to pick up the bracelet and put it on the shelf. Then he cast a glance around the dressing room, ensuring that nothing else was out of place. Almost instantly, his stare fixed incredulously on the yellow Post-it note still affixed to the door of the safe. A couple of swift strides took him to the note; he pulled it off the door, tilting it so he could decipher the series of dates printed on it in Pearl's messy handwriting.

Immediately, he realized what he was seeing. His mouth set in a tight, judgemental line, and he removed a calfskin leather diary from the inside pocket of his sleekly tailored Harris tweed jacket, opening it and smoothing the Post-it onto a page as evidence. Closing the diary once more, returning it to his pocket, Thierry shook his head in silent disbelief as he turned off the lights and stepped out of the dressing room, closing the door behind him.

As he turned, he walked straight into a massive blow to the face that sent him reeling back. His foot caught on the edge of the Persian rug. He tripped, his arms flying up as if to catch onto something that wasn't there, some invisible support, and flailed wildly, beating the air, even as he tipped backwards, sent fatally off balance, his head smashing into the marble edge of the mantelpiece with a dull *thunk*.

It was a horribly muted sound, his thick hair muffling the direct impact of stone against skull. But it was followed by the most almighty racket as, his body limp, he crashed down into the fireplace, scattering the delicate painted fire screen and the poker and tongs neatly arranged in the wrought-iron stand behind it. Metal smashed into the brick, the tools tumbling everywhere.

Angel came tearing into the bedroom at the noise, eyes wide as saucers. He was amazed to see a strange man lying half in the fireplace, half out. But he skidded to a halt, clapping his hands to his cheeks in horror, as he came closer and saw the blood streaming from the man's face, the pool that was beginning to form around the caved-in back of his head.

Pearl was stock-still, still clasping the weapon she had used to hit Thierry in the face, which she had snatched from the mantelpiece in desperation as she saw him preserve the evidence of her attempt to open her mother's safe. It was one of Vivienne's Oscars, shining and sleek, the face and hands of the statue now thickly clotted with blood. Made of solid metal, coated with 24-carat gold, the Oscar was undamaged by the blow. The cartilage of Thierry's nose, however, had smashed, spurting blood, which was now beginning to run down the smooth surface of the statue and onto the priceless rug.

Mutely, Angel took one hand from his face and pointed down at the dripping gore. Pearl looked down, following his gesture, and then shrieked, jumping to the edge of the rug, putting the Oscar down on the edge of the fireplace, where the blood started to trickle onto the brick surround.

'This is all your fault!' she screamed at Angel, relieving her stress and shock, as she so often did, by abusing her son. 'If you'd kept watch, like I told you to, this would never have happened!'

Tears started to form in Angel's eyes.

'Is the man dead, Mummy?' he asked in a pitifully small voice.

'I don't know!' Pearl screeched. She fell to her knees by Thierry's body, but her first action was not to put her fingers to his throat, feeling for a pulse. Instead, she scrabbled in his jacket, dragging the diary out from his inner breast pocket, flipping it open and ripping out the incriminating Post-it, crumpling it and shoving it into her bag. She hesitated for a second, thinking of the jewellery back in the dressing room. There would be no time to put it all back in its place, so why not snatch some advantage from this awful situation?

Jumping to her feet, she ran back into the dressing room, emerging with her palms cupped together to form a bowl piled high with glittering gems. She dropped to her knees in front of her small son, frantically stuffing the jewels into his cargo trousers. Bracelets, earrings, necklaces, brooches tumbled into all the various pockets as Pearl hissed: 'The nasty man tried to kiss Mummy and make her kiss him back, okay? That's what you have to tell everyone. Mummy told him to stop, but he wouldn't, so Mummy had to hit him to make him stop trying to kiss and grab her. Got it?'

Tears were pouring down Angel's cheeks. Usually Mummy didn't like him to cry, but she wasn't shouting at him as she usually did to 'turn the tap off', and he honestly didn't think he *could* have stopped, not when the man who had mysteriously appeared from nowhere was lying there in front of him with more and more blood coming out of him, and nobody trying to help him or make him better . . .

'Mummy, shall I get something to put on his head?' he asked.

'No! He *attacked* me, you stupid boy!' Pearl screamed. 'Don't you remember? You saw him attack me – I was defending myself! And we don't say anything to anyone about these, okay?'

She tapped his pockets, which were noticeably bulging with the swag she had stolen from her mother.

'Not a word! You went to the loo, the nasty man tried to kiss me and I had to hit him, you came out of the loo and saw everything . . .'

'I *do* need the loo now,' Angel sobbed piteously. 'I do need it, Mummy!'

'You'll have to hold it!' Pearl snapped. 'Now, *remember the story.*'

Angel's face was wet with tears now; they were dripping off his chin, just as the blood was dripping from the Oscar, staining the bricks. Pearl's voice softened a little. Still kneeling in front of her son, she reached out and rubbed her thumbs over his cheeks, wiping away some of the tears.

'You're Mummy's good boy,' she crooned to him. 'You're Mummy's favourite boy in the whole world. It's not the first time you've told stories for Mummy, is it?'

'What on *earth* is going on?' interrupted a contralto voice that would have been instantly familiar to half the population of the world. 'Pearl, what are you doing in my rooms? You know I've banned you from making unauthorized visits!'

Vivienne Winter swept into her bedroom with the élan of a woman who had been both a renowned beauty and an international film star since the age of fourteen. She was instinctively theatrical. Only with her closest intimates was she fully comfortable being completely natural – and for Vivienne, who had been surrounded by an entourage from a young age, the concept of behaving entirely naturally was rather different from the average person's.

Pausing just inside the doorway, unfastening her fox-fur tippet and dropping it casually onto a silk upholstered occasional chair, Vivienne stood there, as poised as if she were expecting to be photographed by a horde of paparazzi, surveying the scene before her. Pearl and Angel both turned to look at her, instinctively moving so that they concealed Thierry's body, their faces so guilty that Vivienne heaved a long sigh of gloomy anticipation, wondering what could be the latest mess Pearl had managed to get herself into.

Angel forgot momentarily about the man with the blood on his head and the story he was supposed to tell for his mummy as he stared up at Grandma Viv in wonder. He was always riveted by her when he saw her afresh. He knew not to say this to Pearl – and of course he loved his mummy best – but in Angel's opinion, Grandma Viv was the most beautiful lady in the whole world. Her skin was so smooth and creamy; she always smelt of wonderful perfume; her jewels were like the Queen's. And though Mummy often boasted that she had inherited Grandma Viv's eyes – which didn't make sense to Angel – Grandma Viv's eyes were a deeper, more spectacular purple than either his or Mummy's. He had spent ages comparing them in the mirror, sitting on Grandma Viv's lap, and he knew he was right. But he wouldn't have dreamed of saying that to Mummy either.

He drank in all the details of her appearance. Vivienne's hair was piled up loosely on top of her head in a careful arrangement of curls, her make-up elaborate and carefully applied. Her Donna Karan knit dress hugged her curves and emphasized her tiny waist without any help from shoulder pads. Her Paloma Picasso gold earrings, specially made for her by Tiffany, were set with baguette-cut diamonds.

She was wearing her customary four-inch heels, Italian leather designed for her in Italy by Fiamma Ferragamo. Fiamma's father had made shoes for Ava Gardner, Greta Garbo, Sophia Loren, Audrey Hepburn, Lauren Bacall and Rita Hayworth, but it was Fiamma, fifteen years ago, who had sketched for Vivienne a patent platform pump with a matching grosgrain strip across the toe. Vivienne owned the shoe in a wide variety of colours. For the last ten years, she had been polishing and perfecting her signature style. There was no fudging your age for the public when you had been famous since your teens, and had a daughter at twenty-one; she was known to be forty-eight, and she was intensely aware of the need not to seem to be dressing younger than her age.

She caught a glimpse of herself in the gilded Louis XVI mirror on the dressing table across the room, and her lips quirked in satisfaction. Even faced with her wayward daughter's latest crisis, her own perfect appearance could cheer her up.

So far the day had gone wonderfully: her fitting that morning at Christian Lacroix's *atelier* had been extremely gratifying. She was in Paris to play a duchess in a British/French co-production of a film version of a nineteenth-century historical novel. M. Lacroix had shown her a design for the dress she would wear for the crucial ball scene, together with fabric swatches of gold brocade that had made her smile like a cat presented with a dish of fresh prawns in cream. It would be impossible for the viewer to look anywhere but at her in that shimmering golden dress. Her younger female co-star would be writhing in jealousy. She had expected to come back here in triumph, drink a glass of champagne with lunch, celebrate in style. But instead she had to deal with yet another crisis involving her wretched daughter.

She gazed down at Pearl and Angel, whose pretty faces, upturned to hers, provoked a whole raft of conflicting emotions. Pearl was absolutely forbidden to be in here. Her daughter was not only a spendthrift, but completely untrustworthy. Pearl had stolen many times not just from her mother – which would have been bad enough – but from Vivienne's friends, too.

Mortifying, humiliating; but there was no time now for the 'where did I go wrong?' questions that often tormented

Vivienne. She needed to deal with this situation immediately, without getting tangled up in what-ifs. There would be plenty of time for those later.

'Well?' she demanded, hands going to her hips, the toe of one black patent-leather pump tapping impatiently on the parquet floor. 'I'm waiting! Please explain to me immediately why you're in here, when you know perfectly well you're forbidden to come into my bedroom on your own!'

Angel, overwhelmed by his grandmother's stern tone, blurted out:

'Granny Viv, don't be cross! I needed the loo and Mummy said . . . Mummy thought . . .'

As he spoke, however, he stepped forward, and Vivienne gasped in horror. Part of Thierry's body was revealed, lying at an awkward angle across the fireplace surround.

'My God!' Vivienne exclaimed, not quite believing what she was seeing.

She ran over to Thierry and screamed as she saw the blood, which was no longer flowing from his skull, but had settled into a red halo beneath it. Dropping to her knees, she placed her index and middle fingers against the carotid artery, checking for a pulse – just as she had been taught when, at only nineteen, she had played Sister Fortunata, the heroic nun who nursed plague victims during the Black Death in Siena in the historical epic *No Greater Love*. How the audience had yearned for her to yield to the seductive charms of the handsome Italian actor Gian Maria Volonté, twenty years older than her and in his glorious prime, playing the noble Doctor Luigi whose hands kept meeting Sister Fortunata's over the corpses of plague victims . . . but it was not to be. Rather than allow the young nun to succumb to the pleasures of the flesh, God took her for his own (to quote the final line of the film, as spoken mournfully yet worshipfully by Doctor Luigi) and Sister Fortunata died a martyr's death, although conveniently without any nasty pustules to mar Vivienne's exquisite teenage beauty.

No Greater Love had not been a career highlight for Vivienne (although, off screen, Gian Maria Volonté had been a personal one). Reviews had been scathing, some observing that the medical staff of the fourteenth century seemed oddly familiar with modern practices. Vivienne and Gian Maria had probably been too carefully coached by the doctor who had been hired as a consultant, but she had always taken her roles extremely seriously. Which now meant that, almost thirty years later, she knew exactly how to determine whether Thierry was still alive.

She had her answer after a few seconds, but she held on for several more, unwilling to accept the evidence her fingertips were relaying to her. But even as she resigned herself to the fact that there was no pulse in his pale neck, she noticed that the halo of blood beneath his head was starting to coagulate. The fresh red colour was darkening perceptibly, the texture thickening.

Vivienne had uttered the words many times before on stage and screen, twice in *No Greater Love* alone. But that made it no easier for her to part her exquisitely curved lips and say in disbelief, 'He's dead.'

Pearl shrieked theatrically, unable to deliver a convincing scream of horror because secretly she was hugely relieved. A dead Thierry would be unable to tell Vivienne the true reason Pearl had hit him with the Oscar. Even despite the prompting she had given Angel, Pearl was aware that her mother would believe her assistant's version of events rather than her daughter's.

'He tried to grope me, Mummy!' Pearl said, pulling Angel into her arms, sinking to sit with her son in her lap. 'He wouldn't stop, and I had to hit him to make him! He was saying really creepy things—'

'With Angel right there?' Vivienne said, her voice dripping with incredulity.

Slowly, she got to her feet, her gaze fixed on her daughter. It had taken Vivienne a long time not to be swayed by Pearl's imploring expression, those wide eyes, and the blonde curls and high forehead that she had inherited from her father, a wonderfully handsome actor with whom Vivienne had starred twenty-seven years ago in a completely forgettable movie – so forgettable that she could remember neither the title nor the plot, nor, at this moment, her co-star's surname. He had been as stupid as he was pretty, and although she hadn't meant to get pregnant, she had consoled herself with the reflection that her baby was bound to be absolutely beautiful.

She hadn't, however, anticipated Pearl inheriting her father's minimal brain capacity. Brent, bless him, had been one of those big, handsome lunks, dumb as an ox but sweet as a Labrador puppy, who simply didn't have the range for movie stardom. He had eventually snagged a recurring role in an American soap opera as a heroic surgeon, perfect for his handsome face and limited talents, and Vivienne sometimes hooked up with him when she was in LA. Brent wasn't outstanding in bed, but he was eager to please and had a nice cock, and frankly, sometimes that was more than enough when you wanted to get laid.

Yes, a truly sweet guy. He'd wanted to be involved in Pearl's life, but it had been very difficult, as Brent – what *was* his surname? – had been married at the time, and Vivienne's team of publicists had worked hard to cover up the fact that their client was not only having a child out of wedlock, but with a married man to boot. In fact, Brent's wife, an actress, had been having a contemporaneous affair herself with the producer of a film in which she had just been cast, so no one had really been betrayed at all; but those typical behind-the-scenes shenanigans were always kept secret from the general public, who wanted to believe the lies they were told about true love, fidelity and happily-ever-after among the beautiful people who featured on magazine covers.

One of the reasons Vivienne couldn't remember Brent's surname, of course, was that Pearl had taken hers. Would it have made a difference, Vivienne wondered now, if she'd done what the publicists wanted? They had been desperate for Brent to divorce his wife and marry Vivienne, so they could spin the story of an overpowering love that had caused the two of them to behave badly, but could be excused because Brent was doing the right thing, making an honest woman of his beloved, giving their baby a father.

But the thought of being married at the tender age of twenty-one, especially to a man she didn't care about, had been anathema to Vivienne. Headstrong by nature, spoilt by and from her pampered years as a teen star, she had refused to be tied down to a man she found so boring she often sat on his face just to stop him talking during sex. When she snapped those very words at her publicists, they had been so horrified at the idea of their client impetuously blurting out a remark like that to a journalist that they had promptly backed off any further attempts to push her and Brent into walking down the aisle.

Maybe if Brent had been around, it would have been better for Pearl, she thought. *I wasn't a very good mother. In fact, I was a very bad one. I was always working, always travelling, always out. Brent would have been a much more stable influence than all the nannies who dragged Pearl around from one first-class cabin, one hotel suite to another . . . but it's much too late for recriminations now. I have to focus on the present . . .*

Vivienne was keeping a firm grip on herself, utilizing every ounce of self-control she had learned over her long career. From the moment she had ascertained that Thierry was dead, she had known that this was one of the most important crossroads in her family's life. She had failed repeatedly with her daughter. This time she absolutely had to get it right.

Vivienne took a deep, measured breath as she looked down at her daughter's lovely face. She blamed herself for Pearl's wildness and inability to settle; for the fact that Pearl had never worked a day in her life; for Pearl turning to drugs and drink; even for Pearl's light-fingered tendencies. Vivienne knew perfectly well that she had led Pearl to rely on her financially because she was not to be relied on in any other way. The one thing she had always been able to provide for her daughter was money: an endless stream of money, a positive river of gold that had flowed constantly into Pearl's bank account, only to fountain out from Pearl's hands as soon as it arrived.

And then the fountain had dried up. Pearl had been too greedy – had managed to run up debts even larger than her income, so that she had begged her mother to bail her out. Vivienne had responded by setting up a trust fund for her, letting her know what sum would land in her bank account every month, trying to teach her some financial responsibility. But it had been too late. Pearl had learned too well that the river of money would flow constantly, and was incapable of adjusting to the new reality. Thefts were her way of compensating, and when caught, her justification was always the same: that her mother had been unspeakably cruel to accustom her daughter to unlimited funding and then to expect Pearl, overnight, to learn to live within a budget, no matter how lavish.

'I know what happened, Pearl,' Vivienne said quietly. 'I know why you killed him.'

'I didn't kill him! It was an accident!' Pearl exclaimed, clutching her son even tighter. 'I just hit him because he was groping me, trying to kiss me – it was disgusting – Angel, tell her!'

'The man grabbed Mummy,' Angel said, and his eyes on Vivienne's face were terrifyingly limpid, clear of any signs of deceit. Pearl had trained him all too well. 'He grabbed her and was being creepy and she had to hit him with the statue. She *had* to.'

'What exactly was he doing, Angel?' Vivienne asked gently.

'Trying to kiss her,' Angel said, elaborating on his theme. His mother was stroking his hair now, silently showing her approval, and that egged him on to add: 'He was sort of squeezing her. Mummy was telling and telling him to let her go, but he wouldn't. Honestly. I promise.'

Pearl's hands settled on his shoulders, holding him tight, her thumbs caressing circles on his narrow bones, her head lowered to kiss the crown of his head. He felt himself blossom with pride: Mummy had told him what to do, and he'd got it exactly right. He must have done, because Grandma Viv was nodding, and that would mean that Mummy loved him now more than ever . . .

'Pearl,' Vivienne said, even more gently, raising her gaze from her grandson's face to her daughter's. 'Thierry was gay.'

All the blood seemed to drain from Pearl's face. Both her light brown mascara and the matching eyebrows she pencilled in over her pale blonde hairs suddenly stood out in vivid relief against her chalk-white skin. Angel started to writhe in her grip.

'Mummy,' he said, 'you're hurting me. Mummy, what's wrong?'

Pearl's knuckles were whitening too as she dug her fingers into her son's shoulders. Angel remembered that he was hungry, and that he needed the loo, and he started to whimper.

'Mummy, *please* . . .'

'You're hurting the child, Pearl,' Vivienne said.

Even Pearl's lips looked pale from the shock of Vivienne's revelation. She managed to stammer: 'But he *did* – he did grope me—'

'Turn out your pockets, please, Pearl,' Vivienne said quietly. 'I have to tell Baxter to contact the police, and you don't want to be found with any of my jewellery.'

'Fuck you, you bitch!' Pearl swore furiously.

She let go of Angel, who instantly wriggled away, running to the en-suite bathroom. Standing up, Pearl theatrically pulled out the linings of her jeans pockets, turning around to show her mother that there was nothing in the back ones, then tearing open her bag and dumping its contents all over the rug.

'See?' she hissed. 'You're always suspecting me of the worst! I hope you're bloody ashamed of yourself.'

She put her hands on her hips, her voice rising.

'Are you going to say sorry, Mummy? Well, *are* you?'

The toilet flushed, and Angel could be heard crossing to the sink, turning on the tap.

'What a good boy,' Vivienne said with an odd inflection. It took Pearl a moment to realize that her mother sounded, suddenly, very sad. 'He never used to be that good about washing his hands, did he? As I remember, the last time you both stayed here, we kept having to remind him . . .'

Before Pearl could do anything to stop her, she crossed swiftly to the bathroom door, swinging it open. As Vivienne had suspected, Angel was not washing his hands. Having turned on the tap to cover any noise he might make, the little boy had ducked down in front of the sink and was swiftly emptying the heaps of sparkling gems from his pockets into the cabinet below. Pearl, on her mother's heels, took in the sight and quickly exclaimed:

'*Angel!* What are you *doing*? Did you take some of Granny Viv's jewellery? Oh Angel, how *could* you?'

On hearing these words, Vivienne, who had been keeping iron control over her emotions, turned on her heel and backhanded her daughter so hard across the face with one slap that Pearl was thrown back to the floor, gasping in shock, blood welling up from a cut. One of the many rings that

Vivienne was wearing had been a special gift from Randon Cliffe. It was a magnificent single diamond in an old-fashioned inverted setting, which meant that the *culet*, or point, of the round-cut diamond was facing upwards rather than down. Randon had been told by the jeweller he had bought it from that this was how the first ever engagement ring had been made.

The setting was highly unusual. Diamond experts considered it failed to maximize the sparkle and life of the stone being used, causing it to lose crucial light transmission. But Vivienne had so many jewels that she particularly prized rarity, and she and Randon were both amused by the way the sharp, pointed *culet* drove up from the base of her finger like a knuckleduster. Certainly, it had easily slashed Pearl's cheek open.

'My God, Pearl,' her mother said in tones as cutting as the inverted diamond. 'It's not enough that you're a thief and a killer – you've turned your son into an *accomplice*! You didn't even tell him to go to the bathroom and hide what you'd stolen, did you? He thought that up all on his own, to protect you! How *dare* you blame him for trying to cover up your crime? How *dare* you try to make me believe it was Angel, not you, who stole my jewellery?'

Angel stared in horror at his grandmother. He had never seen Grandma Viv hit anyone before, and it scared him just as much as the man lying in a pool of his own blood. He had hoped, desperately, that if he managed to hide the jewels, Grandma Viv would believe Mummy, would hug her and tell her it was okay; that she had been right to hit the nasty man, it was all a mistake. Grandma would explain it to the police, and everyone would be nice to Mummy and tell her not to worry.

But now he had messed it up by getting caught. He should have locked the bathroom door, but he was scared to lock doors in case he got stuck inside. It was only while he was weeing that he'd got the idea to sneak all the jewellery out of his pockets, because they were bulging and he was scared that Grandma Viv would spot them and blame Mummy – only Mummy had blamed *him*, which was so unfair that he couldn't even find the words to say how unfair it was – and all of a sudden he felt tired and hungry and miserable and angry and guilty and scared, such an overwhelming rush of bad feelings that he thought he could explode with them . . .

He wanted to kick something to let the feelings out; not just kick, but break something, smash it into such tiny pieces that it could never be repaired again.

'You've had your last chance, Pearl,' Vivienne was saying, so icily that her daughter shivered in fear.

'You can't have me arrested,' Pearl said sullenly, not meeting her mother's eyes. 'The publicity will be terrible for you.'

'My God! How many times have I *heard* this?'

Vivienne's wonderfully modulated, theatre-trained voice started low and rose to a throbbing, passionate contralto. It wasn't acting: there was nothing faked about her fury and passion. That was the essential quality of a diva. Her emotions were always utterly real, but the way they were expressed was indistinguishable from one of the more dramatic characters she had played on stage or screen. Her gestures, her vocal control, were all a product of the amount of time she had spent in front of a camera, being observed, being taught to consider herself the centre of every room she inhabited.

'How many times, Pearl? Do you have any idea at all how often you've played that card?' she demanded of her daughter. 'My God, every single time you shoplifted or ran up a huge debt with your drug dealer or got arrested for driving drunk or stole from me or my friends, only to hear, "Oh, but Mummy, you have to hush it up, because otherwise the publicity will be terrible for you!" A man is *dead* because of you, and you're still trying to get me to hush things up! Well, not this time, Pearl. Thierry was worth a hundred of you. He was loyal, trustworthy, thoughtful and as honest as the day is long. Whereas *you* –'

She drew a long, trembling breath, remembering her grandson's presence, and managed to bite back the words that would accurately describe his mother's character.

'You've turned your son into a liar,' she said. 'And you're not even ashamed of that. If you were, you would have tried to protect him. But I just saw you throw him under the bus, Pearl. You tried to make me believe that Angel was a thief! You made the poor little boy carry everything you've stolen!' Vivienne's outrage was increasing with every word.

Pearl's jaw was set defiantly now. 'You can't get me sent to prison,' she spat up at her mother. 'I'll tell all sorts of stories about you in court! I'll make up all sorts of things! I just hit him to get him off me—'

'Probably because he caught you red-handed,' Vivienne said wearily. 'Pearl, your only piece of luck in this entire miserable, tragic story is that Thierry came from a very conventional bourgeois family in Lyon. He wasn't out to them, although they had their suspicions, and, poor thing, they made him so ashamed of being himself he swore he never would be. They treated him very badly. He once told me they said they would much rather have a dead straight son than a live gay one. Well, now they will,' she added grimly. 'And I hope the bastards choke on it.'

She walked over to Thierry's body and bent over him, tenderly stroking his hair, disordered by his fall, from his bruised face into the style in which he had always carefully brushed it.

'Forgive me,' she said softly. 'It's for Angel, not for her. It's so her little boy can grow up without being called the child of a murderess. Hopefully you can understand, because you were so damaged by your terrible parents. I'm trying to make sure Angel does better.'

She leaned over to kiss Thierry's forehead. His eyes were open and sightless, and she slid the delicate lids gently closed with soft touches of her thumbs. Then she walked over to the bedside table, picked up the telephone, and pressed a button.

'Baxter? Please ring Eduard at the studio's PR office for me, please,' she said, her voice composed. An observer would never guess the inner turmoil she was suffering, the guilt she was feeling at letting Thierry's reputation be traduced. 'No, Thierry is . . .'

She paused, unable to finish that sentence.

'Just ring him, please, Baxter. Tell him it's an emergency, and that he needs to come over here right away. Immediately. And bring him straight up when he arrives. And no, Baxter,' she reassured her anxious butler, who had broken into a stream of apologies, 'don't worry. I don't blame you. How could you have turned them away from my front door? It's not your fault. Just tell Eduard to come here *straight away*.'

Her hand was trembling as she set the phone back in its cradle.

'Here's what's going to happen, Pearl,' she said, her voice still steady. 'We'll make sure that this is all covered up, just as you want. The head of publicity from the studio is coming straight over. When he grasps the situation, he'll call whatever police officers he's got in his pocket and they'll arrive primed to believe whatever we tell them. You'll trot out the story of how you struggled with Thierry and fought him off with my Oscar – I doubt you'll even be taken into custody.'

In her decades as a major star, Vivienne had heard of graver crimes than this being covered up by studios. Pearl had, after all, not actually meant to kill Thierry; what she had done would be considered manslaughter under almost any jurisdiction. Vivienne knew of one film star turned director, for instance, who, filming in a third-world country where cash was king, had done considerably worse to a series of barely legal prostitutes. No one reputable would work with him any more, but he had never spent a day in prison for what he had done.

But as Vivienne watched the relief flood across her daughter's face, it was no consolation to her that others had behaved even more appallingly than Pearl.

'Angel will be kept completely out of it, of course,' Vivienne continued. 'Baxter will say he was downstairs. They won't dream of asking a seven-year-old any questions if they don't know he was up here.'

Vivienne noticed bitterly that this comment took Pearl by surprise; it had not even occurred to her to protect her son from having any contact with the police. 'And from now on, he'll be living with me,' Vivienne finished, bracing herself for Pearl's reaction.

'*What?*'

Pearl, who had been sitting on the rug, arms wrapped around her knees, jumped up so lithely that Vivienne had a flash of envy for her daughter's youth. Vivienne kept herself trim and fit with diet and exercise (she was currently keeping her abdominals tight with the *Callanetics* video), but there was no substitute for the flexibility and suppleness she'd had in her mid-twenties.

'You can't do that!' Pearl shrieked. 'What are you saying? Angel's my *son!*'

'Whom I will gain custody of the moment you get arrested for manslaughter – not to mention when you go to prison,' Vivienne pointed out.

This took a moment to sink in.

'You *can't*,' Pearl breathed, clutching her hands at her chest. 'I won't let you take my son away from me!'

'Oh, spare me the amateur histrionics,' Vivienne said with contempt.

'I'll leave those to you, shall I, Mummy?' Pearl said with biting sarcasm. 'You've been peddling them for donkey's years!'

'*My* histrionics are strictly professional,' Vivienne said coolly. 'And they've been keeping you in the lap of luxury for your whole life. Well, that's come to an end too, Pearl. From now on, you will no longer have custody of your son and your trust fund will be cut off. You're on your own. I'll make sure you're not arrested and tried for manslaughter, but that's the last thing I'll do for you.'

This news struck Pearl so powerfully that she couldn't say a word in response; she broke instead into hysterical sobs. Angel, hearing his mother crying uncontrollably, emerged from the bathroom, where he had been hiding, trying not to listen to the fight raging next door. He had retrieved the ruby bracelet from the heap he had been concealing in the bathroom cabinet, wrapped it in a hand towel, and started to crush it with the heavy glass container of cotton wool balls that had been on the bathroom shelf.

This was what had got Mummy into trouble. If he'd just managed to get rid of all *this*, Mummy wouldn't have lied about him stealing the jewellery, and Grandma Viv wouldn't have hit Mummy. And the destruction of something precious and valuable was giving him some relief from the big tight knot of tension in his chest, letting him breathe a little more freely, helping him conquer his overpowering impulse to cry . . .

But at the noise of Mummy sobbing and wailing, Angel was on his feet. He didn't bother to put back the cotton wool ball container, but he did stuff the hand towel and its contents into his trouser pocket, calculating swiftly that there was no way anyone would search him now. Dashing through into the bedroom, he threw himself at his mother, wrapping his arms around her waist, begging her not to cry.

'She's taking you away from me!' Pearl cried. 'She wants to take you away from me for ever, Angel!'

Vivienne leaned forward.

'Pearl,' she said, articulating each word so perfectly that, as they dropped from her lips, they were as clear and sharply pointed as the diamond that had cut her daughter's cheek. 'I will give you a choice. If you tell the truth about everything that happened in this room – about your coming here to steal from me, and hitting Thierry because he tried to stop you – I will support you one hundred per cent. I will pay for the best lawyer. I will look after you when you come out of prison. I will tell Angel that although you did the wrong thing, you are taking responsibility and behaving honestly and that I'm proud of his mother for the first time in her adult life, and I will support him living with you when you're free again.'

She paused, looking at Pearl, whose violet eyes were wide with surprise as she heard this speech. Vivienne waited to see if Pearl would answer her, accept; but no response was forthcoming, and so Vivienne continued with the second part of her offer.

'Or,' she said equally deliberately, 'I will cover this up for you. You won't spend a day in prison, but you won't see your son again until he's eighteen. I will make sure that you don't corrupt him any further. The poor boy has been through enough. God knows what he's seen already, living with you! And now you're using him as an accomplice – making him lie for you, cover up for you! It can't go on.'

Vivienne paused again, but Pearl still remained silent. Ever since giving birth to her son, Pearl had thought of him as her 'get out of jail free' card. He had been an angelic-looking baby, hence her choice of name; and the sight of her holding little Angel, gazing down at him with her sweetest expression, had never failed to provoke sighs of admiration and comments on how much the two of them looked like the Madonna with Baby Jesus in her arms. Whenever Pearl got into trouble, the well-rehearsed tactic of summoning her son so that she could wrap her arms around him and look pleadingly up from his tangle of blond curls, identical to her own, always made a vast difference to whoever had a grudge against her.

What an irony: the nickname Pearl had given Angel was now actually coming true. Just as in the game of Monopoly, the 'get out of jail free' card, it turned out, could only be played once. If you chose to use it, you had to discard it.

I'll get him back, Pearl thought. *Mummy can't actually hold on to him till he's eighteen! She's just throwing threats around because she's angry . . .*

Glancing sideways at Thierry's corpse, Pearl had to admit that her mother had reason to be furious. Pearl had gone too far this time. Of course, properly looked at, Thierry's death had been an accident, and surely, after a while, when she calmed down, Vivienne would realize that and give Pearl custody of her son once again. Pearl would just have to keep herself out of prison and play for time . . .

'You can take Angel for the time being,' she said, doing her best to make it sound like a highly noble decision. 'I can see that I have issues right now I need to work on before I'm ready to be a full-time mother.'

'Mummy!' Angel screamed, looking up at her incredulously. 'Mummy, no!'

'Don't fool yourself, Pearl,' Vivienne said, looking intently at her daughter. 'This is until he's eighteen, and it'll be locked down tight. You'll sign Angel over to me today. The studio's legal team will draw up an agreement for me that you'll have to sign before I organize representation for you. If you think you can refuse to sign it just because I supported your story, think again. I'll not only withdraw my support, I'll tell the police I've just found out that Thierry was gay, which will mean you can rule out any idea of trying to claim self-defence. You have no money for lawyers, and I'll testify against you if I have to. You'll probably end up going to prison for murder.'

Vivienne had no idea whether this was true, but she was sure that Pearl was even more ignorant about the French legal system than she was. By the time Vivienne finished, Pearl was trembling with fear as she absorbed the extent of the threat her mother was making.

'You have to stay with Granny Viv from now on,' she managed to say to Angel, reaching down to prise his hands off her waist. Taking his shoulders, she turned him around so that he was facing Vivienne, and gave him a little push towards his grandmother.

Vivienne managed a smile for Angel, though it was not her best. Pearl gave Angel another push. Obediently, he took a step, and then another, until he reached Vivienne's arms.

'I haven't been a very good mother, Pearl,' Vivienne admitted as she picked up Angel and sat him on the bed beside her, her arm around him. 'I'll take part of the responsibility for you turning out this way. I've neglected you and spoilt you, and that's a toxic combination. I promise you, I won't make the same mistakes with Angel. He's just as precious to me as he is to you.'

Tears were pouring down Angel's face once more.

'Is Mummy going to go to prison?' he asked, twisting his head around to look up at his grandmother.

'No,' Vivienne said, tightening her arm around him for reassurance. 'Mummy's not going to go to prison. But you're going to be living with me from now on, darling. Mummy made a big mistake –'

Over his head, Vivienne glanced once more at Thierry's body, drawing in a steadying breath to cope with her guilt at minimizing his death as a 'mistake'.

'– and now she has to go away and be by herself and think about what she's done,' Vivienne finished, realizing that she was talking about Pearl as if she were a child.

She is *a child*, Vivienne thought sadly as she returned her gaze to her daughter, who was standing there, hands shoved into her jeans pockets, her face as defiant as that of a toddler about to throw a tantrum. *I've kept her a child for far too long. And it's my poor Thierry who paid the price for my failure to be a good mother.*

Baxter was tapping at the closed living room door.

'Madame, the gentleman you summoned is here,' he called.

She knew she should meet them in the living room, prepare them for what they were about to see. At forty-eight, she still considered herself in her prime: she was at the height of her beauty, with work offers still pouring in. And yet, confronted with the death of her secretary, her daughter literally with blood on her hands, and her grandson to bring up, a wave of exhaustion swept over her. All she could do was sit on the bed and watch as Baxter led Eduard into the bedroom. They came to a sudden halt just over the threshold.

'My God!' Baxter exclaimed, his habitual poise completely deserting him at the sight of his colleague's body lying in a pool of blood.

'Baxter,' Vivienne said wearily, 'please take Master Angel away. He's hungry and thirsty and he shouldn't be here any longer.' She fixed her daughter with a bitter stare. 'Frankly, he should never have been here in the first place.'

'Of course, Madame,' Baxter said, wrestling the mask of composure back onto his face with a visible effort. 'Master Angel, come with me, please.'

Angel climbed down from the high bed, and then paused, looking anxiously at his mother.

'Mummy?' he said in a tiny voice, as Eduard stepped to one side, both to allow the child to be removed easily and also to better assess the scene before him, cogs almost visibly whirling behind his eyes. Pearl made no response to her son.

'Mummy?' Angel repeated, but Pearl still couldn't, or wouldn't, answer him. 'I don't want to go!' he persisted, his voice rising now. 'Mummy, don't make me! I want to stay with you!'

Put on the spot, Pearl could not meet his imploring eyes. She stared down at her feet, clad in battered suede Chelsea boots, and muttered, 'Angel, you're going to be living with your grandmother for a while.'

'No!' Angel said, looking from one woman to the other. 'No, please, I want to stay with Mummy! Please, Grandma Viv!'

'Pearl?' Vivienne said to her daughter. 'You still have a choice.'

Pearl bit her lip in fury.

'Angel, you have to stay with Grandma,' she mumbled. 'I've made up my mind.'

'In any case,' Eduard interposed in perfect, but heavily French-accented English, 'this is no place for a child. He must immediately be removed.'

Vivienne walked over to Angel.

'Darling, go with Baxter and have something to eat,' she said softly. 'He'll look after you. We need to talk about grown-up things now, about the poor man who's dead. I have to take care of him.'

'Will I see Mummy after?' Angel asked, his voice higher as he began to panic now, the realization of what was happening sinking in. 'After I have my snack?'

When Vivienne and Pearl fell silent, Angel started to cry yet again. Vivienne gave the butler a nod, and Baxter took Angel's arm gently just as the boy's sobs became audible. He was too tired now, too hungry and thirsty, to have the energy for loud wails; but his heartbroken, miserable, exhausted sobs were much harder to listen to than childish screams of frustration. Angel's little shoulders were sagging, his hands covering his face, his small skinny body so pathetically frail and fragile as Baxter escorted him from the bedroom that no one could say a word. Vivienne, Pearl and Eduard all stood there in silence, listening to the small boy crying, a desolate, mournful sound that resolved itself into one word repeated again and again into his tear-wet palms:

'Mummy . . . Mummy . . . *Mummy . .* '

Chapter Four

London, 2015

'Well, your résumé is excellent, Miss Lavington,' said the sleek, strikingly attractive woman sitting across the coffee table from the job applicant. She put down the folder she was holding and turned to the handsome blond man sitting next to her.

'Do you have any questions for the candidate?' she asked him.

'I do, Miss Delante!' he beamed, his eyes sparkling.

He leaned forward, hands propped on his knees, as his colleague shook back her enviably thick mane of glossy black hair from her smooth face. The configuration of her wide, full cheekbones and delicately tapered eyes spoke of Chinese origins, as did her vellum-coloured skin; but the light sprinkling of freckles across the bridge of her nose, and her eyes, which looked either hazel or green depending on the light, indicated that there was probably a Celtic element to her ethnic make-up. She was perfectly groomed and faultlessly dressed for conducting an interview, in a grey gabardine Joseph trouser suit and a silk blouse whose khaki shade set off her eyes.

'Miss Lavington!' the male interviewer said, fixing the

pretty young woman seated in the armchair opposite him with such a charming smile that she blushed a little, despite her extensive experience. 'As Miss Delante has been explaining, our boarding school is a very exclusive environment. The parents of our charges are sophisticated people from the absolute elite of society. Any teacher we hire must have not only an impeccable CV, but also the social skills to function as a role model for our students. It's our responsibility to select staff members who truly incarnate good character. In so many ways, we are moral guardians.'

Miss Lavington was nodding politely at these words, her hands folded neatly in her lap, seated demurely with her knees and ankles pressed together. Her outfit was perfectly judged: a navy two-piece outfit with a knee-length pleated skirt and a Peter Pan collar in the same shade, the blouse fastened down the front with a series of small covered buttons. Sheer flesh-coloured tights, navy leather shoes with two-inch heels and T-bar straps, and pearl stud earrings were her only accessories. She had parted her blonde hair at one side and drawn it back into a ponytail at the nape of her neck. Her make-up was discreet and her nails painted with a French manicure; her Cupid's bow mouth was glossed in pale beige.

'I definitely feel I can be the kind of teacher you're looking for, Mr Winter,' she said, looking from one to the other of her interviewers. She pushed her dark-framed glasses a little higher up her nose. 'I very much enjoy working with young people, and I would love to think of myself as a worthwhile role model.'

'Good, good!' Mr Winter said approvingly. 'Well, at this

stage of the interview process, what we generally like to do if we're feeling positive about the candidate –'

He glanced over at Miss Delante, who nodded confidently.

'– is to ask you to tell us how you would handle a scenario that quite often comes up, as it were, when we're dealing with young people who are well into adolescence and working through all of the consequent changes that they're experiencing physically and mentally.'

'Excuse me?' Miss Lavington said, her delicate eyebrows drawing together a little in confusion. 'I'm not quite sure that I—'

Miss Delante laughed.

'Don't worry! Mr Winter never uses one word where three will do, I'm afraid,' she said with great friendliness. 'He's always been like this. I joke that he swallowed a dictionary at birth. What he means,' Miss Delante continued, crossing her legs so that the heel of one Gina stiletto rested on her trousered knee, 'is that young people in a boarding school in the Swiss mountains are inevitably thrown together. There's bound to be some sexual experimentation. It's simply unavoidable.'

'Oh, of course,' Miss Lavington said earnestly. 'It has to be expected. After all, they're teenagers, and in a mixed school – although it happens in single-sex schools too—'

Both her interviewers made sounds of agreement.

'So let me pose a hypothesis,' Mr Winter said enthusiastically. 'Suppose that you're the staff member on duty one evening. A young gentleman, one of the students in your charge, comes to you in a considerable state of upset. He's been teased by a girl, because when she kissed him, he was inexperienced and didn't do a good job of kissing her back. Let's say that she mocked him and called him gay.'

'Oh dear,' Miss Lavington said sympathetically. 'Poor thing! Well, of course, the first thing that I'd say is that there's absolutely nothing wrong with being gay and that word should never be used as an insult.'

'Good, good,' Mr Winter agreed. 'And then?'

'How old is the young gentleman we're talking about?' Miss Lavington asked.

'Oh, fifteen at least,' Miss Delante said, lighting a cigarette with a Cartier gold lighter.

'Well,' Miss Lavington said firmly, 'in that case I would say that the next thing to do would be to establish whether he's gay or not. Personally I believe that most of us are fundamentally bisexual.'

This statement was met by more murmurs of agreement from across the coffee table.

'I would probably unbutton my blouse, like this,' she continued, beginning to suit the action to the word, starting with the button at the top, half-hidden under the Peter Pan collar. She took her time, gradually exposing the cream lace demi-bra she wore underneath.

'I would run my hands over my tits,' she said, massaging her nipples with the palms of her hands until the small pink tips, visible through the lace, were fully hard. 'Then, I would see if he had an erection,' she said, smiling. 'That should settle it! Of course, if he didn't, I would be sympathetic and make sure he had a suitable male teacher to discuss the issue with as soon as one was available. Ideally you, Mr Winter?'

Mr Winter gravely nodded as Miss Lavington went on:

'In the short term, I would obviously reassure him, tell him not to be embarrassed, and if he hadn't already come in his trousers –'

They all shared a smile of amusement at this little quip.

'– I would probably give him a quick hand job to alleviate his tension,' she continued. 'Then sit him down, give him a starter lesson in kissing techniques, let him touch my tits and maybe wank off over them. He'd almost certainly get a second erection at that age, and I'd want to make sure he was fully relaxed and feeling better before he left my office.'

'Very thoughtful,' Miss Delante said. 'I'm sure any distressed student would benefit from such a charming experience. Especially spunking over your tits. They really are very pretty. Can we perhaps see – ?'

'Oh, of course!' Miss Lavington pulled her blouse out of the waistband of her skirt, shrugged it off, and reached behind her to unclip her bra. She removed that too. Her breasts were small and rounded, the pink nipples still hard and puckered. As easily as if she was not sitting there topless, she continued: 'In the longer term, I would initiate a programme to make sure the young man was fully trained in all the basics. He would be drilled in fingering me to orgasm, naturally. Then we'd move on to him eating me out, and finally fucking me, as a series of rewards for good behaviour. The idea is to turn him out with a range of skills so that he can eventually go back to that young lady with his head held high and blow her mind. And everything else!'

'Oh, that's a good point,' Mr Winter chimed in. 'The young lady who called him gay as an insult! How would you deal with that?'

'Well, after my initial meeting with the young gentleman,' Miss Lavington said, 'I would send him away – hopefully feeling much better about himself! – and go to find the young lady. I would bring her back to my office and speak to her very severely indeed.'

At the word 'severely', both her interviewers leaned forward with such enthusiasm that she continued: 'I have a no-tolerance policy for that kind of language. I would have to spank her till she learned her lesson, and then I would almost certainly make her lick me out to emphasize the point that we all have bisexual tendencies and they're nothing to be ashamed of.'

'Perfect!' Miss Delante said brightly. 'Don't you think, Mr Winter?'

He nodded.

'Miss Lavington, I'd like you to show us exactly how you would handle that interview with the young lady. Miss Delante, if you wouldn't mind?'

'Oh, my pleasure!'

Miss Delante extinguished her cigarette and stood up, walking with hip-swinging grace around the coffee table.

'I shall take the role of the naughty girl,' she said with enthusiasm. 'We can assume that you've already conducted the verbal tongue-lashing part of the reprimand, and go straight to the physical side of things.'

'You've been a very, very naughty young woman!' Miss Lavington said, promptly standing up and assuming a severe expression. 'How dare you behave like this! Take off your jacket immediately and bend over my desk.'

She pointed to the small round dining table across the

room, with a chair set to each side. Miss Delante removed her jacket and adopted the position, and Miss Lavington administered five hard spanks to her upthrust buttocks.

Miss Delante said breathlessly: 'I'm sorry, Miss—'

'Oh, you're going to be *much* sorrier before I'm finished with you!' Miss Lavington said. 'Your parents are paying a fortune for you to be taught proper manners, and you won't leave this room until I think you've learned your lesson! Take your trousers down. I'm going to spank you till your bum's as red as a tomato.'

Mr Winter was unzipping his own trousers, a happy smile on his face, manoeuvring his hard cock out from the slit in his boxers; Miss Lavington, casting a swift glance over at him, was reassured that she was handling this scenario just as required. Miss Delante dropped her own trousers, revealing a small, flat bottom clad in black lace briefs.

'You naughty, *naughty* girl!' Miss Lavington exclaimed disapprovingly. 'Wearing slutty knickers like that to school! Do you wear those when you suck the boys off, you dirty little thing?'

She gathered the lace briefs in each hand, jerking them to bunch up in the centre of Miss Delante's buttocks, exposing them fully.

'I bet you do,' she said, her open hand coming down with a loud slap on each cheek in turn. Every time she administered a spank, her small bosoms wobbled a little with the effort, and Mr Winter licked his lips in appreciation as he watched the effect. 'I bet you stuff as much cock in your mouth as you can get, don't you, a filthy little thing like you?'

Mr Winter was pulling on his own, watching the scene

with the air of a connoisseur, as Miss Delante writhed and moaned and begged in vain for mercy. Miss Lavington did not stop till, as promised, the nearly-bare bottom before her was bright red and the imprint of her finger marks was clearly visible over its curves.

'There, that looks much better,' Miss Lavington said, stepping back and pulling up her skirt to reveal a cream lace suspender belt holding up her stockings, and a complete absence of any underpants at all. 'Why are you being punished? Can you tell me?'

Miss Delante stood up, rubbing her sore bottom with a satisfied smile.

'For calling a boy gay, Miss,' she said. 'I'm really sorry.'

'Sorry isn't good enough!' Miss Lavington snapped, sitting down on the table in her turn, holding her skirt up at her waist, spreading her legs. 'How dare you be so disrespectful to our gay friends! You can apologize by eating out my pussy like you mean it.'

Eagerly, Miss Delante dropped to her knees in front of the other woman. Miss Lavington sank both hands into Miss Delante's thick, glossy hair, pulling her mouth right into her crotch, starting to moan straight away. Her legs wrapped around Miss Delante's back, her spine arched, and she groaned:

'Oh yeah, you dirty little thing . . . yeah, stick your tongue in my cunt and eat me out . . . yeah, lick my clit like that, lick it hard . . . fuck, yes, make me fucking come, you dirty girl . . .'

Mr Winter lifted his hand to his mouth, spat on it, and replaced it around his cock, pulling and twisting it simultaneously in slow, expert strokes, his own legs splayed, his head lolling against the pillows at the back of the sofa, but still at an angle to enable him to watch the woman on her knees eagerly servicing the one on the table. Miss Lavington's bottom was rebounding now as she came, shoving her pussy into Miss Delante's mouth, the table rocking wildly; it was a good few minutes before the latter pulled back, her lips sticky and wet, and smiled up at Miss Lavington, whose glasses were now askew on her nose and whose blonde hair was starting to fall down around her shoulders.

Miss Lavington, her cheeks flushed, her lips red from where she had bitten them, waited to pick up her next cue. Miss Delante slid her hand down to rub her own crotch, slid her finger inside herself and then inserted it into Miss Lavington's mouth for her to suck.

'I think it's time we played with a naughty little boy,' she said with a conspiratorial grin. 'Don't you?'

'Ooh,' Miss Lavington said, when the finger was removed again. 'I *love* playing with naughty boys who need disciplining!'

'This one needs a *lot* of discipline,' Miss Delante assured her. 'Look at him sitting there with his cock out!'

She strode over to the sofa and slapped Mr Winter's cock lightly, making it bounce and strain towards her.

'For that,' she said menacingly, 'you don't get to come until we tell you.'

She bent down and wrapped her hand around his cock, pulling at it, forcing him to his feet to walk – stepping out of his trousers as he did so – across the room following her. She led him through the open connecting door and into the large bedroom. At the foot of the bed, she stopped.

'Take off your tie,' she commanded, and when he had obeyed, she said to Miss Lavington: 'Pull off his boxers and tie this around the base of his cock. Tight. Like a cock ring.' The large cock swelled even more as soon as she said the words, eager for punishment.

'Ooh, what a naughty boy he is!' Miss Lavington said, pushing her glasses firmly onto the bridge of her nose again. 'He wants it badly, doesn't he?'

'He needs a good spanking,' Miss Delante said firmly. 'He needs to get on his knees on the bed and have his arse tanned.'

'Both of us at once,' Miss Lavington said, managing to give this line just enough of a questioning inflection so that she could be sure it was what her clients wanted.

'*Oh* yeah,' Miss Delante said, taking off her blouse. She was also small-chested, and was not wearing a bra.

There was not only a large mirror behind the king-size bed, but one above it. As Mr Winter climbed onto the bed, his big cock swinging between his legs, the silk tie dangling from it, he was able to lift his head to see both women pull their arms back and start to deliver a long, stinging series of punishing slaps to his tight, round butttocks. Every so often Miss Delante would break off, reach around and slap his cock, making it bounce, pre-cum glistening on its big round head, and every time she did so he groaned in pleasure. Miss Delante was in charge now, Miss Lavington following her cue with professional expertise. They didn't stop until his bottom was as red as Miss Delante's had been, and then Miss Delante said gleefully, pushing him to turn over and lie on his back:

'You suck him off, but don't let him come. He doesn't deserve it yet, the dirty boy. Every time you feel he's getting there, pull back and spank his cock.' She smiled. 'Trust me, he's *very* well-trained.'

Miss Lavington wasted no time, taking off her skirt in a swift motion before climbing onto the bed, kneeling between Mr Winter's spread legs and starting to obey orders, her pretty pink lips spread wide to accommodate his girth. Miss Delante was also on the bed now, still in her stilettos. Having dragged off her lace knickers, she was straddling Mr Winter's face, lowering her shaved crotch onto his waiting mouth.

'Eat me out, you naughty boy,' she commanded. 'Make me come like I made her. I'm going to fuck your face with my pussy right now . . . oh God . . .'

His mouth closed around her, his teeth lightly digging in as he started work.

'Fuck, fuck, *fuck*!' she wailed, gripping the headboard, muscles in her thighs standing out as she braced herself, rising and lowering, hitting peak after peak, watching herself come in the mirror behind the bed, which was angled to give her a view of the entire scene. If she tilted slightly sideways she could see Miss Lavington deep-throating Mr Winter's cock, lifting her head at intervals, gasping for breath, slapping the cock with a carefully judged open palm as she had been instructed.

One last bump and grind, one last long spasm as she watched the scene behind her for an extra thrill, and then she held herself, gasping, in the air, her strong lean thighs trembling; she needed a break, couldn't take any more for the moment. Miss Lavington raised her head alertly as she saw Miss Delante still gasping, her whole body throbbing as she recovered from her series of orgasms.

'I think you should come on her tits,' Miss Delante managed to say, rolling over to lie next to Mr Winter, propped up on the bed pillows. 'Don't you?'

'Oh *God* yes,' he said with enthusiasm.

Reaching down, he took hold of his cock, which was so swollen and red it had looked on the verge of shooting for the last ten minutes. Still with the tie wrapped around its base, he pulled on it hard; it was slick from Miss Lavington's enthusiastically applied saliva, and quivered like a tightly wound spring in his fist. Miss Lavington, always fast to pick up prompts, knelt up between his legs, leaning forwards so that her small firm breasts were directly over the head of his cock; in just a few seconds, Mr Winter was groaning, his hips pumping upwards, his back arching, as a stream of hot milky semen shot upwards in an impressive fountain, bathing her pink nipples as he directed it with an expert hand.

Miss Delante watched in open appreciation as he decorated Miss Lavington's breasts with a lavish coating of almond-scented liquid. Miss Lavington gave every appearance of delight; when, eventually, the last trickle had finally subsided, and Mr Winter collapsed back onto the pillows with a deep grunt of satisfaction, she sat back on her knees, palms over her breasts, making circles on them, rubbing it in, making soft moans of pleasure.

'Well!' Mr Winter said, looking at Miss Delante in the mirror above their heads. 'I think that was a satisfactory interview, don't you?'

'Oh, definitely,' she said drowsily. 'Damn, I want a cigarette and I left mine in the living room.'

'Oh, let me!' Miss Lavington slipped from the bed, walking across to the connecting door without a shred of self-conciousness about the fact that she was clad only in her suspender belt, stockings and T-bar shoes.

'Nice little arse,' Mr Winter said, reaching for another pillow to put behind his back, watching Miss Lavington enter the living room with great appreciation. 'Next time, I want to spank that and then fuck her up it while she eats you out.'

'You want her to stay on?' Miss Delante asked.

'God, no,' he said, yawning. 'You know the old saying, you pay them to leave. But next time you're in town, she can be the schoolgirl. We'll turn her out every which way. You've got a strap-on, right?'

'Honestly, Angel! It's like you don't know me!' she said, faking astonishment.

He laughed, meeting her eyes in the angled mirror.

'Yes – it may have been a while, but some things don't change, eh? Although back then, we had to improvise . . . oh, those cucumbers we used to steal from the school kitchen . . .'

'We were terribly deprived children,' she agreed, smiling at him wickedly.

'Deprived *and* depraved,' he said neatly.

Miss Lavington re-entered the bedroom carrying Miss Delante's pack of cigarettes, her lighter and an ashtray.

'How thoughtful,' Miss Delante said gratefully.

'My pleasure!' Miss Lavington said, dimpling into a smile. 'It really *was*. So, my two hours are nearly up, and . . .'

She tailed off tactfully to allow her clients to express a

wish for her to stay longer, or pronounce themselves fully satisfied.

'That'll be all for today,' the man called Angel said, twisting up on his elbow to take a cigarette from Miss Delante, who was proffering him the packet. 'We're fully satisfied. There's a tip on the mantelpiece for you. You're *very* talented at improvising – I see why your agency recommended you so highly.'

'Oh, thank you!' she said with great enthusiasm. 'I love role play!'

Demonstrating that she understood completely that an escort is paid, above all, to leave after her work is done, Miss Lavington gave the couple on the bed a seductive wink and then removed her skirt from the bedroom floor, her cash tip of five hundred pounds from the mantelpiece and herself from the bedroom, closing the door behind her.

'There's a loo off the living room, right?' Miss Delante said. 'She can wash up?'

'Of course,' Angel said. 'But these girls always carry wet wipes.'

'Ugh, you disgusting male clients with all your leakages,' Miss Delante said, pulling a comic face of disgust.

'Please, Nicole, you love it,' Angel said, grinning. 'I once saw you suck off every boy after a male tennis doubles match at school, and swallow every last drop. And then you did the umpire, too.'

'Mmm, that was Herr Hoffman,' Nicole said dreamily, drawing on her cigarette. '*So* hot! I had the most enormous crush on him. Remember? Big and blond and built like a brick shithouse, thigh muscles the size of hams? I saved him for last. God, I'd never do that again, though, five in a row!

Someone told me a few years ago that the calorie content of sperm is through the roof! It was all very well when I was sixteen – seriously, you can suck guys off all day at that age and not put on a pound.'

'I'm disappointed,' Angel said, sending a curl of smoke up to the mirror above. 'Aren't you going to blow me even once, for old times' sake?'

'Well, maybe for you,' Nicole said, reaching out a hand to tweak one of his nipples. 'For old times' sake. You're in great shape, Angel.'

'I'm vain,' he said negligently. 'I play tennis and squash every day and eat paleo.'

Nicole looked appreciatively down his body. Long, strong limbs and a nicely muscled chest, with a stomach that wasn't rippled with muscle but smooth and flat: a tennis player's body, not a bodybuilder's. He was very well proportioned, the slimness of his hips making his cock look even bigger by contrast, and very smooth – only a light dusting of golden hair on his thighs and forearms, the nest of curls at his groin a deeper guinea-gold, as were the damp tufts of hair at his armpits.

However elegant and lean his body was, though, it was Angel's face that melted so many hearts. He fully lived up to the name his mother had given him on first sight of his delicate features; his wide, amethyst eyes were just as stunning on a grown man as they had been on a small child, and although his fair curls were darker now, deep gold rather than white-blond, they still framed his face like a halo. His features were those of a Byronic hero, with his high forehead, straight nose and full, almost pouty lips the colour of raspberry sorbet.

'You know, I think you're dead wrong about the calorie content of come,' he said, reaching for his phone. 'I'd be a lot fatter if you were right. And look what great bodies gay men have! It's just not possible.'

Nicole frowned as she took this in. Angel was thumbing his phone, tapping those words into a search engine.

'If that bitch did it deliberately,' she said with rising wrath, 'I'm going to – ugh, I don't know what I'll do, but something really, really bad . . .'

'Five to ten calories, tops,' Angel announced cheerfully. 'Thank God. No saturated fat, only one per cent cholesterol, and phew, a very low sodium content. And . . . drumroll, wait for it . . . carbohydrate content negligible. Effectively zero per cent. You've been had, Nicole. Some jealous bitch want to steal your man away from you?'

'That fucking cow,' Nicole said with real venom, sitting up to stub out her cigarette, twisting to the ashtray on the bedside table. She was so slim that her flat stomach barely bulged as she did so. 'I'm going to have to think up something really *awful* to revenge myself.'

'Roofie her and shave her head,' Angel said. 'Go old-school.'

'Honestly, you're right,' Nicole said. 'Remember when I did that to that slut Gisele at school because she was Herr Hoffman's little whore and I was crazy about him? We didn't have roofies then, though. I had to get her really drunk on Martini Dry.'

'Didn't she burn her arse on a radiator?' Angel said, exhaling another curl of smoke. 'Or am I thinking of someone else?'

'No, it was perfect!' Nicole said, cheering up at the memory.

'I got her to drink nearly the whole bottle on a dare, and then when she passed out I shaved her head with Panio's electric razor.'

'God, he was so hairy!' Angel said. 'He looked like he was wearing a black mohair sweater underneath his shirt. Put me off Greek boys for years.'

Nicole giggled.

'Anyway,' she said, 'after I shaved her head I left her there with all the hair just lying around her, but she must have got up in the middle of the night and gone for a wee – all that Martini – and instead of going to the loo, she sat down on the bathroom radiator instead and pissed on it right there, and she burnt her bum in stripes – it was one of those old iron metal ones. She was so out of it she didn't even realize what she'd done till she woke up later and started screeching in pain. Matron had her face down in the infirmary for three days. She couldn't sit down properly for at least a week.'

Nicole smirked.

'And Herr Hoffman liked to do it best with the girl sitting on his lap in her little tennis skirt, so by the time she was fit to go again I'd been in there for weeks fucking him dry,' she finished with great satisfaction. 'He was a bit of a disappointment, actually. Not that big and he didn't last that long. But I still fucked him all the rest of the term, just to piss off Gisele.'

'*So,*' Angel said, extinguishing his own cigarette and sitting up, 'poor little Gisele had stripes all over her arse, did she?'

Nicole flipped onto her stomach and reached back to trace lines down her smooth bottom.

'Like *this,*' she said, watching him with her head turned

to one side on the pillow, her hazel eyes bright. 'And *this*, and *this* . . .'

'I think,' Angel said, his cock hardening as she drew her finger slowly along her buttocks, 'that we should recreate that effect for old times' sake. Don't you?'

'Oh *yes*,' she said, wriggling contentedly. 'God, Angel, we have to talk business! You keep distracting me! I've got this fantastic proposition for you. A massive score. Really, it's a once-in-a-lifetime opportunity.'

'But darling, I don't want a timeshare in Florida!' Angel said, swinging his long legs off the bed.

'Shut *up*,' she said, giggling. 'As *if*. No, it's genius. We could both make a fortune. It's very devious, though.'

'Sounds right up my street,' Angel said as he strolled over to the wall of built-in wardrobes that lined one whole side of the large bedroom. 'You must tell me all about it after I've striped your bottom.'

From one of the wardrobes, he retrieved something that he swished menacingly through the air as he returned to the bed.

'Ooh! A proper cane!' Nicole said in delight. 'Just like Madame Martel had!'

'You won't believe this,' Angel said smugly, 'but it's exactly the same one. I convinced her to give it to me when I left school. I said I wanted a fond memento that would always remind me of her in the years to come.'

'You were always her favourite,' Nicole said. 'Teacher's pet.'

'She let me do some of the canings in my last year,' Angel said. 'You were gone by then, of course. I often used to fantasize it was your arse I was striping.'

'Well, now it is!' Nicole reached forward, grabbed a pillow and slid it under her hips.

'I won't go mad,' he said, running the cane down the cleft of her buttocks, making her writhe a little in anticipation. 'Just a few perfect strokes, some pretty red lines I can look at later while I fuck you from behind. Trust me, I was Madame Martel's best student.'

The cane lifted and came down with a hiss as it sliced through the air and onto Nicole's left buttock. As promised, it was the lightest of touches, far away from anything that could have cut the skin, and it left a straight red stripe, perfectly vertical, which caused the wielder of the cane to smile in satisfaction.

'I think there's room for five more,' he said delightedly. 'Oh, Nicole, you're going to *love* how this looks. Really, it's *just* like being back at school!'

Chapter Five

Tylösand, Sweden – the same afternoon

Christine Smith was sweaty and pink-cheeked, her leg muscles aching, her chest heaving from her long scramble along the crags and rocky outcrops that lined this part of the Swedish shoreline. Glancing at her watch, she was taken aback to see she had been walking – or rather hiking – for almost two hours; she wasn't naturally sporty. Clearly, she had needed to burn off even more frustration than she had realized.

Christine was taking a huge risk being here in Sweden, rather than back in London at her desk at Berkeley, the auction house where she worked. Every day that she woke up in her luxurious room at the five-star Hotel Tylösand, she was digging a deeper hole for herself, because it meant that another twenty-four hours had passed without her achieving what she had come here to do. She was spending money she didn't have, and because she had taken unpaid leave from work, she was depleting her scanty resources without the anticipation of much salary landing in her account at the end of the month.

God knew, even a whole month's salary wasn't exactly a generous sum. Auction houses famously paid their lower-grade staff very little – those jobs were usually taken by scions of rich families, fresh from an Art History degree at Cambridge or the Courtauld Institute, who were supported by trust funds and had rent-free accommodation at the flat in Eaton Square their family used as London digs. Christine had only snagged the post of assistant gemmologist in Berkeley's Fine Gems department because her qualifications were as close to perfect as humanly possible. Birmingham University might not have the glamour of Cambridge or the Courtauld, but its three-year BSc in Gemmology and Jewellery Studies was the most respected degree in her field, and she had been not only the most gifted but the most hardworking student, according to her professors, for many years.

For Christine, there had never been any other option but hard work. Taken into care at five, she had ended up with foster parents whose house was run like a business, taking in as many children as they could with the consideration entirely on how to maximize the stipend they were paid per head. It was a dormitory rather than a home, the children expected to stay out until dinnertime and head straight to their rooms after bolting down their meal – rooms they shared with as many other kids as could be crammed into them.

Christine's escape had been the library during the day and borrowed books at night, headphones in her ears to block out the mayhem of the other foster kids fighting around her, a torch under the covers to read after lights out. When, at fifteen, she had come across a crime novel in which the detective had had to consult a gemmologist at an auction house about whether a diamond necklace was real or fake, it was as if the torch had turned to illuminate her own face. *That* was the career for her, she had known instinctively, and she had never wavered from it. Like a child taking part in a school play and realizing they want to be an actor, or seeing a pianist on TV and suddenly craving to take piano lessons, Christine had known not only that she wanted to be a gemmologist, but that she would have a natural talent for it.

Every decision after that had been made with a single goal in mind: to secure a place on that degree course, to be elected a Fellow of the Gemmological Institute of Great Britain, and to get a job at an auction house, becoming head of her department just like the character in the novel. However, once the dust had cleared and the frenzy of studying, interviewing for jobs and proving herself at work had abated, Christine had looked around Berkeley and realized that her path to the head of department office – the partnership track – would not be achieved with what had worked for her so far, a combination of innate ability and sheer graft.

Because the crucial element she lacked was the range of social connections with which her colleagues had been born. They would routinely hear about estates that were about to become available for auction because of the impending death, say, of a rich great-aunt with an enviable collection of fine art, or ceramics, or jewellery, and they would move in to steer the heirs and executors to Berkeley. In addition, they knew hedge-funders and property moguls who could afford to splurge on lavish purchases. Although Berkeley was increasingly reliant on Christine's abilities for authenticating gems, those skills would not get her promoted. She was watching colleagues who had been hired at more or less the same time as her rise through the ranks in various departments, and it was not because their knowledge of Old Master paintings or Japanese netsuke was encyclopaedic. It was because they drank champagne on Jermyn Street with those hedge-funders, spent weekends shooting grouse with aristocrats, could bring a steady stream of sellers and buyers to Berkeley.

Christine could never compete with their level of access to the one per cent – the people they had grown up with, the ones they had met at private school or university or clubs on Pall Mall. She needed, she gradually realized, to pull off a major coup if she were to stand any chance of getting onto the partnership track; otherwise she would be Berkeley's back room expert forever, her expertise ensuring her a job for life, but one that paid a comparative pittance. And there would be no point in changing jobs. If Christie's or Sotheby's or Bonhams had an opening for a star gemmologist, Christine would definitely be a serious contender, but she would face exactly the same problems there as she did at Berkeley.

So she had applied her brain to the situation, as she had done when she was strategizing how to become a gemmologist: confronted the extent of the task in front of her, calculated what she would need to do to achieve her goal. The trouble was that she had only seen a single genuine possibility, and it was extremely unlikely that she would be able to pull it off. This trip to Sweden was costing her a fortune, and it wasn't as if she had savings to fall back on.

Living in London was horrifically expensive. She couldn't possibly afford a deposit for a mortgage on what Berkeley paid her, and her rent consumed a significant amount of her income. She was already relying on her credit cards, something that terrified her. Her biological family were in and out of prison; she had had no ties to them since she was taken into care. She had been forced to be her own safety net, and it always felt as if she was just one step away from the edge of the abyss.

Already, she was fielding irate calls and emails from her boss, who was becoming increasingly vexed not only at her absence but that Christine, who had pleaded a vaguely described family emergency, wasn't able to give a fixed return date. The appraisals were piling up, and she was the only one in the Fine Gems department who could be trusted with the most delicate and complicated of them. But no one was indispensable, and her boss was beginning to make noises to that effect.

The irony of Christine's current situation had not escaped her. All her fellow guests at the Hotel Tylösand were here, on this stunning stretch of the south coast of Sweden, for rest and relaxation. It was a spa hotel, so even if they were attending a conference in the business centre during the day, afterwards, with typical Scandinavian ease about their bodies, the participants would don robes and head for the huge inside pool and Jacuzzis, the steam rooms, water massage and outside hot pool to unwind. They would each choose a lounger in the glass-walled relaxation room with its panoramic views over the seashore and lie there as if in bed, watching the sun set behind the waves and the stars come out.

Only Christine was tense, on high alert, in the midst of all this luxury and ease, despite the fact that she had never stayed in such a luxurious resort hotel in her life. Even on an overcast September day, it was breathtaking. Her room had a balcony with a stunning view over the sand dunes that sloped down to the grey waters of the Baltic Sea beyond.

Every morning as she pulled back the curtains, the sight of the sky meeting the sea, broken only by the pretty island with its little red and white lighthouse seeming to float just off the coast, gave her precisely the sense of calm and peace that the hotel had been designed to evoke for its guests.

For about a minute, she thought grimly now, as she stood, catching her breath after a steep ascent, on the high rocky outcrop at one end of the wide sandy beach directly below the hotel. *I feel lovely and floaty and peaceful for about a minute, until I remember how much this is costing me and start freaking out that it'll all be in vain. That all my planning and scheming and sneakiness have been for nothing.*

Because I'm beginning to be afraid that even after I've spent all this money, taken time off from work I can't afford and pissed off my boss so much that I'll be lucky not to get the sack when I get back to London, I'll never manage to meet Vivienne Winter . . .

The wind was wild this afternoon, lathering the sea into a frenzy. Waves crashed against the rocks below Christine like hammer blows, the spume hitting the stone then bouncing and tumbling up, twisting in the strong breeze, big white bubbles as frothy as if they had been formed in a high-powered Jacuzzi and then fired from a water cannon. Some, rebounding from the tips of the rocks, flew so fast through the air that they landed metres from the sea on the thick grass and broom close to Christine's feet. She bent down, fascinated, and slipped her hand under one; it rested on her palm, much denser and firmer than a soap bubble, its consistency like whipped egg white, before she pursed her lips and blew it away, watching it turn and flip through the air once more.

I am not *going to see this as a metaphor, hopes and dreams whirling up in the wind then crashing on the rocks*, she told herself firmly. *I'm a sensible, practical person in the middle of taking a calculated risk that might get me sacked with no way to pay off the enormous credit card bill I'm busy racking up . . . Oh God . . .*

Standing up again, she took a deep breath of fresh, cool, salty air. It was wonderfully invigorating, and reminded her suddenly that it had been hours since she ate. The breakfast buffet at the hotel was unbelievable: as well as an omelette station, there was a huge spread of meats, cheeses, smoked salmon, caviar, herring and some other weird fish that Christine was completely unable to deal with first thing in the morning, not to mention any other time. You ordered your cold drinks by pressing a button on an iPad next to a single tap that then miraculously dispensed whatever you had selected; how they did that, she had no idea. It was like something out of *Charlie and the Chocolate Factory*.

And there were two entire tables laden with more varieties of pastries, breads and rolls than Christine had ever seen before. Swedish people clearly loved their carbs. Her favourite was the rye crispbread, baked in a giant circle two feet wide; it was shaped like a wheel, with a hole in the middle to allow the big flat pieces of bread to be slotted over the central spindle of a specially made wooden serving platter, so that you could break off as much or as little as you wanted.

Despite having tucked into a large ham and leek omelette, made to order, with tomatoes and peppers on the side, plus of course the crispbread, Christine was now starving. That was what a nearly two-hour trek would do for you. But it was a huge nuisance, because she was trying to fill up on breakfast – included in the room rate – and eat lightly at her two subsequent meals, in order to save money.

The intention had not been to work up an appetite on her long hike. She had just meant to let off some steam, because hanging around the public areas of the Hotel Tylösand, hoping to catch a glimpse of Vivienne Winter, was driving Christine mad with frustration. Vivienne was staying, of course, in one of the fifth-floor penthouse suites, with her own private terrace for total privacy and optimal sea views. Christine craned her head back to see if she could spot a small figure on the large wraparound, glass-walled balcony at one corner of the hotel building, doubtless wrapped in Vivienne's signature furs. No; the floor-to-ceiling glass windows were all closed. She didn't expect Vivienne to eat meals in the restaurants, of course, but the actress would have to descend to the spa for her daily visits, and that was when Christine was hoping to snatch a word with her, when she was relaxed from a spa treatment and likely to be amenable.

It wasn't a very good plan, but it was all she had. She had visited Vivienne's Mayfair apartment building, but her house-keeper had told her through the intercom that Ms Winter was at her villa in Montreux, and to write to her at that address. Christine had pleaded that she had written numerous letters to both the London and Montreux addresses, contacted Vivienne's various agents and business managers, and heard nothing back; the shrug the housekeeper gave in response to this was almost audible. But then, finding out from an online gossip magazine that Vivienne was in Tylösand for her annual spa trip, Christine had realized that it would be much easier to gain access to Vivienne here.

But no one could sit still indefinitely – especially not a twenty-six-year-old woman on a mission. Not even in such a beautiful spa area, all Scandi simplicity, pale wood, clear glass, and a deep central hot pool with a seating area in which Christine had spent hours so far pretending to read her Kindle while keeping a perpetual eye out for the actress. After days of this, feeling as if she were going to burst out of her skin, Christine had been unable to stay put any longer.

Now, her restlessness burnt off, she looked ruefully down at her trainers, which were as damp and clotted with sand as the treads of the wooden staircase. A thin, fit blonde in full trekking gear jogged past her with enviable ease straight up the path, casting a glance at Christine's comparatively feeble workout clothes – jeans, a too-thin hoodie, and the trainers that had repeatedly slipped on the rocky path. The blonde doubtless meant the look sympathetically, but Christine couldn't help taking it as judgement, and she grimaced in embarrassment at her comparative lack of fitness and suitable attire.

I'm a failure, she thought in total gloom. *I'm spending a fortune for nothing, I'm in the most beautiful place I've ever been in my life but I can't even enjoy it. And I really ought to go to the gym more often! Look how that woman's running up the hill – she's barely breaking a sweat, her face was hardly even pink – God, I wish I was in that sort of shape!*

She knew she should get back, have a shower, take up her vigil again in the spa area. But the fresh air was so bracing, and as soon as the negative thoughts flooded in – fear of never managing to meet Vivienne, guilt about not exercising regularly – the salt breeze seemed to sweep them away again, making her optimistic despite everything. And the damp sand, stretching out in front of her, was so tempting . . .

Christine had avoided walking too close to the water on her outward trek, but at this point her trainers were already wet: in for a penny, in for a pound. So she greeted the impulse to climb down to the beach and start making footprints with absolute delight. Childish, silly fun for a little while was exactly what she needed to help distract her from her gloomy thoughts, and as she ran across the beach she looked back gleefully to see the line her feet had made in the sand.

It was low season, with a grey sky and heavy clouds overhead, a few drops of rain falling now and then: weather unattractive enough to dissuade most people from venturing outside, apart from a fitness freak running up the rock path, or a visiting Englishwoman who was going stir-crazy. There was just one other figure visible far down at the other end of the beach, walking a couple of dogs, distant enough not to see Christine capering around like a crazy woman. She'd never been taken to the beach when she was little, never played as a child on wet sand, trying to get the patterns she was making absolutely perfect, and for a few moments she was genuinely delighted at the fun she was having. It felt like catching up for lost time, an impulsive reward for all the years spent studying rather than playing . . .

She was so absorbed that she was quite oblivious both to how sodden her feet were getting and to the large, black-sheathed figure emerging from the cold waters of the Baltic Sea, just a few metres down from where she was messing around on the beach like a kid. The figure, seeing Christine, stopped to watch her antics, tilting back its face mask and snorkel for a better view. It was a man, built square and solid, his frame blocky, the shiny, sleek wetsuit making him look almost like a mythical hybrid of man and seal rising from the depths of the ocean.

He stood there for a while, seeming unaffected by the cold water lapping around his thighs, the heavy push and pull of the waves. Eventually he spoke, timing it for the moment when Christine had finished a particularly ambitious zigzagging outline. She jumped in total shock, looking around the beach frantically for the source of the voice; only when he repeated his greeting did she swivel round, trainers churning up the sand, to see him standing there in the sea.

'Shit!' she said involuntarily. 'You nearly gave me a heart attack! Where did you *come* from?'

The man opened his mouth, paused for a second, and then said:

'English, yes?' in a strong accent.

'Yes! You really scared me! Isn't it a bit cold to be swimming?'

He said something that sounded like: '*Zdra-stvooy-tye*,' bowing in a comically formal way as he did so. 'I am sorry for scaring! Hello! English good,' he continued. 'English people very good and kind.'

'Um, thank you,' Christine said, baffled now not just about where he had come from, but where this was going. He was wading out of the sea now, and she watched the strong, steady thrust of his heavily muscled thighs and calves through the water with considerable appreciation. The wetsuit clung to him, a second skin that displayed not just his solid torso, his flat stomach and imposing pectorals to great effect, but also his considerable biceps.

I do need to get back inside on Vivienne watch, she told herself, *but this is certainly perking up my day. No harm having a friendly chat with Hot Wetsuit Man, is there?*

'Please, tell me that you are kind English woman,' Hot Wetsuit Man said. As he emerged from the Baltic she saw that he was wearing flippers. The fact that he was managing to walk across the sand in them without looking like a clumsy, waddling idiot was almost as impressive as his musculature.

'I *usually* am,' Christine said warily as he reached her and, to her great surprise, took her hand, sandwiching it between both of his. He stood looking down at her, his mask pushed high on his forehead like a pair of sunglasses, his eyes a light, bright blue, the hair plastered to his scalp a dark rusty gold. He wasn't handsome, but he was hugely attractive, reminding Christine of the film star Rutger Hauer in his prime, with his strong jaw, big, uneven nose and unflinching blue gaze; her foster mother had had the biggest crush on him. Hauer had been blonder, but this man could have been a younger version of him, apart from the copper-tinged hair.

'I am Sergei,' he said, letting her hand go to pound on his chest. 'Sergei from *Rosseeeya*. You say Russia.'

'Um, hello, Sergei,' Christine said, confused but game. 'I'm Christine. It's very nice to meet you.'

'I am from Russian – what you call submarine,' he said. 'You have heard of this?'

Christine wasn't a news junkie, but it would have been impossible to have been in Sweden for a few days and not know what he was talking about. It was on the cover of every newspaper lined up on tables in the hotel breakfast area and in reception, it was the headline of the *Daily Mail* online, which Christine checked in the mornings, and every time she switched on the TV in her room the story was leading the news bulletins. The Swedes were accusing the Russian navy of having sneaked one of their submarines into the territorial waters of the Swedish archipelago; the Russian defence ministry staunchly denied it. There was no photographic evidence, but multiple sightings had been reported. Not only was the Swedish navy out searching for it, but several newspapers had hired helicopters to try to spot the errant sub, as it would be a huge diplomatic incident if its presence could be verified.

So when the diver identified himself as being from the Russian submarine, Christine's jaw actually dropped in shock at the revelation. She tasted salty air in her mouth for a moment before she closed it again.

'You're *what*?' she blurted out.

'I see you know about this!' Sergei said earnestly. 'You stay in hotel there, *da*?'

He gestured to the low, wide central building of the Hotel Tylösand high behind them, a gleaming modern edifice of glass and stone and wood, a triumph of elegant Scandinavian design.

'Yes,' she said automatically, still processing the fact that she had been precipitated into the middle of the biggest news story of the moment. Only yesterday, the media had been fanning themselves into a frenzy over a report that a mysterious 'man in black' had been spotted and reported to naval intelligence, who had diligently tracked him down and discovered him to be not a Russian seaman, but a pensioner fishing for sea trout. But what if the pensioner had been a false lead, and the man in black had been a Russian sailor all along – maybe stranded by some diving accident? What if he was the man standing in front of her right now?

'You are by yourself in the hotel?' he was asking, and Christine nodded, because he was a handsome man who seemed not remotely threatening, his gaze was giving her very pleasant thrills up and down her body, and she was not only by herself, but single. Clearly, she wasn't expecting a long-term relationship with an escapee from a Russian submarine, but he *was* ridiculously attractive . . .

'May I stay in your room? *Pazhalsta?*' the Rutger Hauer lookalike asked anxiously. 'Please yes? They must not find me! I can hide there till I swim back to my submarine!'

For a long moment, Christine could think of nothing but this large, luscious hunk of a man in her hotel room. Showering in her bathroom, wrapping around his waist one of the generously sized towels that would surely however reveal a considerable amount of his well-built frame, padding into her bedroom, barefoot, smelling of the lovely Bigelow toiletries the hotel provided, looking at her with those amazing light blue eyes, smiling maybe the way he was doing now, so appreciatively, as if he found her just as attractive as she did him . . . both of them, at that point, deciding on a very pleasurable activity that would pass the time waiting for his submarine to come and fetch him . . .

Right. And when you get caught sheltering him, which you will, her brain said, *they'll arrest you for being a Russian spy.*

And by the time they realize – if they do! – that you're just some idiot who got swept away by a gorgeous man in a wetsuit, Vivienne Winter will have checked out of the hotel and you'll have no chance at all of getting that precious word with her that you've staked so much on . . . you know that has to be your priority . . .

'I can't,' she said, sounding, as she was perfectly aware, wistful. 'I'm really sorry, but I just *can't.*'

'You could bring me coat,' Sergei said. 'White coat, like they have.'

He pointed up to the terrace with the sunken, heated outdoor soaking pool; a couple of guests were leaning on the balcony, taking in the sea view, dressed in the hotel's white towelling spa robes.

'I take this off,' he said, gesturing to the wetsuit and flippers. 'I put on coat and walk in with you. No one knows who I am! Then I come to your room to hide.'

Christine swallowed hard at the image, once more very vivid, of Sergei peeling off his wetsuit, sheltered by a rocky outcrop, standing there completely naked in his muscular splendour, then accompanying her into the hotel, just the towelling robe to cover his nudity . . .

'I *can't!*' Her voice rose to a pathetic squeak. 'I just can't take the risk. I'm so sorry.'

Sergei hung his large head, utterly disconsolate.

'I have been swim for long time,' he said sadly. 'I am hunger.'

'I can go inside and get you something to eat,' Christine offered; his expression was so disappointed, and he wasn't being pushy or insistent, which of course made her want to help him even more.

'And drink!' Sergei brightened up. 'Vodka! You bring vodka and we drink together on beach – we find quiet place I can hide, we sit and drink and I recite to you Russian poems about beautiful women who are kind and gentle to sailors lost from their ship . . .'

Christine's eyes narrowed. Finally, her brain, rather than other parts of her anatomy, was kicking in.

'Hang on,' she said suspiciously, her tone no longer apologetic. 'You're not trying to tell me that you swam off a submarine in a *snorkel*? You'd have an oxygen tank and a proper mask, surely?'

'I was just doing a, what do you call, reconnaissance,' Sergei said smoothly. 'A quick check to see if the Swedes have found where we are hiding.'

'Right, and your English is getting better by the second,' Christine said, pulling her hand away. '"Reconnaissance"! And a minute ago it was "English people very good and kind!" You're taking the piss, aren't you?'

His English was certainly good enough for him to understand that amount of vernacular. 'Sergei' threw back his head and burst out laughing.

'May I?' he said, reaching out for her hand once more.

Christine held back. 'What's your real name?' she said, trying to sound reproachful, but unable to stop her voice coming out flirtatiously. She knew that her eyes were sparkling, her lips curving into a smile; this was all happening very fast, this handsome man attempting an epic tease as a way to break the ice with her, and the fact that she had spotted it fast and turned it back on him made her fizz with pride at her own swiftness. Of course she should have realized the truth before, but she could scarcely blame herself – when a muscly hunk in a skin-tight wetsuit accosted you on a beach and asked if he could stay in your hotel room, naturally you would be distracted for a while from the likelihood of his story by all kinds of in-appropriate thoughts . . .

'I'm called Tor,' he said, in an accent completely different from the fake Russian one he had been putting on. Now he sounded Swedish, like everyone who worked at the Hotel Tylösand, but with a strong American tinge. 'I'm sorry,' he went on. 'I just couldn't resist. I was thinking as I came back in from my swim about that man in black who the navy was chasing, and how funny it would be if those people up on the terrace thought I was him. And then I saw you, and I wanted to talk to you because you're so pretty and you looked like you were having a great time making shapes in the sand, and I thought it would be so much fun to play the game with you. So the idea to play another game – to pretend I was Sergei from Russia – just popped into my head all at once. Forgive me?'

Tor was still holding out his hand, and because he had been brave enough to stand there with it out for the whole time he explained himself, looking awkward and vulnerable, and also because he was so good-looking and his blue eyes were twinkling in evident appreciation of her quick wits, Christine placed hers once more in his grasp. He promptly raised it to his lips and kissed it.

'I'm not saying that I forgive you,' Christine said, sounding extra stern because her head was spinning a little at the sensation of his lips on her skin.

'Of course not! What was I thinking!' he said gravely. 'I

will have to redeem myself in your eyes after teasing you like that. Will you please have a drink with me this evening in your hotel so we can begin the redemption process?'

Christine hesitated, but it was just because she was calculating when the Vivienne Winter Watch for that day would be over. Christine usually hung out in the spa until eight in the evening, just to be sure that she didn't miss her target; but it did seem rather unlikely that a woman in her seventies would be getting a massage or treatment that would run so late.

In that assumption, as it happened, she was completely wrong. Vivienne had always been a night bird.

'Please say yes!' the man called Tor said hopefully. '*Jag är ledsen!* I'm sorry! That's Swedish, by the way,' he added. 'Not Russian.'

'Thank you, I can tell the difference,' Christine said firmly.

She noticed he was looking quite anxious at her lack of response, and although he deserved some punishment for having tricked her, experience told her that if she left it any longer, the momentum would trickle away. He would think she was playing games – not the fun sort – and become less keen, more wary. That, she knew, was never a good way to start a date. It was Tor's open enthusiasm about seeing her that was so charming, and she mustn't allow that to dissipate by being too cool for school.

'Okay,' she said finally.

'Okay you will come for a drink?' he said with such visible hope for a positive answer that she heard herself giggle in sheer pleasure.

'Okay I will come for a drink. Tor,' she said, and was sure that she had gone a little pink saying his name.

'You are too kind, Christine,' he said, and she definitely felt the blood rising to her cheeks at the confirmation that this was a man who actually listened to a woman, at least to the point of remembering the name she had told him right at the start of their convoluted conversation. He, meanwhile, was positively beaming.

'But not before eight,' she clarified. 'I have, um, things I have to do before then.'

'Of course! I will let you go. Later, you must tell me all the fun things you have done today over cocktails in the hotel bar,' he said, finally releasing her hand. 'I look forward to hearing them.'

He made another little bow and then turned to head off down the beach. More than anything – apart from securing that meeting with Vivienne Winter – Christine wanted to watch Tor walk away, those firm buttocks rising and falling, tight and round in the shiny black wetsuit. But if he turned and caught her staring at his bum, she would be mortified.

Christine was fiercely career-focused; nothing could completely distract her from the mission she had come here to accomplish. But if anything could manage it for a little while – she allowed herself one glance at Tor's square black figure, now paused as he switched his weight from one foot to another, pulling off his flippers, then setting off again barefoot, running one hand through his thick copper-blond hair – if anything could, it would *certainly* be the anticipation of a date with a muscled Viking who had turned out to have a really good sense of humour.

Chapter Six

London – the same afternoon

'Well, darling, I'm thoroughly exhausted,' Angel said, his golden curls spreading against the padded headrest of his whirlpool bath. 'You're to keep your greedy little hands off my cock for at *least* a couple of hours.'

Nicole, lying at the other end of the bath, her shiny black hair dampening as the bubbles rose around them, the dark perfume and incense scent of Tom Ford's Oud Wood bath gel filling the bathroom, gave him a slumberous smile.

'Don't worry, darling,' she said. 'My poor bum is awfully sore. Want to spend the rest of the evening taking tranqs and passing out in front of some bad television?'

'Sounds delightful,' Angel said with great enthusiasm. 'Oh, I've missed you, Nic! Are you in London for a while, sweetie?'

'Yes,' Nicole said as she reached for her glass of chilled muscat. 'I happen to have made Hong Kong rather too hot to hold me for quite a while.'

'God, Nicole, what happened?' Angel asked, one of his elegant eyebrows arching. 'You had such a cosy little berth there!'

Nicole sighed as she took a sip. 'I got greedy,' she said frankly. 'You know I had this lovely setup with my dad?'

Angel nodded; Nicole's situation had been no secret from anyone at boarding school. She was the illegitimate daughter of a high-powered British banker resident on the island, who had maintained a Chinese-born mistress in the city for many years. The mistress had an apartment in her name on the Kowloon Peninsula, a driver and full health insurance; although very young when she met Nicole's father, she had negotiated successfully for the companionship she provided. And when she had, as planned, become pregnant with his child, those skills had been used to great effect for the benefit of her daughter.

Nicole had been educated by private tutors – largely to ensure that she did not associate with anyone who might also know her father's legitimate children – and then sent to Chateau Sainte-Beuve, high in the Swiss mountains, as soon as she turned eleven. Its fees were stomach-churningly expensive, but her father could afford them, and Nicole's mother had set her heart on her daughter having an education equal to anything her half-brothers and sisters were enjoying at their British boarding schools. Nicole's father had made discreet enquiries and been informed, by an executive director who had found himself in a similar situation, that Chateau Sainte-Beuve was famously flexible in its policy about the background of the students it chose to admit, and equally tactful about the parent interviews that most schools usually insisted on conducting.

As Nicole had found on arrival, this was far from being the only flexibility that Chateau Sainte-Beuve's staff and students enjoyed. Most new pupils took to the regime with great enthusiasm; they were, after all, pre-selected by virtue of the school being a notorious dumping ground for children who, though intelligent and well brought up, were not from conventional backgrounds. Angel had been kicked out of five schools before he ended up at the Chateau, but had instantly found it congenial. Vivienne had been full of relief that finally he had settled in a school that gave him such glowing reports – and certainly the institution would not have survived if it had not given its students an education that would enable them to go on to the best of universities. It was just that its methods of employing discipline, and its philosophy on how the students should best spend their leisure time, were extremely unorthodox.

On graduating from Chateau Sainte-Beuve, two years before Angel, Nicole had taken a degree and an MBA in America. She had then returned to Hong Kong – against her father's wishes, as he was now, ironically, the Chief Risk Officer of a hedge fund and even more scandal-averse than he had been when he first started seeing her mother. Realizing this, Nicole, with her mother's acumen, had secured from him, in addition to the monthly income she already received, a luxurious apartment close to her mother's, in return for an ironclad agreement that her parentage would never be mentioned. She had proceeded to establish a small financial advisory company that served as a cover for a range of much more nefarious activities.

'You didn't betray Dear Daddy, did you?' Angel asked now, lighting up a cigarette and propping his elbow on the black marble bath surround, hand high, to avoid it getting wet from the roiling water. 'Darling, never bite the hand that transfers money into your bank account! God knows I've learned that the hard way with Granny Viv!'

He grimaced, an edge to his voice as he pronounced Vivienne's name.

'No, I wasn't that silly,' Nicole said, rolling her eyes. 'I still have my monthly whack from Daddy. But I got involved in an insider trading deal that turned messy. I had to get out fast.'

'Oh dear,' Angel said, quite unsurprised. 'Interpol on your trail, or whatever they call it?'

'No, no, I covered my tracks as far as all that goes,' she assured him, sliding down so her shoulders were covered by the luxuriant bubbles. 'I was the middleman – middle woman – between this trader and the triads. It was perfect! I was totally safe from the police, because no way would the trader ever dare to give away his triad contacts, even if he got busted. Which he did, because he got greedy; but that wasn't the issue. The real problem was that I was fucking the triad guy – one of their White Paper Fans, which means he's on the financial side – and he thought he was the only guy I was seeing. Oops!'

She pulled a comic face.

'So when the shit hit the fan, Mr White Paper Fan had the trader killed in prison when he was waiting for trial – because he found out that I was fucking him too, and got really pissed off. *So*, I obviously needed to get out of town pronto, in case he decided I was next.'

'My God, how lurid!' Angel said, hugely entertained. 'Don't tell me you've brought the triads to my door?'

'No, no,' Nicole assured him. 'He's married to the daughter

of the Dragon Head – that's the big boss. Which meant that we were *ridiculously* quiet about the fucking part. So as soon as I left Honkers, I was fine. He isn't going to reach out to have the Wo Shing Wo – that's the British wing – come after me. That would be giving things away – making it really obvious that it's personal rather than business – because if I'm out of the country and not testifying against him, there's no need to bump me off. I never even said one word to the police there. I'm completely out of the loop.'

'God, Nicole,' Angel said, mesmerized. 'You do know how to live.'

She shrugged. 'Honkers isn't the Wild West,' she said nonchalantly. 'It's not that big a deal doing business with the triads. I just shouldn't go back there for, oh, twenty years or so, unless of course he drops dead unexpectedly. He was really into me.'

'*Not* a surprise,' Angel said appreciatively, taking a drag on his cigarette. 'Not a surprise at all, darling. What was he into?'

'Oh, the usual. Naughty girl sits on your lap and tells wicked stories about boarding school,' Nicole said airily. 'The funny thing is, of course, that most girls have to make them up, don't they, but mine were all true!'

She rolled her hazel eyes.

'In fact, I had to dial down some things, you know? I told him about sucking off the boys' doubles teams, and then Herr Hoffman, but I gave him the impression that they made me do it, rather than me begging them to let me so I could beat that whore Gisele's record.'

'I bet he *loved* your naughty tales,' Angel said, finishing his cigarette and stubbing it out in the large Venetian glass ashtray on the marble surround. 'Pour me some muscat, will you, my sweet?'

Nicole reached for another gold-rimmed dessert wine glass and poured a generous dram of amber liquid into it, sitting up to hand it to Angel. Water poured down her torso, bubbles clinging to her pert nipples, and Angel observed it with approval. He had installed colour-changing lighting in his bathroom, set into the large shower recess under the double sinks and black lacquered built-in cabinets, and as they cycled from golden yellow to greens to blues, purples, reds, and a flaming orange that faded into yellow again, their glow was reflected in the multiple mirrors that lined the walls, catching glimmers off the black marble and lacquer surfaces, creating an instant atmosphere of decadence and seduction. Their wet skin glimmered too, the lighting giving their slightest movement ripples of light and colour that were exquisitely erotic.

'Candles are much too much like hard work,' he had said airily to Nicole earlier, when she exclaimed in pleasure at the effect. 'All that melting wax, and remembering to blow them out when you're all happy and sleepy on muscle relaxants. I always look at the scenes in films with fifty candles lit around the bath and think "Amateurs". You know, school barely banned *anything*, but that "no smoking inside and no candles either" rule was bloody sensible. We'd have burned the place down in a month if they hadn't enforced it.'

Nicole clinked her glass with Angel's and continued, 'So I'm selling my Honkers apartment, and I've got a line on an exciting new opportunity, which is where you come in.' She grinned. 'It's to do with your illustrious grandma.'

Angel raised his eyebrows.

'Granny Viv? Really?' he asked, genuinely surprised, but again with the sharpness that any mention of Vivienne always brought to his voice. 'I'm dying to hear what kind of scam you could be running that involves *her*. She's very quiet these days.'

'You haven't been in touch with her for a while, I'm guessing,' Nicole said.

Angel shook his head.

'Doesn't approve of my lifestyle,' he said, his mouth twisting into an ugly sneer. 'Wants me to settle down. Cut my trust fund payments to the absolute minimum. I've had to hustle and bustle to pad out my income, I can tell you. I've got a big coke deal on at the moment that ought to set me up nicely for a while, but I shouldn't bloody have to toil away like this. When I *think* about what she put me and Mummy through! I shouldn't have to lift a finger!'

Nicole had clearly heard this before, or very similar words. Her head tilted sympathetically, her eyes softened, her lips parted on a soft exhalation; all the classic indications of a good friend who wants to demonstrate concern and understanding, but who knows that there is nothing left to say on the subject.

'So what on earth are you into that involves *her*?' Angel asked, his expression still unpretty.

'It's the jewel collection,' Nicole said.

Angel's sneer deepened, his amethyst eyes cold as the stones they resembled.

'You're not planning to steal any of it, are you?' he enquired. 'Let me advise you against that plan, if so. It never ends well.'

135

'Oh God, no!' Nicole exclaimed. 'Nothing that crude! You know me, darling. I never get my own hands dirty. I wouldn't remotely dream of anything that . . . direct. No, this is all about the auction.'

'The *what*?'

Angel was clearly baffled.

'The enormous auction! She's planning to sell off almost the whole of her jewellery collection for charity – hadn't you heard? Goodness, you two really don't talk, do you?'

Then Nicole shrieked, because Angel had jumped to his feet, sending displaced water flying everywhere. She whipped her glass up to avoid soapy water mingling with her wine, her other hand protecting her face.

'How dare she?' Angel ejaculated furiously. 'How fucking *dare* she? That's my fucking inheritance she's flogging off! I've been holding on all these years playing nice, just waiting for her to finally kick the bucket so that I'd come into everything, and now she's selling it out from under me? That bloody *bitch*!'

The sudden surge of anger made it impossible for him to keep still. More water splashed wildly as he took a big step up onto the wide marble surround, his balls swinging as he did so, and then down onto the plush bath mat. His penis slapped fatly against his long, muscled thigh as he strode over to the heated towel rail and whipped a towel off it, wrapping it round his waist.

'Fuck her!' he said, pacing to the far side of the bathroom, smacking one hand against the black marble sink surround. 'How *dare* she do this? She's screwed up my entire bloody life, and now she's selling off my inheritance to make herself look good!'

Nicole lowered the wine glass and finished its contents in silence. Angel was never rational on the subject of his grandmother. Nicole knew from long experience that there was no point, God forbid, pointing out that the mother who hadn't worked a day in her life and who died of an overdose when he was nine years old was scarcely a victimized, innocent heroine, cruelly mistreated by her own evil mother – which was the picture Angel insisted on painting of Pearl. But it didn't take a genius to work out that Vivienne could not have gained custody of Angel against Pearl's wishes, at least not without a prolonged and bloody court case.

Angel, however, blamed the whole tragedy on Vivienne. In his mind, that terrible day in Paris had been his grandmother's fault entirely. She had kept Pearl so short of money that Pearl had been compelled to steal from her; hired someone who assaulted Pearl, forcing her to defend herself physically; then refused to help her daughter without imposing terrible conditions on her, coercing her into giving up her son. This was Pearl's narrative, of course, in which the words 'She made me do it' were always prominent.

Pearl had seen her son only fleetingly after Vivienne took him into her care. Naturally, she had blamed this on Vivienne, rather than the fact that without Angel to look after there had been no brakes at all on how much Pearl had been able to party, and as a result she was utterly unreliable when it came to scheduling and keeping visits with her son. Her run lasted two years, until she was found by a guitarist with whom she had spent the night face down on the sofa of the hotel suite in which he was staying. The doctor summoned by the hotel officially attributed her death to an overdose, but his private opinion was that Pearl had thrown up and then passed out in the mess she had made. It had not been the combination of drugs and drink she had taken that evening that killed her, but the fact that she had suffocated on her own toxic vomit.

Angel had never been the same since. For all her good intentions, Vivienne had remained just as absorbed by her career and her love life as she was when Pearl was young. Failing to learn anything from the mistakes she had made with her daughter, Vivienne had raised Angel with the same lack of stability, employing a constantly rotating staff of nannies and private tutors as she dragged him in her wake from one continent to another. At eleven he had been sent to a succession of boarding schools; predictably, he had proceeded to cause so much trouble at each one that eventually he had ended up at the Chateau Sainte-Beuve. It might have been described to Nicole's father as a school willing to accept students from unorthodox backgrounds, which was perfectly true; but it was better known among the hyper-rich as a place of last resort for children who had made more conventional establishments too hot to hold them.

Despite the fact that Angel had flourished at his final school like the wicked man in the Bible spreading like a green bay tree, it had not abated his resentment of his grandmother in the slightest. Nothing could.

'I have a way for you to get back at Vivienne,' Nicole said eventually, watching Angel as he strode up and down the bathroom, his jaw set, attempting to work off some of his anger. 'And make good money from the auction. Two birds with one stone.'

'Keep talking,' he said between gritted teeth. 'God, it's taking all my energy not to smash something . . .'

'Okay, I've done some research,' Nicole began, 'and the way these big celebrity auctions work is that an awful lot of the high-ticket items are sold behind the scenes. Most of the sale lots are smaller, less pricey things that sell at auction for way more than their actual value, because people want to be able to say that they own something that belonged to Elizabeth Taylor, or Audrey Hepburn, or Vivienne Winter. I looked up the Elizabeth Taylor auction, and some of the pieces went for over a hundred times their estimate, just because of the provenance. A bracelet valued at twenty-two grand went for over ten times that – two hundred and seventy thousand. A necklace valued at two grand sold for over three hundred grand! And the Taj Mahal diamond, a tiara Mike Todd gave her, a huge ruby ring from Richard Burton – they all set new records. The diamond went for over five million.' She smiled at him. 'You can see I've been busy!'

Angel's full, berry-tinted lips pressed together in frustration as he imagined the vast sum his grandmother's world-famous jewellery collection was bound to realize at auction. Pausing by the recessed bathroom cabinets, he opened one, rifled through a selection of prescription medication and swallowed a small, lozenge-shaped Alprazolam dry with a skill obviously learned through long experience.

Nicole knew him well enough to wait it out. Arguing with Angel never went well: charming as he was, his triggers were numerous, and one of the reasons he had been repeatedly expelled from his previous schools had been his tendency to get into fights. He had been utterly vicious, willing to do anything necessary to win. At the Chateau this energy had been swiftly diverted into sexual games with a distinct BDSM flavour, but nevertheless his fellow students had learned quickly not to provoke him – especially by referring to his mother or grandmother. Even an inadvertent mention could set him off, and he had absolutely no gentlemanly scruples: he'd turn on a girl as fast as on a boy.

Nicole was not remotely afraid of Angel. But she badly needed her latest scheme to succeed, and his help was essential; there was no point antagonizing him by pushing. She would wait patiently until he calmed down enough to hear her plan.

'Give me fifteen minutes,' he said.

Angel almost always spoke in short, elegant sentences; his brief, clipped words were a clear sign of his altered mood. He unwrapped the towel, threw it at the rail and re-entered the whirlpool bath less dramatically than he had exited it. Nicole reached out to the central taps to add some more hot water to the bath, understanding perfectly what he meant: it would be a quarter of an hour until the benzodiazepine kicked in and he was relaxed enough to discuss the matter.

She held out a hand for a cigarette and he obliged her, lighting one of his own. He lay back against the headrest, his curls now dampening thoroughly as the bubbles rose around his skull. They sipped muscat in companionable silence, Nicole's exquisitely pedicured feet toying lightly with Angel's genitals underwater, slow caresses to his penis and balls that were more soothing than stimulating. Soft music played through the built-in waterproof speakers, a trippy, hypnotic mix, and Angel, setting down his empty glass, closed his eyes, his silky blond lashes fluttering down to his porcelain cheeks. He looked ridiculously young and innocent, his pale, near-hairless chest lapped by the water, the lights flickering across his flawless skin.

Eventually his eyes opened once again, fixing on her, a signal that he was ready to hear her idea. No matter how familiar Nicole was with Angel's beauty, it never failed to dazzle her. She had noticed even Miss Lavington – who of course had assumed that sobriquet and upper-class accent for professional purposes; her real name was Dawn Hamblett, and she was from the Black Country – had occasionally looked quite hypnotized, despite her extensive experience, when she was staring at Angel's eerily handsome face.

'As I was saying, the small items go to auction, but a lot of the big sales at celebrity auctions happen in private,' Nicole said. 'Rich people want to make sure of getting the pieces they've set their hearts on. Plus, the famous ones don't want to look vulnerable by bidding on something they're not going to get. It's that Marilyn Monroe song – they want what they want when they want it.'

A glimmer of amusement curved Angel's lips. '*If I gave you the moon, you'd get tired of it soon,*' he sang.

'Exactly! So, I've got a hotline to a major player in the music business who's dying to get his hands on Vivienne's famous rubies – the necklace and earrings that belonged to Catherine the Great.'

'Who is it?' Angel asked curiously.

Nicole hesitated.

'If we're teaming up, we're teaming up,' he observed. 'All in or nothing.'

'Lil' Biscuit,' Nicole said, rather reluctantly naming the successful rapper and entertainment mogul. He had recently married Silantra, the most famous reality TV star in the world, internationally known for her sex tape, frequent nude selfies featuring her generously sized derrière, and the reality show she did with her two sisters, *Sugar Girls*. It went against the grain with Nicole to reveal her contacts, but if she lied to Angel and he found out, she would be in trouble. Her entire plan depended on using Angel's access to pull strings with Vivienne to favour this offer.

'He wants to buy them for Silantra,' she explained, 'then write a song about her and shoot a video with her wearing them.'

'In a thong, sticking her tits out and shoving her bum in the air,' Angel observed.

'*You* know that, *I* know that, but Vivienne mustn't,' Nicole said firmly. 'That's the point. They need someone to broker this: me on their side, you on yours making the deal. They know Vivienne might not be over the moon about the Booty Queen of the World using her name for publicity, so they don't want to approach her directly.'

'I doubt Granny Viv has the faintest idea who Silantra is,' Angel observed.

'Right, and we want to keep it that way,' Nicole agreed. 'So, I have an in with Biscuit's manager, Jamal. We dated a few years ago. When everything blew up at home, I actually went to LA first and gave Jamal a call. I was planning on staying there for a while, but after we got reacquainted, we had a catch-up and I realized I had to come to London and talk to you about this. Silantra's set her heart on getting the rubies, but Lil' Biscuit's saying no way will he buy them at an auction, because he thinks they'll work out it's him bidding through proxies and drive up the price. Plus, he wants the cachet of having done a deal behind the scenes.'

'I'm genuinely impressed,' Angel drawled. 'I'd have thought he wanted to show off by spending a record figure at the auction.'

'Not at all,' Nicole said. 'He's very canny, apparently – always watching the bottom line.'

'So you came to London,' Angel said, 'and looked me up so that I'd pull whatever strings I could to get the rubies for Silantra. In return for . . .'

'Oh, a hefty intermediary fee,' Nicole assured him immediately. 'I pointed out to Jamal that they can't expect to get a discount on the deal. If they want the kudos of having snagged some of Vivienne's most famous jewellery pieces, they'll have to pay the full valuation price plus a markup for the private sale. And a ten per cent finders' fee to us, of course.'

'How much do we have to cut back to Jamal?' Angel asked.

'Nothing,' Nicole said with satisfaction. 'He's getting the sale Biscuit wants – he'll expect a bonus from Biscuit, but we're not paying him a penny at our end. I made that crystal clear. If we can secure Vivienne's agreement, we can drive a hard bargain on the price – and of course the higher it is, the higher our commission. When you're selling gemstones and jewellery, official value is completely meaningless after a certain figure, apparently. Their worth is whatever people are willing to pay for them.'

'You *have* been doing a thorough job, haven't you?' Angel

commented. 'God, I've barely spoken to that old bitch in years. Worming myself back into her good graces is going to be quite a task.'

'You're all she has by way of family,' Nicole observed. 'How difficult can it be? You're contrite, you love her, you want to build bridges . . .'

Angel stood up once more, but this time without creating a miniature tidal wave. Bubbles gleaming on his naked body, iridescent in the colour-changing lights, he reached down to extend a hand to Nicole. The blond curls plastered to his scalp gave him the look of an ancient Greek statue of an athlete, about to throw a discus.

'Time to strategize,' he said as he pulled Nicole to her feet. 'I can't just turn up on her doorstep in Geneva, say "Hello Granny, I've been missing you," and then launch two seconds later into an elaborate pitch about why she should flog her rubies to a rap star for untold millions. Viv may be in her seventies, but she's always been smart and I've got no reason to assume she's losing her marbles. I'm going to have to be *very* cautious. She hasn't trusted me for ages.'

'Probably with good reason,' Nicole said slyly, and Angel laughed.

'Very!' he agreed. 'So let's work on a watertight explanation for why I'm suddenly popping up again. Viv will be suspicious of me and my motives, and if I'm going to pull this off, I'm going to have to carry it off perfectly.'

His eyes narrowed.

'That old bitch owes me so bloody much,' he said, his mood changing abruptly yet again. 'I can't believe she was planning to shaft me like this. She took me away from my mother – poor Mummy, driven to her death by that woman . . . I could kill her. I could strangle her with my bare hands and watch her die, and it still wouldn't be enough to compensate for what she did to me and Mummy!'

Nicole shifted nervously. She had expected that his vicious resentment of his grandmother would have abated over the years. Instead, it seemed to have grown into something poisonous and lethal, fostered in the dark and now calcified into a malformed and twisted weapon, sharp enough to injure anyone. Even the person wielding it.

She averted her eyes from Angel's face, which was momentarily distorted by an expression of pure hate. It was as if a sculptor, having made a clay model for a projected sculpture, had taken violently against the creation, savagely squeezing and twisting its handsome features into a mutilated version of their former beauty. It occurred to Nicole that she was seeing, in a swift visual illustration, the damage that had been done to Angel as a child, the darkness inside him that he had deliberately chosen to cultivate.

He was a young man in the prime of life, unscrupulous and dangerous – pitted against Vivienne, a seventy-three-year-old woman who, no matter how resilient, could not help but be relatively frail and vulnerable. Nicole had put the two of them on a collision course, and she was not going to reach out her hand and steer Angel away.

After all, Vivienne was partly responsible for how Angel had turned out. She would just have to take her chances.

Chapter Seven

Tylösand – later that evening

Christine had stayed in the Hotel Tylösand's spa until a quarter past seven, just as she had planned. Meeting Vivienne was her priority, and no matter how much her thoughts kept drifting to the strapping figure Tor had cut in his clinging black wetsuit, she made sure her eyes were firmly fixed on any doorway through which her target might emerge. The spa was generously proportioned, with a swimming pool large enough to do lengths on the ground floor level, and two Jacuzzis behind it with views over the sand dunes beyond; upstairs was the fitness centre and a central heated soaking pool inside, with another outside on the terrace.

Christine had positioned herself on a lounger by the soaking pool, and in the warm, scented room, her main challenge was keeping awake. The panorama before her was a study in muted shades blending into each other, a watercolour with flashes of metallic paint: the grey slate of the outside pool; the bleached wood of the terrace; the glass balcony walls bordered with steel handrails. And then the sand dunes, flowing up into a breakwater and down on the other side to the seashore, the steel-grey sea and the paler blue-grey sky beyond. Beiges, blues, greys, a softly moving picture, the steam rising from the hot water of the outside pool, the breeze lifting sand and rippling it down the slopes, the grey sea water beyond, breaking against the shore in steady ebbs and flows.

The constant, gentle motion of wind, water and sand had hypnotized the hotel guest on the lounger beside her into sleep. He was snoring softly, his quiet rumbles hardly audible above the fountain streaming gently over the tiled curve of the indoor pool, running off in the channels sunk in either side. Christine sipped cold water and green tea to keep her alert; every so often she ate an apple from one of the fruit bowls placed around the relaxation area. The sharp acid spike made her mouth water in reflex, the sensory jolt helping her to be vigilant every time the door to the staircase opened to reveal who was entering the pool area.

However, yet again, her luck was out. Vivienne Winter did not grace the spa with her presence that evening. As Christine returned to her room to change for her appointment with Tor she had mixed feelings – disappointment mingling with panic at the thought of how large her bill must be by now, swirled round with the excitement of having a date for drinks with a fantastically attractive man. It was awful of her to even think that, having invited her, Tor would pay; but she was almost certain that he would, and at least that meant she could have a few glasses of wine with dinner without worrying about the expense.

The fact that she was going on a date in a foreign country, with someone she barely knew, who she had met in such a random way, took a considerable amount of pressure off the situation. In London, she only really met men through work, where she spent the vast majority of her time; having realized that her value to Berkeley was not in her connections but her abilities and work ethic, she had been living, sleeping and breathing gemmology, wanting to make sure that every single appraisal she did was the best it could possibly be.

Tor had called her beautiful on the beach; she knew she wasn't beautiful, but she was certainly pretty, with a nice figure, and she was asked out quite often by clients and fellow art experts. It had always been hard, though, for Christine to avoid an overly cautious, controlled manner on those occasions. She was trying so hard to fit into the upper-class world of art dealing that she was self-conscious all the time. Her accent, her background, her style in clothes and jewellery, her income level, were all so different from those of the staff and clients of Berkeley that she constantly felt she was in danger of making a social mistake so grave that people would never take her seriously again. As a result, the men who had liked her enough to ask her out found her demeanour much too stiff and rarely rang her again, preferring a woman who would at least laugh at their jokes.

So Tor – not only a foreign man, but met abroad; not part of the Berkeley social set; not familiar with the exact nuances of accent and behaviour that were so important to the British class system – was a breath of fresh air. Tor was certainly not going to judge her for not being posh enough, not 'weekending' in the country, being unable to ride a horse, or having gone to a comprehensive.

She only wished she had known she'd be going on a date when she'd packed for her trip to Sweden. She had brought only a carry-on bag on her budget airline flight, trying to keep costs down as much as possible, and she had packed to impress Vivienne Winter with her professional demeanour, not look sexy for a hot Swedish man with a body made for a clinging wetsuit. Even her swimsuit was demure; she couldn't possibly have her boobs on display as she accosted Vivienne Winter in the spa. Christine had actually bought a one-piece online especially for the purpose, black with a high-cut neck.

Thank God I didn't meet Tor wearing it, she thought. *He'd have assumed I was a nun on holiday!*

She was washing clothes every day to save money on laundry costs. A bra and knickers hung from the shower fitting, a T-shirt over the towel rail, turning the huge marble bathroom into a considerably less glamorous makeshift drying room. At least, however, that meant that the bra she needed for the one cocktail dress she had brought was clean.

Although the dress did not say 'nun on holiday', as it left her arms bare, it was an extremely basic black shift, bought from John Lewis: a department-store version of a designer style, perfectly respectable for auction house cocktail parties, and all that she could afford. Her nails were shellacked in a French manicure – elegant if not exactly alluring – and she piled her light brown hair on top of her head in a sexily dishevelled loose bun that countered the respectable neckline of the dress. There was nothing she could do about the boring black court shoes she had brought, the ones she wore for long days at viewings with barely a chance to sit down. She would have given anything to have her best patent-leather heels with her, the ones that made her legs look leaner and longer, her ankles narrowed, her bum higher and rounder.

But there was no point crying over spilt milk, or shoes she hadn't packed. She lined her eyes with so much black pencil that you could practically see them from the moon, applied three coats of mascara, doused herself in perfume and, picking up her little clutch bag, headed downstairs.

Clearly the universe is determined to make me seem like a really good girl tonight, she thought wryly as she stepped into the lift. *Ladylike dress, grandma shoes. I'll just have to flirt extra hard to make up for it.*

The lift doors opened onto a huge atrium whose white walls served as a background on which to display a stunning collection of paintings and photographs on a grand scale. Placed around the space were various highly modern sculptures on display plinths, plus a large, gleaming red motorbike in what looked like mint condition. It had been explained to Christine on check-in by a proud receptionist that the hotel was part-owned by the Swedish musician Per Gessle of the band Roxette, who, with his wife and business partner, took a lively interest in modern art; they had the biggest collection of photographs by Anton Corbijn in the world.

But as Christine stepped out of the lift, her eye was caught not by the sculptures – or the huge oil painting, as big as a picture window – but a shining, incongruous shape to her left: it was a vintage car parked in the glass-walled lobby. And it certainly hadn't been there earlier in the day. She couldn't help walking over to confirm she was really seeing it: a silver-white Morgan two-seater with red interior, low to the ground, built for speed, its back flanged out aerodynamically, the legend 'Speedster' running along the side. How someone had managed to drive it in and park it so neatly between the supporting pillars of the lobby, she had no idea; the main lobby access was through revolving doors.

Christine stood gazing at it, highly impressed. She was used, of course, to seeing all kinds of art installations for her job, but the audacity of this one, a car that seemed to have driven into the sweeping lobby straight through its glass walls without leaving a mark, was both theatrical and charming. The two young women behind the long wrap-around lobby desk were giggling, their heads together, and Christine assumed they were talking about the Morgan for a moment, until she noticed the direction of their stares; not at the car at all, but the art gallery in the corner of the lobby.

A man was leaning in the open doorway, chatting to someone inside, and as she glanced over at him she felt herself blush. It was Tor, wearing a blue sweater and grey trousers, his copper-gold hair like a flame in the softly glowing lights of the lobby. His throat, bared by the open neck of his sweater, seemed as wide as one of the lobby pillars, and she had a vivid flash of the body underneath his clothes, the solid muscle she had seen outlined by the wetsuit.

He sensed her gaze on him and looked across; pushing off the doorjamb, he strode towards her, beaming. There was clearly no playing hard to get with Tor.

'Oh, you changed!' Christine said cheekily. 'I'm a bit disappointed.'

'Damn, you don't want me, do you? You want Yuri!' he exclaimed. 'Shall I go home and come back in my wetsuit?'

'Maybe later,' she said saucily. 'And it was Sergei, not Yuri.'

'Sergei! Of course!' His blue eyes twinkled. 'I can be Sergei for you. But he's a pretty boring guy.'

151

Christine pouted.

'He didn't seem that boring to me,' she said. 'I was hoping for some Russian poetry, like he promised. About women who are kind to sailors lost from their ships.'

'*Beautiful* women,' Tor corrected, looking down at her with great appreciation. 'I may not remember what Sergei was called, but I know I mentioned beautiful women.'

'We'll have to see if we can find some for you,' Christine said, in such a blatant fish for a compliment that she felt mortified even as the words came out of her mouth.

'Oh, I am very happy with the one I have here,' Tor said, extending his arm, elbow out, in an invitation to link hers through it. She did, heat flooding her body at the physical contact, at the sheer size of his forearm, the warmth of him and the scent of his aftershave – rich and warm, like brandied oranges. He escorted her into the bar, where a table for two was placed beside the fireplace.

'I reserved this,' he said, pulling out the leather armchair for her to sit down. 'I thought you would like to be warm after your cold walk on the beach today.'

'You were colder than me,' she said as he took the chair opposite. 'It must have been freezing in the sea!'

'Well, I didn't have to swim all the way from a submarine,' he said. 'But in any case, I'm used to the cold. I like it.' His white, even teeth flashed bright. 'I love it, in fact,' he added. 'It makes me feel alive.'

'I suppose that's living here,' Christine said. 'It must be very cold in winter.'

God, how boring you sound! she thought. *Why are you talking about the weather!*

Tor shrugged as the waiter arrived to take their order, a bottle of red wine; he, like the receptionists, seemed to know Tor, exchanging some friendly banter in Swedish that clearly went beyond the usual waiter/client courtesies. Tor raised his glass, and Christine matched the gesture. The crinkles around his blue eyes showed his tan, a striation of white lines fanning out on either side, the skin around them a weathered golden-brown. He was just as she'd remembered from the afternoon, easy, friendly, gorgeous, almost too good to be true, and she wasn't up to her best game, not armoured with the dress and heels and bright red lipstick that would make her most confident; she'd only brought the most basic of make-up, certainly nothing sexy.

'Do you come here all the time?' she asked, gesturing around the sleek bar with its shiny black walls and tables, its red lacquered surfaces, its lavishly cushioned seats. It was hung with gold records in glass cases and posters for iconic bands; there was no doubting that the hotel was owned by a musician.

Tor looked surprised.

'No, not really,' he said. 'I travel a lot, so when I'm at home, I like to be at home. I make a fire, listen to music, drink some beer. Watch the sea.'

'But everyone seems to know you here,' Christine observed. 'Is it because you're a local?'

'Ah, okay! I see why you're asking!'

Tor sat back in his seat, cradling the wine glass in his hands. Christine noticed how big they were, and how scratched and gnarled; if he hadn't mentioned travelling a lot just now, she would have assumed he was a carpenter, a roofer, someone used to manual labour.

'So, you know I'm not a Russian sailor called Sergei,' he said. 'But you may think when I answer that I'm teasing you again. I promise you that I'm not, okay?'

'Oh my God, what are you going to say?'

Christine was laughing; she felt it couldn't be too bad, as he wore no wedding ring and had no marks of having just removed one. Maybe he was an actor, famous in Sweden, a TV personality; but she'd met plenty of actors and TV presenters through her work, and they were much more groomed, more slick than this guy. Certainly their hands wouldn't be so ragged and gnarled. She drank some wine and watched him consider his words, with considerable curiosity about what he might be about to reveal.

'Do you want to guess what I actually do?' he asked.

'Um, fisherman?' she tried: there was the tanned, weathered skin, the beaten-up hands, the travelling. Maybe he had one of those boats that went out for weeks on end? She'd seen a TV series about that; it looked terrifying, but Tor didn't seem like he scared easily.

'Oh, nice guess! But actually, I'm an explorer,' he said, and Christine coughed wine painfully out through her nose, the smooth, oaky Cabernet unpleasantly acid when it hit the nostrils. Tor leaned forward, picked up one of the black cocktail napkins and handed it to her, quite unfazed by the sight of red wine dribbling down onto her upper lip.

'Sorry, I didn't mean to freak you out,' he said. 'Do you have something against explorers?'

'No, but it's just such a funny word!' she said, wiping the wine off her face. 'I'm imagining you going to the South Pole with dog sleds!'

Tor reached over and took the glass of wine from her hand as a precaution.

'I actually led an expedition to the South Pole with dog sleds last year,' he said, and waited for her jaw to drop and her eyes to widen before he slid the glass back to her again.

'You're joking,' Christine said, but without much conviction. She recognized the ring of truth when she heard it. She stared at him, a memory rolling back to her of press coverage last year of an expedition for charity: it had garnered vast amounts of publicity because among the group had been not only a sprinkling of famous actors, but the redheaded playboy Prince Toby of Britain.

'Yes, that one,' he said cheerfully, seeing her recognition. 'We got some frostbite, but nothing too serious.'

'I can't think of anything to say,' Christine admitted. 'Apart from okay, I believe that you really like the cold.'

'But I also like to sit in a nice warm bar by a fire with a beautiful woman,' Tor said deftly. 'I'm very flexible.'

Christine was still fairly dumbstruck.

'Sorry,' she said simply. 'I honestly can't think of anything to say that isn't really obvious or stupid.'

'Great,' Tor said, to her surprise. 'Anything's better than you asking me what Prince Toby's like, or saying "Hey, you must be really brave", or "How do you go to the toilet in the snow?"'

'I'll wait a few minutes and then be sure to ask you all those questions,' Christine said, picking up her wine glass.

'From you, I wouldn't even mind,' Tor said with such fondness that she ducked her head towards the glass, suddenly fascinated by the colour of the wine.

'So, enough about me!' he continued cheerfully. 'What do *you* think about me?'

This made her laugh out loud; she found herself kicking off the dowdy shoes and curling up in the armchair. The fire was crackling beside her, bright as Tor's hair, and his crow's feet were crinkling adorably.

'Seriously, though, what are you doing here?' he asked. 'We don't get many foreigners, especially in the off season. Are you here for the spa?'

'It's lovely,' Christine said, 'but no. Although I'm spending most of my time in it.'

'When you're not dancing on the seashore,' Tor observed.

'That was my time off,' she said.

'You're working? This is a great place to be quiet and concentrate. Are you a writer?'

'No, though this would be the most amazing writer's retreat! I'm just –' Christine hesitated. 'It's going to sound a bit weird when I say it out loud.'

Tor picked up his glass.

'I'm going to drink some wine,' he suggested, 'and then when you tell me I can snort it out of my nose to keep you company.'

'Okay, I'm just going to spit it out,' she said. 'I'm pretty much here to stalk Vivienne Winter – she's staying here at the hotel.'

Tor swallowed his wine, rather than spitting it out as promised, but his forehead furrowed, and the crow's feet relaxed so that his eyes were no longer smiling.

'Are you a journalist?' he asked, and for the first time there was a slight cooling of his tone.

'No, no, nothing like that!' she said swiftly. 'It's about her jewel collection. And don't worry, I'm not a cat burglar either. I work at an auction house as an appraisal expert – I'm a gemmologist. I've heard she wants to sell off the major part of her collection for charity, and I really want us to be the auction house she chooses. It would be an amazing opportunity for the company, but honestly I'm mostly thinking of myself and my career. If I brought something this huge to Berkeley, I'd have a serious chance of getting a major promotion.'

Tor nodded slowly.

'But this is not a professional way to do it,' he commented. 'To come to a hotel where she is staying and try to talk to her when she doesn't expect it.'

'I know,' she admitted. 'But I've tried every other avenue I could to get in touch with her, and nothing worked. We're a very reputable auction house, but we're not Christie's or Sotheby's, and her adviser won't take my calls. It's so frustrating! I know I – *we* – could do the most fantastic job for her. We've been established for over two hundred years, we have international offices, we're a hundred per cent reputable, and we'd offer her a much more favourable commission rate than the Big Two. I just want a chance to put my case. Berkeley's case.'

Christine had to stop to catch her breath; she was getting carried away. Tor's expression was still unreadable.

'So I did some research,' she continued. 'I found out she was staying here, and I took unpaid leave from work to come here too. I thought we might bump into each other in the spa – I know it's a bit much to launch into a sales pitch in the sauna, but if we happened to be in the Jacuzzi at the same time and got talking . . . The thing is, I genuinely do

157

think I could do a great job for her. I've got so many ideas – obviously with Vivienne's approval, but I'd want to use social media, work with the press, build up even more excitement for this sale than there was for Elizabeth Taylor's. I've analysed that in such detail – they had a brilliant PR, and it was incredibly well run. I want to build on that and do even better. That sale was in 2011, and things have changed so much since then – I'd start a whole Instagram account for the pieces, and use it to whip up massive excitement for the smaller ones, because those are more likely to go way over the estimated value. I'd . . .'

But at this point, Christine literally did run out of breath. In an effort to convince Tor of her good intentions, she had ended up giving him the pitch that she had been honing for the last week. It had been on the tip of her tongue for days, ready to burst out if she did manage to secure Vivienne Winter's attention for a moment or two, and it had proved unstoppable.

'Sorry!' she said, when she had got a second wind. 'I just wanted to make you see I'm not some kind of nutcase. I'll change the subject. You must be bored out of your mind.'

Tor was pulling his phone from his trouser pocket, tapping on the touchscreen.

'This is your auction house?' he asked, holding it up so she could see the home page of Berkeley's website, austerely old-fashioned, with a stark white background decorated with elaborate blue curlicues and an ugly Gothic font that one did not so much read as decipher. If websites had been designed in the Victorian era, this was pretty much what they would have looked like.

Christine nodded ruefully.

'If you click there –' she indicated the link – 'you'll see me. I'm the appraiser for the jewellery department. My boss is going mental about me being away,' she added ruefully. 'I've got so much work piling up, I don't know how I'll ever get through it.'

Tor chuckled at the thumbnail photo of Christine that came up.

'So serious!' he said, looking at her with her hair scraped back, pearl studs in her earlobes, wearing a black jacket and a white blouse buttoned up to the neck. 'I would not have dared to ask this woman if I could hide in her hotel room!'

'Yes, that's partly why I wanted to meet Vivienne in person,' she explained. 'The partners have this really stuffy image – look at the web design! How would you ever look at that and think: "Oh, this woman's bound to have great ideas for building awareness of the sale through social media!"'

'I see,' Tor said thoughtfully.

'I know it's a real cheek, my trying to snatch a word with her like this,' she admitted. 'And it hasn't worked out anyway. I'm going to have to go home soon, or I'll end up with the sack as well as a gigantic credit card bill.'

She sighed, and finished off her glass of wine.

'Oh well, it was worth a try!' she said bravely. 'I'm sorry, I'm just moaning now and it must be really boring. Let's talk about something else. What's Prince Toby like? I'm dying to know!'

Tor acknowledged this joke with a fleeting smile, but he didn't engage with her invitation to change the subject. Instead he reached out for the wine bottle, refilled her glass and said, 'Excuse me for a few minutes. I promise, I will be back.'

Pushing back his chair, he stood up. Christine tried not to look at the flex of his thighs and the flatness of his stomach, both very much in evidence, before, with a nod, he strode away across the bar. She assumed that he was heading for the toilet. Only after she'd waited for some time did it occur to her that if that were really the case, only some terrible gastric disturbance could explain how long he was taking.

She couldn't quite believe he would simply have disappeared, even if he'd been totally turned off by the information that she was here to stalk an elderly woman. On the positive side, there was Tor's character, as revealed to her so far: he had been nothing but polite and gentlemanly. It was near-impossible to imagine him simply abandoning her halfway through a date without a word of explanation, even in her own hotel bar.

On the other hand, there were the gruesome experiences she and her girlfriends had accumulated in years of going out with guys. Every one of them could trot out at least one terrible dating anecdote. Christine's friend Lauren had once had a man pick her up at her flat and ask through the intercom if he could come in and smoke a joint before they went to dinner. When she said 'No' he had sulked, walked her to the restaurant he had booked in near silence and left her at the table half an hour later, saying he was going outside for a cigarette. He had never returned, and since they'd ordered food and drink, Lauren was stuck with the bill. Another friend, Jen, on a business trip to LA, had met a guy in a bar and taken him back to her hotel – only to have him look at her in her bra and knickers, stammer: 'I'm sorry, I can't do this. I thought you would be more toned,' and leave.

Her present situation was minor compared to those horror stories. Christine was just on the hook for a bottle of wine; she didn't need to even pay for a cab home. She could take the rest of the Cabernet up to her room and finish it that evening as consolation for the date having gone so horrendously awry.

But he seemed so nice, and he said he would be back! she thought miserably, checking her phone yet again only to see that twenty minutes had elapsed. *How long should I wait? Half an hour in total. That's it. Any more and I'll look even more of an idiot than I do now, the girl who every single person in this bar knows got stood up by Tor the Famous Explorer – no, worse than stood up, there isn't even a word for what happens when someone decides halfway through the date that your moral character's so appalling that he can't bear to spend any more time with you—*

'Hello! Here I am again!'

She had been so absorbed in misery that she hadn't even seen him return. He was standing beside the table, holding out one hand to her.

'Let's go,' he said, and Christine was so relieved that he had come back that she took his hand and let him help her to her feet without even asking where they were going.

'But the bill?' she said. 'Don't we need to pay for the wine? I'm—'

'It's all arranged,' he said easily, and she noticed that there was a bottle of Krug in his free hand, plus two glasses. 'Trust me. We're going back to my submarine to drink champagne.'

'Ooh!' she said, managing to retrieve her wit. 'Champagne plus lots of handsome Russian sailors to recite poems to me! You're really spoiling me tonight!'

Tor squeezed her hand in appreciation of this quick response as he led her through the bar and across the lobby. Even though she didn't know what to expect, Christine was taken aback to see they were heading towards the entrance to the spa, which should be closed by this time of night. However, the elegant young woman seated at the desk smiled on seeing Tor and, with a little nod, pressed the button that caused the low glass door to swing open.

Christine sensed that there was no point asking Tor what was going on: he had the air of a man about to spring a surprise. Clearly he had pulled major strings to get them admitted to the spa after hours, especially since he wasn't even a hotel guest.

But I haven't got my bathing suit with me, she thought. *And if he thinks he's going to talk me into stripping off and jumping into a hot tub with him naked to drink champagne, he's got another thing coming. No way is that going to happen, no matter how cute he is or how much he tries to tell me it's normal in Sweden to skinny-dip on the first date . . .*

Tor was leading her up the staircase to the first-floor spa area. As he pushed open the big glass door, his wide body blocked any view of the interior, so that when Christine followed him in she gasped audibly at the sight before her. Because, lounging on the contoured bench in the hot pool, water flowing gently over her ample bosom, her hair wrapped in a white turban, her eyes heavily outlined with black pencil and a champagne glass in her hand, was none other than Christine's elusive target: Vivienne Winter herself.

'So,' purred the unmistakable husky voice, '*this* is the young lady who's been stalking me?'

Christine felt the blood rush from her head. She had stopped abruptly, and Tor's hand in hers was pulling her off balance. She staggered, and was grateful for the first time that she wasn't wearing her high heels, but the sensible court shoes.

'Goodness me,' Vivienne drawled. 'I know I'm no spring chicken, but I didn't realize I looked so terrifying that young women would go into a nervous catalepsy at the sight of me!'

She looked, frankly, stunning. There is a French saying that at a certain age, a woman needs to choose between her *derrière* and her face; if she keeps her bottom and hips youthfully slim, she won't have enough plumpness to her face to keep it also looking young, and vice versa. Vivienne had definitely chosen her face, allowing her figure to ripen out. Her eyebrows were heavily pencilled in to frame her amethyst eyes, and her skin was darker than it had been in her heyday, when it had been famously pale: now she sunbathed regularly, careless about brown spots at her age. The colour not only gave her a healthy glow against the white of her turban and the equally white ruched Miracle Cut shapewear swimsuit, but threw the purple eyes into even more striking relief.

There were candles flickering around the water's edge, clearly placed there at Vivienne's request, as Christine had never seen them on the pool surround before. They struck multicoloured shards of light from the diamonds that glinted against Vivienne's tanned skin: a stack of tennis bracelets and a pair of enormous four-carat, brilliant-cut stud earrings.

And yet Christine realized that journalists interviewing Vivienne had, if anything, been making an understatement when they commented that she had been bedecked in superb, glittering jewellery, but added that the gems had paled in comparison to the effect of her extraordinary eyes.

'I *am* terrified! But you look *amazing*,' Christine blurted out, the words clearly so spontaneous that Vivienne burst out laughing, a delicious ripple of amusement that was so sincere that Christine felt herself relaxing in relief. Tor guided her to sit down on the end of one of the loungers facing Vivienne, and Christine was suddenly grateful for the comparatively long skirt of her dress. It might be dowdy standing up, but sitting down it meant she didn't have to squirm around, dragging down the hem so that Vivienne Winter wasn't looking directly at her knickers.

Tor was ripping the foil off the neck of the bottle of Krug, removing the wire, popping the cork. He had placed the glasses on the pool surround, and he bent over to top up Vivienne's before filling the others.

'Um – I don't understand what's happening,' Christine said, trying hard not to gawk at Vivienne as if she were a rare and exotic animal in a zoo.

Vivienne's smile was enchanting. Christine's head was filled with the kind of clichés that might have popped straight out of commercials for expensive watches, cribbed from poetry anthologies: *a thing of beauty is a joy forever. Timeless splendour never ages.* It really was true. When you were born with this kind of beauty, it never left you. At seventy-three, Vivienne radiated as much allure and charm as she had done at thirty.

'You complained to my godson that you hadn't seen me

in the spa so that you could pounce on me and try to convince me to let your company run my jewellery auction,' Vivienne said, taking her newly filled glass from Tor with a wink of thanks. 'And he knew that was because I was in here right now. I'm a night owl, darling. Always have been. I avoid the spa during the day, but they very kindly keep it open for me after hours so I can indulge myself with an evening soak in here. Then I pop out to the terrace and freeze my tushie off in the night air for as long as I can bear – so good for the circulation! – before I climb into the outdoor pool and watch the stars. I have my whole delightful nightly routine.'

Tor walked over to give Christine her champagne, a grin on his face as wide as the Cheshire Cat's.

'I'm a magic man,' he said boastfully. 'I hope you're impressed with me.'

'I *am*,' she said, still half disbelieving her own eyes.

'*Skål*,' Vivienne said, raising her glass high, and Tor and Christine echoed her toast as he sat down on the pool surround.

'You see, Tor's grandfather was an old flame of mine,' Vivienne explained. 'I used to visit him here in Tylösand – such a pretty little village – and rather fell in love with the place. When he eventually married Tor's mother, I was married to Randon – the first time around – and they sweetly asked me to be Tor's godmother. And since the hotel was revamped, I've become a regular visitor. It's wonderful, isn't it? I'm rather obsessed with the crispbread.'

'Me too!' Christine said with a little unguarded laugh of surprise.

Vivienne sipped some Krug and watched Christine with

attention, clearly assessing everything about her: appearance, manners, bearing, speech. Christine was used to this kind of evaluation, having conducted many meetings with potential sellers of fine jewellery. And she had been preparing for this for days, under much worse circumstances: buttonholing an oblivious Vivienne and begging for a few minutes to do a pitch would be infinitely worse than this situation, in which Tor had already briefed Vivienne on what Christine was hoping for.

At the moment, though, Christine's instincts were telling her to sit quietly and sip champagne, letting Vivienne lead the conversation. She glanced sideways at Tor, and he gave her a discreet nod, confirmation that she was right not to launch into her prepared speech yet.

'Well, you know how to be patient, which is crucial,' Vivienne eventually said with approval. 'So, now I've had a look at you, why don't you trot out the spiel you must have had on the tip of your tongue for days?'

Christine wasn't sure if this was some sort of test.

'Are you sure?' she asked carefully. 'I mean, you were relaxing, having your nightly spa routine with your champagne – would you prefer me to make an appointment for tomorrow?'

'Nonsense!' Vivienne said briskly. 'No time like the present!' She raised her glass to Christine with a gleam of pure mischief in her eyes. 'Let's have it!'

But just as Christine sat up straighter, drew in a deep breath and prepared to work her way as efficiently as possible through her list of bullet points, the door to the staircase opened once again.

'Grandma!' exclaimed a light tenor voice, and the most

beautiful man Christine had ever seen stepped into the room, closely followed by the receptionist from the spa desk.

'Ah!' the beautiful man said, taking in the scene before him. 'How delightful, it's a party! Hello, Tor! Hello, very attractive young lady! Room for one more?'

'Mrs Winter, he said it was an emergency,' the receptionist said nervously. 'I recognized your grandson, of course –'

Angel flashed his wonderful smile at her, acknowledging his status as a staple of the magazine gossip columns.

'– but I thought I should come to check with you as well, just in case,' she finished.

Vivienne's expression was quite unreadable: her training as an actress was suddenly very much in evidence. Christine caught her breath, looking between the two faces, so hauntingly alike. With her hair concealed under a turban, Vivienne's features were clearly visible. In a series of discreet and expensive operations over the years her skin had been deftly lifted and tucked, like crêpe fabric pinned round a dressmaker's model, over the strong framework of her jaw and high cheekbones. The full lips, the straight noses, and of course the extraordinary violet eyes were identical.

On close examination, however – and Christine was blatantly staring – the young man's jaw was stronger, his forehead squarer, the face not quite as heart-shaped as Vivienne's. She couldn't take her eyes from him. A memory of a recent Berkeley fine art auction came to mind, its centrepiece a fourteenth-century painting of the Annunciation, the Archangel Gabriel telling Mary that she had been chosen to bear Jesus. Tall, milky-skinned, with a cascade of golden hair pushed back from his face, the Byzantine-influenced almond-shaped eyes, straight nose and pouting lips: Vivienne's grandson could have been the model for Gabriel.

Christine had researched Vivienne's jewellery collection in great detail. She knew, for instance, that Vivienne's famous pear-shaped pearl, which hung from a choker of pearls and diamonds, had once been part of the Crown Jewels of France. Named the Medici Pearl, after Catherine de Medici, its first owner, it had been worn by both her and Mary Stuart in her time at the French court before it was smuggled out of the country by Napoleon III when he was sent into exile. After being sold off to pay the expenses of his court, it had passed through the hands of a complicated trail of owners before it had been bought for Vivienne by the man she had married twice, the actor Randon Cliffe. Charmingly, and very much in keeping with his generous character, Randon had commissioned a miniature version of the piece for his adoptive daughter, Pearl, so that she could wear it on the day he first married her mother.

So Christine was familiar with Vivienne's daughter's name because of the association with the pendant; but she did not read gossip magazines, and she had no idea what Vivienne's grandson was called. When Vivienne said in a deliberately flat tone, 'Angel. Goodness me. What a *very* unexpected visit,' Christine's jaw dropped in amazement that this gloriously handsome man, who had just reminded her of an archangel, was so perfectly named.

Angel, she repeated to herself, unable to take her eyes off him. *Wow. I didn't even think it was possible for a man to be so beautiful.*

Chapter Eight

Tylösand – the same evening

'So! What's this news that's so important you've barged in on my lovely spa evening, Angel? I was having a very pleasant chat with Tor and that nice girl he brought up to see me!'

Vivienne stared at her grandson with icy composure, her heavily pencilled eyebrows elegantly raised. There had been no continuing Christine's sales pitch in the spa pool after Angel's intrusion. It was impossible to talk business when her grandson was simultaneously apologizing for the interruption and telling his grandmother that he had urgent news. So Vivienne had emerged from the pool with the graciousness of a Roman aristocrat rising from a mosaic bath in her private villa – unsurprising for anyone who had seen her acclaimed portrayal of the scheming Livia, wife of Emperor Augustus, in the film of *I, Claudius*.

Tor and Christine were dismissed with promises to meet up the following day, and Vivienne proceeded back to her suite, regal in turban, robe and her own sheepskin and lambswool slippers. Always careful of her image, she wanted to avoid being seen shuffling through the hotel in the spa's backless slide-ons, like an old lady in a retirement home. Waiting for her was her devoted personal assistant Gregory, part of whose job it was to provide companionship and foot massages as Vivienne wound down for the night.

The assistant was much too discreet to show visible surprise at the sight of the grandson from whom his employer had been estranged for years. Bowing himself out of the living room, he retired to his room in the suite until Vivienne called for him. Gregory, who had worked for Vivienne for many years, was making exactly the same assumption as she was: that Angel, in the throes of yet another financial crisis, had tracked down his grandmother for an emergency loan.

Vivienne smoothed her robe down and took a seat in the centre of the sofa, gesturing at Angel to sit in one of the armchairs. Coldly, she said, 'I suppose you've come to ask for money? That always seems to be what motivates you to make contact with me.'

'No, Grandma,' Angel replied with perfect composure, laced with just a touch of sorrow. 'Take a deep breath. I'm afraid the news I have for you is bad, but it's nothing to do with needing money.'

'Oh, really? Forgive me, Angel, but I've heard tall stories from you before,' Vivienne said. 'And the drama of this arrival feels rather forced to me.'

'I'm sorry for bursting in on you,' Angel said gravely. 'I only got the diagnosis a few hours ago, and I wanted to come and tell you immediately, in person. I didn't think it should be done over the phone.'

'*Diagnosis?* What are you saying?'

The blood drained from Vivienne's cheeks. Angel nodded, his expression growing even more serious.

'I'm so sorry to have to say this, Grandma,' he said. 'But I've come to tell you that I have cancer.'

Angel had wasted no time. As soon as the perfect cover story had popped into his head, in a flash of pure inspiration, he had been determined to deliver it as soon as possible. He had rung Vivienne's manager to find out her current location, telling him he had bad news about his health and wanted to give his grandmother the news in person. On hearing that she was in Sweden, Angel had jumped in a cab to Farnborough airport, booking a private flight to Halmstad airport en route, which the manager had told him was the closest one to Tylösand; its airport was too small to take international scheduled flights.

This impulsive, spendthrift behaviour was typical of Angel. No matter how strongly Nicole had pointed out, her fingers flying swiftly over the touchscreen of her phone, that he could save thousands by taking a flight to Copenhagen or Gothenburg and hiring a driver to Tylösand, Angel had dismissed her concern as ridiculous. He stood to make vast amounts from this auction, he declared confidently, because he was going to insinuate himself back into Vivienne's good graces so successfully that she would allow him to be involved in all the major decisions. Clearly there were vast opportunities for him to rake in finders' fees or commissions, ensuring that prospective buyers secured the pieces they wanted in private sales. Besides, his coke deal was about to come through! He would soon be rolling in money, able to pay off his sky-high American Express Black Card balance in full.

'And anyway,' he had finished, his eyes sparkling, 'if I get a scheduled flight and then have to drive for a few hours, I'll get there too late to see Granny Viv tonight. And I simply can't wait to break the grim news to my beloved grandmamma! Oh, how I'm going to enjoy this! Just imagine if she has a heart attack and drops dead – that would be perfect, wouldn't it? I'd inherit the lot before she had a chance to sell it off!'

'You're a sick puppy,' Nicole had said, lounging on the bed and watching him throw some clothes into a custom-made leather Globe-Trotter suitcase. 'Can I stay here when you're away? I *can* afford a hotel, of course, but this is much more civilized.'

'Oh, definitely, stay here!' Angel had been delighted at the idea. 'We can celebrate as soon as I get back. Start thinking up some creative ways to do that, darling! Why don't you work out some elaborately pervy scenario for us two and that saucy minx we played with earlier?'

'Ooh,' Nicole had agreed, 'that sounds divine! I'll start putting together some ideas . . .'

Even now, as he stood in front of Vivienne, Angel was picturing various possibilities for himself, Nicole and 'Miss Lavington'. But nothing could be read in his facial expression; as far as anyone could have told, butter wouldn't melt in his mouth. His stricken grandmother was looking as closely at his face as if she could somehow read the symptoms there.

'*Cancer?*' Vivienne repeated, her lips trembling. 'Oh my God, Angel! Surely it can't be true! You're so young still!'

Angel was secretly delighted at her reaction, which was even more profound than he had imagined it would be. Her cheeks had hollowed out, her eye sockets were sunken and dark. The carefully tended, immaculately moisturized skin looked grey under her light tan, and her jaw, which she held high to minimize sagging, had dropped, showing a hint of double chin.

'I'm afraid so,' he said. 'I've been through rounds of tests. I didn't want to worry you until it was confirmed. I was hoping the growth was benign. But . . .'

He let this tail off, shaking his head sadly.

Vivienne let out a long, poignant, heartbreaking sob, a theatrical effect she had perfected over the years and which was now so natural to her that it emerged in entirely genuine situations. It was almost unbearably moving. Even Angel, who had no heart to break, was extremely impressed, making a mental note to remember how it sounded for future use.

'And it's serious, Angel?' she asked, her eyes beginning to well up with tears. 'I mean, of course it's serious, it's *cancer* –'

A brave woman, Vivienne had no difficulty facing facts: she despised people who could not talk frankly about disease and death.

'– but what's the prognosis? What did the doctor say?'

Tears were beginning to well up in her eyes. From his trouser pocket, Angel produced a handkerchief made of linen so fine that, as the ancient Egyptian princes used to boast of their clothing, it could have been pulled effortlessly through a finger ring.

'I'm sorry,' he said quietly, handing it to her. 'I'm so sorry, Grandma.'

Angel had spent his private plane ride happily Googling both 'terminal cancer' and 'cancer miracle recovery'. At first he had considered giving himself a skin lymphoma, because this had both of the crucial factors that he needed: he required a cancer that had a high fatality rate, but was also capable of being sent into remission by a surgical operation combined with radiotherapy. He had no intention of embarking on an elaborate attempt to fake having chemotherapy by shaving his head, losing weight, performing exhaustion and poisoning symptoms. A lymphoma, therefore, seemed ideal, as according to the medical websites it was most commonly treated with surgery and/or radiation therapy.

Almost as soon as he had settled on this idea, however, he rethought the strategy. A swelling in the lymph nodes was visible, presumably, as he would have noticed it himself. What if Vivienne wanted to see it? Or if she expected, post-operation, to be shown gauze and surgical dressings? As an experienced and accomplished liar, Angel knew that the simpler you kept your lies, the easier it was to make them believable. Since he didn't want to have to explain away the lack of bandages or scarring on his body to a concerned grandmother, where could he locate his cancer that she would never see the operation site?

The groin, he thought instantly. That was easy – make it cancer of a lymph node in his groin. He would just have to limp a bit, press his hand into his crotch and wince when he sat down or stood up . . .

But why not go the whole way – make it somewhere she couldn't possibly ever see it?

'It's testicular cancer, I'm afraid,' he told Vivienne even more gravely, gloating secretly at his own brilliance. 'They're going to have to operate in the next couple of days. That's why I turned up here so late. I had to come and tell you immediately. It's stage three, I'm afraid. The expert says they don't have effective statistics on the survival rates to give me, as very few men present with their cancer this advanced. But the prognosis –' he took a long breath – 'isn't good.'

'Oh, *Angel*!'

Vivienne's body sagged. He was quick to jump up and take a seat next to her on the sofa, collecting her torso gently into his arms, her tears dampening his shoulder.

'I can't bear it!' she sobbed into his jacket. 'This isn't supposed to happen! First your mother gone so young, and now you getting sick! Grandmothers aren't supposed to survive their grandchildren!'

Angel stiffened at the mention of Pearl. He could barely tolerate hearing Vivienne speak his beloved mother's name; some of the worst fights between him and Vivienne had been provoked by his hyper-sensitivity to any reference to his mother that might present her as not the perfect plaster saint of his imaginings. Vivienne felt his reaction and looked up, clinging to his lapels, her face wet, her eye pencil smudged.

'We *have* to put the past behind us,' she said, catching her breath, gradually regaining control of herself. 'We *can't* hold onto old grievances now, Angel. We're all each other has!'

Pearl had never told Angel who his father was, for the simple reason that she didn't know herself. All she had said, when he had asked her why he didn't have a daddy, was that he was enough for her, and she ought to be enough for him. And then she had either cried or got angry – which had taught Angel early on never to raise the subject.

Brent, Pearl's father, had died several years ago, and

Vivienne had naturally attended the funeral. It would certainly still have been newsworthy to find out that the baby Vivienne had had out of wedlock had been fathered by a married man; but Brent was long retired, and there had been no press coverage that might have raised suspicions. It had been a quiet ceremony at a cemetery in La Jolla, California, attended by his widow (his fourth wife, thirty years younger than him), various ex-wives and children, extended family – and a small group of sobbing, black-clad women who were long-term fans of Brent's work as a heroic neuro-surgeon with an identical, criminal mastermind twin on the daily soap opera *The Beautiful World Turns*.

What Vivienne said was quite true: if she had any distant relatives still alive, she had no contact with any of them. It had never bothered her. She had always believed that one made one's own family in life, and had gathered around her a tribe of gay men with whom she felt infinitely more at ease than she did with her boring straight relatives – or, in fact, any of the straight men she had been involved with.

Apart, of course, from Randon Cliffe. But Randon was long dead, having crashed the Cessna he was flying, drunk out of his mind, on New Year's Eve, impulsively racing to see her in the wake of their second divorce. She had always hated him flying; she knew how reckless a driver he was, and she would never get in a plane if he was at the controls. She had always thought, wryly, after the first terrible waves of grief and loss had begun to abate, that it was typical of Randon to die in the way that would annoy her the most.

'We're all the family each other has,' she repeated, sitting up straight again and dabbing at her eyes with Angel's handkerchief. She said the words without a hint of self-pity; they were simply a statement of the facts. 'I want to support you in any way I can. Is your insurance—'

'So far it seems fine,' Angel said cautiously. It hadn't occurred to him until this moment, but if Vivienne were going to offer him money for non-existent medical treatments, that would be a welcome side benefit of this plan.

'Any extra bills for things that aren't covered, send them straight to Gregory,' Vivienne said, crushing this hope. 'He'll make sure they're taken care of immediately.'

Damn, Angel thought. *Wait, I wonder how hard it would be to fake some bills and set up a bank account with a medical-sounding name? I bet, with her tech skills, Nicole would be able to do that if I cut her in for a share . . .*

'Thank you so much,' he said gratefully. 'I have one of the best specialists in the world taking care of me, but there may well be extras that insurance doesn't cover. I must confess, Grandma, though, it's a very personal area – literally. It's going to make me feel awkward to discuss, err, the details with you –'

I'm a genius, he thought smugly, watching understanding flicker across his grandmother's face. *I'm an absolute bloody genius. No way can she press me to tell her whether I'm having a ball cut off, for instance. This covers me from ever getting caught out.*

'Oh my God! What about your fertility?' Vivienne said, her eyes widening in horror as the thought hit her. The handkerchief fluttered down to her lap; all her attention focused on the fact that Angel might become sterile as a result of the treatments he would have to receive.

This caught him off guard. He paused, swiftly reviewing the various options available to him, considering which would unlock his grandmother's goodwill most effectively.

'I didn't ask,' he said eventually, deciding that the best strategy was to keep his options open. 'It all happened so fast – I only found the swelling two days ago, I had the Harley Street appointment this morning and went straight home to pack a bag and come to find you. I didn't even think of asking that question. *God.*'

He fell silent, as if letting this huge new potential issue sink in.

'I never thought about having children,' he said, watching his grandmother's face intently, 'but this kind of news . . . it changes everything. It makes you think about mortality, time running out . . . leaving something behind you on this earth . . . someone to carry on the Winter name . . .'

With every clichéd phrase, he saw Vivienne nod more and more intently. Her lips were pressed together, her throat working as she tried to fight back a new wave of tears. With each swallow, the huge diamonds in her ears trembled and flashed brilliant light, their platinum setting designed to display the perfectly colourless stones, the highest grade possible. She reached out and took Angel's hands, the diamonds in the bracelets on both wrists equally luminous, set off by her lightly tanned skin and the white robe.

'You're only thirty-two!' she said, her tone piteous. 'I thought there was so much time! And maybe there still is – but I've always hoped you'd settle down one day, raise a family . . .'

For fuck's sake, do you have any idea who I am? Angel

thought, but his expression, if anything, became even more serious: he might have been contemplating the meaning of existence.

'Can they . . .' Vivienne was clearly choosing her words carefully, trying to convey her meaning without embarrassing her grandson with too much personal detail in her questions. She was by no means shy or modest, but she and Angel did not have the kind of close, loving bond established over decades that meant they could talk easily about such intimate physical issues. 'I mean, I'm sure there are procedures that can be done . . . precautions that can be taken before you have to have any chemotherapy . . .' she continued.

'Just radiotherapy, thank God,' Angel said swiftly. 'That's a piece of good luck.'

'Wonderful! Wonderful! But still, in that area . . .' Vivienne swallowed again. 'Before that starts, couldn't they . . . I'm sure they can . . . well, in any case, please, *please* bring the fertility issue up with the doctor immediately, darling. Please. No matter what it costs. You must have the best, most cutting-edge treatment.'

'I will, Grandma,' he promised. 'I have the operation scheduled for two days' time. I'll make sure it all gets discussed thoroughly before then, and we'll do everything possible.'

'And you're having it in London?'

Angel nodded.

'At the Wellington?' Vivienne asked, naming the famous private hospital in St John's Wood that hosted royalty from all around the world for surgical procedures. Nicknamed 'The Dorchester', after the Park Lane hotel owned by the Sultan of Brunei, for the amount of rich, titled Arabs it hosted, with its room-service menus, flat-screen TVs and etiquette-trained staff, it was the closest thing to a five-star hotel experience that one could have while undergoing surgery.

Angel had prepared for this question. If he said he was having surgery at somewhere like the Wellington, or the St John and St Elizabeth, also in St John's Wood, Vivienne would insist on visiting; even if he told her that he didn't want her to come and see him, she would doubtless ring up, or send flowers, and would find out immediately from the hospital reception that he was not listed as a patient.

'It's being done in Harley Street,' he said smoothly. 'As an outpatient. They're taking the lump out under local anaesthetic. If that goes as planned and there aren't unforeseen complications – if it hasn't spread further than they anticipate – then I'll move on to radiotherapy very quickly.'

God, I'm good, he reflected smugly. *That sounded incredibly plausible.*

'I'll come back to London with you,' Vivienne said instantly.

She lived most of the year in Montreux, on Lake Geneva, Swiss residency being by far the most advantageous way to lower her tax bill. Wealthy foreigners were attracted to Switzerland by its fiscal deal permits, which effectively meant that as long as they did not earn income in the country, they not only paid significantly lower taxes than Swiss citizens, but were not required to declare their non-Swiss income and assets to the tax authorities. Although the Swiss government might not make money by taxing the holders of such permits, the presence of vast amounts of celebrity residents naturally meant a large revenue stream for the local economy; and, of course, the property market flourished as foreigners paid ever-increasing sums for their homes.

Naturally, however, Vivienne maintained a place in London too, an apartment in a mansion block on Park Lane; she could be in the country for up to three months a year without incurring British taxes on her income. This was a serious consideration, as with her thriving lines of perfume, skincare, cosmetics and jewellery, Vivienne was earning more now than she had ever done in her heyday as an actress.

'I'll stay in London as long as you need,' she assured Angel, squeezing his hands passionately. 'As long as you're in treatment. This is more important to me than anything else. Anything at all.'

Angel knew exactly what she was saying, and he was deeply impressed with the success of his strategy. The cancer story had been intended as a way to get close to his grandmother again, an excuse for making contact with her so close to news of her jewellery auction leaking out. It was only now that he was seeing its effect on her – including Vivienne's concerns for the possibility of his being able to father her great-grandchildren – that he was realizing that this was a huge opportunity in itself. Vivienne relinquishing her cherished non-resident British tax status for a year would be a huge financial sacrifice. If she was willing to do that for Angel, what else might she be prepared to offer?

'Thank you, Grandma,' he said in his best heartfelt voice. 'I know we haven't been close. But this can be a fresh start for both of us.'

'Yes, Angel,' his grandmother said firmly, her confidence

returning, her chin raising. 'A fresh start. That's what we need. You'll be fine, darling. I know you will. You'll come through this. Honestly, I see it as a wake-up call to both of us in all *sorts* of ways.'

Her eyes flashed as she confronted the future, determining to make the best of it, as she had always done.

'And Angel,' she said, fixing those magnificent eyes on her grandson. 'Tell me, darling – are you seeing anyone?'

Chapter Nine

Tylösand – the next day

'So, tell me about yourself, Christine!' Vivienne said with a smile so friendly that Christine felt as if she had been wrapped in a mink blanket. 'Are you seeing anyone?'

This line of questioning was so unexpected that Christine choked on the foam of the cappuccino she was drinking. To her great surprise, Vivienne had rung her room at eight o'clock that morning, inviting her to breakfast; Christine had thrown herself out of bed, into the shower and then into her best smart-casual outfit with lightning speed, brewing herself a pot of coffee to make sure she was alert for the rendezvous.

She had definitely needed the coffee. The night before, she and Tor had returned to the hotel bar for dinner, Christine a bundle of nerves at having been so close to making her pitch to Vivienne and then frustrated at the last moment. Tor had been eager to reassure Christine that Vivienne would definitely set up another meeting, while Vivienne herself had been the soul of politeness on saying goodnight to Christine. Still, it had been hard for Christine to put aside her anxiety, and she wished now that she had known Vivienne would be calling so soon. As it was, she had drowned her worries in red wine and stayed up much later than she would otherwise have done.

Christine's head had been spinning the whole time; not just with anxiety, but with the unbelievable fact that she had not only met Vivienne Winter, but found her open and friendly – even amused that Christine had practically stalked her by following her to Sweden. Tor, naturally, had been pumped up by his success in helping her, and their conversation had been wild, silly, delightful and giggly: banter about Russian sailors, Tor improvising a silly song about a beautiful woman who, like Christine, had blue eyes, freckles and light brown hair, which had caused fellow diners to look over indulgently as she blushed. One particularly jolly chap actually joined in the chorus.

There had been lots of toasts and clinking glasses, and a second bottle of red wine with dinner; when Tor finally settled the bill and they stood up to leave, Christine had realized instantly that she was very drunk. Her knees had buckled, and she'd grabbed the back of her armchair for support, wobbling so visibly that Tor had practically jumped over to help her, taking her arm.

She had been mortified, but Tor had just laughed.

'Hey,' he said easily, 'you had a big day! You met Vivienne Winter *and* me! I know, who cares about Vivienne when you have me to talk to, right? No wonder you needed to let off steam!'

This made her giggle even as she gratefully leaned on his arm, like a Victorian heroine out for a walk in the park with an admirer. Propping her up effortlessly with one strong forearm, Tor had reached into the jug of water on the table and extracted an ice cube. Holding it to the back of her neck, he laughed again at the shocked expression on her face as the freezing ice cube touched her skin.

'Keep it there till we get you back to your room,' he had said comfortably. 'It'll help.'

Although he had indeed escorted her to her hotel room, there had been no kiss at the door. Christine had been too busy just concentrating on standing up straight and pressing the ice cube to the back of her neck; it did help, but she was still mortified. She usually held her drink better than this. Tor was too sensible and well mannered to pressure a clearly drunk woman for a kiss goodnight, though she did remember his lips pressing briefly to her forehead before he held the door wide for her and told her that he'd ring her tomorrow . . .

The sound of the phone shrilling like a mynah bird so early had been a nasty shock, but Christine was young and resilient: a lukewarm shower and two Solpadeine had worked wonders. Adrenalin was surging through her at the anticipation of the Herculean task ahead. She wasn't foolish or naive enough to think that she could convince Vivienne in just one conversation to agree to use Berkeley as her auctioneers; her goal today was to pull off a successful first pitch, which would open the door to a full series of meetings with the whole Fine Jewellery department, plus the Berkeley partners.

Christine felt like a sprinter ducked and ready with her feet on the blocks, a race car revving up at the starting line. She had been ready for this for days, was champing at the bit to get started with the business meeting; so Vivienne's question about her relationship status took her completely aback.

'I'm not, actually,' she answered, wiping the cappuccino

foam from her lips as tidily as she could. 'Seeing anyone, that is.'

'But you must have plenty of admirers,' Vivienne said, and, if anything, her smile grew even warmer. The extraordinary violet eyes sparkled reminiscently and the lips, less full than they once had been, but still beautifully shaped, quirked up at the corners. 'Oh, the fun of being your age! I had the most *wonderful* times . . . How old are you, my dear?'

'Twenty-six,' Christine said, and saw Vivienne's eyebrows quirk upwards in such a familiar expression that it gave Christine a little shiver of delight; she had seen Vivienne make that same gesture in so many iconic films.

The eyebrows were dyed brown and pencilled in deftly to fill the gaps, Vivienne's eye make-up done with equal expertise. Not even the loyal Gregory was allowed to see her without her make-up and one of her many wigs or turbans. She had been so prudent over the years with skincare and surgeries, having the minimum possible performed: the wattles around her neck removed, and the bags under her eyes and the sag in her eyelids whisked away with blepharoplasty. She knew very well that if her eyes were as astonishingly vivid and almond-shaped as ever, people would barely notice the crow's feet around them.

With the same intelligent planning, Vivienne had eschewed fillers, Restylane and collagen lip implants. She had seen almost all her contemporaries fall victim to temptation, and it seemed that once they started down the filler route they could never stop. It was a slope so slippery it might have been greased with pints of oil. Even Jane Fonda, who had on the whole been sensible with her facial surgeries, was baring her shoulders in evening dresses at seventy-seven and dieting herself to an extreme of thinness that Vivienne found both unflattering and dangerous.

'Twenty-six?' she said, leaning to look closely at Christine. 'You take good care of your skin. And you have young features. You'll age well.'

'Thank you!' Christine flushed. She didn't particularly like her round face and snub nose, but Vivienne was right: they did make her look more youthful.

'You find Tor attractive,' Vivienne said, sipping her own cappuccino.

It wasn't a question, so Christine remained silent, wondering where the conversation was going. They were breakfasting in Vivienne's suite: since Vivienne Winter could not be expected to go down to the buffet, the buffet was, literally, brought to her. In all her meetings with the uber-rich, Christine had never seen anything like this level of VIP treatment. Three separate serving trolleys were arranged along one side of the living room, stacked with selections of the cold cuts, smoked fish, salads, fruit, cheeses and crispbreads which were so lavishly displayed in the restaurant, just in case Vivienne might be tempted to snack on one of the offerings. Christine would not have been entirely surprised to see an omelette station set up in the far corner.

Vivienne had asked her if she wanted eggs, as she was ordering them for herself from room service, but Christine's stomach was churning with nerves, and she couldn't contemplate eating anything cooked. She was also worried about not eating with sufficient elegance under Vivienne's assessing gaze. Instead she had taken slices of cold ham and chicken, and was cutting them into small pieces that wouldn't slip off the tines of her fork.

'Tor *is* very attractive, of course,' Vivienne continued, reaching out for her napkin. 'He's always been a charismatic boy. Wild, too, ever since he was little. He was always climbing trees and getting into scrapes and coming back with blood pouring from some wound or other. All that need to explore, strike out for points unknown! He's never been able to settle – his wife's certainly found that out the hard way.'

Christine, who was politely breaking a piece of crispbread over her plate so that it wouldn't shed any crumbs as she bit into it, heard the snap of the rye bread like a small bone cracking. A chicken wishbone, maybe. Only in this case, her desire would certainly not be coming true.

'Did he tell you he was married?' Vivienne asked, taking a black grape from the fruit bowl, contemplating it for a moment. 'I *do* hope so. He can be very naughty that way. His grandfather was just the same – too charming to stick to one woman. We had a long affair, but I never dreamed that he was faithful to me.'

She smiled naughtily.

'Of course,' she added, 'I wasn't either. But then, I wasn't married most of the time.'

She popped the grape into her mouth and chewed it, all the time watching Christine's reaction.

'Tor *is* very charming,' Christine agreed, setting the crisp-bread pieces down on the plate.

She had suddenly lost her appetite. The breakfast table had been placed in front of the floor-to-ceiling windows onto the terrace, and the view was even more beautiful up here on the top floor of the hotel. She could see the whole of the little island, the sweep of the bay, the steep rise and descent of the sand dunes, the steely grey-blue of the sea and sky melting into each other at the far horizon. The sun was almost visible, its outline radiating a pale haze of light through the cloud cover.

Christine's gaze fell to the beach below the wooden staircase, on which, just yesterday morning, she had been capering around like an idiot – an idiot who couldn't spot a married man who was obviously much too attractive and funny and delightful to be single. What had she been *thinking*? When did it ever happen that you met a gorgeous man on a beach, and he asked you out, made up songs about you and introduced you to a legendary film star, and was actually eligible to boot?

Never. Not once. It was like something out of a film, and now Christine had bumped heavily down to earth.

Determined not to be perceived as a fool by Vivienne, Christine used every ounce of her self-control on keeping any reaction from her face. She was desperate to look as if she had been fully aware of this information, considering Tor merely an amusing acquaintance.

'We had a fun time over dinner last night,' she said as airily as she could. 'He sang some songs with other people in the bar.'

This, she hoped, sounded as if they had formed a group with other diners, rather than sat *tête-à-tête*; certainly, she was not mentioning the fact that the songs had sprung from a private joke, and centred around her beauty.

'Oh good! I'm glad you had a nice evening,' Vivienne said, selecting another grape. 'Tor's so delightful, such a lovely boy. He gets on so well with women that he can't limit himself to only one. I'm sure we both know the type very well, don't we?'

Despite the emotions roiling inside her, Christine could not help but be flattered at the easy way Vivienne – one of the most famous beauties of all time – included her as an equal in this observation.

'Oh, yes! Great company, but not to be taken seriously,' Christine said as lightly as she could.

'Do eat something!' Vivienne said, fluttering her fingers at Christine's plate. 'Breakfast is the most important meal of the day. I was always saying that to Pearl and Angel when they were little.'

Dutifully, Christine dug her fork into a piece of ham and ate it, washing it down with a gulp of freshly squeezed grapefruit juice. A seagull perched on Vivienne's balcony, cawing loudly and making a welcome distraction for Christine. She could glance over at it, allowing the lump of misery in her throat to settle, averting her eyes from Vivienne's all-too-knowing gaze. A knock came on the door of the suite. Moments later Gregory entered, carrying a plate topped by a stainless-steel warmer.

'Your omelette, Vivienne,' he said, setting it in front of her.

'Are you sure you don't want eggs?' Vivienne asked Christine, who shook her head, more than ever disinclined to eat. Gregory removed the warmer and himself in swift succession, vanishing into another room in the suite and closing the door behind him.

'Mmm, delicious,' Vivienne said, looking at the plate. 'So

light. Goat's cheese and shredded leek – I must get my cook to put shredded leek in my omelettes in future.' She picked up her fork. 'So, I'm off to London after breakfast,' she added, quite unexpectedly. 'Cutting short my spa break. Angel has brought me some news that we need to . . . work through there. I'm assuming you're based in London? No reason, of course, apart from your accent.'

'I am,' Christine said quickly, not knowing where this was going but grateful to have the conversation switched away from Tor and onto her job. 'Although Berkeley has salerooms all over the world, of course. New York, Tokyo, Milan and Geneva.' She had left this one for last deliberately, and she saw Vivienne give a little nod of appreciation.

'And you have a detailed proposition for me, I imagine?' Vivienne continued. 'You haven't just turned up with a pretty smile and pleasant social manners?'

'Oh no!' Christine said, taking a deep breath. 'I have a whole proposal for you and your management. I'm suggesting an approach that will take in not only your iconic status as an actress, but a businesswoman with several internationally successful product lines. If we work on the sales and market-ing as I'd like to, we can loop in your perfume, jewellery, even skincare brands, and incorporate them in the sale, so that we can not only derive the highest possible gain from pre-sales and the auction itself, but build your brands even further to increase your revenue with those too. We'll incorp-orate a wide range of social media to publicize the jewellery collection as visually as possible, linking it in with designs from your various products and also, ideally, historic photo-graphs of you wearing them.'

Christine hesitated, then plunged forward with the most crucial element of her pitch.

'My vision would be to have the catalogue run chronologically,' she explained. 'Telling the whole history of your life and films through your jewel collection. My dream title for the auction would be *Vivienne Winter: A Life in Jewels*.'

Did I go too far? she thought, unable to read Vivienne's expression. *Did I make it too personal?* Vivienne had never agreed to an authorized memoir, despite repeated attempts by publishers to offer her millions to sit down with a ghostwriter. She might well recoil from this idea, which would inevitably have a degree of autobiography about it. Christine had done her research, known her proposal might be risky for that reason; and yet the title was so perfect, the concept so striking, that she had not been able to restrain herself from suggesting it.

'I really see this as being much more than just an auction,' she continued, almost stammering now with nerves. 'It's a historic moment, a celebration of your entire career. That's how it will be seen by the media, so my thinking is to get out ahead of that, capitalize on it. Make the catalogue a celebration of all your achievements first, and a sale guide second. That way it'll look much classier –'

Christine caught herself, having learned from Berkeley's posh staff members that actual upper-class people never, *ever* used the word 'classy'.

'Much more elegant and memorable,' she corrected herself. 'I want it to be a collector's item in itself. And that will make people even more eager to bid for the jewellery. They won't feel that we're selling to them – they'll feel privileged just to be able to buy, if you see what I mean! The Elizabeth Taylor jewel auction fetched nearly seventy-five million pounds. I honestly think if you let Berkeley handle yours the way I suggest, we can easily beat that figure.'

She wound down, feeling as if she had been talking for hours. Vivienne's poise was magnificent. She had been sitting serenely, cutting and forking up small pieces of her leek and goat's cheese omelette, all the way through Christine's pitch. Now that Christine had finally come to a halt, Vivienne took another bite of omelette, washed it down with a sip of ice water, reached for her cappuccino cup – and then, to Christine's barely suppressed agony, drank from that too, her expression entirely neutral, prolonging the suspense to a point that Christine felt nervous sweat beading on her palms. She slid her hands to her lap, scrunching the linen napkin to absorb the dampness, wadding it into a tight ball that she squeezed hard to stop her begging Vivienne pathetically for her verdict.

'My goodness,' Vivienne finally said, with that superb raise of her eyebrows. 'You're even more efficient than I was imagining! What an excellent pitch! And you managed to get that first part out almost in one breath! I'm definitely intrigued.'

She set down her cup.

'I need to hear more about this very persuasive concept of yours,' she continued. 'I think you should come back to London with me today. You can break down your ideas for me in more detail on the plane.'

Christine stared at her, speechless.

'Angel will be travelling with us,' Vivienne said. 'Or rather, we'll be going with him. He's organized a private flight. I want him to work on the auction too, so it'll be convenient for us to hear you talk about it when we're all together.'

She glanced at Christine's plate.

'You don't seem very hungry. Have you finished?'

Christine nodded mutely; she was far too worked up to have managed to eat more than those first few bites of ham. She couldn't believe what she was hearing. The revelation that Tor was married, that she had been foolish enough to start falling for a man who was clearly too good to be true, had knocked her off balance. Reeling from the news that her judgement was severely flawed, she had summoned up every ounce of energy to nail her pitch to Vivienne, remember everything she had planned to say and deliver it in the right order, sounding infinitely more confident than she felt. Having succeeded beyond her wildest dreams, she suddenly felt exhausted.

'Well, in that case, why don't you pop back to your room and pack your bags?' Vivienne suggested. 'We'll meet in the lobby in an hour. Gregory's already seeing to my cases and settling the bill – which includes yours, my dear. No arguments, please, it's a drop in the ocean to me. Take it as a tribute to your enterprise and ambition. Oh, and don't worry about getting peckish later – there's always plenty to eat on board private planes!'

She favoured Christine with such a blinding smile that its recipient was grateful she was still sitting down; if she had been standing, she was sure her knees would have buckled even more hopelessly than they had in the bar the night before. Vivienne Winter was paying her hotel bill, inviting her to travel on her private plane and talk in detail about her ideas for the auction! It was unbelievable, a dream come true! Christine needed to assign Tor firmly to the past tense, where he belonged, and concentrate on the blessed, miraculous fact that she had achieved the unthinkable: convincing Vivienne Winter to seriously consider Berkeley for her jewel auction.

'I hope,' Vivienne said as Christine stood up to follow her instructions, 'this is going to be the start of a simply delightful . . .'

She paused for a moment, choosing the right word.

'Relationship,' she finished.

And for a split second – so fast that Christine was sure, afterwards, that she must have imagined it – one of Vivienne's eyelids flickered down and up again, her lips quirking as she executed the tiniest and most subtle of winks.

Chapter Ten

London – very late the same day

'She wants *what*?' Nicole demanded furiously. 'I don't *believe* this! Are you fucking kidding me?'

'It all happened so fast!' Angel said, practically giggling. 'It's a whirlwind romance!'

'This is *ridiculous*!' Nicole had her hands on her hips. 'You go away for one night and come back practically *engaged*?'

'Hey, hey, let's not put the cart before the horse,' Angel said, walking over to the lavish built-in wet bar of his living room. 'Shall I mix us a nightcap? I'm feeling rather celebratory! What about a Negroni? Sweet but bitter at the same time. That should suit the mood *you* seem to be in, darling.'

'I'm just . . .' Nicole searched for the right word to sum up her emotions, and after a while, found it in vocabulary picked up from a fellow student at the Chateau, the son of an East End entrepreneur. 'Gobsmacked,' she finished.

'Well, you look fantastic,' Angel said, meeting her eyes appreciatively in the mirror behind the bar, then running his gaze up and down her body. Nicole was clad in a clinging red silk negligee that lifted her small, perfect breasts and presented them to the viewer as if they were miniature vanilla cupcakes in crimson wrappers; over it she wore a matching silk robe, trimmed and sashed with deep burgundy silk velvet. Her feet were bare, and her pedicure was immaculate.

'Love the nail colour,' Angel observed.

'The colour's called "Coca-Cola",' Nicole said, tilting one hand from side to side so he could see the red glitter inside the black polish, the same shade as her toenails. 'Clever, isn't it?'

'Charming,' he said as he reached for the gin and Campari. 'The whole ensemble.'

'I'll really miss Honkers,' Nicole said, sighing. 'All my clothes are custom-made, you know? I designed a lot of things, or had them copied from pictures. The tailors there can do anything, anything at all. And the material's the best in the world. Everything I have on is copied from a La Perla catalogue, customized for me. And look! The colour goes with my stripes!'

Swivelling round, she lifted the hems of her negligee and robe, showing off the marks from the caning Angel had laid on her the day before.

'Mmm, sexy,' he purred. 'You must take a look at the bite marks you made on my bum. I think those are coming along nicely too.'

'We're quite a pair, aren't we, darling? Like peas in a pod,' Nicole cooed, letting the silk fabric fall. Gliding forward, she picked up the ice tongs and dropped ice cubes into the two lowball glasses in which Angel was mixing their Negronis.

'Nicole,' Angel said, and there was a rapier point to his voice now. 'Let's not play the betrayed wife game, shall we? Before you came back into my life so agreeably a couple of days ago, we hadn't seen each other in years.'

'Oh God, I'm not *jealous!*' Nicole said airily, taking the heavy-based glass from Angel's hand, swirling the sunset-coloured liquid, making the ice cubes clink. 'I just don't want to be cut out of the deal! I brought this to you, after all – you must admit that. You wouldn't even have known about the auction if it weren't for me.'

'I don't quite see the issue . . .' Angel began, strolling over to the built-in window seat with its view over Knightsbridge and, in the distance, Hyde Park. He lounged elegantly on the dark grey suede cushions.

'This isolates me from the centre of things!' she protested.

'But Nicole, the whole idea was that I was going to be the liaison with Viv, while you had the contacts with Silantra and Big Cookie,' Angel said, taking a long drink of his cocktail and smacking his lips together in relief as the alcohol hit his bloodstream. 'I don't see how this changes anything.'

Nicole ignored Angel's play on Lil' Biscuit's name. 'Because now Vivienne's going to have you chained to the side of this auction girl!' she said petulantly. 'That wasn't the idea at all!'

'Not *all* the time,' Angel said patiently. 'I have to have my "radiation treatments" and recoup from them, remember? There'll be plenty of time with all my "doctor's appointments" for our fiendish plotting. And fun times. Lovely fun times.' He winked.

'Is she going to join in, do you think?' Nicole asked, brightening up a bit. 'You know how much I like to play with another girl.'

'God, no,' Angel said flatly. 'Even if Christine would want to, that's simply not possible. It has to be all romance, hearts and flowers, true love and monogamy forever, at least as far as she knows. I'm supposed to be making her fall in love with me and knocking her up in quick succession – or even the other way round. The main thing Granny Viv cares about is a great-grandchild. She's made me promise to have my sperm frozen – I presume so that if the cancer knocks me off, that'll be her second line of attack.'

Nicole raised the glass to her lips. The flaming Negroni blended with the colour of her negligee and robe, a striking contrast to her matt-beige skin and silky black hair. 'Who saw *this* coming when you decided to give yourself cancer!' she said rather bitterly.

'Certainly not me!' Angel riposted. The light was behind him, which gave him an advantage. Eyes narrowed, he took in Nicole from head to toe, but this time with no sexual motive at all. He was assessing her mood, her unexpected reaction to the news, working out how best to handle his co-conspirator.

'I'm just surprised,' she said, walking over and curling up opposite him on the wide window seat, 'that you didn't mention you had a girlfriend who was the perfect contender for this role. That would have kept it in the family! We could have played the loving couple, maybe even faked a pregnancy . . . it would have been so much more plausible than this idea that you seduce some little nothing from an auction house in a couple of weeks and convince her to let you do her bareback . . .'

But she stopped, because Angel was laughing so hard that he had to set down his glass on the lacquer coffee table.

'What?' she said crossly. 'What did I say? I'm simply suggesting that it would have been a much better option! As your girlfriend, I could have slipped into the middle of a lot of things . . . got more closely involved with all the ins and outs of the pre-sales . . .'

'*Darling!*' he said, when he could speak again. '*Look* at yourself!'

He gestured at the seductive picture Nicole made in her silk and velvet lingerie.

'Do you really think I could trot someone who looks like you over to Granny Viv as the woman who's going to make me turn over a new leaf and go respectable?'

Angel was not going to say out loud that Nicole's entire appearance signified high-class call girl or professional mistress, but it was most definitely what he was thinking. Vivienne, an astute judge of character, would have sniffed her out in seconds.

'I wouldn't dress like this to meet your grandmother!' Nicole said indignantly. 'I'm not an *idiot!*'

'Even in your best demure dress,' Angel said gently, 'you ooze sex, sweetie. A man doesn't settle down with you. He asks you who you want to share for a threesome, and gets stuck in. As it were. Come on; you don't want to be taken for wife material, do you?'

Nicole frowned as much as her Botox would let her, which meant two tiny parallel lines forming on either side of the top of her nose.

'I could act it!' she snapped crossly.

'She'd run a background check on you,' Angel said in a happy inspiration, as he could see that Nicole was taking his comments in a worse spirit than he had intended. 'And that would be bound to pull up at least some of your activities in Hong Kong. One of the things that makes her so keen on the auction girl is that she's so respectable and career-oriented. You should have heard her banging on about her ideas on the plane! I must say, a lot of them were very good, but she never shut up for a second. And Viv seemed to be eating it up with a spoon. She thinks the girl'll make an excellent candidate for motherhood. She likes her work ethic – says it'll balance out the fact that I haven't got any.'

The mention of a background check had stopped Nicole dead in her tracks; she bit her lip, perfectly well aware that this was the last thing she wanted to happen.

'So what's the plan?' she said eventually, drinking more of her cocktail.

'A two-pronged attack,' Angel said, fishing out his pack of Davidoff cigarettes from his jacket pocket. 'First, I go and get my sperm frozen, or whatever it is they do with it, in case I pop my clogs. This is all by the by, of course – I'm not actually going to do that, but I'll tell Viv I have. She wants to know that if I die, she can buy some eggs, squirt it in them and make some grandbabies. Ideally, however, she's hoping I'll stick around, turn over a new leaf with a nice girl, and bring the brats up myself as a doting father.'

He lit a cigarette.

'This particular girl isn't *mandatory*, of course,' he added. 'But she ticks all the boxes, and because I've scared Granny Viv shitless with the cancer diagnosis, and the idea that I might not have much time left, she's doing everything she can to throw us together. If she's happy with the auction house, the plan is for me and Little Miss Christine to work on the research together, so I'll have something to keep me grounded while I'm sick, using Granny Viv's charming phrase. Meanwhile, I'm taking Little Miss out to dinner, working my magic, fucking her seven ways to Sunday with condoms that I've put a hole in, and Bob's your uncle!' Angel took a drag on his cigarette.

'She'll be on the pill, surely?' Nicole said dubiously.

'Darling, I don't want to knock her up, do I!' Angel said, throwing his arms wide rhetorically. 'That's Granny Viv's take on things! The whole condom idea was hers, naturally.'

'My God! She really is a piece of work,' Nicole said with grudging respect. 'She actually suggested you poke holes in condoms?'

'Yes! You see?' Angel's eyes narrowed. 'No one bloody believes what she's capable of but me! I've seen her in action and I know *exactly* what she's like. She's utterly unscrupulous.'

The apple doesn't fall far from the tree, does it? Nicole thought, but was far too sensible to say out loud.

'So you're not going to knock her up, but you're going to sweep her off her feet?' she summarized instead.

'Exactly. Oh, and Granny Viv doesn't want me to tell her anything about the cancer diagnosis either, of course,' Angel said airily.

'She's using this poor girl like a surrogate without even telling her!' Nicole said, reaching out for a cigarette. 'For all she knows, she could be pregnant in six months by someone who's about to die!'

'I *told* you!' Angel said, his voice rising. 'I *told* you what she's like!'

'So . . . is she attractive, this Christine girl?' Nicole said in a faux-casual manner that didn't deceive Angel for a second, but did at least succeed in distracting him from his anger and resentment towards his grandmother.

He drew on his cigarette and considered Nicole thoughtfully. It occurred to him that she seemed to be assuming quite a lot on the basis of a very short reacquaintance. They had never been boyfriend and girlfriend at school; fixed pairings had been unusual there. He had barely seen her since, just bumped into her at the usual round of parties from St Moritz to St Tropez; and though they had had sex whenever the occasion arose, they had been nothing more than fuck buddies.

Now, in the space of barely twenty-four hours, here she was: installed in his apartment, proposing a complex scheme to wrangle kickbacks for access to his grandmother's jewellery, and acting as if they were long accustomed to plotting together.

Angel didn't trust Nicole as far as he could throw her. He had no automatic assumption that she would, as she had promised, split the commission from Lil' Biscuit and Silantra fifty-fifty; but then, nor did he intend to cut her in equally on anything he might be able to make without her knowledge. And now that he would be working on the auction preparation so closely, his opportunities for kickbacks had expanded still further – which was ideal for him, but less so for Nicole.

'Oh, she's perfectly nice-looking,' he answered, in a careless way that matched the tone of the question. 'Viv wouldn't accept anything less mingling with her own precious genes.'

In his opinion, Christine was much better than nicelooking. At the least, she definitely had potential, although her clothing was much more buttoned-up and dowdy than

Angel preferred. His mental observation that Nicole looked like a high-class call girl, elegant and slutty in equal measure, had been entirely favourable. That black dress Christine had been wearing the night before at the Hotel Tylösand had been horrendous, more suitable for – he searched in his head for a dowdy profession, and settled on the most stay-at-home, dandruff-covered one he could think of – a female crime writer's rare night out than a young woman with an excellent figure visiting a chic hotel.

But he wasn't going to be fool enough to tell Nicole that he was very much looking forward to peeling off Christine's boring outfits, finding out the precise dimensions of the nicely shaped curves that lay beneath them, and ravaging those curves in every conceivable way. He imagined his dick deep in her mouth, those big blue eyes wide in concentration, her cheeks sucking in as her lips and tongue worked his shaft.

Instantly, his cock hardened. Oh yes, having to fuck Christine on his grandmother's instructions would be no hardship at all. He had seen a sprinkling of freckles over the modest décolletage revealed by Christine's demure cocktail dress, her bare arms; as he contemplated exactly where more might be scattered over her naked body, hidden in her secret clefts and declivities, waiting for him to find them, his balls tightened too. Angel was an eternal seeker of variety.

Even if he hadn't found her attractive, however, Angel would have seduced Christine simply for the pleasure of cutting out Tor, whom he had always intensely disliked. There was something so bluff and hearty about Tor, so jolly and cheerful, which women seemed, inexplicably, to find attractive. Being practically the same age, the boys had been forced to play together as children after Vivienne had taken custody of Angel. It had seemed like a perfect idea for her to visit Sweden as regularly as she could so that her grandson and godson could play together while she continued her affair with Tor's grandfather.

Typical Vivienne, Angel thought sourly. *Pretending she was dragging me over there for my welfare, when in reality it was all about her convenience. I hated every moment. They kept making me play outside with Tor, and I bloody hate the outdoors. It's dirty and messy and you're always getting scratched.*

Tor had been the most enthusiastic of hosts. His physical competence and sense of fair play had always annoyed Angel intensely, as had Tor's persistence in attributing the best motives to Angel's bad behaviour. Tor's sympathy and consideration for Angel's status as an orphan after Pearl's death, his insistence that Angel have first choice in playing with Tor's toys, had often made Angel want to punch him in the mouth. And Vivienne had never stopped praising Tor's lovely manners, his patience with Angel, his willingness to share – all of which had naturally infuriated Angel even further.

His visceral dislike for Tor would probably never have abated: Angel could hold a grudge forever. But Tor's achievements as an adult were salt rubbed into Angel's wounds. Tor was regularly in the news, his handsome, smiling face in newspapers and magazines, his arm round a brave amputee whom Tor had helped achieve their dream of reaching the South Pole, or skiing down Everest, or something equally pointless. The sight made Angel want to punch Tor in the mouth all over again.

It had been obvious last night at the spa how interested Tor was in Christine. Angel hadn't seen that light in Tor's eyes since they were eight years old and Vivienne had given Tor a Scalextric set, an order custom-made for him, based on the roads around Tylösand. Angel had done his best to systematically break as many pieces of that set as he could, and Tor had forgiven him every single time, which had driven Angel near-insane with suppressed fury.

Oh yes, Tor had been as enthusiastic when he looked at Christine as he had been at the age of eight, holding the miniature red pick-up truck that had the same licence plate as his father's, his eyes sparkling with pleasure. That in itself would have been enough to make Angel want to swipe Christine away from under Tor's nose – just as he had 'accidentally' pulled the licence plates off the truck and buried them in the garden. He'd turn Christine inside out until she forgot there was any other man in the world but him. And every time he shot in her mouth and watched her swallow it down eagerly, every time he heard her beg him to fuck her in the arse, scream as he lubed her up, slid in his cock and started to pump her like a cheap whore, his physical pleasure would be immeasurably heightened by his triumph over a man he had always, frankly, hated.

Angel wondered whether Tor had fucked Christine already; he thought it unlikely. Tor prided himself on being a gentleman, and they had only met yesterday afternoon. He would have limited himself to kissing Christine at the door to her room. It wouldn't have mattered to Angel – in fact, he would positively have preferred it if he was following Tor. Smugly, he felt sure that his experience in an extremely wide range of sexual activities would beat out his childhood rival in this adult field of competition. He would have enjoyed doing to Christine everything that Tor had done: better, longer, with extra twists.

Sadly, however, it was now too late. Vivienne had summoned Angel to her suite immediately after dispatching Christine to pack her things. She'd briefed him not only on her expectations that he would, ideally, seduce and impregnate Christine, but explained that she had cleared the way for him by telling Christine that Tor was married. This was technically correct, but Tor and his wife had been separated for enough time that the wife had a new boyfriend, and they were currently working through a non-contentious divorce process. However, even if Tor tried to correct the misunderstanding, Granny Viv had apparently convinced Christine that he was a playboy who would do anything to get a woman into bed. Christine wouldn't believe a word he said.

Angel had, reluctantly, to give Granny Viv credit. She was a nasty, devious old bitch with her hands too tightly wrapped around the purse strings, but she thought fast and effectively. With that well-calculated lie about Tor, she had ensured the road to seducing Christine was wide open to Angel. He imagined Christine's white freckled legs in the same state, Christine's fingers between them, strumming herself wetter and wetter as she pleaded for Angel to fuck her, and smiled as his erection butted against the seam of his trousers.

'Nic, darling, seeing you in that ragingly sexy outfit's given me the most enormous stiffie,' he lied, tracing his hand over the outline of his swollen cock. 'Why don't you come over here and give me one of your signature blow jobs? That'd be *just* the thing to make me forget all about that boring little bitch.'

Nicole could not resist a challenge, nor an opportunity to mark territory that she seemed to consider rightfully hers. Finishing her Negroni, she tossed back her superb mane of hair and went down on her hands and knees, crawling seductively across the window seat towards him. Angel unzipped his trousers in readiness.

'I'm going to suck you like a Dyson,' she said, running her tongue around her lips.

She slid the middle finger of her right hand into her mouth, dampening it thoroughly, before removing it and giving him a narrow dark stare positively laden with naughtiness.

'You'd better take those trousers right off,' she purred, her eyelashes fluttering. 'I've got plans for your arse, too.'

'Oh, Nicole, you really are a treasure,' Angel sighed, obeying her instructions and lying back on the window seat, his hips tipped up to give her full access.

'Don't forget it,' she said with just a lacing of menace before her mouth closed around him just as tightly as she had promised, hot and moist. Angel sighed even louder as she began to work him with her tongue, her hand slipping below his cock, tracing up his perineum, provoking a series of moans from him as she started to trace circles round his arsehole.

'Fuck, no, I won't forget this,' he groaned, his hips bucking, Nicole taking all of his dick into her mouth with the practised ease of a woman who had learned to override the gag reflex at a very exclusive Swiss boarding school. 'Jesus, you've got to be one of the best cocksuckers in the world . . . you should give lessons, you really should . . .'

Nicole purred again, the reverberations delicious around his cock, her hand splayed wide so that her thumb could tickle his balls. He wondered how to deliver the revelation that she couldn't stay on in his apartment. He would have to court Christine as if he were the kind of man who had turned over a new leaf from his playboy days, and having Nicole slinking around the place in red silk lingerie wouldn't exactly convey the necessary impression.

He'd have to think carefully about how to handle the eviction notice, though. He wanted to keep Nicole sweet, make sure she understood that he was being forced to do this because of his grandmother. Not only did he need Nicole's contacts to broker the deals for Vivienne's jewellery, but he would be loath to lose the opportunity to have regular sex with her. It was rare to find a woman every bit as perverted and debauched as he was, and he had been looking forward to having a great deal of fun with her while she was in London.

Her finger started sliding into him, reaching for the exact spot he was yearning for her to touch, even as her tongue lapped his cock as if she were licking the topping off an ice cream. He heard himself starting to moan, to plead for her to finish him off, to start sucking him hard, pump her head up and down the whole length of his cock, but he knew she would draw it out longer, because she would enjoy the sound of his begging too much to stop any time soon.

Yes, he'd have to tread very carefully with Nicole's delicate ego. Because no way was that little milk-faced Christine going to be able to give him a blow job half as good as this one.

Chapter Eleven

London – two weeks later

'I can't believe this,' Christine said to Vivienne, staring at the huge, pear-shaped pearl with unabashed awe as she held the heavy pearl and diamond choker in both hands. 'I genuinely can't believe I'm touching it!'

She shook her head in wonder.

'We studied it, of course, for my gemmology degree,' she went on. 'But I never thought I'd be this close to it! The Medici Pearl – wow, it's legendary. Literally legendary. Worn by Catherine de Medici, Mary Queen of Scots, Empress Eugénie . . . and now Vivienne Winter!' Christine finished wisely, having learned quickly that Vivienne's preference was for attention to remain focused firmly on her. 'What a pedigree! It's unbelievable.'

'Sadly, I don't wear it any more,' Vivienne observed, reaching out one ring-laden hand to touch the enormous pearl with her index finger. 'Chokers emphasize my jowls, I'm afraid – even after having had them picked up and stapled back by Dr Chout. These days, I rarely wear necklaces at all. And my bones are fragile now: I can't wear the big pieces for any length of time. Just putting the tiaras on makes me wince at the weight. Hence the auction. Why let all these beautiful pieces just gather dust in the vaults?'

Christine was used by now to Vivienne's occasional paralysing frankness, and had learned that Vivienne did not expect her interlocutors to demur when she spoke honestly about her age or appearance.

'You could have the pearl taken off and reset,' she suggested instead. 'On a longer chain, perhaps.'

Vivienne shook her head.

'No, it was on the choker when Randon gave it to me,' she said simply. 'So I couldn't possibly change the setting. I can't control what happens once I've sold it, of course. But while it's in my possession, it remains as it is.'

Her expression softened, her eyes misting over. Christine could have sworn that they had changed colour, darkened to a deeper purple, as Vivienne remembered the love of her life, Randon Cliffe.

Vivienne settled back in her chair, her hands resting on the wide padded arms. It was a yellow chintz pattern that had been fashionable in the 1980s, the last time Vivienne decorated this apartment. The place was a luxurious time warp, all gilt furniture, swagged and tasselled curtains and wall-to-wall carpeting. Vivienne might enjoy the stripped-down, Scandinavian chic of the Hotel Tylösand for a spa visit, but she liked her various homes plush and her furniture overstuffed.

The apartment was on the top floor of a huge Park Lane villa, and had been Vivienne's *pied à terre* for decades. It seemed small to her after her lakeview mansion in the hills above Montreux, but she loved its views over Hyde Park, which was eternally so lush. It was exactly how she always remembered London from abroad: the beautiful green spaces at its centre, breathing out oxygen; the wide, gracious avenues that bordered them; the red buses gliding along the avenues like ships down a river.

At that moment, however, Vivienne was not seeing the spectacular view. Her eyes were closing as she travelled back into the past. She had no memories of Randon in this apartment, which had been a conscious choice. Shortly after his death she had sold the house in Brompton Square in which they had lived, on and off, during the ups and downs of their two marriages. It was impossible for her to stay on at that address knowing that he would never come back to it, never bang open the front door in the way that always drove her crazy, calling to her to come down and stroll across the Brompton Road with him, hand in hand, heading for San Lorenzo on Beauchamp Place, where there would always be a table for them in the glass-roofed courtyard.

They would settle into San Lorenzo's wicker armchairs, eat risotto with king prawns or linguine with clams washed down with huge quantities of prosecco and Gavi dei Gavi. Randon would always finish the meal with a Sambuca *con le tre mosche* – aniseed liqueur with three coffee beans at the bottom of the small shot glass, the 'three flies' that represent health, happiness and prosperity.

Oh, San Lorenzo! Vivienne had barely been back since he died. Mara Berni, the co-owner, had died a few years ago, but Lorenzo and the rest of the family were still there, running the restaurant and its offshoots. However, just as Vivienne had been unable to stay on in Brompton Square, she also could not bear to revisit one of the places she had been happiest, where she and Randon had talked and laughed and gossiped and kissed and reminisced about the times they had spent together in Italy; those glorious times, filming *Nefertiti* while falling in love.

God knew, Randon and she had had plenty of fights at San Lorenzo too, arguing and squabbling and throwing insults, inevitably when they had too much drink inside them. Sometimes the fights sparked a bout of lovemaking, sometimes the throwing of glasses and bottles, sometimes both. Vivienne had stormed out several times, ignoring Randon yelling at her not to be a stupid bitch and to calm down – how she had hated it when he told her to calm down! – his wonderfully resonant, RADA-trained voice carrying across the entire restaurant.

People who had been surreptitiously watching them bicker would turn and stare openly at the spectacle of Vivienne Winter, her black hair bouncing, her magnificent bosom thrust high like a prow and bedecked with diamonds, those violet eyes, rarer even than the diamonds she was wearing, sparkling dramatically, a fur thrown over her shoulders, teetering on her heels tipsily, making one of her notoriously theatrical exits. Randon would drain his glass and slam it down, swearing loudly, vowing that this time he wouldn't fall for the silly bitch's penchant for throwing scenes; and then, seconds later, would stand up, swearing even more loudly, pull a wad of cash from his pocket – San Lorenzo, famously, had never taken credit cards – throw it on the table, and follow in her wake.

No matter how high the celebrity attendance was on one

of those evenings – and its regulars at that time had included Mick Jagger, Eric Clapton, Joan Collins, Hugh Grant, Sophia Loren, Madonna and Princess Belinda – the restaurant would fall quiet, listening in silent ecstasy to Randon Cliffe outside in the street, bellowing sonorously to Vivienne Winter that if she got mugged it would be entirely her own idiotic fault and she shouldn't expect him to replace her damn jewellery if she acted like a stupid bloody cow wandering by herself around London with a fortune round her neck.

The fights had only worsened with the years. They had never been able to live together successfully. Both had fantasized about domesticity, but had been unable to attain it with each other. On set, in hotel suites or rented villas, they had lain in each other's arms and talked poetically about how wonderful it would be to have some time off work in a home of their own.

However, every time they had actually made the attempt, it had been a disaster. They were too alike – too spoilt and volatile and selfish and temperamental – to make compromises. Vivienne was able to settle down with Dieter, her second husband, in later life because his nature was extremely compliant, letting her have her own way in everything – and because, in her late fifties, she was less inclined to have sex with any other man who might tickle her fancy. Before then, she had never been faithful for any length of time. Both she and Randon had been instinctively promiscuous, which was one of the reasons they had both taken so easily to the gypsy-like, itinerant, opportunity-filled life of the working actor.

Vivienne's reputation was legendary. She had befriended her gay co-stars and seduced the straight ones, racking up such a list of conquests that she left Grace Kelly, that well-known libertine, in the shade. Single motherhood had not slowed Vivienne down at all. Her daughter had lived entirely at her convenience, brought up by nannies in the basement flat of the Brompton Square house, a fully contained apartment with a separate entrance so that Vivienne would never need to see Pearl unless she wanted to.

Randon had been adorable with Pearl when she was trotted out to spend time with her mother and stepfather, dressed up, looking like a little cherub; he had taken great delight in seeing her mauve eyes widen in wonder and excitement as he gave her the choker he had especially made for her, a miniature of her mother's, right down to the dangling pearl. The nanny in residence at the time had expressed concerns about the latter, worried that Pearl would pull it off and try to swallow it. Randon had shrugged magnificently and asked what harm that would do her.

'We'd just make her poo in a bowl till it came out the other end,' he said, and Pearl had giggled so hysterically at this idea, she got the hiccups.

Predictably, Pearl had sold the choker decades ago, when she had run out of money; however, the jeweller to which she had taken it had been sharp enough to contact Vivienne immediately and offer it to her at a premium. Still, what Vivienne had paid then to reunite the two pieces was a drop in the ocean compared to what they would be worth together now, either as an auction lot or a private sale.

Christine laid Vivienne's choker back in the velvet-lined tray on the coffee table, carefully arranging it next to Pearl's smaller one. It was a poignant sight, the child-sized piece of jewellery, when one realized that the mother was still alive but the little girl for whom it had been made was long gone.

Vivienne cleared her throat, easing herself upright again.

'I was just resting my eyes for a moment,' she said with a slight defensiveness, and Christine nodded politely, accustomed by now to keeping quiet during the times that Vivienne nodded off or lost herself in memories. The best thing to do, Christine had learned, was to act as if the lapse had only lasted a few seconds, and continue the conversation where they had left off.

'I was wondering – do you have any personal photographs of you wearing the choker?' she asked accordingly, and was surprised when Vivienne let loose with a laugh that was almost raucous, bubbling with amusement.

'Randon took some,' she said. 'God, how he loved that camera! It was a Kodak Instamatic, one of the first that had flashbulbs you didn't have to change every time. They sent it to him hoping for publicity – we were sent so many things then by all sorts of companies, it was a constant stream of gifts – and it succeeded beyond their wildest dreams. He was never without it.'

Christine's eyes widened.

'Vivienne!' she exclaimed; the actress had insisted Christine use her first name, and Christine was surprisingly comfortable with the intimacy. Vivienne was so warm to her, so friendly, that by now it seemed natural. 'Why didn't you tell me this before when I was asking about photographs?' Christine went on, leaning forward eagerly. 'You know this is a big part of our strategy for getting the absolute most out of the sale, selling the exclusive rights to use photos from your private collection with you wearing the piece! And ones taken by *Randon Cliffe* – wow, that would be a treasure trove!'

She looked closely at Vivienne, and took in the sheer naughtiness sparkling in the actress's eyes. Vivienne's bone structure was so wonderful, the facial work she had undergone so effective, that it was easy to picture her as that film star who had been given lavish jewellery as tribute to her beauty and talent, posing for her lover in photographs that had never been seen before . . . because . . .

'*Oh*,' Christine said, understanding kicking in.

'*Exactly*,' Vivienne said with relish.

'But how did he manage to get the film developed?'

'He did it himself,' Vivienne said. 'His house in London had a lab in the basement. He'd have put one in mine, too, but Pearl and her nanny were down there, thank God, so he couldn't muck around with chemicals at Brompton Square. He was very careless, always dropping things on the carpets and getting them stained, and I had some absolutely priceless Persian silk runners in that house . . . Anyway, the lab! You'll have seen those in old films. The room was red-lit, to avoid overexposure, and he had to soak them all in that developing liquid or whatever he called it. Extraordinary to think how technology has come so far! Now I can't step outside the house without people wanting selfies with me! And they expect me to wait around while they put their phones on those wretched sticks!'

She mused, then added: 'I'm always fascinated by what people choose to invent, and when. Did you know, we didn't have adhesive sanitary pads until the 1970s? They put a man on the moon before they thought to sort out a woman's most basic needs.'

'That's *shocking*,' Christine said, horrified. 'What did you keep them on with?'

'Big safety pins with white plastic heads!' Vivienne recounted with unholy glee. 'Imagine, having pins so close to your privates! They made belts for you to attach them to. It was utterly revolting. And a nightmare if you were in a film that needed tight-fitting clothes, of course.'

Christine was used by now to Vivienne's going off-topic. She was completely lucid, but she loved to chat about anything that popped into her head, and she was genuinely fascinating. Fortunately, Christine had plenty of time to listen to her, eventually gently steering her back to the subject under discussion: the provenance of her jewellery collection, together with the anecdotes and, hopefully, the photographs that would help to sell each piece.

Vivienne had stipulated, on contracting with Berkeley to give them the auction rights, that she work principally with Christine. It had been a triumph, more than Christine could possibly have hoped for. She had immediately been promoted, given a significant raise and her own office, and allowed to hire another appraiser, whose work she would supervise. In addition to that, it was agreed that her entire working time until the auction – which was scheduled for New Year's Eve of that year, at their Geneva sale house – should be devoted to Vivienne's collection. Christine was assembling the catalogue, arranging valuations, putting lots together to appeal to private collectors and liaising with potential buyers – including, crucially, the big jewellery companies, all of which wanted to buy back the pieces they had made for Vivienne. The publicity would be spectacular and enduring; those items of jewellery would be on perpetual display, lent out to museums and special exhibitions, used forever to link the brands' names to one of the most glittering film stars of all time.

Cartier, De Grisogono, Bulgari, Van Cleef et Arpels, Tiffany: Christine was working with them and many more. They wanted to meet Vivienne, to hear her stories about their pieces, have their directors photographed with her. Christine's strategy was to offer access to Vivienne only if their offers proved high enough. She was packaging the pieces enticingly, with as much documentation as she could put together. A tiara from Cartier made for Vivienne was already spectacular, for instance, but the fact that it had been a gift from Vivienne's lover the Sultan of Dijar – and that she had worn it to the 1977 Oscars and not only been photographed in it with Faye Dunaway, who won the Best Actress award that year for *Network*, but put it on Dunaway for some pictures of them larking around at the after-party – was priceless.

Christine had already explained this to Vivienne, but the way photo rights worked for commercial purposes was that they belonged to two entities – the photographer and the subject. Although the images could be accessed on photo agencies' websites, any company wanting to use them for advertising would have to get permission from both the subject and the photographer, and pay whatever fee they negotiated. If Vivienne not only had photographs of herself taken by Randon, but owned the photographer's rights to them – which hopefully would have passed to her, under Randon's will – this would be a goldmine for the auction.

Seeing Christine's eagerness, Vivienne smiled at her affectionately.

'You're being very patient,' she said. 'But you're absolutely dying to know if I still have any of the nudie pics that Randon took of me wearing nothing but the jewellery he gave me, aren't you?'

'*Yes*,' Christine said, with such fervour that she blushed. 'Sorry, I don't mean to sound pervy . . .'

'They were just for us, of course,' Vivienne said. 'I have boxes and boxes of them.'

Christine realized that she was clasping her hands together as if in prayer, her eyes lifted ecstatically to the heavens.

'Of course, I'm not saying I was naked in *all* of them!' Vivienne continued. 'But as I said, they were just for us. I used to look at them all the time after he died, to remind me of him. I took some of him, too, when I could prise that thing out of his hands. And he wasn't the best at developing – not all of them came out well.'

'That wouldn't matter!' Christine couldn't help her voice rising. 'That wouldn't matter in the least if you *still had the film!* Because we could print new shots from the negatives! Nothing rude, of course – we'd crop them, we wouldn't show people anything inappropriate—'

'Oh, that's true, you could reprint them,' Vivienne said vaguely. 'I never thought of that.'

And now she did look her age.

'There have been so many photographs of me,' she commented, almost wearily. 'And many taken by men who loved me, too. Yes, I adored Randon, but there were other men I loved as well, plenty of them, and they all shot me from time to time. Not naked photographs, though. Randon was the only one I would ever trust enough for that. I knew, without a shadow of a doubt, no matter how much he swore at me or called me a silly cow or stamped out of the house yelling that he'd never come back in a million years – or cheated on me, not that it wasn't a two-way street as far as that went – I *knew* that I could take my clothes off and writhe around on a bed while he took photos of me, and they would never, ever end up in anyone's hands but our own.'

Christine watched Vivienne, fascinated, as her eyes once more seemed to take on an almost ombré sheen, deepening in colour, the effect caused by her pupils widening as she remembered the wild times she had had with Randon.

'Oh, and there are photos of him naked too,' Vivienne added wickedly. 'I wouldn't let him have it *all* his own way! He had the most amazing penis,' she said dreamily. 'I really should pull those photos out now and look at them for old times' sake . . .'

'Oh, you should!' Christine said, after recovering from the momentary shock of hearing Vivienne Winter talk so non-chalantly about Randon Cliffe's penis. She was agog at the idea of a secret treasure trove of erotic photographs of these two iconic film stars.

'Actually, you should in any case,' she added, the business side of her brain kicking in. 'Those are a valuable part of your estate, and obviously you won't want them to fall into the wrong hands after you're . . . after you're . . .' Since she was neither a solicitor specializing in estate planning and will writing, nor a financial adviser needing to discuss a client's asset disposal after their eventual death, Christine didn't quite know the right words to use about this delicate subject.

'At the least, you should definitely make sure you know where they are, and that they're safe,' she continued, after a pause. 'And consider whether you're okay with us using any for the sale. Honestly, I wouldn't be doing my job if I didn't encourage you to give us some for the auction . . . think of the money that could bring in, and of course it's all for charity! Where did you say the boxes of photographs were? And the negatives?'

'Goodness! I'm not sure,' Vivienne said blankly. 'It's been so long . . .'

Her voice tailed off. Christine waited to see if she would finish the sentence, but no more words were forthcoming. Vivienne was gazing out of the windows that looked over Hyde Park, but it was clear that in her mind's eye there was quite another vision, some memory she was replaying for herself. Her eyes were half closed, her eyelashes fluttering, and a little smile was playing around her lips.

Sitting quietly there in silence, watching Vivienne reminisce, images flooded into Christine's mind too. Vivienne at fourteen in her breakout role, cast as Juliet in a film of *Romeo and Juliet*; the producers had cast a young drama student as Romeo, focusing more on his looks and chemistry with Vivienne than on his acting ability, and she had acted him off the screen. He had barely been heard of again.

A young Vivienne playing Stella in *A Streetcar Named Desire*, vivid and sexual and passionately attracted to her husband, the brutal Stanley Kowalski. Vivienne as Anne Boleyn to Richard Burton's Henry VIII in *Beloved Queen*, portrayed as madly in love with a young Warren Beatty as Henry Percy, the love of her life. Beatty had been totally miscast, but the sexual charge between him and Vivienne had been off the charts. Even so, it hadn't prevented the film from flopping, with critics pointing out the multiple historical inaccuracies.

But it was still watched avidly for the love scenes. Vivienne, who had been having an affair with Beatty at the time, was positively luminous, glowing and vibrant with desire. The crucial scene where – dressed in cloth of gold, her dark hair looped and pinned into a golden net heavily decorated with pearls, more pearls dangling from her earlobes – she danced with Henry Percy at a court masque while both Henry VIII and Henry Percy's wife looked on, realizing slowly why their spouses were incapable of returning their affections, was one of Vivienne's most famous moments as an actress. Yearning and guilt, love and sorrow: the changing expressions that flitted across her face in the course of the dance had been exquisite.

And then, of course, Vivienne as Nefertiti in her diaphanous white floating dress and high blue war crown, a gold collar round her neck so elaborate and studded with gems that very few women in the world could have carried it off. Vivienne with Randon Cliffe, perpetually bare-chested, one of the few co-stars who possessed enough manly charisma to balance out Vivienne's sexual allure. Vivienne and Randon on screen together in the first heady rush of their love affair had felt almost too raw, too naked – as if they were together in private, and someone had filmed them without their knowledge.

Christine had made it her business to watch as many of Vivienne's films as she could before going to Sweden on her mission to court her for the auction. The images of Vivienne as Juliet, as Stella, as Anne Boleyn, as Nefertiti, were still vivid in her mind as she looked at Vivienne now: seventy-three years old, her eyes closed, but on her lips a smile identical to the blissful expression of her fourteen-year-old Juliet, looking down from the balcony at her long-forgotten Romeo. Of Anne Boleyn, young and in love, still believing that she could marry Henry Percy and become Countess of Northumberland, betrothing herself to him in a secret ceremony that she would later be forced by Cardinal Wolsey to deny. And above all, of Nefertiti, finally coming to life as a woman after long, barren, passionless years with her husband, when Randon Cliffe's Horemheb forced himself on her in a way that would certainly be labelled sexual assault nowadays, but at the time had been regarded as one of the most romantic film scenes ever committed to celluloid.

Christine found it tremendously moving to see Vivienne, her skin now so soft, so delicately lined, her features blurred by age, still experiencing emotions as rich and vivid as they had been in her heyday. Was it Randon she was remembering, or one of her multitude of other lovers? It might even be Dieter – a man who could not have been more unlike Randon.

Dieter, with whom Vivienne had stayed until his death several years before, had been a multimillionaire Swiss businessman who abhorred the spotlight and was happy to play second fiddle to his hugely famous wife. He had preferred to stay in the Montreux mansion while Vivienne travelled the world with her gay entourage: appearing as a judge at film festivals, making guest appearances on TV shows, and promoting her ever-increasing range of perfumes, jewellery and skincare. Dieter ran her companies from behind the scenes, and he never minded how much she needed to travel to publicize them. Much as he loved Vivienne, having her in Montreux on a twenty-four-hour basis would have been extremely exhausting for him.

The naked photos of her and Randon won't be in Switzerland, Christine deduced. *Surely she wouldn't have taken them to the house she shared with Dieter, where he lived full-time while she travelled the world. He could easily have come across them, and she wouldn't have wanted that.*

It's by far the most likely scenario that they stayed here in London . . . and I could make a start on looking for them right now.

Chapter Twelve

London – a short time later

Vivienne was definitely sleeping; reveries of her glory days had led to a comfortable afternoon snooze. Her bosom, draped in a green silk blouse with a flatteringly high pussycat bow at the neck, was rising and falling slowly, steadily, her exhales audible, almost stertorous, the heavily mascaraed lashes fluttering with the rhythm of her breath.

I could just have a quick look around . . .

It wasn't being sneaky; it wasn't spying. Christine had full access to Vivienne's jewellery collection, and possessed the security code to both safes so that she could continue with the job of cataloguing the huge collection even if Vivienne were not at home. The catalogue was to be chronological – Christine's concept for it had been approved by both Vivienne and the chairman of Berkeley. It was to be called *Vivienne Winter: A Life in Jewels*, just as Christine had suggested, and it would be as detailed as she could possibly make it. Her career was now entirely linked to this auction, and she was working on it during every waking moment.

Every moment, of course, that she wasn't spending with Angel.

Normally, this would have been the worst time of all to

meet a new boyfriend. Christine would have embargoed any attempt by any other man, no matter how eligible, until the auction was successfully concluded. *Even Tor?* she found herself wondering, and dismissed the thought of him with great firmness. It was beyond annoying that memories of his smile, his sense of humour, his body in that tight black wetsuit, insisted on popping back from time to time. She had absolutely prohibited her brain from thinking nostalgically about a married man who had acted like a single one, and she was extremely irritated when it refused to obey her.

Although she had to admit, she never thought about Tor when she was with Angel. When Angel was present, it would be impossible to think about another man . . .

But Christine wouldn't allow herself to think about Angel, either. Not at work. He was much too distracting. Her thighs clenched together and she swallowed hard; if she started remembering the most recent night she had spent at his apartment, she wouldn't get anything done. Angel was like a drug. In a way, it was lucky that she had such a crucially important job to do at the moment. Under normal circumstances, she would struggle to concentrate at work at all.

He had dropped so suddenly and shockingly into her life that she still had a hard time believing that he was real. He might almost have been the angel he resembled from the painting of the Annunciation, flying down on gilded wings to transform her existence; but while Gabriel had brought Mary news that she had been chosen to bear Christ, what Vivienne's grandson brought was considerably more devilish. Although angels and demons had always been closely linked in mythology, of course; wasn't Lucifer himself a fallen angel?

In any case, Christine was still wrestling with the fact that Angel had chosen to land next to her. Men like him simply didn't get serious about women like her. They dated super-models, socialites, actresses.

However, Nathan, a gay colleague of Christine's who was managing the social media aspects of the auction, had told her that very handsome men were often like peacocks. Because they wanted to be the acknowledged beauty of the couple, they preferred to settle down with women who were not as attractive as they were.

'Just think of yourself as a peahen, and enjoy looking at Mr Handsome,' he had advised, not entirely helpfully. 'Look at all the gorgeous actors whose wives are just nice-looking, or a bit dumpy! Rock stars go for supermodels, but there are plenty of actors out there who score a ten and whose wives are just a five. Seriously, check out the gossip mags and you'll see. Not that I'm saying you're a five – you're definitely at least a seven.'

'Wow, thank you, Nathan,' Christine had said, reeling slightly. 'I *think*.'

Since then, she had flicked through some online gossip sites and seen the truth of Nathan's theory. Plenty of peacock actors with comparatively peahen wives, who tended to have been make-up artists or waitresses, for some reason, before their marriage. It wasn't exactly flattering, but since she had no idea where her relationship with Angel might be heading, and didn't have a spare moment to wonder about it, there was no point dwelling on it. She was just too busy with the arduous task of organizing *Vivienne Winter: A Life in Jewels*. Christine had promised Vivienne that she would top the total achieved by the Elizabeth Taylor jewel auction. If they didn't make more than seventy-five million pounds, she would take it as a personal failure.

There was no question, however, that she and Angel were in a relationship. She had slept over at his penthouse for more than half of the previous week and had, at his suggestion, brought over an increasing selection of clothes and toiletries. Vivienne was already referring to Christine as Angel's girlfriend. And the fact that she was, unbelievably, dating *Vivienne Winter's grandson* made Christine feel as dizzy as if the room was spinning around her.

Stop! she told herself; this always happened when she thought about Angel. *Think about the photographs! Where are the photographs? That's the only thing you should be concentrating on right now!*

Tiptoeing out of the sitting room to avoid waking Vivienne, Christine walked through the flat to the dressing room – almost as large as the bedroom itself. Its door stood open, as did the door of both safes. Christine was in and out of them all day with jewellery boxes. As a precaution, Vivienne's insurance company had insisted on stationing a security guard in the entrance lobby of her apartment, who did nothing all day but play games on his phone and check the bags and pockets of anyone leaving the flat.

Christine had become accustomed much faster than she would have expected to having access to the glittering, Ali Baba-like treasure chest that was Vivienne's entire jewel collection. It had been flown in from her houses in New York, Montreux and Los Angeles to be assembled, for the first time ever, all in one place. Intimately familiar with the contents of the safes by now, Christine knew that the large boxes on the lower shelves, big enough to contain a store of photographs and negatives, held the tiara collection. And valuable as those photographs were, she didn't think that Vivienne would have chosen to store them under lock and key in a safe so full of jewellery boxes that space was precious.

Still, Christine was reasonably sure that they must be in London. Vivienne had told her that Randon's photographic lab had been at her house in Knightsbridge; Vivienne would no doubt have cleared it out carefully after his death, ensuring that all of the saucy photographs and negatives were in her possession. And it would be logical for them to have accompanied her on her move to Park Lane. Vivienne would surely not have put items as compromising as naked images of herself and Randon into storage. They were far more likely to be tucked away somewhere in this flat . . .

She searched the dressing room to no avail. There were no boxes of photographs and negatives among the vast array of Vivienne's extraordinary collection of clothing and accessories. Clicking her tongue in frustration, Christine turned to leave the room, her brain racing with speculation as to where the photos might be.

'Oh!' she exclaimed in surprise as Angel, stepping into the dressing room, caught her around the waist and pulled her to him firmly. His mouth came down hard on hers, his tongue sliding past her lips, his hands descending to cup her buttocks, pulling her against him even tighter so that she could feel his penis stirring at the contact.

'Well, hello, little kitten,' he said eventually. 'Fancy bumping into you here!'

'I know,' Christine managed. 'So unexpected to find me at my job!'

'I didn't actually come by to see you,' Angel said cheerfully, releasing her. 'You're just a bonus. I have some news for Granny Viv.'

'She's fallen asleep,' Christine said.

'I know,' he said. 'I just popped into the living room and saw her passed out and lightly snoring. Is that happening often, may I enquire?'

'Oh, she nods off sometimes, but it's not a big deal,' Christine said, wanting to reassure Vivienne's loving grandson that his grandmother seemed in excellent health. 'She was having a trip down memory lane, and it turned into an afternoon nap, that's all.'

'How do you find her?' Angel asked. 'Mentally, I mean?'

'Sharp as a tack,' Christine said. 'She does wander off sometimes when she's telling me stories, but she always catches herself and comes back. I don't have to prompt her. I mean, for her age, she's amazing.'

'She'll go on forever, won't she?' Angel observed, and his mouth twisted into what Christine would, under any other circumstances, have considered a cynical smile. 'Like her own diamonds. She's just as tough as they are, and just as hard. She'll probably outlast us all.'

'You sound almost . . .' Christine began, frowning, but Angel cut her off, reaching a finger out and caressing her under her chin as he would a cat.

'Pretty Christine,' he said. 'My little kitten. It's nothing. Sometimes I remember my mother, you see. She was so young when she died. It always seems brutal to me that while Granny Viv's the ultimate survivor, my poor mother wasn't.'

'I'm sorry,' Christine said, her frown dissolving. Of course he hadn't meant to speak harshly of Vivienne; she could see how close they were, how much Vivienne adored him. His mother's death had been a tragedy, and naturally it would be poignant for him to see Vivienne growing old so gracefully when Pearl hadn't even made it to her thirtieth birthday.

She wanted to say more, but it was so hard to speak with Angel stroking her on the highly sensitive, soft skin of her jaw. He had a way of finding parts of her body that no other lover had ever caressed, bringing them to such vivid life that she would be acutely aware of them forever afterwards.

'Don't worry, little kitten,' he said, his finger sliding down, expertly unhooking the top button on her blouse to slip down the cleft of her cleavage. 'I'm fine. More than fine. You have a way of making all my cares disappear.'

He undid the second button.

'I'm going to make you purr,' he whispered. 'And then maybe caterwaul.'

'Angel, no!' she protested. 'I'm at work – Gregory's around—'

'So? Everyone knows I'm your boyfriend. God, I loathe that word,' he added in parentheses. 'And it's a union blessed from on high by Her Holiness Vivienne Winter. I can't *tell* you how much she approves of you, kitten. Says you're doing the most fantastically thorough job.'

'Really?'

Christine's blue eyes glowed. While she knew how hard she was working, it was wonderful to hear Vivienne's appreciation confirmed. Christine did not come from the kind of privileged background that took praise for granted. She regularly noticed how the aristocratic employees of Berkeley's accepted compliments on their work as their due; she couldn't imagine herself ever receiving praise without basking in it.

'My God,' Angel said, manoeuvring her back her round the corner of the wall and into the dressing room, 'I think you look more excited by Granny Viv's saying how intelligent and hard-working you are than me telling you I'm going to sit you on her dressing table and make you come like a train.'

'Angel, *seriously* – this is *totally* unprofessional—'

'Oh please, kitten. Granny Viv's even keener on you as my girlfriend – ugh, equally ghastly word – than she is on you in your professional capacity, if that's possible. I'm sure she'd be nothing but delighted to know that I'm servicing you and keeping you happy. God knows, it's not like she hasn't had plenty of fun in her time!'

Shutting the door, he picked Christine up by the waist, sat her on the central island of the dressing room, and pushed her legs apart with the confidence of a man to whom no woman has ever said no. From the first, Angel had acted as if her body was his toy to play with, and he was so sure of himself that Christine, to her surprise, had found herself going along with whatever he wanted.

It was as if she had been struck by lightning twice on one day. First there had been her meeting with Vivienne in Tylösand; and then, by the time their private plane had landed in London, she had effectively gained not only the job opportunity of her dreams but the boyfriend too. Angel had been hugely appreciative of her pitch for the auction, lavishing her with compliments, both personal and professional, while Vivienne had clearly endorsed his attraction to Christine by telling the two of them to go to celebrate once they had dropped her in Park Lane.

Angel had taken Christine to the rooftop bar at Galvin's on the twenty-eighth floor of the Hilton, just a few doors down from Vivienne's mansion. The views of London from that height were breathtaking. They drank French 75s, a sharp-sweet mixture of champagne, lemon juice and gin, talked about everything and nothing, and by the time Christine reluctantly said that she needed to get home so she could be ready to break the amazing news to her bosses at Berkeley the next day, she had been in thrall to Angel. His beauty, his charm, those amazing violet eyes that, when trained on her – as they had been for practically the entire time – made her shiver like a rabbit hypnotized by a snake; a rabbit desperate for the snake to consume it whole.

Angel had not eaten her up that night, however. He had taken her and her suitcase home in a black cab all the way to Acton, pulling her onto his lap and kissing her for the entire drive with expert, leg-trembling skill. He had accompanied her to the door of her flat, naturally carrying her suitcase. Then, instead of the final goodnight kiss she was eagerly expecting, he had slid his hand up her skirt, tweaked the lace of her underpants and whispered in her ear:

'I'll take you out to dinner tomorrow night. Don't wear any knickers.'

Christine had managed barely any sleep that night at all

in anticipation, and the next night, of course, she had got even less . . .

'You're wearing knickers again!' Angel said now with great disapproval, having pushed her skirt up.

'Angel, I'm at *work*,' Christine said as firmly as she could, considering that her legs were parted and his fingers were now splayed around her crotch, holding it as he might a piece of fruit he was about to consume. 'I need to behave properly and focus, and I don't feel serious about my job without knickers on! I'm wearing hold-up stockings because you like me to, and that's enough of a nuisance . . .'

'But I like to think of you knickerless at all times,' he said, and though he had promised to make her purr, it was he who sounded like a cat. 'So that I can pop by here and slide a finger up you whenever I feel like it.'

She opened her mouth to tell him that this auction was her most important ever, indubitably the most important one she would ever have in her career; that if he hadn't been Vivienne's grandson, she would have told him that she couldn't start a relationship with anyone during this crucial period. That she didn't want him dropping in to seduce her when she was in the middle of cataloguing his grandmother's jewels, because it was horribly distracting. That she didn't want him treating her like a toy.

And yet, as he closed his fingers tighter around her and started tracing slow circles with his thumb exactly where she wanted to be touched, not a word of that perfectly reasonable speech issued from her lips. Instead she heard herself moan, a sound of complete surrender and abandon. She reached out to circle his neck with her arms, bracing herself on his chest, her head on his shoulder, gasping as he flicked his thumbnail against her most sensitive point in a series of snaps that for some reason sent her crazy.

'I'm not going to take your knickers off,' he said against her ear, the feel of his lips exquisite torture. 'I'm not going to put my fingers up you, and I know you want them there, don't you? You want them there really badly. You feel empty without them. Tell me.'

'Yes,' she sobbed into his shirt, squirming against him. 'Yes, I want them, please, *please* . . . do it, please do it . . .'

'If you'd been good and not worn knickers, I'd be finger-fucking you right now,' he said, biting her earlobe hard and tracing one finger up and down the edge of her knickers, teasing her, slipping underneath just enough so that she could feel his touch beneath them and then retreating as her hips jerked forward, her body pleading for him to keep going, trying to show him how wet and needy she was.

'*Oh* no,' Angel mocked her. 'This is your own fault. If you'd been good, you'd have half my hand jammed up inside you, making you come all over my fingers, you dirty little bitch. But you don't get that. Not today. You get to come, but not to get finger-fucked, no matter how much you beg and plead and cry . . .'

She was begging now, her mouth damp against his shirt, her words incoherent, her hips still jerking. His thumb returned to the circles it had been tracing over the fabric, tight and even and faster and faster until her whole body juddered and clenched and she wailed her release into his shoulder, bouncing on the polished wooden top of the dressing table, hearing a seam in the lining of her skirt tear as she spread her legs.

'That's right, kitten,' Angel said, and even as she obeyed, she was amazed at his self-control, the cool possession in his voice, his ability to stand back, as it were, and watch from a distance as she completely lost control of herself. 'Come like a fucking train, just like I said you would.'

He flicked her with the nail of his index finger now, right on her nub, and although it smarted, it made her come again immediately, much to her surprise. She clung on to him for dear life as he alternated thumb circles and nail flicks against her, randomly, so she never knew what was coming next, heard herself pleading with him to stop, to slow down, even as he worked her to orgasm after orgasm.

'This is *my* game, kitten,' Angel said, biting her earlobe again, hurting her even as he brought her once more to climax. 'You play by my rules. No knickers next time, right?'

'No, Angel, no – I promise – please, *please* stop, it's too much . . .'

Tears were forming in her eyes when he finally showed mercy. His hand left her crotch, and he pulled back from her a little, taking in the sight of her as she panted for breath, her shirt partially unbuttoned, her skirt shoved up above her knees, eyes glazed and eye make-up smudged, lips parted. His erection was swollen and prominent, pushing at the fly of his trousers, but he showed no need to attend to it.

She pointed at it. 'Do you want me to—'

'No, no,' he said airily. 'You need to get back to work! You don't have time for any more games. We can save that for later.'

'I don't know how you hold out like you do for your "games", Christine observed. Her body was slowly coming back under her control; she started to button up her shirt. 'It's like you can choose exactly when you want to come.'

'If you'd had my very specialized and particular boarding school training, you'd understand,' Angel said, smiling reminiscently. 'You wouldn't have fitted in there, kitten. You're too sweet. They'd have made mincemeat of you.'

'They would not!' Christine said crossly, slipping off the centre island and smoothing her skirt down, checking to see if the outer material had ripped as well as the lining. 'I went to a really rough school, and my foster home wasn't exactly the Ritz.'

'Oh yes? Playground games with kicks and hair-pulling, maybe a stabbing or two?' Angel said. 'What does that teach you, apart from not annoying the kids who have knives?'

Christine was feeling the back of her skirt. It seemed intact, but she needed to make sure.

'Can you see if there's a rip?' She swivelled round to show him the back.

'Let's see . . .' He bent over, straightened the back seam, and then, even as he said: 'No, you're all fine – as respectable as ever,' his fingers pincered on one buttock like a lobster claw closing, so hard that she yelped in pain. She was immediately aware that he had deliberately bruised her.

'See?' Angel said, his voice full of amusement. 'If you'd been to my school, you'd *never* have made a noise when someone pinched your bum. We used to take turns doing it to each other until we all learned to keep as silent as mice. And then we'd check each other's bruises to see who'd made the best one. My technique's impeccable now. You'll see, later. You'll have a lovely pair of them, finger and thumb.'

'That really hurt!' Christine complained, rubbing her bottom.

'Pain and pleasure, kitten,' Angel said gently. 'Pain and pleasure.'

'You play too rough sometimes, Angel,' Christine said, still cross, pushing past him to open the dressing room door.

'No such thing,' he said lightly, dropping a kiss on her neck. 'You'll learn. So, what are you working on today?'

'Oh!'

Christine's expression immediately lightened, her resentment forgotten as she told Angel about her search for the photographs, spilling out her excitement at the revelation that they existed.

'Do you know where they are?' she finished. 'Have you seen them anywhere around here? Of course, not *seen* them – I mean, they're of your grandmother! – but do you have any idea where they'd be?'

'Didn't Granny Viv tell you?'

'She pretty much drifted off and fell asleep while I was asking her,' Christine said. 'Maybe she's woken up, now, though.'

'No, she'd be calling for you or Gregory if she had,' Angel said. 'It's teatime – she'd be screaming for her pot of Earl Grey and lemon shortbread biscuit from Fortnum's. Come with me, kitten.'

He took her hand and pulled her out of the dressing room in his casually imperious way. They went into the octagonal central foyer, hung with a pair of enormous, elaborately curlicued Venetian glass chandeliers, a riot of gold and yellow and blue, specially made by the glassblowers of Burano for this hallway. Set around the walls were console tables holding matching glass vases, each three feet high: transparent glass swirled with ribbons of the same shades of blue and yellow, holding great sheaves of yellow roses.

Angel crossed the foyer, heading for the dining room at the back of the apartment. Rarely used now, its long mahogany table and set of twelve matching chairs, and its pair of marble-topped console tables, both topped by imposing silver candelabras, had the air of having been long abandoned, even though they were impeccably polished and shiny. It was like walking into a stately home that had been turned into a barely-visited museum.

A huge mahogany credenza anchored the back wall, its glass-fronted cabinets holding Vivienne's priceless china collection. It had been one of the few pieces she had brought from Brompton Square; she had always kept its doors locked when she lived there. She and Randon had so often thrown things at each other in anger: she'd been determined, at least, that the gold-rimmed Sèvres dinner set which had belonged to Madame de Pompadour wouldn't get smashed in a drunken rampage.

'If I show you where those photos are, will you do something for me?' Angel asked, and Christine said 'Yes!' instantly, before she'd thought it through.

'Wait, hang on . . .' she added quickly, but he was already laughing.

'Do you know how to deep-throat?' he said, chucking her under the chin again.

'Yes! I mean, I've definitely . . .'

'Ever lain with your head over the edge of the bed and taken a big cock all the way down your throat?' he said. And then he winked. 'I have. At school. I told you it was a highly educational period of my life.'

Christine felt the blood rise to her face. Angel had dropped hints before, but this was the first explicit reference he had made to having sex with men.

Well, boys, really, she thought. *Other boys. That does make a difference. And it was boarding school, after all – you hear stories about posh boys messing around at school, and then they grow up and don't do it any more, do they?*

Or do they?

Christine resolved to ask Nathan cautiously, generally, without bringing Angel into it, what he thought of the possibility that you could suck cock in your teens at school but basically be straight. She had an uneasy feeling that his answer might not be exactly what she wanted to hear. It wasn't that she had any prejudice against gay men at all – God knew, that would have been difficult in the art world. But what if Angel were bisexual, and wanted to have sex with men while being in a relationship with her?

You really can't worry about this now! she told herself firmly, adding it to her increasingly long list of Things to Think About After the Auction.

'I'll teach you proper deep-throating tonight,' Angel said. 'There's a trick to it. I'm going to love watching your eyes go big as I bury my cock in your mouth. You'll think you can't take it all, but you will. I'll have you gargle with some hot water before to loosen you up.'

Christine's eyes widened in shock, but Angel had timed his words perfectly, following them immediately with a dramatic reveal. He bent down, unlatched two of the lower doors of the credenza and nudged them open to show, inside, a stack of several big storage boxes. Vivienne's cleaners were thorough, so there was no dust or cobwebs around the boxes, but they were clearly decades old, the pattern dated; as Christine dropped to her knees to start pulling them out, her heart racing in excitement, she could see that the metal that trimmed the edges of the box was tarnished with age.

'Oh my God,' she said, 'oh my *God* . . .'

'*Just* what I'll be saying later as I fuck your mouth, kitten,' Angel said, as he hefted the first box up onto the dining table.

But Christine was dragging out the second box and opening it eagerly, gasping at what she saw as she lifted the lid.

'Oh *wow*,' she said, as reverently as if she were looking at a holy relic. 'Oh wow, this is *incredible*.'

The box was full of photographs stacked in piles, with a big brown envelope at the back. It had once been held together by elastic bands, but the rubber had dried out and broken over the years, and lay in discarded coils at the bottom of the box. Pulling out the envelope, Christine confirmed that it was full of strips of negatives; she knew what they looked like from watching old films.

The photographs were tired and old now, their gloss faded, their edges bent and wrinkled. Carefully, Christine picked up the top stack of one file and started going through it. It was a treasure trove. Vivienne in full make-up, her hair set in thick black ringlets, a champagne glass in her hand, laughing, back from a party probably, looking a little tipsy and hugely happy; Vivienne with a bare, un-made-up face, drinking coffee on a balcony overlooking the Amalfi coast, and giving the finger to Randon for some reason. Vivienne naked, sprawling on a huge bed, its white sheets thoroughly rumpled, her arms spread wide, her hair a dark pool framing her face.

It was supposed to look spontaneous, but Christine could tell it had been staged to some degree: Vivienne's hair was arranged in perfect coils, as if they had been artfully spread out around her face, and her outstretched limbs were equally symmetrical. Christine imagined Randon standing on a chair with his Kodak, issuing directives, jumping down to move a lock of hair or the bend of a knee, before climbing up again to start snapping away, while Vivienne gazed up at him with such absolute love and adoration in those wonderful eyes, every pore of her body radiating the self-confidence and relaxation of a woman who has just had world-class sex.

It could not have been more clear that they had just made love, but Christine had the feeling that the jewellery Vivienne was wearing had been donned afterwards, because she was literally draped in a king's ransom of rubies and diamonds, the necklace as big and ornamental as one of the collars she had worn when playing Nefertiti, the bracelets as wide as cuffs. The tiara was as large and lavish as the one Princess Belinda had worn on her wedding day. No one could possibly have sex with that amount of metal and stone fastened around her body, not without being cut and bruised, and Vivienne's skin was smooth and perfect, not a mark on it, in this photograph taken years before Photoshop was invented.

And although she was slim, her waist small, her limbs long, she was much curvier than was currently permitted for a leading lady. Vivienne's breasts were large and full, her hips voluptuously rounded, and the small swell of her stomach was visible from above – by no means as concave as would be required nowadays, when actresses needed not just to fit into size six sample dresses, but to be as toned and buff as heptathletes. Just thinking of the women's bodies that were featured in magazines nowadays – the tightly abbed singers in tiny bras, the reality 'stars' starving themselves to be photographed in minuscule bikinis in Ibiza – made Christine immediately aware of her own small but protruding stomach. Even when Angel had been making her come just now, in the dressing room, a tiny part of her had been trying to suck her stomach in as much as she could . . .

Christine dragged her thoughts away from her own body issues with resolution. If nothing else, she had been staring at this photograph of a naked Vivienne so long that it was beginning to feel a bit pervy. She leafed through more of the photos; they were randomly stacked, as if someone had piled them into boxes without any attempt to sort them. There were pictures of Vivienne laughing on the ski slopes, all fur and diamonds and huge goggles, Vivienne in the swimming pool wearing a tiara – *wonderful* – and then Christine came across one that she initially thought was a mistake, something snapped and printed out by accident. She stared at it, baffled: it looked like an oddly shaped finger with a ring on it. Then she giggled in embarrassment when she realized what it actually was.

Not a finger at all, but a penis. A large, erect penis with

a long string of white pearls looped around it, its full juicy head protruding proudly from its decorated shaft, the pearls trailing into the thick mass of tight black curls at its base, draping over the full balls below.

Well, we can't use this one! Christine thought, still giggling. *Imagine putting this in a catalogue – I think the partners would have heart attacks!*

She couldn't stop staring at it. How often did you get to see the penis of one of the most famous actors of all time, let alone fully erect and decked out with matched pearls, each as big as the tip of her little finger? It looked like a 1920s-style strand, made long enough to take a short loop around the neck and let another one dangle down over the bosom.

Christine's professional memory flicked back to a similar strand sold at Christie's last year: over a million dollars, bought by the Earl of Rutland to celebrate his wife, the Countess, having given birth to twin daughters. A modern version of the British aristocrats who had married American brides in the nineteenth century to restore their family fortunes, the Countess, who owned a gigantic American fracking empire, had brought multiple millions to the marriage, which had restored the crumbling Rutland stately home to its former splendour. A million dollars was small change to the Earl. Christine made a mental note to approach the Rutlands as possible pre-buyers for the auction; they really should have been on her list already.

The Countess had had quite a reputation for wild partying before she married. She would probably have loved a copy of a photograph Randon Cliffe had taken of his private parts – it was obvious from the angle of the shot that the owner

245

of the penis had been the one holding the camera. But Christine was going to have to screen this kind of picture very carefully. There was no way anything too sexual could make it into the auction catalogue, and if they decided to sell the rights to any of them, extremely strict conditions would have to be imposed upon the buyers.

I'm definitely going to have a 'no engorged private parts rule', though, Christine decided firmly. *Not even in, err, private sales. Goodness, I never thought I'd use those words in a professional context!*

If there were images of Randon naked, she wondered, how would she and Berkeley deal with that? Christine was sure that the partners would take the old-fashioned view that a nude woman's body was much more acceptable, more artistic, than a man's; she had even been informed earnestly by an older partner that women did not like looking at naked men.

Because the men who run things don't like the idea of comparisons being drawn between their willies and the ones on screen, Christine thought cynically. *Well, if there are naked ones Vivienne wants to sell, I should pitch this as a celebration. Make the nudity almost incidental, suggest that people are being vulgar if they focus on the fact that Vivienne and Randon happen not to have many clothes on, if any . . .*

Vivienne would surely be in favour of that approach. Christine looked down at the photograph again, still amazed by its existence.

'Oh my God, it's a prehistoric dick pic!'

Angel plucked the photograph of Randon's pearl-draped penis from her hands.

'Can you believe it!' he marvelled, staring at it

appreciatively. 'Talk about early adopters! God, that's a *very* nice cock, I must say. One sees why Granny Viv kept going back to him, doesn't one?'

'*Angel* – that's your grandma!' Christine protested.

'Oh, come on. It's not like you weren't thinking it too,' Angel said cheerfully.

After Angel's comments about sucking cock at school, this line of conversation made Christine distinctly uncomfortable. She reached into the box and picked up a photograph of Vivienne on top of another stack, one she was sure would distract him; it was a head shot of her wearing the famous pearl and diamond choker, her black hair drawn back to show it off.

'You know that Randon had a miniature version of the choker, right down to the hanging pearl, made for your mum?'

Angel's nod was the briefest sketch, but Christine was too excited to notice.

'I'd love to find a picture in here of her as a little girl wearing it!' she enthused. 'There are lots of photos of Vivienne and Pearl in them, of course, but a behind-the-scenes one would be incredible. We're selling the chokers together as one lot.'

Angel plucked the photograph from Christine's hands, gazing at his grandmother wearing the choker, the enormous pearl sitting at the hollow of her throat, opalescent against her equally smooth and pearly skin. To a gemmologist, the word 'priceless' was mere hyperbole: there was a value to everything, although often that was simply whatever a client was prepared to pay. Randon Cliffe had bought the choker for fifty thousand pounds in 1975. Today, Christine had tentatively estimated the value of both chokers at eleven million. Much more, if the rights to this private photograph of Vivienne were included.

'Mummy had to sell her choker because Granny Viv cut her off,' Angel said, his tone hardening. 'And as soon as she did, Granny Viv bought it back for her own collection but didn't give Mummy a penny, even though she knew how desperate things were. My grandmother's always cared about her jewellery more than she does her family. No wonder Mummy died the way she did. She knew her mother didn't give a shit about her.'

'Oh Angel! I'm sure that's not true! I can see how much she loves you!'

Jumping to her feet, Christine embraced him wholeheartedly, wrapping her arms around him and squeezing tight.

Naturally the subject of his dead mother would be hugely painful for him. Never before, however, had Angel articulated the awful belief that his grandmother was responsible for his mother's death. This was the first time that Christine realized how damaged he had been by his upbringing, and it made some of the doubts she had had about him seem much less important.

Of course, she was aware that Angel had been living with Vivienne at the time of Pearl's death because of the latter's drug addiction; and she had gathered, from things that Angel had let slip, that the transfer of custody from mother to grandmother had been extremely fraught. Angel had been sent away to school rather than staying with his grandmother, and his stories from that period in his life were incredibly lurid. He had never had a job in his life, lived off a lavish trust fund, and had a reputation as a high-living, modelizing playboy. Charming as Vivienne was to her, Christine couldn't help realizing that Vivienne had done almost as poor a job of bringing up her orphaned grandson as she had previously done with her daughter.

To Christine, Angel seemed like a hero from a romance novel: too handsome, too debonair, too sexually skilful to be real. Now, she understood why. All the modern romantic heroes had dark pasts with which they struggled, were flawed and damaged by their tragic childhoods. Their shiny, perfect facades were just that: facades. A crucial piece of information had just fallen into place for her.

Christine often flashed back to that extraordinary day when she had been interviewed by Vivienne in the morning in Tylösand, and courted by Angel in the evening in London; the day when her mundane, everyday life had morphed into something out of *Hello!* magazine crossed with *Vanity Fair*. It had never seemed completely real to her before. Cinderella stories did happen in her profession: she knew a young woman who had been on the front desk at Berkeley when a newly divorced Greek billionaire walked in, decided Gemma was precisely what he wanted in a second wife, and whisked her away on his private plane to his private yacht. In itself, that would just be a business arrangement: a beautiful blonde trading her looks for his money. But the billionaire was charming, and Gemma really had fallen in love with him. When she popped in to visit her ex-colleagues after a year and a half, accompanied by a nanny pushing baby Spiros in a top-of-the-range Bugaboo pram, Gemma had been clad from head to toe in Chanel, dripping with diamonds and flushed with happiness.

The world of fine art was full of rich men looking for trophy wives. Galleries and auction houses – and their feeding grounds, the art history faculties of universities – were well known for being stocked with employees much more attractive than those found in other professions. After all, if you stripped away the elaborate language and exquisitely polished manners, galleries and auction houses were in the business of selling – and salespeople were statistically better looking than the average person.

Even though Christine had been hired as an expert, rather than front-desk arm candy – and there was the male version of that, too, slender sprigs in perfect tailoring and silk ties, with butter-yellow hair even silkier than their ties – she had quickly realized that her girl-next-door looks didn't hurt. Every single male Berkeley partner or director, and every male client over forty, had taken an interest in her that was best described as inappropriately avuncular. Looks could be so misleading. Her big blue eyes, her freckled snub nose and her rounded cheeks gave her an air of freshness and innocence that made most men assume she was a sweet girl from a nice, sheltered suburban home, part of a close and loving family. Just as people looked at Angel's dazzlingly handsome face, his poise and charm, his confidence, and naturally thought that he had been cherished and coddled for his entire life by an adoring grandmother.

The Winters might be rich and famous, but as a family they were seriously flawed. Pearl had chosen drugs over her son; Vivienne had abandoned him to a boarding school with some sort of bizarre sexual regime. No one had looked out for Angel, just as no one had ever looked out for Christine. That must be why he had chosen her, Christine realized, out of all the women he could have dated: because, instinctively, he had sensed how much their backgrounds mirrored each other's.

Angel might never have had to work for a living, but he had been forced to survive in other ways. No wonder he had some sexual tastes that were barely on the edge of acceptability; look what he had been through! He talked about his school experiences as if it had all been a wonderful game; but how was it possible for a boy his age to go through that without coming out warped to some degree?

This wasn't a fairy tale – or at least not the Disney kind, with all the raw, bloody edges smoothed over, the neglectful, cruel parents sanitized and nothing real left from the original, gruesome Brothers Grimm versions. The revelation brought Christine an overwhelming sense of relief. She didn't want to be a passive, grateful Cinderella, raised up to dizzying heights by a perfect Prince Charming. Instead, here was something she could actively do – she could help Angel and Vivienne reconcile, encourage them to heal their wounds. They were, after all, the only family each other had.

'I'm so sorry about your mum, Angel,' she said, kissing his neck. 'I'm so sorry you grew up without her, and that bad things happened to you. But honestly, your grandmother really does love you. Whenever she talks about you, her eyes light up. I really hope you two can sort things out and you can forgive her for what happened with your mum.'

'You're a nice girl, Christine,' Angel said, patting her head. 'A genuinely nice girl.'

Christine flushed with happiness, her arms round his neck, her head resting on his chest. If she could have seen his face, however, she would have had a very different reaction. Angel's eyes were crossed, his features contorted into a gargoyle grimace.

Oh Lord, how long do I have to put up with this? he was thinking. *God help me, she's seeing me now as some sort of wounded soul that needs saving, and I'll have to play along with it so Granny Viv keeps the money fountain flowing. All this vanilla sex is driving me mad with frustration. I can't wait for Nicole to get back from Atlanta so I can really let loose! One little bruise on her bum, and Christine acts like I flogged her for an hour before hog-tying her and fucking her up the arse.*

Which, frankly, isn't the worst idea in the world . . .

His cock was hardening at the image. She'd be crying, of course, pleading with him to stop, those big blue eyes wet with tears, her make-up smeared, her pale buttocks striped and welted as he held them open, her helpless wriggling making him even more excited as he lubed her up . . .

It was a stroke of luck, all things considered, that he found Christine very attractive. It was partly to do with the impulse to see how far he could push her, how many dirty, perverted sex acts he could coax and coerce her into performing; he certainly never needed to picture another woman in order to get an erection with Christine. He was already counting the hours until he could drape her over his bed and sink his cock deep into her throat, just as he had told her he would.

But as soon as Nicole returned from Atlanta, where she was meeting Lil' Biscuit and Silantra, Angel would be ringing up the escort agency and booking that pretty blonde who liked role play for a threesome that would make the last one look as tame as – well, as most sex with Christine.

Hearing footsteps in the hallway, he immediately got his facial expression under control. As Vivienne came into the foyer, he was gazing down at Christine with a tender light in his eyes.

Vivienne sighed in pleasure at the sight of them. It was exactly what she had planned, and Vivienne adored it when things went according to plan. She had neatly separated Christine from a romance that had been burgeoning with Tor, pushed her firmly into Angel's arms, and here she was, well on the way to finding herself pregnant with Vivienne's first great-grandchild . . .

Christine pulled back on seeing Vivienne. Pink-cheeked, embarrassed, she babbled apologies about hugging her boyfriend during work time, which turned into a stream of excitement about the photographs and urgent pleas for Vivienne to go through them with her as soon as possible. Vivienne nodded with a smile, but she was barely listening. She was looking back and forth between the two of them: her near-mythically handsome grandson, and pretty Christine with her clever brain, sweet nature, and colouring that was similar enough to Angel's to mean that any children he fathered with her would not look too different from the Winter template.

Frankly, Christine could have been one of myriad young women of breeding age with the right looks, a good job and a nice personality. She had simply happened to be under Vivienne's nose when she had been told that Angel might die, that his fertility might be compromised, and an impulse had stirred in her that was as violent as it was unexpected: the terror that her genes would die out. She was like one of those disgusting rich men who fathered children late into old age on nubile young things. Fear of mortality was countered by the need to reproduce, to leave something behind when one left this world. That impulse had worked fast in Vivienne. She hadn't hesitated for a moment in telling Angel she would be raising his monthly trust fund payments significantly, as well as giving him a large lump sum, the day he told her Christine was carrying a Winter baby.

Fear of mortality, of course, was also the reason for the jewellery auction – it was really nothing to do with charity. Vivienne's seventieth birthday a few years ago had been such a depressing milestone. And, although she hated that she was now well into her eighth decade, the issue upsetting her the most was how little interest the media seemed to have in her decades' worth of achievements.

Vivienne Winter had once merely had to leave the house to be surrounded by reporters and photographers; these days, she'd be lucky to get a feature that didn't spend most of its copy discussing whether she'd had plastic surgery. It drove her mad that they never asked the men about surgeries, despite the fact that so many of her male contemporaries had clearly undergone more carefully executed nips and tucks over the years than Leonardo DiCaprio had dated Victoria's Secret models.

Now, however, reams of press and TV would be generated

about her glamour, her generosity, the talent and beauty that had allowed her to acquire so many extraordinary pieces of jewellery. Her advancing age would be much less important than the celebration of her life and career. Christine's suggestion of *A Life in Jewels* as the title for the catalogue had chimed perfectly with Vivienne's own vision of what the auction signified to her.

Looking at Christine busying herself with the boxes of photographs, Vivienne nodded in approval.

I want her pregnant by the end of the year, she decided. *I've told Angel he gets a million on me hearing she's pregnant, five when she gives birth to a healthy baby. And he'll have to marry her. I want my grandchild raised in a stable, two-parent household. She'll have to give up work, of course. I don't want a career woman farming my grandchild out to nannies. God knows, I don't see Angel as one of those modern fathers with the baby carrier on his chest!*

They'll get another five million and a house on their marriage. Notting Hill, maybe, with a nice garden: close to Mayfair, so I can visit whenever I want. And another baby in a couple of years, maximum.

This was all, of course, predicated on Angel's 'cancer' going into remission. He had told Vivienne that the radiation treatments were going extremely well, that the doctor was already cautiously optimistic, and that he would be able to have sex with Christine without contraception soon after the end of the radiotherapy, news that Vivienne had greeted with delight. She was refusing to believe that Angel would not survive. Her plans were entirely centred around this illness being a momentary blip, something that would be remembered in a year or two merely as the catalyst which had not only miraculously reunited her and Angel, but given her great-grandchildren.

Vivienne would allow Angel six months, once he had been given the all-clear by the doctor, to see if Christine could get pregnant. If not, he would have to move on and find someone who could. Or maybe – Vivienne debated this – Christine could undergo IVF. Trying for more than one baby at once would be the most efficient strategy. But either way, the timetable must be kept, the quest for a great-grandchild be rewarded with success.

And if there had been a way to pay a doctor extra to ensure that the baby had the Winter amethyst eyes, Vivienne would have done it without a moment's hesitation.

Chapter Thirteen

Atlanta – the next day

'Oh my *God*,' the most famous reality star in the world breathed, as she studied the close-up photographs of Vivienne's pearl and diamond choker. 'Bae, *look* at the size of that pearl!'

'It pops great against that black velvet,' her husband drawled, one big finger touching the image of the Italian pearl hanging from the choker. 'It'll be way better on you than some skinny white chick.'

'It *so* will,' Silantra sighed in ecstatic contemplation. 'What should I wear with it in the video?'

'I kinda think a white leather bikini?' Lil' Biscuit said, knitting his brows in contemplation.

Husband and wife both tilted their heads at the same angle, thinking it over. Their marriage was entirely one of convenience, arranged by their management teams as efficiently as a matchmaker bringing two clients together, linking their hands and giving them a gentle nudge down the aisle. However, it had been pleasant for the happy couple to discover that they had more in common than an unquenchable craving for fame. In fact, they shared three major interests: they both loved spending money, watching basketball (which was lucky for

Silantra, as the fact that her husband's boyfriend was a basket-ball player meant that she was contractually obliged to attend a considerable amount of games) and dressing Silantra up in ever more extravagant outfits.

Lil' Biscuit liked to see Silantra looking as sluttish as possible. As he had put it to Silantra: if he were a woman, he'd dress like a hooker every day of the week. And now that Silantra was married, she could wear clothes that Sondra, her momager (both mother and manager) would have ruled out when she was a single woman. After Silantra had rocketed to fame with a scandalous sex tape, Sondra's strategy had been to present her daughter as a nice girl who got her freak on in private but was relatively ladylike in public.

Now, however, Silantra was free to totter out of the house in seven-inch heels, spilling out of a bandage dress bought two sizes too small to show off her latest implants, ten thou-sand dollars' worth of Russian hair extensions tumbling down her back. In interviews, she explained in a manner as demure as her outfit was revealing that, as a loving wife, she was dressing to please her husband, who liked to see her looking 'feminine'. She and Lil' Biscuit – and his boyfriend Gray, when he was around – spent many happy hours assembling outfits for her that made her look, as Gray put it, like Russian Hooker Barbie.

'She's like our own RealDoll,' he said to Lil' Biscuit once. 'Only we don't want to fuck her.'

'Or maybe we get a diamond bikini made for you to wear for the video,' Lil' Biscuit eventually said, still staring at the photograph. 'Like one of those Vicky's Secret catwalk shows. That kinda thing always gets tons of press. You know, like that actress who wore that dress made of pearls to the Oscars a couple of years ago? Thousands and thousands of pearls, worth, they said, maybe a million. Hell knows how she was supposed to sit down in it, but that's not the point, right?'

But Silantra, who only ever looked at photographs of herself, shook her head at this. Her expression was blank, but that was par for the course: her face was so full of Botox and fillers that it could barely register anything. Even when she had an orgasm, pretty much all that happened was that her eyes and mouth got wider.

'I'd *love* a diamond bikini,' she said. 'But not when I'm wearing this. It would be, like, too much. Like, the choker would get so much attention, and so would the diamond bikini. So why do them both together, when we could get two episodes of the show and two sets of magazine covers instead of one?'

'Great point, babe!' her husband agreed, grinning in pleasure at the fact that, as always, he and his RealDoll Russian Hooker Barbie were so happily synchronized. As far as he was concerned, he and Silantra would be mated for life, one of the few happy Hollywood couples that would go the distance. What better beard could he possibly find?

He leaned back, spreading his arms along the back of the gigantic sofa and flashing a dazzling white smile at Nicole, who was sitting quietly on the opposite sofa, waiting until he chose to address her. Diamonds sparkled in his ears, bright as spotlights against his deep chocolate skin, which was moisturized so thoroughly that it gleamed as richly as the leather sofa. More baguette-cut diamonds flashed at both wrists: stacked rubber bracelets, prototypes made to his own design, each set with a pair of one-carat gems. Lil' Biscuit loved jewellery and was always looking for more ways to incorporate it into his outfits; he was planning to roll out the commercial sale of the bracelets later that year.

'Hey,' he drawled to his wife, looking over at one wrist complacently, turning it a little to see the precious stones glitter against the black rubber settings. 'The guy who did these for me told me they make these diamond dresses for runway shows and value them at a cool mil for the publicity, but the diamonds they use are so tiny they ain't worth nothing. It's all a con. There's a hell of a lot of work that goes into sewing all the tiny bitty things onto the dress, but they get it all sweatshopped so they don't pay anything for it.'

'I'd *love* a diamond dress,' Silantra said enthusiastically.

'We could glue it on to you, and let the paps go crazy trying to catch a shot of you flashing 'em something by accident,' Lil' Biscuit mused.

'I could unstick it a little, right at the end,' Silantra suggested. 'Do a little wiggle and flash a bit of nipple. Then I could, like, pretend to be shocked, and you could be all, *Oh honey, are you okay?* and maybe take your jacket off and lend it to me to cover up. And then we could film us coming home, like I'm upset and you're hugging me and saying *No, it's cool, I like to see you dress up all sexy, honey*. Mom says those scenes rate really high. And afterwards it could be an in-joke between us. Like, I could say *Oh honey, isn't this too revealing?* when I'm, like, trying something on in a store, and you could say *Hey, at least it isn't that diamond dress!* and we could laugh.'

The show was the only subject on which Silantra spoke

for any length of time, and Lil' Biscuit, respecting her long experience with constructing and parcelling out her life for the TV cameras, was nodding seriously as he listened to her.

'Great idea,' he said. 'I like it.'

Silantra smiled, one of the few gestures her face was able to perform. It came slower than usual, however, as she had recently had extra collagen injected into her lips and she was still getting used to how they moved.

'I know Mom decides what scenes we'll do,' she said. 'But I've been, like, watching her for years now, and you get a sense of what's gonna work, you know? When I watch TV I'll see a scene and think "Oh yeah, we should totally copy that." Like that jacket thing. I saw it in an old movie. Old movies are my favourite.'

She paused to consider why, her eyelashes flickering.

'They're slower,' she eventually concluded. 'And everyone speaks real clear, so you can hear everything they say. I like that.'

It was so normal for husband and wife to not only have other people present as they talked, but TV cameras running too, that neither of them demonstrated the slightest trace of self-consciousness or embarrassment at having ignored Nicole. Lil' Biscuit looked down once more at the glossy photographs scattered on the coffee table, and then, finally, at Nicole, saying, 'So we need to talk about the bottom line here.'

Nicole nodded. She was quite aware of how A-list celebrities functioned: everyone else was a satellite around their sun, a bit player who could be summoned and dismissed like a servant. For Biscuit and Silantra to break off a discussion about which of Vivienne Winter's jewels they wanted to acquire, to engage in a conversation about diamond dresses, publicity stunts and future scenes for their reality show, was entirely typical.

She had been occupying her time quietly sipping from a glass of mint-infused Fiji water, which she now set back down on the leather coaster, monogrammed with Biscuit and Silantra's initials, that the maid had placed on the glass coffee table in front of her. The table, too, was decorated with the initials L, B and S, etched into the centre. Pretty much everything in Biscuit and Silantra's Atlanta mansion was similarly adorned.

'I understand that you want to secure some of Ms Winter's pieces ahead of the auction,' she said to Biscuit. 'So we need to discuss the protocol for how this works. As I'm sure you're aware, it's standard at this kind of high-level auction to negotiate private sales for pieces, especially ones that we'll package together. Like the choker, for instance – it's being sold as a lot with the "baby" one.'

Silantra nodded eagerly at the mention of a baby. She was already imagining the stream of selfies she could generate from the image of her and a future daughter – they had decided to do gender selection, as in market research surveys of their fans, Silantra and Biscuit having a girl had polled much higher than a boy – wearing their matching pearl and diamond chokers. Having a baby or two was definitely the next step in her career. Silantra had been envious for a long time of the magazine covers her sister Shanté could snag simply by stepping out in public with one of her photogenic little children, not to mention the endorsements and freebies Shanté was constantly offered.

Silantra speculated on how much she would be able to ask for a magazine cover holding her little girl in her arms. She'd been told that Angelina Jolie and Brad Pitt got four million dollars for their *People* pictorial of the first view of their baby Shiloh Nouvel, and almost the same from *Hello!* in the UK. Surely she and Biscuit would score at least that much?

'No one knows how high the bidding will go, of course,' Nicole continued. 'The only comparable auction of this magnitude was Elizabeth Taylor's jewellery sale in 2011, and prices in the art and precious gemstone markets have definitely increased across the board since then. The chokers are one of the highlights of Vivienne's collection. They have everything: the history of the Italian pearl, the fact that they were gifts from Randon Cliffe to Vivienne at the height of their love affair . . .'

Silantra sighed. This was such good stuff, her fans would love it! She was still pissed that Nicole wouldn't let this scene be recorded for the show, even though Lil' Biscuit had explained that they were cutting a deal, and that couldn't be filmed. Silantra had observed that her mother would normally handle this by shooting a completely scripted scene that bore no relation to what was really going on; but Biscuit had reluctantly said that their entire meeting with Nicole needed to be top secret, to avoid jeopardizing the sale.

'We've valued the two pieces at fourteen million,' Nicole was saying. 'Pounds, not dollars. And I've just heard that there are amazing, never-before-seen private photographs of Vivienne and her daughter Pearl wearing the chokers together – taken by Randon Cliffe.'

'Wow,' Biscuit said, his perfectly threaded eyebrows rising. 'That's quite something. So you'd be selling . . .'

'Both the model rights and the photographer's rights, bundled together,' Nicole clarified, a smile of pure satisfaction on her face. 'It's a real coup. The legal situation has been checked. Vivienne was the residuary legatee under Randon Cliffe's will, which means that everything he didn't specifically name goes to her, and there's no mention of his photographs in the will. So they're hers to sell.'

'We'd want some real classy, glamorous shots that Silantra can recreate,' Lil' Biscuit specified. 'And some cute ones of her and the kid, for the future. With exclusive rights to use 'em, locked down tighter than –' he reached over to pat Silantra's hip – 'my lovely wife's butt.'

Nicole smiled at this quip with appropriate amusement.

'I can arrange for photos to be scanned and sent over for you to choose from,' she said. 'But they'll significantly add to the cost of the deal. And I must make it clear that if Ms Winter is going to consider side deals, rather than putting items into the main auction, there has to be a premium for that privilege.'

Lil' Biscuit eyed her narrowly, an impressively intimidating stare he had honed on the streets and perfected in multiple music videos where he played a range of highly heterosexual bad-boy gangbangers, draped in nearly nude women.

'What kinda premium we talking about?' he asked.

'Let's say if you take the chokers and four photographs, eighteen million,' Nicole said, keeping her voice as steady as if she were on a checkout counter at a supermarket pricing tinned tomatoes, not negotiating a multimillion-pound deal. 'And two extra as a finder's fee.'

'Whoa,' Biscuit said, but his expression did not alter; he was too experienced a negotiator for that to happen. 'Pretty steep finder's fee.'

'I have a direct line to Vivienne's grandson Angel, who's working with the auction house involved,' Nicole said. 'No one else has that kind of clout. He's her only surviving relative.'

'And we can verify this how?' Biscuit asked, steepling his fingers and contemplating the gigantic emerald ring he had bought himself on becoming engaged to Silantra, a twin to her own. As he had said nonchalantly in numerous interviews, he believed in equality, and that meant men being able to wear big-ass engagement rings as well as the ladies.

'We can set up a Skype whenever you want,' Nicole said. 'Angel can also make himself available for a meeting here, if you'd like.'

'And how do we know you're not just setting me up for a bidding war?' Biscuit continued. 'Get an offer from me and go try to play that off against some other rich dude, or three?'

'I've done business with Jamal plenty in the past,' Nicole said. 'I'm sure he's vouched for me.'

'You've fucked Jamal plenty in the past,' Lil' Biscuit said, his voice even.

'I have,' Nicole riposted, 'and we both thoroughly enjoyed it.'

'Oh, I'm sure,' Lil' Biscuit said, grinning.

'You're *very* sexy,' Silantra said, nodding, in the manner of a high-class prostitute professionally approving the appearance of a work colleague.

'Thank you!' Nicole said, accepting the compliment in exactly the spirit in which it was meant. She was dressed in a sleek white pencil-skirted dress – sleeveless, to show off her Pilates Flow-sculpted arms – accessorized with a sleek gold necklace that had been an extremely costly present from her triad lover. The dress was figure-fitting but not tight, and its neckline was demure; it would have been a poor negotiating strategy to challenge Silantra for the title of sexiest woman in the room.

'But whether I've fucked Jamal or not,' Nicole continued, 'I wouldn't have got near this meeting with you if he hadn't known I was legit. I hold up my end of a bargain, I don't change the terms we've agreed upon. I may fuck dirty but I do business clean.'

'Hah! That's a really good line!' Silantra exclaimed. 'We should use that on the show!'

Lil' Biscuit reached out and patted her thigh, a little absently.

'Eighteen mil,' he said, his eyes on Nicole. 'In dollars.'

She shook her head.

'Twenty. In sterling. I have no wriggle room on this one – they're so iconic. The big Liz Taylor pieces all sold for millions more than their appraisal value. Your only other option is to take your chances at the auction.'

'We don't bid at auctions,' Silantra said, with the air of repeating a line she had heard from her husband many times. 'It looks weak.'

'I've seen auctions on TV,' Biscuit said. 'Staff lined up sitting there on phones, talking to fuck knows who, taking bids. How'm I supposed to know that they're not just running up the price I'm gonna end up paying?'

'It *is* strictly supervised,' Nicole said. 'But of course, I take your point.'

'I only make deals I can see the shape of,' Biscuit said bluntly. 'Auctions ain't like that.'

Nicole's heart raced as she sensed the deal was within her grasp.

'And I want a tiara too! At *least* one!' Silantra exclaimed, torpedoing her husband's attempts to play the negotiation as coolly as possible.

She was wearing a cropped tube top that started an inch below her cleavage, and stopped an inch above the base of her breasts. Her stomach was a miracle of liposuction, and her spray-on silver leggings clung to her generous thighs. She was the definition of an hourglass figure, balanced on spike heels she had been trained to wear since the age of thirteen and on which (as the viewers of her sex video could testify) she could balance in an impressive variety of positions. Silantra looked exactly like an off-duty porn star, which, effectively, she was; but as she gathered up her thick mane of hair and held it on top of her head, staring at her reflection in the floor-to-ceiling windows, picturing how she would look in one of Vivienne Winter's iconic tiaras, her expression was as dreamy and beautiful as a Disney princess waiting for her prince to ride up and place a large and expensive crown on her head.

'We'd need to meet Ms Winter as part of the deal,' Lil' Biscuit said firmly to Nicole, 'and of course get some photos with her. Ideally, shoot the scene for the show.'

'Photos will be fine,' Nicole assured them. 'The auction will be held in Geneva, at the end of this year. You'll be invited to that, of course, and as major buyers, you'll also have access to a private meet and greet with her, where you can take all the photographs you want. I'm really not sure about shooting it for the show, however. I very much doubt that would happen.'

Nicole could not have spoken more politely. But it took every ounce of self-control she had not to show, even by the roll of an eye or the raise of an eyebrow, how outrageously unlikely this request was. *Are you joking? Never in a million years would Vivienne Winter appear on a reality show, let alone one whose star is most famous for her sex tape!*

'But we have to film it!' Silantra exclaimed. 'If it's not on film, it didn't happen! That's what Mom always says.'

'It's *just* possible we could film the meet and greet, but I doubt there would be a release to use it on the show,' Nicole said; she wouldn't promise what she was sure she couldn't deliver. To her relief, Lil' Biscuit nodded and dropped the subject of filming, realistic enough to know how unlikely the request had been.

'I'm assuming the two mil commission you mentioned is a flat fee?' he asked.

Nicole allowed herself a little smile of irony at this hopeful question.

'I'm afraid not. We've priced each item with a separate commission,' she said. 'Obviously if you're planning to take more than one item, the figures are open to a degree of negotiation. And the fee is payable in quite a different manner to the price of the items, of course.'

'Of course,' he said with irony to match hers. 'Cayman Islands account?'

'Something of the sort,' Nicole said with great sweetness. 'And it's payable on signature of the contract, as is the sum agreed on for the jewellery.'

'Yeah, I assumed that,' he drawled. 'So let's cut the crap. Tell me – since it's not exactly a secret who's handling this auction – why exactly Jamal thinks I should be talking to you and paying you a finder's fee for each piece we take, rather than getting him to call up the auctioneers and cut a deal with them? Is my manager taking backhanders from his fuck buddy?'

Nicole smoothed her skirt down carefully, taking her time, looking down at her hands rather than Lil' Biscuit's face.

'This is Ms Winter's legacy,' she said. 'She's going to use the considerable proceeds of the sale to endow her charities. But it isn't just about money, and there are a great deal of interested buyers. She's expressed to the auction house representatives that she wants them to only present her with truly respectable potential purchasers.'

Thank God for Silantra's sex tape, she thought, seeing Biscuit shoot a swift glance at his oblivious wife. *That's what's scoring us these huge finders' fees – they genuinely do need Angel to vouch for them, to get over the amateur porn issue.*

'Okay,' Biscuit said, nodding slowly in acknowledgement. 'I get it.'

'You'll meet Angel, of course,' Nicole assured him. She felt as if she had been holding her breath for minutes on end, and could finally let it out in a huge surge of relief. This was actually happening – the single biggest score of her life. 'The idea is that you come to London in a month's time, and Angel will introduce you and Silantra to the auction organizers. Don't be concerned, it won't be an interview process – it'll be guaranteed by then that you're accredited buyers, as long as it's understood between us that a finder's fee will apply to each piece. You'll be able to look at the jewellery itself before you make your final decision—'

'Will I be able to try it on?' Silantra asked, perking up as if she were an animatronic robot programmed to come to life at the word 'jewellery'.

'Oh, of course!' Nicole smiled, imagining the extra fees that would flood in as Silantra, in London, found more pieces that she absolutely *had* to have. There was no need for Nicole to stress the point that Angel's endorsement of her and Lil' Biscuit as buyers could be withdrawn at any time before the deal was done. It was implicit, and Biscuit was far too intelligent not to understand exactly how the situation stood.

Nicole's entire body was now flooded with excitement, but she was careful to look as poised as if this were just one of many high-profile deals she organized on a daily basis.

'Okay, it's a deal,' Lil' Biscuit said with a smile. 'And you better not fuck this up. You got that? When I agree a deal with someone, it goes through just like we said it would.'

He was still smiling, but his tone changed so completely on the last sentence that it took all Nicole's self-control to avoid showing some reaction to it; Biscuit had slid seamlessly from affability into utter menace without altering his expression one iota. It was his most powerful negotiating technique. He let his opponent think that they had reached an agreement, that there was nothing more to be said – then, just as they relaxed in relief, he hit them with a verbal threat backed up by his impressive physical presence.

A gay man growing up in a violent and homophobic environment, even a closeted one, had to be extra tough to survive. Biscuit had hit the gym for hours on a daily basis, building himself a suit of body armour that was intimidating to anyone who might be an enemy. As so often happened with men, his youthful musculature had hardened into impressive solidity in his thirties. He weighed two hundred and thirty pounds, with nine per cent body fat, and regularly practised both Indonesian martial arts and t'ai chi. As he looked Nicole straight in the eye, still smiling, and repeated, 'Yeah. You better not fuck up,' she was suddenly acutely aware not only of his size and his strength, but his power.

'I absolutely won't,' she said, bowing her head deferentially. She sensed that she was by no means the first person who had found herself feeling compelled to show Lil' Biscuit an extra degree of respect. 'You don't just have to take my word for it,' she added. 'You have Vivienne Winter's own grandson to back me up.'

'And he better not fuck up either,' Biscuit said, the smile, if anything, intensifying. 'He could be the grandson of the King and Queen of England, and he still better not cross me in a business deal.'

Nicole met his stare calmly. She wasn't intimidated, because she had no intention of doing anything nefarious this time around. Earlier this year she had faced down triad members, been interrogated by Hong Kong police and been confronted by the father of her triad lover's wife, come to warn her that she had two days to leave Hong Kong for good. Lil' Biscuit, tough though he was, could not compare to that level of intimidation. And in this situation, she was completely innocent of any wrongdoing – which certainly hadn't been the case in Hong Kong. Her gaze was limpid, her conscience clear.

Silantra, reaching for her own glass of water and carefully adjusting the gold-embossed coaster so the monogrammed initials faced her, shot a look up at Nicole from under her free-range mink eyelash extensions. Even with Silantra's irises concealed by blue-tinted contacts, Nicole read the message she was sending with a distinct frisson of surprise, followed almost instantly by a wash of pleasure.

'I got a really tight filming schedule for the next month,' Silantra said, seemingly apropos of nothing. 'Mom and my sisters get in tonight from LA, and we're shooting a lot of scenes about Shanté leaving her babydaddy for real this time.'

'Is she really going to leave DuWayne?' Nicole couldn't help asking. No matter how much she knew the whole show was entirely scripted, she followed it as she would a soap opera.

Silantra's beautiful shoulders rose and fell in a gesture of utter disinterest.

'Who knows? Whatever,' she said. 'It's Mom's decision, and it's Shanté's season arc, not mine. *Anyway*, I'm like super-busy at the mo. But I was thinking, when we come over to London to, like, see the jewellery and everything, you'll be there too, right? It'd be nice to, like . . .' She teased the conclusion of this sentence. 'Hang out,' she finished.

Nicole hadn't realized that Silantra liked girls as well as boys, but the glance Silantra sent her with these last words, together with the flicker of her tongue over her lower lip, could have no other interpretation. Silantra was coming on to her. Nicole slanted her eyes over at Lil' Biscuit to check how she should respond to this; to her relief, he was looking positively benign.

'I'd *love* to,' Nicole said with enthusiasm that was quite unfeigned. Silantra was not only very attractive, but having viewed her sex tape, Nicole was aware that she was also flexible, enthusiastic and a generous bestower of her favours.

'Well, how nice that you two girls are getting along!' Biscuit drawled with the satisfied smile of a gay man who has just seen his wife efficiently arrange her own holiday fun, freeing him up to do the same for himself. 'This could be the start of a beautiful friendship, right?'

Chapter Fourteen

London – one month later

'Mr Biscuit! How lovely to see you again!' Angel said delight-edly, arms thrown wide. 'Are we European? Do we kiss? Or shake hands? Or perform the American manly "one-and-a-hug", where we do a half-embrace and then pat each other's backs? I'm afraid I can't do any of those complicated hand-bumping greetings, but you could teach me one, if you'd like?' He ventured the most fleeting of winks, and murmured, 'I'm sure there are quite a few things you could teach me.'

Nicole, standing beside him, nudged him sharply in the ribs. Angel always liked to push the boundaries; he never felt more alive than when he was dicing with danger. But he had kept his voice just low enough on this sally for his target to be able to overlook it, and the meeting Nicole had organ-ized with Lil' Biscuit and Silantra at Angel's penthouse earlier that afternoon had gone swimmingly.

To Angel and Nicole's great pleasure, Biscuit and Silantra had clearly spent a great deal of time poring over the beau-tiful sale catalogue Christine had produced. When Silantra pulled out her copy of *Vivienne Winter: A Life in Jewels* from her one-of-a-kind, custom-made Birkin bag, which had her own face painted on it by a famous Japanese artist, the catalogue had been so bristling with pink Post-it notes that Nicole had been hard put not to let out an audible sigh of happiness. Silantra's wishlist comprised not only the chokers but two tiaras, several sets of earrings, three bracelets, and a parure consisting of a necklace featuring five cabochon emeralds, a huge emerald brooch that could also be worn set into a tiara or bracelet, and a pair of drop earrings.

The prospect of the finder's fee awaiting him if he successfully convinced Christine to accept a bundled offer for all of these extremely expensive pieces had brought an exquisite smile to Angel's face. Seeing it, Silantra had blinked those mink eyelashes and fixed him with a look of such naked appreciation that Angel had instantly fantasized about nailing the deal by nailing her.

'Subject to her husband's approval, of course,' he had said to Nicole afterwards.

'Excuse me,' she had replied, 'I already have a longstanding date with her, don't forget!'

'So? We love to share, don't we? But do you think Mr Biscuit wants me for himself? I wouldn't mind that at *all*. Do you think they share, too? As Joey said on *Friends* when Ross was torn between two women: "I have two words for you. Threesome." Or foursome, in this case.'

'I'm always up for some fun,' Nicole said cautiously, 'but they'd have to give *very* clear signals and initiate. We can't risk anything messing up the deal.'

'Hmm; I wonder if he's a top or a bottom,' Angel pondered. 'Statistically, he's more likely to be a bottom, of course. And I'm always up for anything, naturally! Did you think he was cruising me?'

'I couldn't tell,' Nicole said frankly, 'and that hardly ever happens. He plays his cards really close to his chest.'

'And what a lovely big chest it is,' Angel said approvingly. 'No steroids or HGT for him, you can tell. Just home-grown American beefcake. Yum.'

'Be *very* careful,' Nicole warned. 'Jamal told me Lil' Biscuit once hung a music executive out of a window by his ankle. On the twentieth floor.'

'This is the main difference between you and me, darling,' Angel pointed out. 'I'm a sociopath, and you're not. I don't get scared.'

'Be *extra* careful, then,' Nicole said, rolling her eyes, 'because you don't pick up the warning cues!'

Happily, this evening, at the launch party being held to celebrate the start of Tor's expedition to the Andes, Lil' Biscuit and Silantra were all smiles. They looked simply magnificent, like a cross between Hollywood and African royalty. Both Biscuit, in a floor-length white alpaca coat and tailored white silk suit, and Silantra, wearing a white jumpsuit with not much back and even less front, were bedecked in gold and diamonds from head to toe.

Inspired by the vintage photographs of Vivienne in the auction catalogue, Silantra's hairstylist had been tasked with piling her Russian-sourced locks on the crown of her head and augmenting them with extra plaits, forming a pedestal around which a tiara could be pinned. The tiara had belonged to Greek royalty, which made it far less interesting to Silantra than the ones she was about to buy from a famous film star; Silantra had only the haziest idea that Greece was even a country.

Angel had welcomed the striking couple to the launch with great appreciation. Having kissed Silantra's hand with a considerable flourish and a half-bow, causing her to let out a sigh of delight at his courtliness, Angel had turned to her husband and launched into the question of how he wished to be greeted by another man.

Lil' Biscuit grinned in amusement at Angel's sauciness.

'I like the handshake,' he pronounced, having considered for a moment. 'It's traditional, and we're in Britain. We should be traditional.'

He extended one large, well-manicured hand to Angel, who took it carefully, as it was bristling with large and expensive rings. Just as Angel was about to let go, Biscuit's second hand closed over Angel's, engulfing it in a warm, firm cage as he manoeuvred the smaller man a little to the side, towards him.

'There a VIP room here?' he asked. 'Or a private office? Somewhere we can have a word, just you and me?'

Angel's blond eyebrows shot up. 'Certainly!' he said with unabashed cheerfulness. 'That would be a positive pleasure, Mr Biscuit.'

'You know it ain't actually "Mr Biscuit"?' the man in question asked, as he dropped Angel's hand and followed him through the melee. The guests at this exclusive party were far too sophisticated to press for autographs or selfies, but they openly gawked at Lil' Biscuit, who strolled through the crowd just like a visiting monarch, his coat hanging open, relishing the attention, the diamond-encrusted fob watch hanging from a gold necklace as thick as his thumb catching the light with every step he took.

The bouncer stationed by the cordoned-off VIP area was

already jumping to unhook the velvet rope as Angel and Lil' Biscuit approached.

'Huge fan, mate,' he said worshipfully as Biscuit passed him.

'Thanks, man,' Biscuit said with a nod, in the manner of a potentate acknowledging a lowly subject, his coat swishing like a cape as he took his rightful place in the VIP section. The launch was being held in the Rumpus Room bar of the newly renovated Mondrian Sea Containers Hotel, on the south bank of the Thames next to Blackfriars Bridge. The views over the river and its beautiful bridges were breathtaking, and there was an outside terrace from which they could be appreciated with a cigarette in hand.

The layout was open-plan, with huge, dramatic half-moon red leather banquettes, punctuated with crimson and purple velvet 1920s-style swivel armchairs to create intimate seating areas. A corner had been arbitrarily roped off to make a VIP area that had very little standing space. However, it was de rigueur at any celebrity party for there to be a section for the most A-list of the A-list guests to gather, no matter how cramped and awkward it was. Much as the VIPs might complain about being gathered in an area so small they could barely turn around, they would have been infinitely more annoyed by the lack of it.

Prince Toby, fourth in line to the British throne, his cousin Princess Sophie, and a couple of members of their entourage were sitting on one of the banquettes, giggling at some private joke. They looked up as Angel entered with Lil' Biscuit, and both Toby and Sophie waved to Angel. He waved back, holding up his hand to indicate that he wouldn't be joining them immediately; instead, he walked with Biscuit to a pair of armchairs in the far corner. Biscuit disposed himself on one of them, his silk suit gleaming under the display of glittering puffball lights hung overhead, their reflections in the huge panel of the glass roof above them doubling their effect.

'What can I help you with, Mr Biscuit?' Angel asked, hitching up the knees of his immaculately tailored Savile Row suit and taking a seat facing the entertainment mogul. 'Do you mind me calling you that? I feel silly just saying "Biscuit". And I can't say "Lil". It sounds like you're a house-maid from *Downton Abbey*.'

'I used to like that show,' Lil' Biscuit said meditatively. 'But it kinda lost its way at the end. The plot stopped making sense. I watch it in reruns on mute,' Biscuit added. 'To see the costumes and the interiors. I wanna do a video based on it. I'm gonna be the Earl. Black Downton. Real high concept.'

Angel nodded encouragingly, quite aware that Lil' Biscuit hadn't requested a semi-private moment with him to chat about a British television show.

'My friends call me James,' Lil' Biscuit said, seemingly on a tangent. 'Cause that's my name.'

He was surveying Angel carefully, his lids half-lowered over his dark eyes, his head tilted back at a casual angle. One hand played with his fob watch, setting off facets of multicoloured light from the diamond setting as if he were trying to hypnotize Angel.

'Let me guess,' Angel said. 'I'm not supposed to call you James.'

'Damn right,' Biscuit said with great cordiality. 'You can keep calling me Mr Biscuit. It sounds cool in an English accent.'

'Anything sounds cool in an English accent,' Angel pointed out. 'I could just sit here and say "bollocks" a lot, and you'd probably enjoy it.'

'You got me there,' Biscuit said, nodding. 'I would. Maybe you can do that later.'

'I'm beginning to feel a bit like your court jester,' Angel said cheerfully. 'I should have one of those things on sticks with bells I could wave as I caper around.'

'The vessel with the pestle has the brew that is true,' Biscuit said, taking Angel completely by surprise. 'Danny Kaye, *The Court Jester*. Great movie.'

He leaned forward, clearly having decided that it was time to get to the point.

'It's about my wife,' he said, a swift turn of his head from side to side ensuring no one was close enough to hear their conversation; behind them was a glass wall with views of the rooftops behind the hotel. 'She likes Nicole, so that's all fine and dandy. But she likes you, too.'

'How nice,' Angel said demurely. 'I find her very attractive, naturally.'

'Yeah, I kinda got that vibe. You got a girlfriend, though. The auction chick. So, no pressure.'

Angel winked. 'Oh, I can definitely work something out,' he said. 'Without Christine being aware of it, of course. She's much too bourgeois for anything this . . . sophisticated. It must be obvious to you that the introduction fee you're paying to Nicole and myself is a very hush-hush subject, not to be mentioned to Christine? She's very conventional – takes her job terribly seriously. Any mention of it would compromise the whole deal.'

It was Biscuit's turn to nod. 'Goes without saying,' he agreed.

'I can see that you're very discreet,' Angel said. 'Nicole and I share that quality. We've known each other since school, so we go back a very long way, and we have a long tradition of keeping quiet about a whole variety of things . . . in fact,' Angel added, chancing his luck, 'I'm personally capable of being *completely* discreet about absolutely *anything* at all. And I'm terribly open-minded.'

Biscuit met his gaze with a long, dark, impenetrable stare that acknowledged Angel's offer while giving nothing away.

'Something to bear in mind for the future,' he said.

'Hi, Angel!'

Princess Sophie, wearing a short miniskirt and a wide smile, plopped herself down in Angel's lap. The way she was sitting made it immediately clear that if she were wearing any kind of underwear, it was the most minimal of thongs. Biscuit, accustomed to women displaying themselves in an attempt to attract his attention, gave the lower portion of her body a brief glance. Avoiding it pointedly might have aroused suspicion about his true preference, and no straight man would have resisted the temptation to look up a young and nubile princess's skirt if given the opportunity.

'You've been totally *hogging* Lil' Biscuit!' she complained. 'And we're all so excited to meet him!'

Biscuit's eyes flickered over the rest of Sophie's party, in particular the handsome, red-headed Prince Toby, whose freckled good looks were reminiscent of his boyfriend Gray's. 'Well,' he drawled, 'I'm kinda excited to meet you all too . . .'

'I can't believe you're going on the expedition, Ange!'

Sophie said. 'I never pictured you as Action Man – outside the bedroom, that is!'

She grinned knowingly. Sophie's tastes ran primarily to working-class white boys, but she had dallied with Angel on and off for years; they were old friends and fuck buddies.

'Oh, it really isn't a big deal,' Angel said languidly. 'We're not having to pull sleds across the Arctic and panic about losing fingers to frostbite, like Tor did with Toby on their polar jaunt. We camp out with full provisions, no foraging for whale meat, nothing sordid, and we do a series of challenges wearing Go-Pros. We'll be competing in races and climbs, all of which Toby or that action-star actress will doubtless win. I'm just eye candy, frankly.'

'But it's so not you!' Sophie persisted. 'You hate camping, the outdoors – you bitched that whole time we went to Glastonbury, and you had one of the posh tents with beds and outlets you can plug your phone into and everything!'

'Those toilets!' Angel said with a reminiscent shudder. 'Boutique camping, my arse! I swear, for the money I paid they should have scattered rose petals in the bloody toilet bowl every morning.'

Biscuit snorted with laughter.

'I hear you, man,' he said. 'I take a helicopter in, do my set and get the hell out. Straight back to my five-star hotel.'

'I still don't get why –' Sophie persisted, much to Angel's annoyance.

'Oh, Granny Viv's doing so much for charity with this auction,' he said. 'I suppose I felt I should do my bit. And I know Tor and Toby already, of course, so it'll really be like an adventure holiday with some mates, getting extra publicity for Granny Viv's jewellery sale – not that she needs it.'

'So, do you want to join the guys in the VIP area?' Nicole was asking Silantra, as they took ginger and green tea martinis from a tray proffered by a waiter who was doing his best not to gawp at Silantra's lavish cleavage.

'Sure,' she said, glancing over to make sure that her husband had had enough time to convey to Angel the message that he was more than welcome to have sex with Silantra. 'I'd *love* to meet the prince.'

'And that's Princess Sophie as well,' Nicole said. 'The tall blonde on Angel's lap. Two royals for the price of one.'

'Wow, this is amazing!' Silantra said, heaving a sigh of sheer happiness. 'I'm at a party with, like, *two* members of the royal family!'

'You'll get on with Sophie,' Nicole said, grinning. 'She's a real party girl though not as much as she used to be. Did you hear about her getting caught out having this big orgy in a villa in Ibiza? Toby was there too, and it was all on film, apparently – lots of coke – anyway, *really* dodgy, and the palace got furious and clamped down on them hard. Prince Hugo was livid. It wasn't long before his wedding, and the publicity was awful. So ever since, they've taken a bit of a chill pill.'

'You gotta be careful when cameras are rolling,' Silantra agreed. 'There's, like, no point recording yourself fucking if you can't make money from it, right?'

Nicole, who had quite forgotten about Silantra's sex tape, started to stammer an apology, but Silantra shrugged it off with a swift rise and fall of one slim, smooth, mochaccino-tinted shoulder, almost completely revealed by her jumpsuit.

The garment had been designed specifically to show off her assets; her round, bolt-on breasts did not need the same support natural ones did, and thus the back of the jumpsuit was so low it showed hints of her buttock cleavage as she moved. Fine gold chains, studded with diamonds in an echo of Biscuit's necklace, hung from the halter at the nape of her neck, the lowest chain almost skimming that cleavage too. The entire outfit was a miracle of engineering.

'This way,' Nicole said, steering Silantra towards the VIP section.

'Is that Angel's girlfriend?' Silantra asked, as they passed a cluster of guests that included Christine. She was with a couple of colleagues from the auction house, wearing a black dress as demure as Silantra's outfit was *outré*.

Nicole could barely repress a sneer at Christine as they passed. Crucial as Christine was to their plans, the whole scenario of Angel pretending to be falling for her was proving extremely annoying to Nicole. It meant she couldn't crash at Angel's, and instead had had to take a short-term lease on a flat which, because of London prices, was costing her a small fortune. It also meant that Angel was unavailable at least half the time, which was frustrating. And despite his protests to the contrary, Nicole had the sense that he was enjoying fucking Christine much more than he admitted. It had been a long time since Angel had had a fresh little thing to corrupt; maybe not since their schooldays, when the upper years had picked out playthings from the new intake, bartering for them with their classmates, just as they themselves had been selected back in the day.

However, breaking in a newbie wasn't Angel's fetish. He

liked experienced women, ones who, like Silantra, were no stranger to strap-ons, role switching and bondage play. So it struck Nicole as odd that, when she brunched with Angel after Christine had spent a night with him, he always looked so relaxed, so sleek and satisfied. It was as if introducing that drab little snub-nosed thing to, say, some bog-standard concept like double penetration had been much more fun than any wild and raunchy idea Nicole could conjure up.

Odd, and exasperating. And the most infuriating part of all was that Nicole could tell Christine was not really in love with Angel. She was dickmatized, as Nicole put it. Sexually obsessed with Angel and his endless box of tricks, thrown perpetually off balance, and thus made vulnerable by not knowing what was coming next; and also hugely flattered by what she believed to be the monogamous attentions of such a handsome playboy, who seemed to have reformed his wicked ways just for her, and whose hugely famous grandmother was encouraging the relationship with everything she had.

Like a fucking romance novel, Nicole thought, her lip curling in contempt. *But those guys aren't the kind of husband material Christine and Vivienne want Angel to be. Men like that don't settle down with a nice girl and give up all the pervy stuff overnight. Quite the opposite. Not only do they want to keep doing all the naughty things they enjoy, they always need more. They have to go further and further to get their thrills.*

It wasn't that Nicole wanted to be exclusive with Angel, nor that she was in love with him. Nicole didn't operate on either of those levels. But when she was fucking a man, she expected to be the most important woman in his life. Both the trader and the triad White Paper Fan had been sexually obsessed with her, willing to take any risk she demanded in order to keep her around, and that was just how she liked it.

She wasn't foolish enough to expect that level of infatuation from Angel: they were equal playmates. But she wanted to be the acknowledged mistress – not sitting back while her co-conspirator had more fun training up an innocent like Christine than he did with her.

He'd get bored with Christine eventually, of course. But by then, Nicole would have got her revenge for the insult he'd given her . . .

'Yes, that's Christine,' she confirmed to Silantra. 'You've got your meeting with her tomorrow, at the auction house. She's the gemmologist there. It's a very convenient connection,' she added pointedly, wanting to underline the fact that Christine's attraction for Angel was in large part the link to the jewellery sale.

Silantra nodded, her blue-tinted gaze slicing up and down Christine's body, making it clear she had exactly the same opinion of Christine's outfit that Nicole did.

'They exclusive?' she asked.

'She thinks so,' Nicole said. 'But then, girls like her always do, don't they?'

Silantra rewarded this observation with a dazzling smile.

'You're funny,' she said. 'And I love your boobs. They're like my sister Shanté's, before she had the babies. Real small and pretty.'

'Thank you,' Nicole said, returning the smile.

'You and Angel . . . ?'

'We like to have fun,' Nicole said, her voice now lowered, as the bouncer lifted the rope to the VIP area and gestured them in.

'We're gonna have a lot of fun later,' Silantra said in an equally quiet tone, letting the hand that wasn't holding the martini glass slide down Nicole's arm in a brief caress. 'I've been looking forward to it.'

'Angel could join us,' Nicole suggested. 'If you'd like. I don't know if your husband . . .'

'Oh, he does his own thing,' Silantra said carelessly. 'We all got our own thing, right?'

'Oh, I'm sure you and I have *lots* of things,' Nicole said, and although Silantra was quite a few inches taller than her, the two women's eyes met in such understanding of the message being conveyed that they might for that moment have been twins.

Christine glanced over as Nicole passed by with Silantra. She couldn't help admiring Nicole's peach suede dress, the way it clung to her slender figure, and the diamond and gold chains trailing down Silantra's smooth, flawless bare back. They were way out of her league, those women; they saw their looks as one of their greatest assets, willing to spend vast amounts of money as an investment to help those assets appreciate. Silantra's face now was by no means the one she had been born with; the work she had had done was calculated to ensure she could be filmed from every conceivable angle.

As Nicole and Silantra entered the VIP section, Christine noticed someone else inside whom she very much wanted to talk to. The rose-gold hair of the Countess of Rutland, arranged in the American-beauty-queen style she favoured, tumbling down her back, was unmistakable. Christine had seen her at jewellery auctions before, but, as a mere appraiser, had not had the status to approach one of the reigning queens of London society.

Although Christine was in correspondence with the Countess's publicist about the possibility of the Earl and Countess viewing Vivienne's collection, so far she had not managed to make an appointment for them. Often, publicists perceived their job as blocking enquiries to their clients rather than facilitating them. Christine had known, however, that they would be likely to show up tonight, as Edmund, the Earl, was an old friend of the younger generation of the royal family and the Rutlands were well known for the many charities they supported.

The rules of social contact at this kind of occasion were clear. Christine would need to be introduced by a mutual friend if the Rutlands were in the main party area – but once in the VIP section she could approach the Countess as an equal, the fact that she had access beyond the velvet rope vouching for her status. Angel would get her in; she was looking around for him when a voice behind her rather tentatively said: 'Christine?'

Stupidly, she felt her heart pound fast as, instead of looking for her boyfriend, she turned round to greet a married man – a man who had completely failed to mention his relationship status when he had picked her up on a beach, invited her out for drinks, and generally behaved in a manner calculated to make her think that he was exactly what she had been looking for all her life.

'Oh, hello, Tor,' she said, looking as composed as she could manage and keeping her voice flat.

She had seen him already, across the room, and assumed that they would probably exchange a few words at some stage. It was ridiculous how nervous she had been at the prospect, considering not only that she had been on good terms with him for less than twenty-four hours before Vivienne's revelations, but that she was now in a relationship with someone else. Still, in the black tie he was wearing for the launch, he looked so dashing. There was something compelling about a man in black tie: it flattered even the worst of bodies and made the best look godlike. Tor, having spent the last month getting into top shape to lead his upcoming expedition, naturally fell into the second category. His shoulders were wide, his waist as narrow as his solid build could achieve; his natural tan shone against the crisp white shirt and black grosgrain bow tie.

'You look lovely,' he said with great sincerity.

But then, she reminded herself, he was a master at sounding sincere. *And at seeming available! Don't fall for it again!*

It was shocking how genuine he seemed. There was a soft light in his blue eyes, as if everything around them had faded to nothing when he saw her. Vivienne had told Christine that Tor was a practised flirt, unable to settle with just one woman; but that kind of man was more like – *Angel*, she thought now. If Angel found himself alone in a room, he would flirt with one of the walls. And he would make that wall blush pink with pleasure if it could, even though it knew that as soon as someone walked in, Angel would forget it had ever existed.

But Tor was worse – much worse. Because the wall would genuinely believe that Tor only had eyes for it, and its heart would be truly wounded when he turned away.

'Thank you,' she murmured, smoothing down the boring black sheath dress she'd chosen because it was suited to a professional occasion at which two of the Berkeley auction house directors would be present. Still, at least her accessories were elegant. Vivienne had insisted on giving Christine a set of aquamarines and diamonds set in white gold – drop earrings, a bracelet and a necklace; inexpensive, Vivienne had assured her, just a little trinket to say thank you for all her hard work on the catalogue. The set must have cost several thousand pounds, however, and the shade of aquamarine so exactly matched Christine's eyes that she almost suspected Vivienne of having bought it especially for her, rather than having found it while going through her collection.

The simple dress set the aquamarines off perfectly, and Christine had pulled back her hair to show off the earrings; they made her feel sophisticated. When you knew you were wearing real, rather than costume, jewellery, you carried yourself differently, pegged your chin higher, felt as if your neck was actually longer. Christine had been feeling elegant until this moment, poised and suitably ladylike; but Tor's gaze on her now was so melting, so appreciative, that she suddenly felt as dazzling as Silantra or Nicole, with their body-hugging outfits and superbly honed bodies.

'You look nice too,' she added lamely.

'It seems so funny that I haven't seen you since that day in Tylösand,' Tor said simply. 'It was such a good evening.'

'I got so drunk!' she said apologetically. 'I never really

thanked you for introducing me to Vivienne. It's been the most amazing thing for me. Thank you so much.'

She was stuttering out short sentences, but at least she was managing to speak, and it was true that she never had thanked him properly.

'Thank me for introducing you to Vivienne – and Angel?' Tor said, his mouth twisting into a rueful smile. 'That was a mistake of mine.'

Christine's whole body heated up with a mixture of embarrassment, delight and anger. How dare he talk like this, make her feel this way, when he was totally unavailable for anything serious? Even if he did eventually leave his wife, he would be off-limits to Christine forever. A married man who could convince a woman that he was truly interested in her was much too dangerous to date.

'You lose 'em the way you got 'em,' one of the girls at the foster home with her had once snapped at Christine, when she guiltily confessed her interest in a boy at school who already had a girlfriend. Christine had known exactly what she meant. Her decision to go out with Angel and yield to his insistent courtship had been partly motivated by the strength of the impression Tor had made on her – the need to block out thoughts of him by putting another man in the place she would have liked him to be. The girl at the foster home hadn't said 'The best way to get over one man is get under another' – that had been someone on her gemmology course – but it was equally good advice.

Only, clearly, it hadn't completely worked. Christine stared at Tor, unable to summon up anything to say that wasn't as aggressive as 'How's your wife?', while he continued:

'You left Sweden so fast! I did understand, of course. I'm happy it worked out so well with you and Vivienne. You must have done a really good job of convincing her to go with your company.'

Christine nodded silently.

'I thought you might leave a note for me, though,' he said, and now he had the nerve to look downright reproachful. 'With hotel reception, saying how to contact you. I made them check again and again. I thought you must have left something for me and they lost it. And then I rang your auction house, and I left messages on your answering machine. But you never returned them.'

He reached up and ran a hand through his hair, a restless gesture that caused bits of it to stand up oddly, dislodged from the style into which he had painstakingly combed it.

'I know that Angel is a very handsome man,' he said simply. 'I see that any woman would like him, and I'm not saying that you owe me anything. I was happy to introduce you to Vivienne. There is no obligation, nothing like that. But I would have liked a phone number for you. A chance to see you again, visit you in London, make you laugh some more. Sing you some more songs about Russian sailors.'

Christine had heard enough. '*You should sing those to your wife!*' she hissed at him, driven to distraction by the way he was pretending to be just a nice guy she'd dumped the second a gorgeous millionaire hove into view. Not only that – he was daring to do this in a public place, surrounded by people, impeding her from screaming insults at him and slapping his face for this brain-fuck mental manipulation he was trying to pull on her.

'What?'

Tor's eyes widened, becoming almost circular, white showing all around the irises. It was funny; he looked positively clownlike. Christine would have laughed if she hadn't been so incensed by what he was trying to get away with – trying to make *her* feel guilty, when he was the married one.

'Your *wife!*' she said, her voice rising now. 'Tell it to your *wife!*'

One big hand closed around her elbow – gently, but firmly enough that when he turned her around and propelled her with him across the room, towards the balcony, it was impossible not to follow. It was weird; if he had been gripping her arm, she would have thrown him off, but being held by the elbow felt somehow as if he were guiding her to a place that she wanted to reach. And she had to admit, she *did* want to get to that place, the one where he actually had some sort of explanation for what he was trying to sell her . . .

'Okay, you are right. I am married,' he said, once they were outside in the cool fresh evening air. The lights of the bridges over the Thames were glittering below them: boats gliding past, dinner cruises, the Thames Clipper, little tugboats, marine police, all lit up like Vivienne's jewels cast onto the rippled grey velvet of the water. The terrace was cleverly designed, with a high glass windbreak and long narrow tables on which guests could set their drinks and ashtrays. Tor moved along inexorably to the far end, nodding at the glamorous guests smoking and drinking, the TV presenters, the actors who supported the charity, the rent-a-celebs who would turn up anywhere for free drinks and whose famous faces would guarantee coverage of Cut Out Cancer's event in the papers tomorrow.

'I *am* married,' he repeated as they reached the far end.

Christine wouldn't look at him. Instead, she stared out through the sheet of glass at the far end, watching Blackfriars Bridge as an overground train stopped at the platform in the centre of the span, tiny people getting on and off. Christine wished she were at the station, heading home. Yes, she'd be alone, her head spinning with misery and anger and confusion, but at least she'd be avoiding this horribly awkward conversation. Tor was clearly about to try to convince her that his being married wasn't a big deal, that his wife didn't understand him . . .

'But we have been separated for a year and a half,' he added. Christine was staring at her own reflection in the glass, but now her eyes flickered sideways to Tor's, by her side, his coppery hair glinting in the sunshine like a coronet. She watched his face intently as he continued: 'My wife has a new boyfriend. She's pregnant with his baby. So you see, yes, it is the truth that I am married – but things are not so simple as that sounds.'

Christine was still not ready to look at him directly.

'Eva lives in Halmstad,' he said. 'It's where we come from. She's a small-town girl – she never wanted to travel much or see the world. We were together from school, and though my father and mother tried to tell me it was too early, we loved each other and wanted to get married young.

'We were very happy for a while, but then I started to be away more and more. I got a job with a sportswear company, I built up their promotions with all sorts of crazy stunts

– jumping off cliffs, things you do in your twenties when you're young and stupid – and then I was asked to go on expeditions to promote the company. Soon, this turned into a job planning and leading them. I was away more and more, and Eva hated that. Neither of us would change for the other, and that was okay, you know? We're the people we were supposed to be. But we were scared to admit it . . . until one day I came back from a trip after a couple of months and she told me she was in love with a guy she worked with, and I thought: "Yes, that's right. That's what should happen. She should be with Bo. He's a nice guy and he'll be better for her than I am."'

He shrugged.

'Eva pretty much moved out the day after that. I'm happy for them. We sorted it out fine – no one was in a big hurry to get the divorce papers organized, and I was travelling so much, it was difficult to manage things. But now she's pregnant, we have to get on with it.'

Christine felt suddenly wobbly, all tension dissolved. She turned round slowly, resting one hand on the table beside her. She realized that she believed every word Tor was saying. Why would he bother to concoct such an elaborate explanation, when it could so easily be disproved? Everything was on the internet nowadays. The only reason he might have for lying to her was if he wanted to get her into bed tonight, before she had a chance to Google him and find out the truth; but he hadn't tried to rush her in Sweden, and he wasn't doing it now. If he were, he would be paying her more compliments, maybe putting his arms around her. But Tor was just standing there, telling her his story – no pressure at all.

'Okay,' she said, still confused about the ramifications of this information, but wanting to show him that she accepted his story.

'I understand why you wouldn't leave me a phone number now,' Tor said, 'and why you didn't return my messages. But what I don't see is who told you – *Oh.*'

He cleared his throat.

'So. Angel told you I was married,' he said. 'Well. English people say all's fair in love and war, but—'

'No, it wasn't Angel!' Christine blurted out. He was her boyfriend, after all, bizarre though this situation was rapidly becoming, and he had never said a bad word about Tor; she felt compelled to defend his reputation.

Tor frowned in confusion.

'Not Angel? But—'

'It was Vivienne,' she admitted.

That was all Christine was going to say. She certainly had no intention of telling Tor that Vivienne had not only misled Christine about the truth of Tor's marital status, but deliberately informed her that Tor was a playboy who would never be content with just one woman. It wasn't just that Vivienne was his godmother; Christine was aware that the career opportunity of a lifetime was tangled up in this. If Tor were to confront Vivienne about lying to Christine – because as he stood in front of her, those clear blue eyes fixed on hers, it was impossible for her to credit Vivienne's description of him as promiscuous by nature – Vivienne might withdraw her insistence that Christine be the person at Berkeley to run the jewellery auction.

Having spent a good portion of the last month and a half

by Vivienne's side, Christine knew that Vivienne was by no means a compulsive liar. Clearly, the reason she had misled Christine about Tor was so that Christine would drop any interest in him and consider going out with Angel, mystifying though it was that Vivienne would care about that. But until the auction was done and dusted, Christine would have to be very careful not to jeopardize her big break.

'*Vivienne?* But why would she do that?' Tor exclaimed, thunderstruck. He showed all his emotions so transparently. It was impossible, in his presence, to believe he was a master manipulator.

'Please, you can't say anything to her,' Christine said hastily. 'I'm in the middle of the build-up to the auction – we have major buyers in town, and they'll be meeting Vivienne if everything goes well –'

She glanced over at Lil' Biscuit and Silantra, who were now on the balcony together with Prince Toby and Princess Sophie, who had come outside to smoke. Angel and Nicole were by their side; it was an intimate, cosy little group.

'No, no, of course not,' Tor said, frowning deeply. 'But still – she is my godmother! So she knows very well that Eva and I are divorcing, about the baby she is having with Bo . . .'

He stopped, a thought having struck him.

'Ah,' he said. 'So.' His hand went up to ruffle his hair some more. 'So,' he repeated. 'I think that my godmother decided that it was time for Angel to find a girlfriend, and she thought that you would be good for him.'

He nodded, confirming the theory to himself.

'I am very fond of Vivienne, but I must be honest and say that she is the kind of person who thinks about herself first

– and second. And maybe also third. You know that she had an affair with my grandfather, long ago? Well, sometimes she would get bored, and come back to Tylösand, and start things up again. He could never say no to her, and it made my grandmother very unhappy. And then she would leave after a few days, and my grandfather and grandmother would have to pick up the pieces. Of course, it was my grandfather's fault too. My father would talk to me about it, just a little. He would say that once you have made a choice of a woman, you should not behave as my grandfather did. But, you know, she is Vivienne Winter, and it was difficult to resist. My mother would say there are lots of other men in the world, ones who aren't married. I agree with her.'

He pulled a face.

'It was difficult. My grandfather is dead now. My grandmother and he had many happy years at the end, and when Vivienne would come to the hotel, it would just be tea he would be invited to, nothing else. Still, he would go, always. And my grandmother was not so okay about that. Difficult, as I said.'

Christine believed this. It was impossible to spend time with Vivienne without noticing that her wonderful reminiscences were seen entirely through her own lens. Vivienne was superbly entertaining, full of saucy observations, deliciously frank; but the one thing missing from all her anecdotes was empathy for anyone but herself.

'Vivienne is used to getting what she wants,' Tor added. 'If she wanted you for Angel, she would not hesitate to – well, bend the truth.'

'I was thinking the same thing. But why would she choose

me?' Christine said, genuinely taken aback. 'I'm just a normal person. I mean, look who Angel hangs out with!'

She gestured over to Princess Sophie, most of her long, slim body exposed by her tiny Pucci minidress, and Nicole in her glossy, chic glory, sleek black hair like a sheet of silk down the back of the peach suede dress, her limbs glowing with gold-flecked dry oil.

'Why wouldn't she want him to date one of *those* girls?' she questioned. 'I mean, he's been out with Princess Sophie!'

'Oh, I know Sophie a bit,' Tor said, with a little smile. 'She is a nice girl under all the silliness. But she is not the kind of girl you want for your grandson, not yet. There is still too much . . . silliness. You – you are a grown-up with a job, not a spoilt rich girl with a trust fund. I could tell that as soon as we started talking about your work. I know those women, and many more like them. They don't have careers. They marry well, and they do it often. I understand completely that when Vivienne talked to you, and she saw that Angel liked you – because I noticed how he looked at you, it was obvious at once – she would think that here was a woman who would be good for him.'

He searched for a way of summing up, and found it.

'You are a serious person. Even though you like to dance on beaches.'

'I wasn't *dancing*!' Christine cringed, even though she couldn't help giggling at this. 'I was making shapes!'

'It did look quite a lot like dancing,' Tor said.

She giggled again, and it wasn't because he was teasing her. The energy between them was so intense now that it was making her nervous.

'Tor,' she began, and instantly he said: 'Yes, Christine?' and took a step towards her, which didn't help things at all. The breeze had picked up. She could feel it on the back of her neck, cooling her down, and she was hugely grateful for it, as she was sure the blood was rising in her cheeks. Tor's cheeks were growing redder, too; and above the crisp white shirt collar, his carefully shaved neck was coming out in blotches. She wasn't the only one here who was nervous.

She shouldn't have said his name. There was a special power invoked when you called someone by their name, to their face; it intimated that the message you were sending was going to be important. You used it when you were telling someone off, breaking up with them; being – well, as Tor would put it, serious.

And as Christine was aware, this was probably the worst place in the world for this conversation. They might be in a little enclave at the end of the balcony, but they were fully visible to everyone inside the Rumpus Room through the floor-to-ceiling glass wall. Additionally, Christine's boyfriend was at the other end of the balcony, not in the kind of compromising *tête-à-tête* in which she found herself, but in a large and friendly group. Her boyfriend – who also happened to be the beloved grandson of the woman who was responsible for the stratospheric rise in Christine's career, and who was clearly invested in seeing Christine and Angel as a couple.

She took a step back, her shoulders pressing against the glass behind her.

'This isn't the time,' she said. 'I can't. I have to make the auction happen. You know how much it means to me.'

'Of course,' he said instantly. 'Yes, I understand.'

He rubbed his neck with his fingers; the blotches were still growing.

'And you have the expedition – with Angel –'

'Yes, with Angel,' Tor agreed, and there was a certain light in his eyes that made Christine feel that Tor was thinking that when they were both up a mountain in the Andes, he would know, at least, that Angel was not in bed with Christine.

'Well, hello, you two! Should I be jealous?' came Angel's light tenor voice, and his gold curls gleamed in the light of the setting sun as he appeared at Tor's side – taller, more slender, and even more blindingly beautiful by contrast with the craggy-jawed Tor.

'What *have* you two been gossiping about all this time?' he asked. 'Let me guess – me? Tor thinks I'm going to be a terrible liability to him on this expedition!'

He flashed his most charming smile as he lightly took hold of Tor's shoulders, turned him to one side, and slid past to wind his arm around Christine's waist.

'No need to worry about me, though, Tor,' he said, still smiling. 'I've been training like a positive Olympian this last month, haven't I?'

'You have.' Tor nodded. 'I've been impressed.'

'I know you only agreed to take me on because Granny Viv made an *enormous* donation,' Angel said airily. 'But I'm going to be a tremendous asset to the team, I promise. I won't try to do more than I realistically can. I'm sure there'll be some days when you and Toby will be all gung-ho – you're all so *very* fit after going to the North Pole, or was it the South? – and I'll have to go off for training walks by myself rather than make the rest of you hoick me up mountains and down crevasses . . .'

Angel's desire to join Tor's expedition, which he had announced a month ago, had taken everyone aback. Angel's explanation was that a friend of his had been diagnosed with cancer, gone through treatment and been declared in remission, and that Angel was so relieved by the news that he had spontaneously decided to participate in the Climb Against Cancer, bought in by a large donation from Vivienne.

It had not been easy for him to convince Vivienne to help with this; she would much rather have had him safely at home, recuperating from the after-effects of his 'radiation treatments'. But Angel had begged her for the contribution to the charity, saying that he felt morally obliged to help out after his illness, and promised her that his doctor had not only cleared him to be active, but commented that exercise, plus the clean mountain air, might be very beneficial to his recovery. He'd be careful, he promised his worried grandmother. He would not engage in any of the more extreme challenges. But he genuinely felt that being a part of the big fundraising expedition would be such a positive act that it would kick-start his recovery, psychologically as well as physically. Angel was sure, he told Vivienne, that he would return healthier than he had ever been, ready to start a family with his waiting girlfriend, and he had been so persuasive that Vivienne had reluctantly conceded.

Christine had been very moved by Angel's story, which she had naturally accepted at face value, as had Tor; Angel was certainly gung-ho about heading off with the expedition. It had made her deeply impressed with Angel, that he would throw himself into such exhaustive training with very short notice to pay some kind of debt to the universe on his friend's behalf.

Angel had been nothing but enthusiastic and positive about the challenge ahead of him. He had been working out with a personal trainer and with Tor. When he wasn't in the gym, or eating the five carefully planned, high-protein, slow-release-carbohydrate daily meals designed for him by the expedition nutritionist, he was sleeping.

He couldn't drink, and he had hardly any energy left over for sex – a first, he had told her. They talked on the phone, but spent very little time together. Christine had been surprised by how disappointed that had made her. Angel's company was nothing short of dazzling: constantly entertaining, constantly stimulating, always taking her by surprise.

And although Christine was perpetually wary about what was, as it were, coming next sexually, dating Angel was such a thrill ride that she craved him when he was absent. He was the risky, dangerous bad boy that you knew you shouldn't get serious about, because he would never stay; he'd tie you up, do all sorts of shocking things to you, make you beg and plead for more, and then disappear. But the twist in the tale was that Angel *was* staying. He called her his girlfriend. Christine had been mentioned in the gossip columns, the *Evening Standard*, the *Mail*, the *Tatler*, as his latest conquest. It was as official as it could possibly be; Vivienne had already mentioned Christine spending Christmas with them in Geneva.

From calling him a peacock, Christine's colleague Nathan had moved, grudgingly, to talking about Angel as a unicorn, the mythical creature in whose existence so many women wanted to believe: the romance novel hero who reformed his wild playboy ways for the sake of a nice woman. How could she possibly resist that?

Angel ran a hand through Christine's hair, turning her face to his so that he could drop a kiss on her lips.

'My poor darling,' he said, his fingers caressing her cheek, straying down to the sensitive place on her neck that he knew by now sent a shiver through her entire body, touched a string that pulled up right between her legs. 'I've been neglecting you horribly with all this expedition training! But it won't be much longer. We're back in a few weeks, and then I'm going to whisk you away for a long weekend. Granny Viv and Berkeley can surely spare you for that long! Venice, maybe, or Capri. Somewhere really romantic, where we don't have to see anyone but room service waiters for the entire time . . . wouldn't that be wonderful? Maybe even Tylösand! That would be rather lovely, wouldn't it? To go back to where we met?'

Even as Angel was stroking Christine, making her body respond to him with his expert touch, he was talking to her but looking at Tor, a little smile on his perfectly shaped lips as he taunted Tor with the mention of his home town. And even as Christine tried not to close her eyes in pleasure at the feel of Angel's hands on her, knowing that if he wanted to take her into a bathroom now and push her up against the wall and lift her skirt, she would let him – more than that, would pull up her skirt herself, undo his trousers, pull out his cock – she was still intensely aware of Tor so close to her, so attractive in such a different way from the man who had his arm around her waist now, his fingers tracing her jawline.

Her body was hot, melting, and more confused than it had ever been. She didn't know who she wanted. No, that was a lie; she wanted both of them. She raised her eyes to Tor's face and saw his mouth twist, his jaw set hard as he turned away from her and Angel, walking over to greet a group of sponsors who were chatting further down the balcony. For a moment, she imagined herself naked with both Tor and Angel, taking both of them at once; that made her even hotter, even more confused, and she found herself turning to Angel, hugging him, mainly to press her face into his shoulder and hide it from anyone who might be looking over at her.

'I *have* been neglecting you,' Angel murmured into her ear, biting and licking it, his breath deliciously hot and stimulating. 'What a terrible boyfriend I am! And darling, I can't see to your needs tonight! I have to get some rest before leaving tomorrow. I'm so sorry. Will you take care of yourself tonight? Fuck yourself silly with your Rabbit and think of me while you're doing it?'

Christine mumbled a yes, even while the image of Angel and Tor naked having sex with her consumed her imagination.

Work, she told herself, taking a deep breath, trying to recover some composure. *I'll concentrate on work until the auction. It's good that Angel's going away – it gives me even more time to focus. I have a major negotiation with Lil' Biscuit and Silantra tomorrow! I need to get my sleep to be fresh for that . . .*

She had no idea, of course, that Angel's plans that evening did not involve getting an early night before the flight to La Paz the next day; instead, he and Nicole would be engaging in a lively threesome with Silantra, ensuring that she was in the best of all possible moods for the meeting with Christine at Berkeley. Swiftly, Angel speculated whether it was safe to leave Christine alone that evening, considering the interest that Tor was still showing in her. He was ridiculously persistent, annoyingly so. Tor and Christine had only met each other once, yet the chemistry was evident: Angel had seen them talking to each other on the balcony, and instantly seen what was going on. They were like two magnets trying to snap together, prevented by a force field. Tor had been almost vibrating with yearning to reach out and take her in his arms.

It made Christine even more attractive to Angel. There was a specific and consuming pleasure to fucking a woman who was desired by a man one intensely disliked. Angel actually wished he didn't have a prior engagement with Silantra and Nicole: how he would have enjoyed spending the night with Christine, looking down at her as she deep-throated him, just as he had taught her; once he'd shot his load and she'd licked him clean, he'd eat her out in turn, oil her up and slide a string of anal beads inside her, pulling them out slowly as he made her come.

And with the other hand, just as she was coming hard, he'd reach up, catch one pink pointed nipple and pinch it hard enough to make her scream. He knew that the pain was no delightful extra for her, that she accepted it only because the pleasure was so intense, and that gave him even more of a thrill – the delight of constantly forcing something on her that she didn't want.

Nicole didn't understand why he was still enjoying sex with Christine so much: well, this was why. Never before

had he had a regular partner who did not share his predilec-
tion for mixing pain with pleasure, but found the pleasure
so intense that she accepted the pain as the price she had to
pay for it. How much he could make Christine take, how
far he could push her, were questions he was pursuing with
the utmost enthusiasm.

Would she eventually stop protesting at the marks he
delighted in leaving on her in return for the flood of orgasms,
the thrill of not knowing what his clever fingers would do
to her next? Nearly two months in, he still relished the frisson
of seeing those big blue eyes widen in surprise when he hurt
her and made her come simultaneously, the freckles stand
out on the bridge of her nose, the flush in her cheeks, the
O her pink lips made as he pinched her and fucked her and
made her scream.

Leaning over, he whispered to her what he would have
planned for them that evening, if he could, and watched as
her nipples hardened under her dress, visible even though
she was wearing a bra – *unlike Silantra and Nicole, those
filthy sluts*, he thought, his cock in a pleasant state of engorge-
ment for all three women. He knew Christine wasn't in love
with him, but he couldn't have cared less. It was enough that
she was mesmerized by him. She might not love him, but
she wouldn't leave him, not unless he let her.

And he wouldn't let her. Vivienne's promises of huge
financial bonuses for the wedding and births of the children
were very compelling. Angel, naturally, had an ulterior
motive for joining Tor's expedition – one that had nothing
to do with cancer, and everything to do with a financial
emergency that not only required his presence in that part

of the world, but a plausible cover story to explain it. God only knew whether the emergency would be resolved; even if Angel managed to pull off the whole tricky business, most of the monetary return was already earmarked to settle his gambling debts.

So he needed to have his trust fund fully reinstated, plus every penny of those promised lump sums from Vivienne. What else did his grandmother have to spend it on, after all? She wouldn't be amassing more jewellery, and her business empires were still bringing in a huge income.

Besides, by marrying and knocking up Christine, he would drive Tor insane with frustration and jealousy. Big, muscly Tor with his tight buttocks and his sweet nature! How Angel would enjoy watching Tor's reactions at Angel and Christine's wedding, when Tor saw Christine swelling up with Angel's baby, holding it in her arms! He would be able to torture Tor with this for years to come. Poor Tor was the opposite of Angel, a serial monogamist who needed to be in love to have sex with someone. Tor had been with his childhood sweetheart for donkey's years, and now he was plainly nursing a huge crush on Christine.

Which makes her extra-precious to me, Angel thought, finishing up his stream of sex talk to Christine, having reduced her to a near-puddle of frustrated desire. *But I'll have to keep her away from Tor until I've sealed the deal. She likes him too much, and he's much more suited to her than I am. Two nice vanilla people just longing to settle down and get married and bake cookies together in a house with a white picket fence while never having sex with anyone else for the rest of their lives. God, I feel sick at the mere idea . . .*

Angel would propose, he decided, on his return from the Andes as a triumphant, cancer-fighting action hero; sweep Christine off her feet, get Vivienne to lavish her with attention, turn the screw so that she didn't feel she could say no. It would be a new game, keeping a woman who wasn't in love with him and who was half-yearning for a man Angel loathed. A game, Angel realized, that he could play for years with Christine and Tor as the main pieces, and his and Christine's children as the pawns. What fun he was going to have!

Sighing with happiness, Angel planted a kiss on Christine's head.

'Darling,' he said, reaching for a cigarette with his free hand. 'I am literally going to count the hours till I get back from the Andes and can see you again, I tell you. We are going to have the most *amazing* reunion. Think of me, celibate for all that time! Can you *imagine* the head of steam I'll have built up for you? My God, I won't let you out of bed for days!'

He felt her tremble in his arms, and smiled triumphantly over her head at Tor, who, though now talking to Prince Toby, had been unable to resist a glance back at Angel and Christine. Angel raised the hand clasping the cigarette packet and waved it at Tor, rather regally.

Goodness, I have a long to-do list, he reflected. *Pay my gambling debts, propose to Christine, snag a mansion from Granny Viv, grab the marriage bonus as well as half the finder's fee from Lil' Biscuit and Silantra – oh, and the no-doubt hefty sum the gossip magazines will pay for exclusive photo shoots and interviews of our engagement and wedding . . . and I'll get Granny Viv to set me up with some promotional job at her foundation so I can travel a lot, avoid spending more time than I have to with my wife, ensure I get plenty of fun on the side . . .*

It wasn't exactly how he had pictured the next few years of his life. But after all, he had been rather in a rut, hadn't he? This new game plan presented him with a whole range of interesting challenges. And Angel did dearly love a challenge.

Chapter Fifteen

The Andes – two weeks later

The two men wrestling on the edge of the snowy clifftop were fighting for their lives. Their grunts of exertion were audible and with each one, a puff of breath formed in the ice-cold air: hot, brief clouds that were testimony to both the sub-zero temperature and the intensity of their struggle.

It could have been the climax of an action film. They both had film-star good looks, though in very different styles: one was lean and taut, the other stockier and solidly muscled. Each was trying to get a grip on the other's Arctic parka, but their hands, encased in windproof gloves, kept sliding off the slippery fabric as they battled for supremacy. Their protective face masks were pulled back, revealing their grimaces of concentration as they grappled clumsily, both acutely aware of how near they were to the brink of the mountain and the lethal drop directly below.

The more heavyset man was wearing wolfskin gloves, and that advantage finally enabled him to grab the other by the padded collar of his parka and hold on for dear life. Both hands dug in with great strength, the rough animal pelt clinging to the fur trim of the collar. He forced his opponent to look at him as he yelled into his face:

'What the hell are you doing, you idiot? You're going to get us both killed!'

The speaker's features were craggy and strong. His eyes were a piercing bright blue, as light and clear as the sky above them, which seemed almost bleached by the reflection of the snow-covered peaks of the Andes mountain range. His square chin was covered by a magnificently thick coppery beard worthy of a Viking or a Tudor monarch, the sunlight glinting off the rose-gold hairs, his forehead corrugated in disbelief as he shook his adversary, head tilted back a little to look up at him.

'Oh, no!' the taller man said lightly. 'Not *both* of us.'

He was dazzlingly beautiful, his face, as striking as a Michelangelo marble statue, framed in a cluster of curls, with a classically straight nose above a full, pouting mouth. His pale cheeks were flushed with exertion but his eyes were dancing with excitement; he seemed somehow to be enjoying the adrenalin rush of this life-and-death struggle, even as a bruise started to blossom on one of his high cheekbones. Although he, too, was sporting a beard, it was much lighter than the other man's, as if the lower part of his face were dusted with gilt.

The Viking shot a glance down at the icy ground on which they were standing, perilously close to the brink. Below it was the fissure of a jagged crevasse hundreds of feet deep, rocky outcrops tumbling down its side as if frozen in place by the heavy covering of ice, myriad blades pointed upwards to impale anyone unlucky enough to fall over the edge.

'That's crazy,' he said, frowning even more deeply. 'Are you on that stuff of yours? You're talking like a madman. Let's both take a big step back, okay?'

He jerked his head behind him, indicating the relative safety of a rock-strewn plateau. Relative to their present position it was a suntrap, the ice much less thick there. Clearly he was calculating that even if the fight continued beyond this standoff, a fall from the plateau would not be life-threatening.

'Spoilsport,' the Michelangelo statue said; but he acquiesced, letting the Viking guide him, still gripping his collar, a couple of steps back. The copper-bearded man let out a long, slow breath of relief as, their parkas brushing closely together, moving slowly in their heavy, snow-crusted boots as they found purchase on the stony, ice-covered ground, they inched away from the killer drop.

'Okay,' the Viking said, letting his hands fall, his expression still serious. 'So we need to—'

But he never finished his sentence. As soon as his grip loosened, the Michelangelo, in one swift, elegant movement, dropped to one knee and immediately rose again, now with something in his hand. He might have been a dancer, so smooth and choreographed was the flow of his body. His back heel anchored into the ground, simultaneously pushing back and driving him up again in one long line that ran right up his legs to his torso, twisting now, the motion pushing to his arm, which whipped out in a tightly controlled gesture. It all happened so fast that the other man barely had time to grimace in disbelief, his words dying on his lips as the fist-sized stone the Michelangelo had picked up from the plateau floor crashed into his opponent's left temple.

It connected with an audible smash of rock against bone. The copper-bearded man staggered, his fur-lined hood tumbling back from his face. But he was as tough as an ox – or the Viking he resembled – and managed to stay on his feet, his legs spread wide, even as one hand rose to his forehead and came away wet with blood. He roared in anger, surging towards the Michelangelo, his wide shoulders ducked to charge him.

The lighter, faster man, a matador to his opponent's bull, held his ground until the last possible second and then sidestepped, dancing onto one foot, raising the other to plant the sole of his boot into the Viking's side, kicking him with all his force to send him reeling off balance. As the Viking, arms outstretched to try to save himself, hit the ground, the Michelangelo narrowed his beautiful eyes in swift, lethal assessment – and then, with an overhand throw, flung the rock he still held against the now-bare and vulnerable coppery head.

The Viking went down under the blow, his forehead striking the stone ground. Either that impact, or the rock to the back of his head, knocked him out. He was motionless, his big square body limp inside its insulating layers of wool and down and Gore-Tex, unable to defend himself further.

'I *did* say "not both of us"', Angel observed to the lone condor that was riding the thermals, wings outspread to a magnificent three-metre span, soaring above the peaks across the wide crevasse. 'Is it my fault he couldn't listen properly?'

He waited, however, a good minute more, ducking over to observe the blood trickling from Tor's forehead and clotting in the thick red-gold thatch of hair at the back of his head. He was extremely cautious, wanting to be absolutely sure that that Tor wasn't faking unconsciousness, setting a trap for Angel to come close so that he could take him off guard, regain the advantage, grab an ankle and send Angel twisting off balance.

But the blood continued to flow, and Tor stayed exactly where he was, his head at an angle on the stones. Finally, warily, Angel stepped forward and shoved the body with his foot, rolling it closer to the precipice. It was heavy, a dead weight, but it yielded under a firm push. Emboldened, Angel gave another shove, grunting with the effort, and then another, until finally he bent down and slid one gloved hand under Tor's back, the other under his solid buttocks, clad in windproof trousers.

Slowly and carefully, because of the slippery fabric, he tipped the body away from him, turning it on its side over the last few rocks, then onto its face, rolling Tor like a carpet closer and closer to the edge of the mountain. Eventually, with a last big grunt of exertion, he heaved Tor's still-breathing body over the edge of the cliff. His abdominals clenched, controlling the movement with every bit of his strength to ensure that the effort of tipping the body into the crevasse didn't send him over with it, too.

Angel expected to hear a crash of some sort, a solid *thunk* as bone and muscle and thick clothing layers smashed onto the jutting rocks below – but no sound came. Kneeling on the icy brink, he craned his head over and saw the body shooting away down a fissure in the rock, as fast as if it were travelling down a long ice slide. He smiled in pleasure, aware that the eventual impact would be even more devastating when it came.

'Enjoy the ride,' he observed. 'That's really *quite* the ski jump.'

He stood up, dusting the snow off his knees.

That was the trouble with decent chaps, he thought meditatively. They expected everyone else to fight clean. Poor Tor. A stint at Angel's boarding school would have done him a world of good; he'd have learned to get down and dirty with the best of them.

He readjusted his mask, fastening it across his face once more; the wind whipping across the plateau was especially painful with the sweat drying on his cheeks.

Time to retrieve my goodies, now Mr Clean's out of the picture for good, he thought. Behind the mask his smile was radiant now, positively angelic: his lips slightly parted, his eyes dazzling. As he turned and began to carefully clamber down the narrow, rocky trail they had followed from their base camp up to the mountain in search of privacy for their sensitive conversation, he found himself humming a cheerful tune:

'*He'll be coming down the mountain when he comes, he'll be coming down the mountain when he comes . . .*'

It took him a few moments to realize not only why that particular song had popped into his head, but that he had unconsciously modified the words; when he did, the smile of pleasure behind his face mask was positively devilish. He was on top of the world, literally and figuratively.

Angel's plan, when he'd embarked on this expedition, had never been to kill Tor. That had been mere collateral damage

– entirely Tor's own fault for poking his nose in where he didn't belong. However, once Angel had concluded that he would be obliged to push Tor off a cliff, there was absolutely no task in life that he could have enjoyed more. He would freely admit that watching Tor's unconscious body tip over the icy edge and slide away down the steep, rock-strewn slope had been one of the most pleasurable experiences of his life so far.

Who's best at outdoor games now, Tor? he thought happily. *It's all very well to train by pulling tyres around all day long on ropes like some stupid macho man, but those big muscles didn't help you in the end, did they?*

To be fair, though, Angel had to acknowledge that he had had a significant advantage. Tor had not realized until the very last moments that he was truly fighting for his life.

What a fool, Angel reflected. *Really, what a total idiot. Didn't he realize how vitally important this was to me?*

But then, Angel too had been a fool, he had to acknowledge. He had been both complacent and smug. He had underestimated his opponent, failed to realize that Tor had become suspicious of Angel's motives for joining the charity expedition. It had been such a stroke of luck that this was the area to which the trek was headed that perhaps Angel had been too careless, too buoyed up by his good fortune.

Six weeks earlier, the news had reached Angel in London that the prop plane carrying a shipment of pure cocaine in which Angel had invested a great deal of money had gone missing shortly after taking off from a discreetly located Bolivian airstrip. No one knew what had caused the plane to crash onto an Andean peak, where it had eventually been located via GPS tracking. Its pilot and co-pilot had probably died on impact; there had been no radio contact from them. Satellite images showed, however, that the body of the aircraft was intact, and since the peak was very high and no one was looking for the plane but the members of the syndicate who had organized the flight, the neatly wrapped bricks of pure cocaine would, hopefully, be safe for a little while, until plans could be made for their retrieval.

The original intention had been for the plane to land and unload its precious cargo on the small island of Curaçao, just off the Venezuelan coast. There the bricks of cocaine would be packed into a shipping container, boxed up with a large quantity of loose ground coffee to confuse any sniffer dogs, and loaded onto a cargo ship bound for Liverpool. It was a familiar route. Certain authorities at both the airstrip and port of Curaçao were used to turning a blind eye to this particular traffic, and although Liverpool could be more problematic, the sheer volume of shipping containers travelling through its docks meant that the risk of detection was fairly minimal.

Unfortunately, the plane crash had derailed these well-laid plans. It was impossible to carry the coke bricks overland back to the airstrip to start again with another plane; the route was far too dangerous, as most of it lay in a rival syndicate's territory. Angel, who had invested in these shipments successfully in the past, had a great deal at stake with this one. The plan was for him to turn over the entire stack of coke to the casino with which he had huge gambling debts: they would pay off the other investors, cover the full balance of Angel's debts, and give him a credit balance for many future hands of blackjack and poker.

So Angel had decided that he was going to bring back the cocaine himself. He had come up with the ideal solution: he would tag on to Tor's upcoming expedition to the area, providing him with the perfect cover to retrieve the precious goods. There was so much equipment in the camp that, with judicious bribes to a couple of expedition staff, Angel could easily conceal all the coke in extra duffle bags labelled with his name. Camouflaged as climbing gear, the bags would be shipped back to the UK along with everything else at the end of the trek. Customs at either end were bound to wave it all through; what could be more respectable than an expedition for a cancer charity in which Prince Toby of Great Britain and the internationally famous action star Missy Jackson were participating?

Unfortunately, Tor had turned out not to be quite as oblivious to Angel's manoeuvres as Angel had assumed he would be. Angel had calculated that Tor would be completely absorbed by organizing the various races and climbs – but Tor must have had some brains to go with all that brawn. Angel's frequent sorties from their various camps, to liaise with the Bolivian locals in the pay of the drug barons who had located the crashed plane, had not gone unnoticed.

It had been such a simple and effective strategy! The Bolivians had unloaded the coke from the plane onto a mule train, and, knowing the mountains extremely well, tracked the progress of Tor's expedition from a safe distance, contacting Angel every day to give the GPS of the latest rendezvous point. Angel had found a daily opportunity to sneak away, carrying the bricks of coke surreptitiously back to camp and concealing them among his climbing gear.

Clearly, however, Angel had been so flushed with success that he had grown sloppy. In the first few days he had been extremely careful to ensure no one saw him leaving camp, but after that he must have let down his guard enough for Tor's suspicions to be aroused. Tor had followed Angel yesterday and seen him with the Bolivian mule handlers, sliding four bricks into his backpack. And Tor was clearly a better actor than Angel would have thought possible, because he had said not a word yesterday. Instead, biding his time, he had waited until Angel sneaked out of camp today, followed him once again and intercepted him on his way to meet the mule train.

Practically the first words out of Tor's mouth had been concern for the reputation of his expedition. He couldn't let it be tarnished by a drug-smuggling scandal – not just for the sake of the charities he supported, but for his long-term sponsors, who would withdraw funding the second a story like this broke in the press. He had, therefore, chosen to lead Angel to a secluded place in order to confront him, a high plateau where they could be sure they would not be overheard by any expedition member.

And that was Tor's big mistake, Angel thought now, a smile playing around his full, rosy lips. *He gave me a peak to push him off. Not only that – nobody saw the two of us together! I can sneak back into camp and eventually act as worried as everyone else when we all begin to realize that Tor's gone missing.*

I mustn't be the first person to notice. That would be much too suspicious. No, I'll wait till several other people are realizing that he isn't around, and get in on the act then.

Now he was humming 'Come Fly with Me', the Sinatra song. The lyrics about floating down to Peru were perfect.

'Who knows?' he speculated aloud. 'Maybe that's where Tor ended up! It's a *long* way down that mountain, he might have bounced off a couple of peaks and landed in Peru . . . "*Once I get you up there, Where the air is rarefied, We'll just glide, Starry-eyed . . .*" Until I push you off, of course! Oh well, all good things must come to an end . . . That's a song too, of course.'

The steep descent needed to be negotiated carefully. Angel's mountaineering boots gripped well, his natural athleticism standing him in good stead as he worked his way down, the face mask pulled back so he could see the crevices his gloved fingers needed to locate and dig into. By the time his feet were back on solid, if icy, ground, he was humming 'Skyfall'.

Music to throw people off mountains to! he thought happily. *I'll make a playlist when I get home in memory of dear departed Tor . . . Hmm, what else could I put on it?*

He mulled the question over on his hike to the location where the mule team was holed up. By the time he reached the clearing, he had assembled a list of songs: 'Free Falling' by Tom Petty, 'Wind Beneath My Wings' by Bette Midler, 'Slip Slidin' Away' by Paul Simon, and 'Push It' by Salt-n-Pepa. Angel had never killed anyone before, and he definitely felt that the event deserved some form of commemoration.

And not just the playlist. I really should have some sort of private Goodbye Tor ceremony every year on this date – throw something off a hilltop in commemoration, while drinking champagne . . .

He was to meet the mule team at the same site where they'd been the day before: a cave twenty minutes' hike from base camp, tucked away in a fold of the mountain, extremely discreet. In the interests of security, they hadn't even lit a camp fire, lest the smoke be spotted by a curious member of the trek. So Angel had no advance notice that once he rounded the clearing, the entrance to the cave gaping dark and dank before him, he would find it empty.

His heart stopped for a moment. This had never happened before. The muleteers had always been one hundred per cent reliable. What could possibly have gone wrong?

Tor! he thought immediately. *Tor's behind this somehow! That bastard got to them first and scared them off!* Although it was just possible that a rival drugs syndicate had discovered the location of the mule train and relieved them of their cargo at gunpoint, it was simply too much of a coincidence that Tor had just confronted Angel about the existence of the cocaine bricks, and now the rest of them had disappeared.

Words Tor had yelled at him on the mountain plateau came back to Angel with heightened significance.

'This stops *now*!' Tor had shouted. 'Trust me, I'm putting an end to it today! It is *over*!'

Clearly, Tor had meant this more literally than Angel had realized. He had already banished the muleteers, doubtless with dire threats. Angel slipped off his glove, pulled out his phone and sent off a text telling them to come back, but he doubted he'd get a response.

God damn him! he thought furiously, his good mood completely dissipated. *That fucking bastard!* He had already retrieved most of the coke, but there had been about fifteen more bricks to take back to camp, and he needed every single one of them.

He'd have to get in touch with the Bolivian contact who had organized the muleteers, and tell him to send them back; and he could scarcely do that by texting him that he'd just shoved his expedition leader off a cliff. So he'd have to concoct some ridiculous story that would be plausible enough to convince the guy. This would be difficult in itself, because he would be furious that Angel had been busted by another expedition member. Yes, his contacts would want to complete the deal, get their product to market; but they were understandably risk-averse. Angel would really have to rack his brains to come up with something that would regain their trust.

Livid, he kicked the wall of the cave so hard that if he hadn't been wearing extremely solid and well-made climbing boots, he would certainly have broken a toe. All thoughts of music to throw people off mountains to were forgotten; Angel's only idea, as he stamped back to camp, cursing with every breath, was that he bitterly regretted not waiting until Tor regained consciousness before kicking and rolling him off the mountain top. He wished Tor had felt every bump, every bone-breaking bounce off the rocks, the terror of the final, fatal impact waiting for him that would pound his body into, hopefully, an unrecognizable, pulpy mess.

Bastard! Damn fucking interfering bastard! I suppose it's too much to hope that he woke up halfway down that gorge, damn him, and realized exactly what was happening . . .

Angel was still simmering with resentment by the time he clambered down the final descent and saw the tents of the base camp, pitched in the lee of a sheltered valley. One goal of this trek was to take the participants on various climbs, reaching personal bests for which each member was individually sponsored; that day Prince Toby and Missy, together with four of the army veterans, were making an ascent, guided by Tor's highly trained team. Tor himself, naturally, had been supposed to lead it, which was why Angel had felt so safe in absenting himself from the camp and slipping away in the opposite direction from the climb. With very little fixed-rope climbing experience, he wasn't expected to complete summits with the rest of them.

No one had returned yet from the day's activities, and the camp was quiet. Angel crossed swiftly to his tent, but even as he reached it, João, one of the guides Angel had been bribing to overlook the growing stash of coke in his tent, came over to intercept him, his face tense and set.

'Angel,' he started, indicating with his head that they should walk back, away from the pitched tents. You never knew who was inside one, able to hear what you were saying. They navigated back over the pegs and guy ropes to a safe distance before João, biting his lip, blurted out: 'Tor went through your stuff when you were having breakfast. I think he took – you know. He carried out a couple of *big* bags. I didn't get a chance to tell you until now – he was watching you, and I just didn't think it was safe to talk – I didn't want him to know I knew what was going on—'

'*What? Fuck!*'

Angel dashed towards his tent, heart pounding. He had to hop, skip and jump over the guy ropes, and as he got there he tripped over a tent peg, bashing into it with the same foot that he'd kicked against the cave wall. This time he did break his toe, but he would only notice that hours later. Then and there, the shock of João's information was overwhelming, all he could think about. He skidded into the tent, fell to his knees in front of his pile of gear and knew immediately that João had been right. Tor had, in one stroke, removed every single brick of coke Angel had painstakingly accumulated during the last few days.

João came in after him, shaking his head as he took in the sight.

'I couldn't do anything,' he said, *sotto voce*.

'Did you see where he went with it?' Angel hissed, turning on João, his face white and his eyes glittering with utter menace.

João gulped. 'Away,' he said unhappily. 'Like, away from camp. And then he came back twenty minutes later and there was nothing in the bags.'

'*And you didn't come and tell me?*' Angel's voice was like a knife now.

'I tried! You were with Prince Toby and Missy and you practically told me to fuck off! And then you sneaked away and I was right over on the other side of camp, so I couldn't get to you in time!' João said. 'I thought Tor was with the climbing group, but I just heard he told them to go ahead without him . . .' He trailed off, backing away defensively from Angel, who looked more like a cornered animal than a human being at that moment, crouching down, teeth bared, eyes wild.

Angel had to acknowledge that what João said was true: João had indeed attempted to lean over and talk to him, and been abruptly told to come back later. Angel had not wanted bothersome interruptions as he sat forking up breakfast stew in a cosy threesome with the prince and Missy, a delightful continuation of the cosy threesome they had enjoyed the night before. Toby had proved disappointingly resistant to any direct physical contact with Angel's genitalia, but there had been more than enough variety to keep the three of them entertained, even with the constrictions of not being able to strip fully because of the icy temperature. The diesel space heater was effective, but outside of the high-tech Rab sleeping bags, which had cost six hundred pounds apiece, it was decidedly chilly, and the participants had only bared the parts of their body that were strictly necessary. Angel and Missy were already planning a rerun, hopefully with royal participation, in the much more congenial surroundings of the hotel in La Paz when they returned there at the end of the expedition.

But even without getting naked, it had been tremendous fun. Missy didn't suck cock with the Dyson-like ability of Nicole, but her rimming technique had been absolutely superb. The expression on Toby's face had been priceless as she made him shoot his load, to his own surprise, much sooner than he had expected, with an unexpected couple of nicely placed fingers up his arse. And if Angel hadn't actually managed to touch Toby's cock or have Toby touch his, he had at least managed to position himself so that he got royal sperm all over his face. Which was certainly, as he had joked to Missy afterwards, one to tell the grandchildren.

Just a few hours ago, he reflected bitterly, everything had been so perfect! Angel and Missy had been plotting for days to seduce Toby into Missy's tent for some unorthodox fun, and had finally managed it, to their great satisfaction.

Rumours about Toby's propensity for group sex had definitely been proved correct. He had barely needed any encouragement at all to double-team a very satisfied Missy. Angel hadn't actually had 'threesome with a royal' on his bucket list, but it was nice to know that he could add it on and then smugly cross it off.

It had all been going so well! Even if Nicole were screwing him on the Silantra and Lil' Biscuit deal, which she surely was – he'd have scored a little extra in her place, too – the amount she had told him was his fifty-fifty cut was a nicely hefty sum. He had been about to rake it in. He had managed to convince his sharp-eyed grandmother that he had thoroughly turned over a new leaf, and that the radiation therapy had treated his cancer effectively; he'd assured Vivienne not only that he had kept it a secret from Christine, but that his fertility had not been compromised.

I'll have to get married the day after I get back to London, just to get my hands on that money from Viv! How else am I going to settle my damn gambling debts?

He stood up.

'Get the fuck out,' he said to João, so harshly that the guide practically ran from the tent. Angel's eyes were still glittering like a feral animal's, his lips drawn back from his teeth.

Jesus fucking God, I'll be lucky if those bastards just break my legs. The amount I owe them, they'll be more likely to throw me out of my own window face first onto the railings below, like that property tycoon who crossed the Russians last year.

He remembered that man all too well: an ex-tycoon who had been caught in a vice, because he was being sued by his ex-wife for millions in child and spousal support. Her lawyers had been digging in precisely the places he didn't want them to look – and that was what had triggered the Russians to shut him down, in case their extremely dodgy deals were exposed in the process.

It had been the main subject of gossip and speculation during the last weeks of the unfortunate man's life, everywhere that mattered: the Mayfair casinos, the private members' clubs like Annabel's and George's. Plus Cipriani and Scott's restaurants – which might as well have been members' clubs, given that their clientele was so exclusive and regular, their best tables allocated only to favoured customers.

The tycoon had been a walking corpse, his face increasingly grey, the meagre hair he had left growing whiter by the day, the lines on his forehead so deep they looked as if they had been made with an etching tool. And there had been plenty of opportunities to watch him disintegrate, because he'd been out every day in one of the most beautiful patches of London, the five-minute walk from Claridge's to Berkeley Square, down Mount Street to South Audley Street. He'd stayed till closing every single night at one or other of the clubs or gambling dens in that area, knowing he was safe in company.

But he'd had to go home sometime. You always did. They'd got him in the end, waited for him in his top-floor flat off Grosvenor Square, staged it to look like a suicide to satisfy the inquest, and sent a clear warning to anyone else that when you did business with the Russians, you didn't call down unwanted publicity on your head.

Angel's breath was coming in spurts of fury, laced with

naked fear. The thought of that short, brutal fall, the iron spikes of the railings coming up fast to meet him in the most terribly medieval of deaths, was scaring him shitless. It was a horrible reflection that Tor's death – sliding down a gorge, unconscious, presumably to die with no awareness of what had happened to him – would be far, far preferable to what was waiting for Angel in London if he didn't come up with a fast way to settle his debts.

Chapter Sixteen

London – the next day

Absorbed as Christine was in her work, the noise in the outer office was loud enough to make her lift her head. Doors banging one after the other, chairs pushed back; it almost sounded like a scuffle, and that was unheard of in the sedate atmosphere of the Berkeley headquarters just off New Bond Street. Christine was expecting the Countess of Rutland, who was scheduled for a mid-morning appointment to view pieces from Vivienne's collection; but the Countess would surely not be causing this kind of commotion.

It was a much-anticipated meeting. To Christine's delight, after she had drunk a ginger and green tea martini at the expedition launch party and steeled herself to go up to the group that comprised Lil' Biscuit, Silantra and the Countess, the latter had been both charming and approachable. Christine had been strategic, greeting Silantra and her husband, mentioning how much she was looking forward to showing them the pieces the next day, which had naturally led to the Countess expressing interest too; as Christine had suspected, her publicist had not let her know about the gem sale.

The Countess had immediately been eager to see the jewels, but had not given any indication about what she might be looking for, which made Christine's task much more difficult. If she had been asked to pull out the tiaras – the Countess certainly dressed glamorously enough at charity balls to be in the market for one of those – or the big necklaces, which she had the stature to carry off, that would have been a start. But the Countess had airily said that she wanted to see everything, and that was problematic, because people always tended to buy more if they were looking at a selection carefully curated for their tastes.

The eye simply became exhausted after viewing too many things, even beautiful ones. It was like eating a ten-course tasting menu: always too much, no matter how perfect the food. By the end, you felt a little sick: you pushed the last plate away, you couldn't finish; you disliked yourself for eating everything, and the restaurant for bringing you all those plates and the matching wine pairings, no matter how excited you had been at the prospect of all that deliciousness a few hours before.

Jewellery, fine art, sculpture: the principle was the same. If the Countess of Rutland really did try to look through the entire contents of the two safes containing Vivienne's jewellery, she would burn out halfway through and possibly end up not buying anything. Christine needed to find a way to pre-select in advance. Having done extensive Google searches for images of the Countess out on the town, she had instructed her assistant to pull the most lavish pieces she could find, with certain stipulations. The Countess tended to wear jewels so large that, like many of Vivienne's, they almost looked fake. Her favourite stones were diamonds, white and pink and yellow. Nothing with a cabochon cut, nothing that wasn't multifaceted. The Countess loved glitter and shine: after all, she had spent years in the beauty pageant world, where less was never, ever more.

And no brooches, Christine had specified. Very few Americans ever understood brooches: they got confused when it was explained to them that they could also wear them as pendants, as central settings for tiaras. European royals were used to jewellery that could function in various different ways, wishing to show their loyal subjects that they weren't being over-extravagant with the money they had amassed from conquest, ruling and intermarriage. There were entire sites online dedicated to the analysis of which royal gems a queen or princess was wearing. What was once a girdle in late-medieval times had morphed into a necklace, the pieces taken out to shrink it down turned into a pair of earrings and a bracelet; diamond drops from a button tiara could be detached and suspended on a chain to be worn around the neck. It never hurt a monarchy to show that it was using its inherited wealth wisely.

But modern Americans, much as they loved the history of their jewels, had absolutely no interest in wearing them flexibly. They wore no sashes across their dresses, unlike royalty at state events, so had no need of brooches to pin to them. Christine was running through the final list for the Countess, who was due in forty minutes, when she heard the commotion outside and realized it was headed towards her. Moments later, to her great surprise, Vivienne Winter herself swept into Christine's office.

As always, Vivienne was impeccably dressed when she left the house, in a silk snake-print blouse and grey pencil skirt that showed off her still excellent legs, her feet shod in suede courts. Over this was thrown a charcoal mohair coat trimmed with dark green ermine, and Vivienne's earrings were pear-shaped emerald drops set in platinum, echoing the green of the fur. Her wig today was a layered long dark bob, her make-up perfect.

Her eyes, however, were stretched wide like a frightened animal's. The black-mascaraed lashes emphasized their unbelievable amethyst colour, but her expression was panicked, her face white under her foundation.

'Christine!' she panted. 'I've just had a phone call! Have you seen the news? Heard anything?'

Gregory, behind her, was also visibly distressed. He was carrying Vivienne's handbag, a grey leather Vuitton that looked surprisingly good with his slim-cut navy suit and Bond Street-slick level of personal grooming.

'What is it?' Christine was on her feet immediately. Something must have happened on the expedition. It hadn't been supposed to be dangerous: it wasn't a trek across the Arctic or an ascent of Mount Everest. But they were climbing mountains, abseiling down cliffs, racing each other for charity challenges. There couldn't help but be dangers in those activities, and just because Angel had been fine on Skype yesterday, laughing with Prince Toby and Missy Jackson as they joined him in chatting to her, that didn't mean he hadn't had a bad fall today . . .

She dashed around her desk to take Vivienne's outstretched hands; the next thing she knew, she was enfolded in a hug, and through the layers of expensive fabric she could feel how frail Vivienne's bones were, how delicate. Vivienne looked so much younger than she was because of the make-up, the wigs, the animal-print shirts and dresses that looked dashing, but whose flowing lines and elaborate prints covered skin that was looser than it once had been. She was a mistress of the little tricks that women of a certain age use to camou-flage their weaker points, tricks that Christine so often noticed with admiration and filed away for future use.

However, with Vivienne's arms wrapped round her, so thin and fragile, her body so light against her, it was impossible to forget that Vivienne was in her seventies. It was a strange contrast, the glamour of Vivienne's signature scent in her nostrils, rose and musk and pepper and orange blossom blended together by an exclusive French parfumier, the expen-sive fur of her cape collar tickling Christine's cheek, and then the delicate, old-lady bones . . .

Christine looked over at Gregory and met his eyes, which were full of concern for his employer. Vivienne was gulping for breath against Christine's shoulder, not exactly crying, but clearly trying very hard not to do so.

'Vivienne . . . is it Angel?' Christine asked, her heart racing. 'Is he all right?'

'It's not Angel!' Vivienne pulled back, fixing Christine with those marvellous eyes. It was surreal to see her in this entirely genuine state of emotion, when Christine had watched her on screen so often acting fear and anguish. It did not make Christine doubt Vivienne's sincerity – instead she felt as if she, Christine, had been whirled into a film in which Vivi-enne was starring.

'It's *Tor*!' Vivienne babbled. 'He's missing! They're searching everywhere, but he went off by himself for some reason yesterday and never came back – he didn't tell anyone where he was going, so they don't really know where to look – he could have fallen, he could be lying at the bottom of a cliff with a broken leg – starving, dying of exposure, knocked out so they can't hear the search party calling him . . .'

'Oh *no!*'

Christine's knees buckled. She had been holding Vivienne up, taking her slight weight, more than she realized; when she crumpled, Vivienne did too, and it was only the desk behind her that saved them. The loyal Gregory rushed forward to take Vivienne's waist, steadying her, and as Christine started to cry, Vivienne did too.

'Get them some water!' he snapped at Nathan, who was standing by Christine's office door, agog. 'And shut the door.'

Gregory guided Vivienne to the big Chesterfield leather guest chair as Christine sagged against the desk, both hands clutching its mahogany frame. Vivienne collapsed into the Chesterfield, her coat puffing out around her; Christine's fingers were gripping the edge of the desk so hard that they left marks on the leather set into its top.

'The more time that passes,' Vivienne said softly, lowering her hands, twisting them nervously in her lap, her rings glinting marvellously, 'the longer it takes them to find him . . .'

'Oh, *don't*! They *must* find him soon!'

Christine was finding it impossible to believe that Tor could have made a mistake catastrophic enough for him to disappear like this. She had seen pictures of him on a daily basis in so many of the photos and videos released by the expedition; Tor's team was highly sophisticated technologically, crucial nowadays for fundraising and satisfying the sponsors. They not only employed a photographer/videographer on staff, but the expedition members were all required to post photos and clips to Twitter, Facebook, Instagram, Tumblr, Vine and Snapchat, enabled by the latest in satellite phones.

The images had been joyful. Laughing faces framed in fur hoods; Missy Jackson, looking so stunning completely make-up-free that she would be swamped with lucrative offers to endorse skincare products; short action videos; photos of the camp food, all helmed by Tor's calm, smiling presence. Tor was the quiet alpha, the centre of the group. As Toby, Missy and Angel, the glamorous popular kids, clowned around together, staging silly shots of themselves pulling faces at the food or 'rescuing' each other from dire emergencies, Tor could usually be seen in the background, checking kit, talking to staff, working away.

There was a wonderful video of him coaching Toby up a steep climb, shouting encouragement, giving him confidence, yelling at him not to give up when he slipped and hung from the rope; Tor had abseiled down from the top of the cliff to show Toby the way, swarming up with ease, demonstrating where the hand- and footholds were, giving Toby the nerve to start the ascent again. Once more at the summit, Tor had leaned over the edge and reached down a hand so that Toby could use it to pull himself up the last couple of feet; and, having dragged himself up, Toby had hugged Tor as fervently as if he were a long-lost brother, slapping him on the back, unashamedly thanking him and swearing enough in his relief at having made it that the videographer had had to blur some of the words he used.

Christine had watched that clip over and over again, thinking muddled and tangled thoughts about Tor that made her feel horribly conflicted. During the later part of the launch party, Angel had barely left her side; but there had been a moment when she had been waiting to retrieve her coat from the cloakroom and he had slipped away for a minute to arrange something with Nicole, who was apparently taking Silantra on to a club. It was then that Tor had found her, having waited patiently for his opportunity.

'Can I see you when we come back from the Andes?' he asked. 'Just – to talk?'

'Yes, of course,' Christine had said at once. 'I'd love that.'

Then she'd realized she'd accidentally used the word *love*, and been unable to say another word; while Tor, nodding, had backed away as swiftly as he'd seized the opportunity to snatch a word with her. It had been odd and awkward and stealthy, because there should have been no reason for Tor to speak to Christine behind her boyfriend's back, and they both knew it.

Christine had kissed Angel with extra passion that night. She would be working the next day when the expedition left, and wouldn't be able to attend the press conference or wave him off at the airport. She had felt guilty, torn, stupid: after all, she had been Angel's girlfriend for nearly two months, loved his company in and out of bed, while she had hardly spent any time with Tor at all. She barely knew him. He was a fantasy, an action man who had walked out of the sea; but that was why it was impossible, now, to imagine serious harm coming to a man as physically fit and competent as Tor.

337

Instinctively, she dropped to her knees on the carpet in front of Vivienne, once more taking the older woman's hands.

'They'll find him, Vivienne,' she said, her voice not quite steady. 'They'll find him, I'm sure. Every one of them will be looking for him, and they won't stop until they do.'

'He's my godson!' Vivienne said in a cracked little voice. 'He's my godson, and he's so very like his grandfather Arnvald . . . almost the spitting image. Oh, Arnvald as a young man, I remember him so well . . .'

After the revelation that Vivienne had lied to her so smoothly, so convincingly, about Tor's marital status and his attitude to fidelity, Christine naturally viewed Vivienne in a different light. Happily, she no longer needed to work in Vivienne's Mayfair apartment, in close contact with her; she had been as professional and efficient as always, while avoiding any one-on-one contact with her.

Now, however, Vivienne was neither scheming nor lying. She was a weeping old lady, the grandmother of Christine's boyfriend, and it was impossible for Christine not to comfort her. Gregory was pulling tissues from Vivienne's bag, handing them to Christine, and the two women dabbed their eyes. Nathan returned with the water and Gregory intercepted him, drawing a side table over next to Christine and placing the glasses on it, the perfect assistant, trying to render every aspect of his employer's life as smooth as possible, even the grieving process.

'You should have seen Arnvald!' Vivienne was saying as she patted round her eyes, trying not to smudge her make-up. 'Such a strapping, wonderful man, so full of life and health – just like Tor turned out to be. Tor could have been his double. How can he be gone? How is it possible? Dear God, this is bringing back so many memories of Arnvald in his glory days . . . how heartbroken I was when he died! It was like a part of me had gone with him! That's what happens, you know – because when they're still alive, you can reminisce about the wonderful times you had together, but once they're gone, you feel so lonely because you can't share those memories any more . . .'

Christine slid her eyes sideways at Gregory, who was now standing by the closed door, guarding it from incursions. His expression was as deferential as usual, showing not a flicker of surprise that Vivienne had managed to turn the focus of Tor's disappearance to herself.

'What exactly happened, Vivienne?' Christine asked, breaking through Vivienne's self-absorbed stream of consciousness. 'What did they tell you? Have you talked to Angel?'

'He rang me,' Vivienne said. 'Just now. He said that he hadn't wanted to worry me before, but they'd been searching for Tor since yesterday evening, when he wasn't back in camp for dinner. They've called in the Bolivian air force for helicopters for a search – it's going to be on the news and he wanted me to know beforehand. The helicopters will be there as soon as the sun's up . . .'

The UK was four hours ahead of Bolivia; it was mid-morning here, which meant dawn should have broken there by now.

'Let me see if I can get him on Skype,' Christine said, standing up and going round her desk to her computer.

Her fear for Tor was a big stone at the pit of her stomach, but so was her anger at the sheer selfishness Vivienne was displaying. Right now, Tor was just a symbol of a man Vivienne had loved, whom she had used mercilessly. She had taken Arnvald from his wife like a toy she wanted to play with, then thrown him back when she got bored of the game.

Perhaps it was naive to expect empathetic behaviour from an actress who had been on a pedestal for the vast majority of her life, worshipped and venerated, rarely contradicted, almost always getting her own way. But this latest revelation of Vivienne's true nature meant that Skyping Angel would give Christine a break from comforting a woman who seemed much more concerned with her own past loss than the fact that Tor was in severe danger.

It was with a racing pulse that she listened to the phone ring, and when the call was answered and Angel's face appeared on screen, she let out a breath of relief. Turning the screen around, hoicking the base of the computer clumsily on the leather top of the desk, she manoeuvred it to an angle that would allow Vivienne to see him from where she sat.

'Christine?' Angel was saying. 'Christine, are you there?'

'Yes, hold on . . . Vivienne's here too . . .'

She returned to Vivienne's side, perching awkwardly on one wide arm of the chair, ducking her head so that Angel could see her beside his grandmother.

'I had to come and be with someone,' Vivienne said to Angel. 'I couldn't just sit there on my own, all shaken up with worry.'

Angel was unfastening the mask from his hood so they could see his face. There was a light sprinkling of snow on the fur trim of the hood, a few flakes falling softly around

340

him; the rising sun was bright behind him, making it hard to read his expression, but his voice was as hoarse as would be expected considering that he must have been out searching all night, calling Tor's name.

'There's no news yet,' he said. 'We've been out since sunset last night with torches and flares. The air force is sending two helicopters – they should be here any minute. The snow hasn't helped, but it seems to be slowing down now that dawn's broken.'

'What could have happened?' Christine asked, leaning forward. 'Where could he *be*?'

Angel threw his gloved hands wide. Looking at the view around him, Christine could tell that he was at the base of a gorge; a sheer sheet of rock rose to his left, and behind him a valley stretched out, outcroppings of grass alternating with stony patches.

'We're spread out and searching as widely as we can,' he said. 'But it's a complete mystery. Tor went off by himself, instead of supervising a climb, and no one knows why, although he did sometimes go out to recce areas by himself for future climbs. There aren't rock falls here or avalanches, and he's incredibly careful – nothing should have happened to him. I saw him on his way out of camp when I was up higher on a bit of a walk myself, so I knew where he was heading – that's helped a lot, because we were able to pretty much rule out some areas for searching—'

'He must have fallen and knocked himself out,' Vivienne said. 'Or maybe a stray rock hit him. It can't be that serious, can it? He'll come round, he'll hear you all calling . . . he'll find his way back to camp . . .'

Angel nodded confidently. He was walking, the phone in his hand jigging as he picked his way over the stony ground.

'We've thought he might have miscalculated somehow, fallen some distance, which is why we couldn't originally find him,' he said. 'His team are sure he'd have never actually tried a tricky climb on his own – he was very safety-conscious. But it's possible he was recceing, going along a ledge, and a bit of stone gave way beneath his feet, so we've climbed down to lower ground to see if he's here. He was wearing padded clothes, which could have helped to break a fall and keep him warm overnight. It's just that the longer it goes on, the more we really need to find him . . .'

Vivienne let out a heartfelt sob.

'I'm sure you will!' Christine said bravely. 'He's so tough! He's probably heading back to camp now while you're out searching for him.'

'Absolutely,' Angel said breezily. 'We'll tear him a new one for giving us the scare of a lifetime, and we'll have forgotten about it by this time tomorrow! God, we'll tie one on tonight! Major hangovers all round! Oops—' He stopped dead. The screen flickered wildly, as if Angel were waving the hand that was holding it around, flapping it back and forth.

'Did you find him? Do you see him?' Christine almost shrieked, the tension unbearably high.

'No, it's just some bloody sheep! I'm shooing them away from the bottom of the cliff . . . we've got sheep herders out looking for him too. You wouldn't believe how high up they graze them here . . . massive great flock, too, like a carpet . . .'

Angel tilted the phone so that Christine, Vivienne, and Gregory behind them could see a scrubby flock of large sheep, dirty yellow-brown rather than white, milling around in a dense pack almost at waist height to Angel. They had obviously found a thickly grassed area in the stony terrain and didn't want to move: Christine could hear the bleating as Angel tried to make his way through them.

'Go on,' he was saying to the animals, 'go and have a drink – look, there's a stream right there . . . It's weird,' he said, lifting the phone back to his face. 'So many extremes here. Cold at the camp, still snowing, but running water down in the valley and sunshine coming through the clouds. That's giving us hope – if Tor's down here somewhere, knocked out, he won't have frozen overnight. It must be a good fifteen degrees warmer down here. Bloody cold at night, though. I'm only just warming up.'

'Oh, yes! He must be down there, having a sleep – well, almost like a sleep . . .' Vivienne said in prayerful tones.

The screen showed Angel's torso now, his bulky bright red jacket with the expedition logo on the right breast; he had tipped back his head, looking up into the sky. There was a loud buzzing, which Christine realized must be the arriving Bolivian air force helicopters.

'The helicopters are coming!' she said, doing everything she could to keep her voice calm. 'That's great! Vivienne, can you hear that?'

'Two of them, right above us,' Angel confirmed, bringing the phone back to his face. 'I have to go. I'll get in touch as soon as we've found him, I swear. And don't turn on the news! They'll get wind of this and start speculating and there'll be all sorts of reports that may not be true – they might get your hopes up, or worry you . . .'

Shouts in the distance got Christine sitting up straighter, hoping that they meant Tor had been spotted. Angel disabused her immediately.

'I've got to go,' he said. 'They're yelling at me to walk faster – we're trying to cover as much ground as possible, steer over to areas where the helicopters might not get a clear view.'

'Of course, of course –' Vivienne's hands fluttered as she waved Angel goodbye. Christine mouthed a goodbye as the image faded.

'Now the helicopters are there, it's going to be all right,' she said firmly, in an attempt to convince herself. 'That's really great. It's good news, Vivienne. They're bound to find him now.'

Someone was knocking at the office door. Gregory glanced from Vivienne to Christine and, at her nod, went to answer it.

'Christine, I'm so sorry,' her assistant said nervously, putting her head round the door, torn between the demands of one celebrity inside with Christine, and another who had just arrived. 'I know you're having a meeting with Ms Winter. But the Countess of Rutland is here for her appointment . . .'

'Yes, of course!' Christine said, standing up, relieved that she wouldn't have to spend any more time with Vivienne. She couldn't have stood any more talk about Vivienne's affair with Tor's grandfather and how sad it was making her that Tor might be lying dead at the bottom of a Bolivian mountain, because of his resemblance to Arnvald. 'Please show her in. Vivienne, I'm so sorry, but there's nothing we can do – I have to take this meeting.'

Gregory was helping Vivienne up, a tactful hand under one elbow. She hadn't even taken her coat off; she came to her feet ready to leave, as it were, her expression dazed.

'They'll find him,' she said, looking at Christine, her great purple eyes like headlights. 'They'll find him, won't they?'

'Hey,' the Countess could be heard saying as she and the assistant approached Christine's office, her accent now, after a few years of living in the UK, a transatlantic blend of her native American and her husband's upper-class English drawl, 'if this isn't a great time I can go get a coffee, you know? I would just *love* to meet Vivienne Winter, I'm her biggest fan – but if there's some sort of crisis going down . . .'

Vivienne visibly transformed herself on hearing these words, standing up straight, pushing strands of her wig back from her face, arranging it as expertly as if she were looking in the mirror. She breathed in deeply, and when she exhaled she had assumed the public face of Vivienne Winter, international film star, about to accept accolades from a titled businesswoman who was a staple of *Tatler* and *Vanity Fair*'s social columns. Seeing that she had fully collected herself, Gregory stepped back, which was the signal for Christine to nod at her assistant to show the Countess in.

'Oh, Ms Winter!' the Countess exclaimed, sailing in with pageant-competitor grace, all rose-gold hair and magnificent bosom, her beautiful face enhanced by every possible treatment and make-up artifice available to millionairesses. Her level of grooming was American, not English, and in the years she had spent on this side of the Atlantic, she had not made the slightest concession to the more casual way that British women tended to present themselves. She might have been a television presenter just walked off set, her mane of hair bouncing, her make-up blended and perfected to a professional standard.

'I'm your biggest fan!' she assured Vivienne with superb charm and delivery. 'I know everyone says that, but I truly am! I'm so excited about the opportunity to become part of your legacy. You simply are the greatest movie star who's ever lived.'

This was perfectly judged. Vivienne immediately blossomed, extending a hand to the Countess, who took it and pressed it with a bow of her head that indicated vast quantities of humility and respect. Christine watched them exchange pleasantries while Gregory and Christine's assistant hovered behind them like attendant servants from a Restoration comedy; Vivienne graciously complimented the Countess on her enormous pink diamond engagement ring.

Christine felt as if she had taken huge amounts of tranquillizers. She might have been viewing the scene through a thick sheet of glass. Nathan appeared at the door, unable to resist this opportunity to witness an encounter between two such glorious and unashamed divas. His expression was ecstatic as he took in the sight of Vivienne and the Countess earnestly discussing the four aspects of precious stones – carat, cut, clarity and colour – while Vivienne tilted the Countess's left hand from side to side to see the faceted depths of the central diamond.

And far across the world, Christine thought, *Tor is lying unconscious – at best – after spending a night in the open, urgently needing medical attention.* Would the searchers find him fast enough? What if he had seriously injured himself, and was bleeding out? What if he had a catastrophic head trauma, and would never recover from a coma – or had broken his back and would never walk again? Tor, so active, so alive, walking out of the cold grey Baltic sea two months ago the picture of health and vitality – the image of him handicapped, crippled, comatose even, brought such a lump to Christine's throat that it was hard to breathe.

If he got gangrene, if he had to lose a limb, Tor would be fine. She knew that instinctively, could picture him as an inspiration to everyone in the same circumstances – competing in the Paralympic Games, finishing triathlons triumphantly on a prosthesis, letting nothing hold him back. But what if he were paralysed? What if he never regained consciousness and stayed alive, but in a coma?

She realized that she was clasping her hands together, praying with everything she had that neither of those terrible fates was in store for him.

Please, don't let that happen to Tor. Please don't let him be a vegetable. I couldn't bear that for him.

She pictured Tor in a hospital bed, tubes feeding into his comatose body; Tor in a wheelchair, a shell of himself like the actor Christopher Reeve, once so strong and beautiful and healthy playing Superman; then, after a riding accident, a quadriplegic, only able to drink through a straw and to talk with visible effort.

Let them find him soon, let them find him alive. With some bones broken, maybe, but no more than that. Let them find him very, very soon . . .

She had no memory, afterwards, of her meeting with the Countess. For the rest of the day, every time her phone rang she jumped as if she had been given an electric shock. Ironically, considering that it was a call from Angel she was awaiting, she collected a series of bruises on her upper thighs from tearing across her room, bumping into the corner of her desk if she were away from it, racing to see if it was Angel with good news.

The updates that did come through were inconclusive. The search area was widening, including the side of the mountain that had originally been ruled out, as Angel had told everyone he had seen Tor heading in the opposite direction. But Tor was not found that day, nor that night.

Every member of the expedition – as well as every sheep herder for miles around the plateau, drafted in with money upfront, plus a rich reward offered for finding Tor – worked tirelessly, moving in wider and wider circles, recharging their torches in relays all through the night. The next day dawned and the Bolivian air force's helicopters returned, flying until the last rays of sunlight had drained from the plateau. For forty-eight more hours, the search continued, the exhausted expedition members now sleeping in shifts, Tor's second-in-command organizing them with grim efficiency. The Bolivian army sent a division to help find Tor, as the government was increasingly concerned about the bad publicity that would result from such an experienced mountaineer going missing in such mysterious circumstances.

But not even the army could help. After five days, the second-in-command called off the search, declaring that Tor could not have survived without food and water for this amount of time under the climactic conditions high in the steppes of the Andes. In silence broken only by the wind whipping their jackets, the expedition members dismantled the tents, packed up their gear, broke camp and started the trek back to the village, where a phalanx of ancient Land Rovers waited to take them back to La Paz.

They flew straight back to London. A paparazzo who had bribed a worker at the private airfield managed to capture a few grainy pictures of Prince Toby, Angel and Missy Jackson, grey-faced, thin, drained with stress and fatigue – a far cry from the happy, laughing images of them that had been uploaded to multiple social media sites just a few days before.

If Tor had been found with a broken back, permanently paralysed, that would have been horrific, but at least it would have been conclusive for everyone who cared about him. No matter how much they tried to tell themselves that he had probably had a fast death – falling into a narrow, inaccessible gorge, perhaps, and dying on impact – the lack of certainty was a burden the expedition members felt they would carry for the rest of their lives. Prince Toby and Missy genuinely looked as if they would never recover from the horror of the last few days.

And although Angel had pulled off a successful murder, Tor had turned out to be his nemesis. With his coke destroyed, and the mule train unable to make contact with him to give him the rest of the bricks because of the search for Tor, Angel was returning home to real danger. There was no satisfaction in having killed Tor, not when Angel still had to face the music as soon as he landed. On his way back from the airport he had been supposed to stop by the private casino in Paddington, drop off the coke-stuffed canvas duffle bags and take the bounty off his head. Now he would face the toughest negotiation of his life.

If anything, his expression in those paparazzo photographs was even more stressed than Toby's and Missy's. They were dealing with the death of someone who had been very close to them; Angel was confronting the imminent possibility of his own.

Chapter Seventeen

London – one week later

'Nothing will ever relieve our feelings of guilt and sorrow. Those of us who were there and failed to find him will always feel that we let him down by not bringing his body home. To his parents, we tender our most profound apologies and our regrets, our humble contrition, that we were unable to find their son.'

Sobs were heard in the right front pew, Tor's mother and father clinging to each other, unashamedly crying. Both were solidly built, with the weatherbeaten skin of people who spent a great deal of time outdoors. Tor might have inherited his clear blue eyes from either one of them, but his red hair had clearly come from his father, whose crop was thickly greying now, a copper coin under silver water. Christine, seated beside Vivienne in the opposite front pew, snatched glances at the two of them. The resemblance they bore to their son was so compelling, and it was the closest she would ever come to seeing him once more.

Angel's voice was soft yet carrying, his light tenor perfectly pitched as he continued:

'Tor was a bright, shining star. He was a tireless leader who always lifted us up when we were down. He gave us energy when we were tired, convinced us we had strength we didn't know we had. We managed to complete feats of endurance we never thought we could accomplish, and that was down to Tor pushing us, telling us not to give up, reminding us that the charities we were supporting needed us to give everything we had. He was wise and careful. He kept us safe, never forcing us beyond our limits. If any injuries happened, it wasn't on Tor's watch. It was because one of us was careless with a cooking stove –' he tilted his head at Prince Toby, seated beside Missy, his arm around her – 'or wasn't looking where she was going at camp, and stumbled over a guy rope . . .' Now his gaze moved to Missy. Both she and Toby let out strangled gulps that were a mix of laughter and sobs.

Angel continued, 'Or, like me, banged my stupid head on a rock face wandering around staring at condors and not looking where I was going.'

This was how Angel had explained away the bruise on his face caused by his fight with Tor; Missy, Toby and the other expedition members acknowledged it with nods of recognition.

'Tor took great care of all of us who depended on him for our safety and our lives,' Angel continued, his sincerity utterly believable. 'His sweet, open nature, his wonderful sense of humour, which kept us all in stitches, his strength, his innate nobility – I genuinely feel that I could stand here all day listing the qualities that made him so unique, such a hero. But I've spoken long enough. And no matter how much I say, I could never fully describe what the world has lost with Tor's passing. So I'm yielding now to my beloved grandmother, Tor's godmother, who's known him since he was born and will be speaking for the family, at the request of Tor's parents.'

Bowing his head sympathetically to Tor's mother and father, Angel paused for a few seconds, keeping his head ducked, the blond curls tumbling forward, letting the silence gather. The mourners gathered in St Elfrida's Parish Church lowered their heads too; when Angel eventually looked up again and stepped down from the lectern, there was a collective release of breath, a little shuffle as everyone resettled themselves in their pews.

As Angel helped Vivienne up from her seat, handed her up to the low podium on which the lectern stood and sat back down next to Christine, she reached out to take his hand, squeezing it tightly, conveying how proud she was of him. Tor was gone, and whatever they might have had together had vanished with him. While Angel had, by all accounts, been a linchpin of the search for Tor, working tirelessly, refusing to rest until he was literally dropping with fatigue.

She had heard as much from Missy and Toby, who had both turned up at Angel's penthouse the afternoon they'd landed in London, finding that they couldn't face being separated after the intense bonding experience of the expedition and the frantic hunt for Tor. They had hung out until late into the night, drinking, smoking, crying, mourning.

Naturally, there had been no mention of their threesome with Angel: 'what happens in the tent stays in the tent', as Angel had joked. Instead, Missy and Toby had raved about Angel to Christine: how intensely he had thrown himself into looking for Tor, so much so that he had almost fainted with exhaustion, and had had to be practically strapped down to his cot to force him to sleep for a few hours.

This was perfectly true. Of course, what none of the other

expedition members knew was that the reason Angel had been looking for Tor so frantically was because he was terrified that Tor might somehow, miraculously, have survived the fall. Concealed in Angel's jacket pocket throughout the search had been a small rock with a nastily pointed edge, which Angel was ready to bring sharply down on Tor's head should he find Tor anything but satisfactorily dead.

Angel was still in shock that Tor had not been found. Clearly, the crevasse into which he had thrown Tor's unconscious body had been an even longer slide into the abyss than he had realized, leading God knew where. Tor must have taken one hell of a ride down that slope to end up so deep at the base of some rock fissure that not even the hovering helicopters could spot the bright pop of his red jacket through the stubby undergrowth. Angel could only guess that Tor, tumbling down the mountain, had precipitated a rock fall of shale and stone that had come to rest on top of him, burying him as it settled.

Angel hadn't known that he had the resources to drive his body as hard as he had done over the five days of the search. But then, he had never killed someone before. You lived, you learned. And mainly, what he had learned from this experience was that murder was surprisingly easy. As Christine took his hand and pressed it affectionately, as he closed his fingers around hers and turned to give her a loving glance, he was already wondering how soon after she'd had the second child he could stage an unfortunate accident for her.

He was going to have to marry her, no question about that. His gambling contacts had been predictably furious at him turning up at the casino empty-handed; he had been forced, to his huge chagrin, to turn over the deeds to his ski lodge in Verbier in order to clear his debts, and he doubted the sale value would cover the full amount he owed them. He was skint, as the finder's fee from Lil' Biscuit and Silantra would be heavily depleted by his other debts. The marriage bonus and gift of a Notting Hill mansion, together with the reinstatement of his full trust fund income, would settle him nicely, and once Vivienne had been presented with an adorable grandchild, the money tap would keep on flowing. But, unquestionably, he needed money now.

However, there was also the long-term future to be considered. Vivienne had mentioned a bonus for two children, but after that he doubted she'd keep forking out a comparably big wodge for any more arrivals. And Christine's value would drop precipitately as soon as there were no more financial incentives for him to keep her alive. When Vivienne stopped coughing up more millions for the next heir to the Winter gene pool, it would be more than time for Christine to pop her clogs.

Divorce would be out of the question. Any half-decent divorce lawyer would hold his feet to the fire, especially because Vivienne was insistent that the mother of her grandchildren stop work to bring them up at home. Angel would lose vast amounts of his money in alimony payments if he was required to keep Christine in the style to which she would have become accustomed as a stay-at-home mother. No, much better for her to perish in tragic circumstances on – perhaps – a hike they took together. Pushing someone off a cliff had worked so well for him already; why not try it again?

Angel would ensure, of course, that he had absolutely no motive for killing Christine. He would seem a devoted husband and father, with no hidden lovers coming out of the woodwork. This could be achieved by limiting himself sexually to men on the down-low who wanted to keep their proclivities secret, and could therefore be relied upon not to spill the beans to any police officers who might come sniffing around. And Nicole, naturally. Nicole could always be trusted to be a hundred per cent discreet.

Looking up at Vivienne at the lectern, Angel wondered how long she could possibly live. *Probably forever*, he thought bitterly. *But even if Viv does shuffle off her mortal coil sooner rather than later, I'm still pushing Christine off that cliff.*

He had a sudden wave of sympathy for the ex-tycoon who had refused to pay his wife her alimony, and ended up murdered by the Russian mob in consequence. Divorce really was shockingly expensive.

Silver-tongued Angel had delivered his eulogy to Tor completely impromptu, but Vivienne was an actress who needed a script, and there was one written for her by her publicist waiting for her on the lectern, printed out in extra-large type. From the moment she cleared her throat, ensuring she had the absolute attention of everyone present, and said, 'We all loved Tor so very, *very* much,' a collective sigh ran through the gathering in St Elfrida's. Her mellifluous, beautiful voice was pitched to carry right to the back of the church, while still making her listeners feel that she was speaking intimately to each of them. The mourners seemed to sag with grief, as if Vivienne had given them permission to yield fully to their emotions, to relax their stiff upper lips.

She was dressed, as always, in a beautifully judged outfit, a black suit with a dark purple silk blouse. Huge amethysts, surrounded by diamonds, shone in her ears, and there was a matching pendant at the neck of the blouse; enough jewellery to show respect, but not so much that it distracted from the seriousness of the occasion.

Her eulogy had been carefully crafted, but that hadn't been strictly necessary. Vivienne could have read out a Wikipedia entry on how to unblock drains and the mourners would have been equally spellbound by her presence, her charisma, her voice, throbbing with grief. Halfway through, people who had been gravely respectful at Angel's tribute were openly sobbing; by the end, Tor's parents had pretty much collapsed.

Down-to-earth country people, they had simply not felt up to the task of addressing such a celebrated crowd, studded with film stars and more than one member of the royal family; Princess Sophie, clad for once in a skirt that fell below her knees, was seated on Toby's other side. Ironic though it was that Vivienne should be delivering the main eulogy, considering her long-term affair with Arnvald, she gave a wonderful performance. By the end, there was not a dry eye in the house. Angel was more than capable of crying on command.

The vicar gave a final blessing, which was barely heard; it served more as an opportunity for the mourners to calm themselves down and apply tissues to their eyes. Vivienne, who had cried a little herself, had been experienced enough to wear a toque hat to the service, pinned carefully to her wig. Now she lowered its attached veil to disguise puffy eyes whose make-up was a little smudged. Many other women, who hadn't taken this precaution, glanced at her wistfully.

The veil had more than one benefit: as she rose to her feet once more, Vivienne adjusted it to fit neatly under her chin, concealing any loose skin in that area.

'I'll have Gregory take me home,' she said to Angel and Christine as they moved back down the aisle, among the last people to leave. 'I'm utterly shattered. I need to rest.'

'Of course, Grandma,' Angel said, patting her hand, which was clasping his arm.

'It always takes so much out of me now, performing in public,' Vivienne said ingenuously. 'Signings for my perfume and jewellery are much easier – I'm sitting down, and I can just smile and thank everyone and pose for photos. But reading from a script really tires me out these days. My eyesight simply isn't as good as it was, and I do worry about getting words wrong, you know?'

Christine could only be grateful that Tor's parents were preceding them up the aisle, the vicar walking with them and offering condolences in a quiet voice, so that they were unable to hear Vivienne comparing her eulogy for their dead son to a performance. Outside, the waiting photographers called the names of the celebrities they saw exiting the church, but in more muted tones than normal out of respect for the occasion; still, a buzz had started as soon as the vergers opened the church doors, a rumble like a volcano starting to erupt, the first dark drops of lava trickling from the crater. Although Vivienne was a draw, the overwhelming focus was on the newly formed couple of Prince Toby and Missy Jackson.

Tremendous speculation had been raging in the press over the relationship between the prince and the action star, not just because Missy was famous, but because she was mixed-race. A love affair between a handsome scion of the British royal family and an actress who had not only conducted many fight scenes in her underwear, but was half African American and half Latina, was making the world's media salivate. What if the relationship lasted? What if Prince Toby proposed, and the two adorable little princesses born to Prince Hugo and his bride Chloe were presented in due course with a cousin who was the first-ever non-white addition to the royal family?

Toby and Missy had not been seen out in public together since the return from the expedition a week ago. The palace had issued a dignified press release stating that Toby was grieving for the death of his friend and colleague, and would appreciate privacy at this difficult time. Certainly, he had not been seen at any of the Chelsea nightclubs he would normally be frequenting. Missy had technically been staying in a suite at the Langham Hotel, but the paparazzi had been tailing her limo every day as it left her hotel around lunchtime, after her daily workout, and drove to the gates of Kensington Palace, where Toby had an apartment. As late as the paparazzi waited outside the gates, Missy had never emerged before the next morning.

The couple were not hand in hand as they walked back down the aisle, but their bodies were almost touching, shoulder to shoulder, hip to hip, as they moved in synch. Missy paused in the narthex of the church to blot away the last of her tears. Her extraordinarily smooth complexion was barely marred by the fact that she had been crying. There were shadows under her eyes, but they only made her skin seem more lucidly translucent, her eyes more sloe-like.

Toby looked at her worshipfully. Missy was the same height as him, and as he reached a hand out to smooth a tight curl from her forehead, their eyes met in mutual empathy.

'Do you two want to come back to ours?' Angel asked Toby, patting his back sympathetically. 'We've got a car park in the basement of the building. You can drive right in so you don't get snapped getting out of the limo.'

'Thanks, mate,' Toby said, but he waited for Missy to make the decision.

Christine noticed Toby deferring to Missy, as she had done over the last few days when she and Angel had been invited to Kensington Palace for quiet dinners in Toby's apartment. Toby had fallen head over heels for Missy, jumping up when she came into a room, rushing to get her anything she needed. It was very sweet. Having only known Toby by reputation as a wild party boy, this quiet, devoted boyfriend was quite a contrast from what Christine had been expecting. It was as if Tor's death had made Toby grow up overnight, realizing that it was time to start taking life seriously.

'I just want to rest,' Missy said softly. 'I've cried my eyes out and I'm getting the worst headache.'

'Whatever you want, darling,' Toby said, taking her hand. 'Your place or mine?'

But Missy's attention was elsewhere: she was staring admiringly at Vivienne. Quite deliberately, Vivienne had delayed her arrival at St Elfrida's until just before the start of the memorial service, never missing an opportunity to make an entrance. Her gracious progression down the aisle had been in the *grande dame* manner, the veil on her toque hat raised, nodding to the faces she knew, acknowledging the murmurs of recognition and awe with an appropriately sad smile. Missy, therefore, had not had a chance to be introduced to her, and the young actress looked thoroughly star-struck even in these circumstances.

'Ms Winter, I just wanted to say how incredibly moving you were,' Missy said, managing not to gush. 'I've been crying for so long now, ever since we heard Tor was missing, and I thought I was all done. But honestly, as soon as you started to speak . . .' She wiped away another tear. 'You really brought him back. I could see his face in front of us all over again.'

Vivienne, whose speech had been full of platitudes and generalizations, smiled charmingly at this tribute.

'You're very sweet,' she said. 'And I hear from Angel how hard you looked for my godson. I thank you with all my heart for everything you did for Tor, you and Toby.'

'Oh, not at all,' Toby said swiftly. 'Nothing to thank us for. We're so sorry we couldn't bring back—'

'Toby, *don't*,' Missy said so strongly that he immediately stopped, and mumbled apologies for his reference to the fact that they did not have Tor's body to bury. 'I *can't*.'

Vivienne cast Missy a glance of approval that she had Toby so firmly under voice control.

'It's terribly hard for all of us,' she said, taking her gloves from Gregory and sliding them on. 'If you will excuse me, I must find my car. I'm simply in pieces from all of this.'

'Of course,' Missy said in a hurry. 'I just wanted to—'

Vivienne held up one gloved hand to stop her, in a neatly executed diva gesture.

'Darling, not now,' she purred. 'But Toby must bring you to see me soon in Mayfair.'

'Oh, that would be amazing!' Missy exclaimed as Vivienne, assuming a suitably grave expression, looped her arm once more through Angel's and glided out through the arched doorway – pausing between the stone columns of the portico, and using them as a frame to give the waiting photographers a perfectly composed shot. Only after a minute did she begin to descend the steps to her waiting limousine.

Christine hung back, gesturing to Toby and Missy to go next. She would have felt hugely self-conscious walking out before them on her own, hearing the sighs of disappointment from the paparazzi and the public as she made her way down the steps and across the fenced-off area in front of the church. Ever since the early days of her association with the Winter family, she had had more than enough of that feeling on red carpets and press conferences. It was like being an extra on the set of a film: invisible at best, a nonentity at worst.

As the prince and the film star appeared on the church portico, shadowed by Toby's bodyguard, there was an eruption of excitement. Toby's press secretary had been briefing the media that Toby and Missy were spending time together after their return from the Andes to recover from their grief, while Missy's publicist had been planting stories in the American tabloids confirming that the two of them were romantically linked. Both sides, however, had strictly instructed Toby and Missy not to be seen holding hands, let alone kissing in public, as it would look as if they weren't sufficiently sorrowful about their friend's shocking death.

Missy had considered her funeral look with great care. It needed to be restrained and elegant, to convey her eligibility to become a princess, but also high-fashion enough to gain approval from the online commentariat. The Givenchy dress and Jimmy Choo low-heeled slingbacks had been sourced for her by a very expensive London stylist, and her pearl earrings came from Garrard's, Crown Jewellers for a hundred and sixty years, the acme of respectability. As she walked down the church steps by Toby's side, a tall, slight figure in head-to-toe black, the clicking of the cameras was almost deafening.

The bodyguard moved forward to hold the car door open, Toby chivalrously gesturing for Missy to go first. Her publicist, up before dawn in New York to watch the coverage in New York on *E! News Live*, sighed blissfully in the knowledge that one just couldn't buy this kind of publicity, while speculating on whether, if Toby and Missy did marry, the palace would let her keep working if she agreed not to shoot any more action scenes in her underwear.

Christine waited a few more minutes before leaving St Elfrida's. If she let the camera crews and mourners disperse a little, she calculated, she would make it through the crowd faster; and as she eventually emerged, she saw she had been right. The TV vans were being packed up and the onlookers who had come to gawk at Vivienne Winter, Prince Toby and Missy Jackson were turning to walk away, their heads ducked as they posted their photos to social media.

Angel was also on his phone, talking urgently in a low voice, but he waved at Christine as she hurried by, miming that he would call her later. She nodded, but kept walking quickly; the sheer volume of work she had to get through was overwhelming, and she would be at the office late again that evening. So she missed hearing Angel snap impatiently:

'Fuck it, Nicole! What do you mean, you're not around?'

'I'm getting on the Eurostar in a couple of hours,' Nicole drawled. 'I have a rendezvous with Silantra in Paris, believe it or not. She's there for costume fittings for her next tour and she wants me to keep her company this evening. Aren't I lucky?'

'Room for one more?' Angel said, turning away from the depleted crowd to make sure he wasn't overheard arranging a threesome at a memorial service. 'God, I really need some major kink. I've been having to do the whole perfect-boyfriend-in-mourning thing with Christine, and it's driving me mad. I need to go crazy tonight.'

'Why don't you ring up that service and get that girl in again?' Nicole suggested. 'She was lots of fun.'

'I can't mark her, though, not without a huge extra charge,' Angel said in frustration. 'Which I can't bloody afford right now. I can't even afford their normal fee, frankly. I'm in such shit, Nicole. Even what we're going to make for the finder's fees isn't enough to bail me out of this hole. Okay, it's short-term, but until I get married I have to be really careful with money. Viv won't come across with any more till then. I'm totally buggered.'

'Or not!' Nicole said flippantly. 'Poor Angel, you can't even pay for someone to bugger you! But I'm afraid Silantra won't be okay with you coming along. She has to be super-careful at the mo. Biscuit's skating a bit close to the wind, apparently – he's had to pay off a tabloid that got a story on him and his boyfriend, so major discretion needed all round. It's fine if I visit her – she's booked me a separate room in the hotel just to be careful – but she can't have a chap sneaking into her suite overnight. Much too risky. Oh, and she's seriously considering taking even more pieces! That means extra fees on those, so—'

'*It's not enough!*' Angel said, much more sharply than he had meant to. The words echoed loudly against the stone walls of the cul-de-sac where the church was located, and some stragglers from the funeral service turned their heads in surprise to see the man who had just given such a moving eulogy shouting angrily into his phone. The location was ideal for weddings, baptisms or memorial services for well-known people, as access to the church could be cordoned off by the police. But the cul-de-sac meant that there was nowhere to have a private conversation, no side streets for Angel to turn down.

'Look, I can't talk here. I'll meet you at the St Pancras champagne bar for a drink before you go,' he said, lowering his voice again. 'When's your train?'

'Seven,' Nicole said. 'I can make it there by five thirty. Drinks on me,' she added teasingly, 'since it sounds like you can't even manage those . . .'

Angel arrived at St Pancras early, repeatedly checking his watch. By the time Nicole appeared – strolling down the length of the long promenade and turning every head in her belted purple trench coat and knee-high black suede high-heeled boots, a large and square-bottomed black leather tote bag slung over her shoulder, her hair pulled back into the smoothest and glossiest of ponytails – he was clasping his fists so tightly that his impeccably manicured nails were digging into his palms.

Nicole was pulling a sleek silver carry-on bag stuffed with

sex toys and skimpy lingerie, in anticipation of the evening she was planning with Silantra. As she reached Angel's booth, she pulled a face at the glass of champagne he had ordered for her.

'You have that,' she said, pushing it over the table to him and sliding in, propping the case against the side of the seat. 'I'm going to be practically naked pretty much as soon as I get to Paris, and I don't want stomach bloat from the bubbles.'

Very unusually at the understaffed bar, a waiter arrived at the table almost immediately, staring reverently at Nicole.

'Grey Goose and lime,' she ordered, choosing a bubble-free, zero-calorie drink option. 'Double shot of the vodka in a tall glass, then squeeze a whole lime into it. Lots of ice.'

As he shot away to fulfil her request, she raised her eyebrows at Angel.

'*That* one wants to be spanked,' she observed. 'I can always tell when—'

'Nicole, I don't have time for banter,' Angel hissed at her. 'We need to work something out. Something else – something more . . .'

The champagne bar at St Pancras station was the perfect location for a clandestine conversation. The high vaulted glass ceiling, the trains rumbling below, the glass walls of the walkway down which the bar ran, the constant stream of passengers pulling cases swiftly along, the low-level clink of glasses and babble of conversation, the spacing of the booths, all meant that it would be impossible to eavesdrop, as long as the people in question kept their voices low. Even a directional mike would have failed to pick up what Angel and Nicole were saying; there was simply too much background noise.

'We? What's this "we" shit, white boy?' Nicole drawled.

'What?' Angel looked both baffled and angry.

'It's an old joke,' Nicole explained. 'The Lone Ranger and Tonto are riding along and suddenly they come to the top of a ridge and below are all these Native Americans, with bows and arrows, and when they turn around there are more behind them. It's an ambush. So the Lone Ranger says: "Hey, what are we going to do, Tonto?" and Tonto says: "What's this 'we' shit, white boy?" and rides down the hill to join the other guys.'

'That'd be funny if I felt like fucking laughing,' Angel said, finishing his champagne and reaching for Nicole's just as her drink arrived.

'I do have an idea, actually,' Nicole said, flashing such a smile at the waiter that he tripped over his own feet, but waiting to continue until he had left again. 'It could score us an absolutely enormous amount of money, but it's on the wrong side of the line. So far, we've been completely legal. Yeah, your grandma wouldn't like it if she knew we were charging introduction fees, but it wouldn't get us arrested. But *this* . . .'

'I don't give a damn,' Angel said intensely. 'Granny Viv's never going to make trouble for me. I'm all she has.'

'Well, it could dump your girlfriend in deep shit,' Nicole said. 'Get her sacked, maybe even send her to prison.'

'Meh; if we make enough from it, I won't need her any more,' Angel said, drinking half the second glass of champagne and signalling the blushing waiter for a third. 'And then I don't give a flying fuck what happens to her, do I? Actually, it would be a *huge* relief not to have to go through with this whole marriage-and-kids nonsense that Granny

Viv's trying to dump on my head. So what exactly are we going to do? Steal some of the jewellery, and frame her for it if anyone finds out?'

Nicole smiled a cat-like, V-shaped smile.

'Exactly,' she said. 'And here's how we do it.'

She pushed her drink aside so she could lean further across the table as she unspooled the plan she had in mind. Angel mirrored her posture, elbows on the table, violet eyes wide with anticipation as he listened eagerly to every word, not the slightest scruple popping into his head.

After all, he had killed one person already, and had planned to marry a second, impregnate her a couple of times and then kill her too. Absconding with items of Vivienne's jewellery, and possibly getting Christine arrested in consequence, was a mere bagatelle by comparison.

Chapter Eighteen

London – the same evening

'Darling! What a dull girl you're being, all work and no play!'

Angel appeared in the door of Christine's office, sparking with energy like a live wire. His blond curls were slightly sweaty, his cheeks flushed and his lips as red as if he had just bitten them to bring extra colour, as women used to do before the advent of lipstick. He was brandishing a bottle of champagne, his eyes even brighter than the glittering foil that crowned it.

There was an urgency about him, a fizz that held as much promise as the champagne. If Nathan had been present, he would have sighed with equal admiration of Angel and envy of his lucky girlfriend.

Christine's first reaction, however, was irritation. She was working late, as she would have to do most evenings in the run-up to the auction; she had planned to stay in the office for at least another hour. But the instant she saw Angel, she knew she wouldn't get any more work done that night. When he wanted something, he pushed until he got it; he was incapable of taking no for an answer.

To be honest, though, it wasn't as if she could say no to him once he put his hands on her. As soon as he touched her, any objection would melt away; not only that, but her consent would turn swiftly into begging for more, because she was so desperate for him to finish what he had so tantalizingly started. The way he would withdraw his hands and mouth and cock just as she was frantic for them had become an intrinsic part of the pleasure for her, as she suspected it had been for many, many women before her. And since she knew that she would not only let him position her however he wanted, fuck whichever part of her he wanted, but plead for him to do so, she might as well go along with it straight away and save time – maybe afterwards she could get some more work done at home . . .

How practical of me! she thought with a half-smile. Pushing away the inventory on which she had been working, she started to stand up.

'What, no resistance?' Angel said, tilting his head to one side. 'No implorations for me to come back later so you can take some more time on your terribly important paperwork? No complaints about me having talked my way past the night watchman by bribing him with insider gossip about Granny Viv's wild times back in the day?'

'I think you could talk your way past anyone,' Christine said, her smile deepening as she reached for her suit jacket, which was hanging over the back of her chair.

'What are you doing?' Angel said, striding round the desk, pulling the jacket from her grasp and throwing it across the room. 'You need fewer clothes on, not more.'

'Angel, not *here*! It's my office! Really, I don't want to do it here!'

She wasn't concerned about being caught. By this time,

nine thirty in the evening, the building was empty apart from the night watchman, and he only patrolled between the front desk and the back door access areas to the security-controlled basement, with its safes and alarmed doors protecting the auction house's extremely valuable lots. That wasn't the reason for her objection. This was her workplace, and if she let Angel have sex with her here, she would always have that image in her mind. It would make it much harder to separate the two areas of her life, clear her mind and focus one hundred per cent on what she had to do to earn a living.

She opened her mouth to explain, ask him to change his mind. And then it occurred to her that her pleas might make his behaviour even more outrageous. That had happened in the past, when she'd asked him not to finger her in his building's lift; he'd responded by pulling her skirt right up to her waist, panicking and humiliating her even as she cried out in release, pounding against his hand as he brought her off. What if he pulled her out into the main office and started fucking her there, where the guard could see it on CCTV? He was more than capable of bending her over a colleague's desk and screwing her where it might be caught on tape. At least in here there were no security cameras to film them having sex.

This is your boyfriend, a little voice said. *This is the man you're committed to, and you can't even trust him to respect your workplace . . .*

Already Angel was pulling at the buttons of her blouse, tugging at them with such impatience that the fabric was ripping.

'Don't,' she heard herself gasp. 'Angel, don't . . . I need to

371

wear that when we leave . . . can we wait, can we do this at yours – even in the limo . . . *please* . . .'

'I've waited all day,' he said, dragging the blouse down over her shoulders. 'I've waited all bloody day, sat through that bloody service, and I need to fuck you right here, right now. You'll love it. You always do. Take your knickers off and spread your legs.'

He kissed her, his hands hard on her breasts, squeezing them, pinching the nipples, his tongue so deep in her mouth she couldn't talk any more. It was instinctive now, her reaction to him; she was wet instantly, had been pretty much the moment he put his hands on her. No, even before. She had got wet the moment he had told her he was going to fuck her. Her knickers were damp, her abdomen hot as molten metal.

Already, as he pulled back and said: 'Do it. Take them off,' against her mouth, flicking her nipples to hard points, her hands were obediently lowering, pulling up her skirt, catching the lace edge of her knickers with her thumbs, taking the waistband of her tights with them, working them down over her buttocks.

He was pressing her back against the desk, her hips leaning into it for balance, making it hard for her to get enough space to pull her pants down. It was quite deliberate: he kept kissing her, his hands covering her breasts, his erection shoved into her crotch, making her wild for it, so that she was sobbing with need and excitement even before the knickers finally came free, sliding down her legs, taking the tights with them too. Her lower body was wriggling frantically. She was trapped from the hips up, couldn't use her hands any more, had to writhe and reach one foot to hook around the fabric, balancing on the other leg, fighting against him to do what he wanted, playing yet another of Angel's games.

'Have you done it?' he said, and she sobbed a yes, widening her legs, her skirt hiked up now to her crotch, everything bared to him, waiting for him, desperate for his fingers or his cock, so damp and ready he could just enter her now and she would cry in relief at being filled. That was how his games worked so powerfully; they were often a complete substitute for foreplay.

'Good girl,' he said, standing back between her spread legs and reaching over for the bottle of Pol Roger. Deftly, he pulled off the foil, unwrapped the wire twist, popped the cork without his usual care not to spill the foam. Instead, as soon as it began to spurt, he lowered the bottle, reached between Christine's legs and slid the fingers of one hand into her. Just as she started to moan and pound herself against him, his fingers widened her, splaying her out, and the next second she felt the cold shock of the bottle neck pushing inside her. Icy, acidic bubbles surged out, tickling her, making her giggle and gasp at once.

Angel was pushing her down, one hand holding the bottle, the other flat on her stomach. Once he had her prone on the desk, her legs in the air, he began to tilt the bottle, more champagne flowing into her, filling her up. It felt extraordinary, shocking, the bubbles like live things inside her, bursting and fizzing. The bottle itself, filling her up too, was hugely satisfying. She realized she was riding it as if it were Angel's cock, something that, before meeting Angel, she would never have done, would have thought utterly humiliating. It was even more humiliating that she wailed with disappointment as he pulled it out, unable to bear being empty even for a moment.

Angel grabbed a book from her desk, a big reference work on historical jewel settings, and shoved it under her bottom, angling it high to keep as much cold liquid inside her as possible. Swiftly, he unzipped his trousers, pulled out his cock and shoved it into her, hard and fast, groaning at the contrast of his heated skin against the iced champagne.

'*Fuck*, yes!' he said. 'Jesus, your cunt is so fucking hot and cold at the same time – can you feel it, can you feel my cock getting you hot again –'

He took the bottle, upended it to his mouth, drank and drank. Christine already knew it wasn't the first drink he'd had that day by the wildness of his actions, the frenzied way he was fucking her, his cock positively bouncing inside her. Her buttocks were thudding against the book, its corners digging in, starting to become painful. She'd bruise if this went on any longer.

She tried to sit up a little, shift herself so the book wasn't hurting her, but Angel immediately pushed her back again.

'Stay down!' he commanded. 'Here, have a drink!'

He shoved the bottle against her mouth, the champagne flooding out, almost choking her; she coughed and sputtered, trying to swallow, but it was hard to manage lying flat on her back. The bubbles ran up her nose, made her sneeze, and all the time Angel was ramming her, forcing her bottom into the hard edges of the book with every stroke, which was really beginning to hurt now.

Christine coughed again, finding it increasingly difficult to breathe. Scared of choking on the bubbles, she managed to curl her head and shoulders up as if she were doing a situp. This time Angel didn't push her back down, much to her relief; instead, he grabbed her shoulders and pulled her up to an awkward half-sitting position, the book still wedged under her. It was digging in even more now that her full weight was on it. She gripped his arms for balance, trying to lift herself a bit off the sharp leather corners of the book, but she couldn't, and the more she squirmed, the more it hurt.

'You're going to love this,' he said, and now that she was looking into his eyes she realized that he wasn't home. He was more animal than human, the whites of his eyes showing all round his purple irises, his hair moist with sweat, champagne trickling from his mouth. His hands slid up her shoulders to her neck. The next thing she knew, they closed around it, his thumbs digging into her windpipe.

Suddenly, Christine's bottom digging painfully into the hardback book was the least of her concerns. She was blacking out so fast she barely even had time to panic. Her hands came up to push at his arms, dark spots dancing before her eyes. She tried frantically to keep them open even as she struggled to breathe; sight and breath seemed inextricably linked, as if losing one would also mean the loss of the other.

Christine had always known Angel was stronger than he looked. The hands around her neck were a vice, closing inexorably. Her fingers reached up, trying to pry them off, but it was like pulling at the iron bars of a gate. The dark spots swelled fast, merging into blackness. Her head felt as light as a balloon as the oxygen deprivation hit.

Her body went limp in Angel's grasp, her eyes fluttering closed, and as soon as it did, he released the clutch on her neck, holding her loosely now to keep her head upright. The whole time, however, he continued fucking her, maintaining a steady, even rhythm that he would be able to keep up for a long time. The frenzied need with which he had entered the room was entirely channelled into this, one of his favourite games, and one at which he had had a great deal of practice.

After a few seconds, Christine's body convulsed as she gasped for air, her eyes snapping open. As soon as this happened, Angel lowered one hand between her legs and strummed her in the way he knew would make her come. The convulsions started instantly, her whole body throbbing with the powerful orgasm. Angel laughed out loud as he watched her eyes snap open wide. She looked absolutely overwhelmed by what was happening to her, the sheer intensity of all this sensation.

'I told you you'd love it,' he said. 'You come *so* fucking hard after a choke! God, *look* at you!'

Christine couldn't respond. Her entire body was in spasm, her bruised throat was struggling for air, her eyes were rolling up so that she could barely see. And all the time Angel was driving his cock in and out of her, overloading her with stimulation. His shirt was damp, beads of sweat standing out on his chest, his cheeks hectic with colour. He was right: she was coming with such force she thought she might faint again from the strength of it.

Desperately, she struggled to keep conscious as the orgasm and Angel's cock rocked her back and forth. When it finally subsided, and she'd managed to catch her breath to some degree, she tried to get some words out, to tell him to let go of her, to stop, that it was all too much; but she couldn't. Her throat hurt too badly. She was in shock. And then once more his hands closed around her windpipe, carefully avoiding her carotid artery, his thumbs shutting off her air supply again, and she panicked even more, thrashing wildly.

She was weaker, however, with much less ability to fight. Her heels drummed uselessly against his buttocks, and he took that as encouragement, not that he needed it; when she came round again, it was to another explosive orgasm. She was dizzy beyond belief, dazed, confused, experiencing the orgasms now as a kind of erotic torture.

Angel had always mixed pain and pleasure, psychological as well as physical, gradually breaking her into his range of tastes and play, teaching her to understand, if not enjoy, the way the two could be blended. This was way beyond anything he had done previously, however – not just unexpected, but utterly terrifying. Although she knew that he wasn't planning to kill her, just playing with her in a cat-and-mouse game, the panic felt just the same as if he were genuinely in the process of murdering her. The total loss of control, the violent assault, the orgasms he was forcing on her were turning her own body against her, so that she appeared to consent physically when she would never have done so verbally.

Tears formed in her eyes and started to trickle down her cheeks. Christine would have been even more horrified, if it were possible, to realize that the sight made Angel's cock swell even more. He wasn't normally a tear fetishist. There had been people at school who had absolutely got off on it:

one boy couldn't come until his partner was sobbing, had insisted that his girls wear loads of black eye pencil, guaranteed to run down their faces in spectacular fashion as they cried from a good spanking.

Some childhood memory he'd been obsessed with recreating, as Angel remembered, its roots in something dark and dirty and sad, as with so many freakish desires. He had been a ridiculously handsome young thing, a French count called Gilles with a sexy accent and an excellently sized cock. There were plenty of girls who longed to cry for Gilles; in the hopes of enticing him they would pile on the MAC eyeliner until they looked like they had black eyes, and spider their eyelashes with non-waterproof mascara.

It had been a school trend that gradually got out of hand until finally, even the notoriously permissive headmistress had been forced to announce at assembly that she had had quite enough of half the female students of Chateau Sainte-Beuve making themselves up to look like Gothic Barbies, and she was banning heavy eye make-up for the rest of the term. She had glanced pointedly at the English literature teacher when she said this; the teacher was sporting enough kohl around her eyes to make it clear that she too would be happy to cry black tears for Gilles.

Angel hadn't previously cared one way or the other if his sex partners cried at the exquisite torture he applied to them. But there was something about the tears falling over Christine's childlike face, filling the round blue eyes, blurring the sprinkling of freckles over her hot red cheeks, dripping into the wide O of her mouth as she gulped in air, that clenched his balls and made his cock even harder.

How Tor would hate to watch this, Christine coming over and over again as she sobbed, as Angel choked her and screwed her brains out! A vivid fantasy of Tor strapped to Christine's desk chair, unable to move, straining at his bonds in rage and frustration as Angel's hands closed once more round Christine's neck and tears spurted from her eyes, sent Angel over the edge sooner than he had planned. He roared in pleasure as the hot sperm gushed from him, mingling inside Christine with what was left of the Pol Roger. And as he came, he found himself fantasizing about pulling out his cock and letting Tor have it smack in his face, shooting all over him.

'*Shit*,' he grunted at this wonderfully pornographic image. '*Shit, that is so fucking hot!*'

In Angel's imagination, Tor bellowed his fury as Angel came on his face, shaking the chair with his efforts to break free. It was fantastic. Angel almost regretted killing Tor before he'd managed to make it come true.

'Oh, bollocks,' he muttered as the spasms subsided, realizing that he had kept Christine under too long. That was what happened when you did a gram of coke and drank a lot of brandy shortly before you started fucking: you got carried away. He'd gone to his club after meeting Nicole, celebrating her clever plan, already counting on the millions they'd score from stealing some carefully selected pieces of Vivienne's jewellery, bumped into some friends and spent the time partying with them, working himself up to a height of sexual tension before arriving to get his release with Christine.

He took his hands off her throat immediately, careful to support her head. It had only been fifteen seconds, at his best guess; he'd seen people out for longer than that for no ill-effects. Red marks were beginning to form on her neck, thumbprints that would be bruises tomorrow. She'd need a high-necked top; but it was winter now, that wouldn't be a problem.

He slapped her face lightly to bring her back to consciousness, one smack on each cheek. Christine stirred, letting out a long, guttural rasp for breath, her chest heaving, her eyes flying open as if she had been resuscitated with a vigorous bout of CPR. She flailed in Angel's grasp, her hips pounding upwards, sent into orgasm yet again as her body slammed back into consciousness. The spasms sent his cock sliding out of her, dripping on the carpet, but he remained between her spread legs, arms round her, holding her up.

'That was amazing, wasn't it?' he said complacently. 'You'll see – when we do that again you'll come like that every single time you wake up. It's an automatic trigger. I helped you along the first few goes, just to get you into the swing of things, but pretty quickly your body just starts doing it on its own. They *were* massive orgasms, weren't they? You looked like you were having the most fantastic time.'

Christine let out a long, hacking cough. Angel took the bottle from the desk, pleased to see that there was still some champagne inside it.

'Mmm, it tastes of you,' he observed, drinking from the bottle neck. 'Want some?'

Christine shook her head.

'Still a bit overcome,' Angel commented with the voice of experience, finishing the Pol Roger. 'I do envy girls, I must say – you get the multiple orgasms. I'd almost rather have those than a cock, much as I love fucking people.'

Christine was struggling to speak, her words coming out as if her throat were coated with sandpaper.

'I didn't . . .' she managed. 'I didn't want . . .'

'Honey and lemon and rum,' Angel said knowingly, dropping the empty bottle into the waste basket. 'Always the best thing after you've been grappled. We'll get you a hot toddy at mine. I'm *fairly* sure I have lemons.'

Christine shook her head again. Despite the pain of her bruised larynx, she was determined to speak; she brought up her hands, pushed Angel back so she could slide off the desk and stand. Her features contorting with all the emotion she couldn't put into her poor throttled voice, she said:

'*Never.* Never coming back with you again. It's over.'

Chapter Nineteen

London – later that evening

'Christine! Christine, you have to let me in! Christine, please! I know you're in there! I'm not leaving till I get a chance to talk to you!'

Angel and Christine had never spent any time at Christine's flat. Angel had only visited it once, in fact: that first time when he had taken her home in the limo, after their flight back from Halmstad. Why hang out in a cramped one-bedroom flat in Acton when they could be in Angel's sprawling Knightsbridge penthouse instead? So although Christine had had a key to Angel's flat and the code to the apartment block's front door after barely a week together, he had never needed the same access to her place. Now she was extremely grateful for this – and also that, as a security measure for a woman living on her own, she had chosen to rent a second-floor flat rather than a garden or ground-floor one.

Unable to get in, Angel had been ringing her doorbell for the last twenty minutes, pleading into the intercom. With no success, he had escalated his attempt to see Christine: he was standing in front of the house, calling up at her, and the neighbours were starting to notice what was going on.

'Christine, I know you're in there!' Angel yelled. 'Please, I just want to talk to you! We can't leave it like this!'

'What the fuck is going on?'

The man who lived below Christine, a grumpy old codger who rarely seemed to leave the house, had shoved up his sash window and was leaning out. Christine had been standing behind her half-drawn curtains, but now she peeked around them, feeling more confident now that there was a witness. Despite it being November, Angel wasn't wearing a jacket, just the white shirt and black trousers he had donned for the memorial service, his throat bared to the chilly autumn night. His fair curls were pushed back from his handsome face, and his eyes were glowing like precious stones, his expression agonized.

'Jesus,' the grumpy man said in shock. 'Who are *you*?'

'I'm in love with the woman who lives above you,' Angel said seriously.

'You *what*?'

'Christine!' Angel called. 'Christine, please just come to the window so I can see you!'

The two girls who shared the ground-floor flat cracked open their living room window.

'Um, hey, can I help?' said one of them, and then, involuntarily, as she took in the sight of Angel: '*Hi.*'

'*Hi*,' echoed her flatmate, face pressed to the window. 'Wow. You are *gorge.*'

Christine knew which one it was: Jenny. Always pissed in the evening, too drunk to find her keys, banging on the window to wake up the other one, Laura, to let her in. From the sound of Jenny, she was well on her way: she was slurring her words. Christine pushed her window up a little, cold air flooding in, and leaned out. She couldn't continue ignoring Angel, not with the whole house involved, but she couldn't call the police on Vivienne's grandson, either. There was the sale to organize, and Vivienne was not likely to want Christine working on it if she'd had Vivienne's grandson arrested for harassment . . .

Her throat was still sore, but she had been sucking cough drops and, yes, drinking honey and lemon and rum since she got home. Much as she hated to admit it, Angel had been right: the drink was soothing the bruised lining of her oesophagus. So she could croak out without too much trouble: 'I'm sorry, everyone. Angel, please go away.'

'Christine!'

Angel's eyes lit up, his arms opened wide. It was like Romeo seeing Juliet at her balcony, and Jenny positively cooed to see it.

'Please let me in!' he begged. 'Please, Christine, just for a few minutes!'

'If you don't let him in, I bloody will,' Jenny slurred.

'Shh!' Laura said furiously. 'Shut *up*, you pisshead! Christine, are you okay?'

'I won't go till I see you,' Angel said. 'I'll sleep in the car if I have to. Please, Christine! Please let me explain what happened!'

'It's Prince Charming who needs to shut up,' said the grumpy man. 'I'm not having him out there all night yelling.'

'Christine, shall I call the police?' Laura persisted.

Christine's heart sank. That would be just as bad as her ringing them herself. And what if the press got hold of the story? Angel's name was so famous, it could easily ring a bell with someone at the police station who wanted to make some money by ringing the papers . . .

'No, thanks, it's okay. I'm coming down,' she said.

She didn't want to let him into the flat, but what else could she do? She couldn't sit on the stairs and talk to him there, not with Laura and Jenny doubtless all ears to hear the drama – and with the responsible Laura probably also keen to make sure Christine wasn't being abused by Angel. If they found out who he was, the story of him choking her – on the night of Tor's memorial service, too – would be too juicy to keep to themselves. So she led him up the stairs and gestured at him to go inside, but left her front door open as an escape route. She indicated that he should sit on the sofa, across the room, and she took one of the kitchen chairs so that the table was between them.

'Christine, there's no need for this,' Angel said gently. 'I would never deliberately hurt you.'

Christine reached up to the high neck of the knitted sweater she had pulled on as soon as she got home, dragging it down to show him the marks in the soft hollow of her throat, reaching around her neck.

'You *strangled* me!' she said, putting huge amounts of reproach and disgust into those three words; her throat hurt her too much to form long sentences.

'This is what I completely don't get! I thought you *liked* it!' he said, shaking his head in surprise. 'You were coming so hard!'

'That made it worse,' she got out.

'*Worse?*' Angel's hands went into his hair, tangling it wildly.

'I don't understand! How can that make it worse? You had such a great time!'

'I was *scared*!'

The mug of hot toddy was on the table, and reluctantly, Christine picked it up; she didn't want Angel to have the satisfaction of seeing that she was following his advice. But if she was going to have to talk, it made all the difference.

'I didn't want it,' she said, after taking a long sip, wincing as the warm liquid went down; it hurt to swallow. 'You *strangled* me.'

'Not strangling – it's choking! Breath play! Christine, you kept coming, you loved it when I put the bottle up you, you loved it when I poured champagne inside you and fucked you.'

'The book hurt me,' she said. 'My bum on it. I have bruises.'

Angel looked genuinely baffled. 'I've *often* given you bruises,' he said.

'And that's weird too!'

'You can give me all the bruises you want,' he said enthusiastically. 'Seriously, you're more than welcome!'

Christine felt like pulling out her own hair. He genuinely did not understand what had happened, why she had got so hysterical in her office, threatened to call the security guard if he didn't leave; he assumed that she had had a fantastic time just because he had made her come. But to her, as she had tried to convey, the fact that she had had so many orgasms made it worse, as if he had used her body against her. It felt as if she had been raped, made even worse by the fact that her rapist was completely convinced that they had shared not just a consensual sexual experience, but a truly excellent one. They were in two entirely different worlds.

'Don't want this,' she managed. 'Don't want choking.'

'But you had such a good – fine, okay!'

Seeing her furious expression, Angel swiftly changed tack, raising his hands pacifically.

'Look, we don't need to do it again,' he assured her. '*Ever*, if you don't want to. I'm sorry I didn't ask you before I tried it. Honestly, I just didn't realize. I've done *lots* of things that you really liked, and that I didn't ask your permission to try beforehand, haven't I? Like in the bath, when I put the soap up you and then—'

'Could have said no then!' Christine got out. 'Or said stop. Could *breathe*!'

It was killing Christine that these were the longest sentences she could manage; she wanted to gush out streams of accusations, explanations of why what he was saying was so very wrong, but her throat simply wouldn't let her.

'I see that! I get it!' Angel leaned forward eagerly. 'I'm sorry! Of course you couldn't! But we've always had such an amazing time in bed – right from the start, there was such chemistry, wasn't there? I can't keep my hands off you, and you always seem to want it so much . . .'

But at this, her eyes narrowed. Realizing quickly that talking about how much she wanted sex with him when she was throwing a massive hissy fit about what he had just done to her was not the best tactic, he halted and reassessed the situation.

No sex talk, he thought. *That's just pissing her off. Time to bring out the big guns. It was time anyway – no point waiting any longer . . .*

He took a deep breath.

'I love you, Christine,' he said, his voice soft now, hypnotically convincing. 'I think I fell in love with you almost as soon as I met you. You're so different to the other women I've been with, so genuine, so real. I've been wanting to tell you for a long time, but I was worried that you'd think it was too fast. You must have known, though? You must have known that you were the one for me?'

He leaned forward, careful not to seem intimidating, or as if he were going to lunge for her and start throttling her again. His eyes were wide and so magnetic that she couldn't look away, despite her intense confusion at this declaration of love from the man who had choked her hard enough to leave bruises all round her throat.

'You're the one,' he repeated. 'I mean that with all my heart, Christine. I'm in love with you. I want to marry you. I wanted to propose before I left for the expedition, but I thought it would be too much for you with how hard you were working on the auction, and it wouldn't be the right time. I wanted it to be the best moment of your life, not something that would stress you out. In fact –'

God, this is good, he thought smugly. *This is great. I'm the king of improvising under pressure. Look at her! She's absolutely dumbstruck – the stupid cow believes every single word!*

'– I was going to propose on New Year's Eve, at the stroke of midnight, after the auction,' he said. Even by his standards, this was superb, and it was hard for him not to smirk at his own cleverness. 'Celebrating everything you've achieved, starting the new year together, hand in hand. Vivienne knows how I feel about you – she's been my confidante, and she's over the moon about it! She was so hoping you would say yes and let her help to plan the wedding . . .'

Christine almost dropped the mug she was holding; it wobbled dangerously, rattling as she set it down on the table, her hand shaking in shock. Just as with the sex earlier that evening, everything seemed to be flipping around. One minute she had been having an amazing time, the next he'd gone crazy and started to strangle her. And now this conversation, which she had thought would end with him accepting that she was breaking up with him, had taken the most bizarre turn. She couldn't speak but it wasn't because of her sore throat; she was struck dumb with amazement that Angel had just proposed to her.

'I'll never touch you in a way you don't like again,' he was saying fervently. 'I'll always ask you in advance, well in advance, if there's anything new I want us to try. I'm so sorry, Christine – I never meant to hurt you! I just wanted to make you happy, make you come, give you the best time imaginable! My God, this is *not* how I imagined telling you I loved you, let alone proposing marriage! I've fucked up so badly!'

Angel's hands were clasped in front of him pleadingly, but he wasn't coming towards her, trying to touch her, kiss her, use his devastating physical attraction to convince her to listen to him; he was behaving as respectfully now as he had failed to do earlier. And he looked incredibly beautiful, and equally contrite.

'School fucked me up, Christine,' he said quietly. 'Sexually, I mean. I've hinted at it before, but I didn't want to tell you what really went on there. I was too ashamed, too embarrassed of what I went through. If I told you half of the things they made me do, you'd be horrified. Orgies, teachers with students, every kind of experimentation you can imagine. I was very young when Granny Viv sent me there, and I didn't stand a chance. What we did today – what I did to you – that was so normal at school I didn't think twice about it. The things that went on – the things that were done to me . . .'

He shuddered.

'I can't tell you,' he said, his head ducked as if in shame. 'You'd never look at me in the same way again. I don't want you to see me as a victim. And I wasn't just a victim, either. I became a participant, a willing one. When people do sexual things to you, part of you starts to like it, even to crave it. It's sex, after all. I found myself wanting them to keep doing those things to me, perverted though they were. I was at the age when you're curious about sex, wanting to experiment. And my God, I got dropped into the lion's den! Be careful what you wish for! There wasn't an experience in the world they didn't try there!'

Angel flicked up a swift glance through his thick lashes to check how this was going down with Christine. To his great satisfaction, he could see that she was reacting just as he had hoped. Clearly, she needed more than the proposal; she hadn't fallen into his arms, hadn't burst into tears and said she was the luckiest girl in the world and yes, yes, she would be his bride. So he had made another lightning-fast calculation. He would deal with the sex issue about which she was being so tediously bourgeois by pleading extenuating circumstances, playing the victim in an attempt to elicit sympathy from her.

It was working perfectly. Her eyes were wide with shock. For the first time since she had opened the front door, there was no anger and resentment in her eyes. Instead, he detected both growing horror and compassion at what he was telling her.

'Christine, I'm trying to be completely honest with you,' he lied smoothly. 'You deserve that. Here's the truth: the worst part is that by the end of my time at school, I enjoyed absolutely everything. I was completely taken over by the sex games that were played. Nothing was off-limits, nothing. What I did to you today was done to me more times than I can count, and I was a good student. I learned how to do everything that had been done to me. I took pride in it, pride in those special skills the older pupils taught me. And that's what warped me, what made me capable of doing that to you today.'

He put a throb in his voice for the next part.

'I don't know where the limits are any more,' he said sadly. 'Today has shown me that. I need help.'

Tears were pouring down Christine's face, tears for the little boy who had been so ill-treated and abused. The sight reminded Angel of how she had cried as he choked and fucked her on her office desk, and the memory gave him an instant erection. God, he'd come so hard, shot right up inside her, flooded her with hot spunk and champagne! It had been a truly excellent fuck. And if the stupid bitch weren't so ridiculously middle-class and inhibited, they'd be doing it again right now, her sitting on that table with her legs spread so he could ram his cock inside her, his hands wrapped tight around her throat, the orgasms ripping through her one after another . . . she'd loved what he'd done to her, the hypocritical bitch!

That was the whole bloody problem in a nutshell: she'd loved it so much, she'd got an attack of the guilts afterwards. Some of the kids at school had reacted like that at first, before they settled into things. But not Angel. He'd taken to everything like a duck to water. His nickname had been Oliver Twist at the Chateau, because he'd always asked for more.

He shifted to make sure she couldn't see his erection, feeling that it wouldn't quite chime with the sob story he was selling her.

'I can't expect you to forgive me,' he continued, after he'd let her cry for a while and managed to get it to wane by thinking about his grandmother. That did the trick fast. 'I can only tell you I love you and I need you. I can't believe I did this to the woman I love.' He shook his head, his expression sorrowful. 'I'm so fucked up,' he went on, his voice cracking. 'I'm damaged, maybe beyond repair. How could I ever think that you could love me back?'

Angel calculated that he'd done enough; it was time to make her come to him. And the way you always did that with a woman was by walking out the door. He stood up.

'I'm going, Christine,' he said. 'I should never have come here. I'm too messed up, and you deserve so much better than me. You deserve a man who can give you the moon and the stars, not a damaged bastard like me. Even if you loved me like I love you, I wouldn't be worthy of it.'

Too far? he wondered. *Too romance novel?* But no, she was looking at him now, full-on, her eyes yearning, her face wet with tears. As he headed for the door, making sure that he trod a careful loop around where she was sitting, she made a sound that was almost a grunt; it would have been a cry if her throat hadn't been so damaged. She flew out of the chair and ran towards Angel, grabbing his arm to stop him leaving.

'I'm so sorry that happened to you at school!' she managed to say. 'So sad . . . so wrong . . .'

'Oh Christine, I don't deserve you!' he said, bending to plant a swift kiss on the top of her head. She was hugging him tightly, both arms wrapped around his waist. 'You're my good angel!'

It was a huge relief that she could no longer see his face. Keeping up that sombre, pious, apologetic expression had been torture, especially when he was furious at her hypocrisy. She'd come more times than he could count! She'd spread her legs for him, panted like a dog, bucked like a horse, come like a nun finally getting a proper seeing to, the dirty, stupid, pathetic little bitch!

And then she'd forced him to enact the most ridiculous contrition scene. Angel was amazed at some of the nonsense he had just spouted. He'd sounded like a hero from one of those novels women loved, where the handsome young billionaire had a secret past full of appalling abuse that had scarred him so badly only the love of the impoverished, innocent virgin could melt his hardened heart and teach him true love. Jesus, she really was a stupid bitch if she'd fallen for *that* . . .

'Prince Charming', that old man in the flat below hers had

called him. Well, this Prince Charming was willing to bet that the Ugly Stepsisters would be much better fucks, much less complaining and whiny, than bloody dishrag Cinderella here. The less attractive ones were usually much more sexually adventurous; they knew they couldn't rely on their looks to keep a man's interest, so they developed excellent skill sets. The Ugly Sisters would almost certainly double-team him with great enthusiasm, peg him senseless, give him a really thorough spanking – do some of the work for a bloody change, unlike this one, who simply lay there without ever thinking that perhaps *he'd* like to get fucked, just for once. She was too selfish to even put a finger up his bum! And then she had the nerve to complain when he got a bit carried away!

He couldn't dwell on his grievances, however. He pulled himself back from the brink, drawing in a deep breath that he knew Christine would read as his emotional distress at the revelations he had just made to her. He had really pulled out all the stops in his plea. He couldn't afford to lose her, not now – not when things were so precarious financially. Not only would his marriage to her trigger his grandmother to fork out a heavy wodge of capital; but for his and Nicole's latest scheme to work, he needed Christine to still be in place at Berkeley as his loving girlfriend, not an estranged, resentful bitch, chippy about having some bruises on her neck instead of on her bum.

'Can I hug you back?' he said softly into her hair, not a trace of his thoughts showing in his voice. 'Would that be all right? I don't want to do anything that you're not sure about.'

She nodded against his chest. He enfolded her in his manly

embrace, just like the hunky billionaire in the romance novels. My God, he'd have to pretend to go to therapy now, be endlessly contrite, bring her bloody bouquets. Would he have to read some of those damn books to work out what to do? Didn't the heroes of those novels spend half the time brutally ravishing the heroines over their own desks and giving them multiple orgasms, anyway, just like he'd done with her that evening? What the fuck did the stupid bitch *want*?

Christine was pulling him towards the sofa; he could safely assume that this meant she'd fallen for his story hook, line and sinker. Thank God for the milligram of alprazolam he'd taken a short while ago. He normally just took half a pill, but he'd been so hyped up after the coke and the sex and the stupid bitch's hysterical freakout that he'd known he'd need more than usual to calm him down.

Still, Angel really hadn't expected that she'd make him work this hard. He'd assumed that an apology, followed by some light teasing about her overreaction, followed by a coy admission from her about how much she'd enjoyed being throttled and fucked to all those world-class orgasms, would fit the bill. Instead, she'd refused to let him in, made him shout like a barrow boy in the street in the freezing cold, forced him into a humiliating speech painting himself as a pathetic victim, and practically trapped him into an engagement where every sex act was going to have to be fairly vanilla, because she'd probably throw fits now every time he wanted to leave a mark on her.

Christ, if this marriage actually happened, he'd have to make so many compromises . . . watch her get pregnant twice, pretend to be excited both times about seeing her body become distorted and unpleasantly swollen, her breasts leaking . . . ugh . . . and then the stinking babies around the house, too . . . he'd have to invent some childhood trauma, blame his inability to bond with the babies on the separation from his mother, make it all Granny Viv's fault yet again . . .

Angel sank down on the sofa, still doing the manly embrace bit, letting Christine's head rest on his shoulder.

'I'll do anything,' he said, channelling Prince Charming again – the modern Prince Charming, the one with the whip and the heart of gold. 'I'll get help. I'll give you all the time you need. But I'll never stop loving you.'

Christine raised her head at this, her face so damp and smudged with tears that he risked removing one arm from around her and using the cuff of his shirt to blot them away.

'I've made you cry so much today,' he said so tenderly that, not for the first time, he thoroughly regretted not having become an actor. He had inherited not just his good looks from his grandparents, but their histrionic talent as well. My God, he had managed to turn this entire situation around, convincing Christine that he was a damaged soul madly in love with her – and he had improvised the whole thing! Not for the first time, he was hugely impressed with himself.

'Please don't shed any more tears over me, Christine,' he said nobly. 'I'm not worth it.'

'You *are*!' she said, as he had known she would, and she turned her head to kiss the wrist that was dabbing her tears. 'You *are*! What happened to you was so wrong . . . so bad . . .'

She hacked out a cough, which lasted a while. Angel thanked God he'd throttled her so hard that last time; it meant she couldn't spill out an endless stream of nonsense about him being a victim.

'Can't believe your grandmother sent you to that place,' she managed. 'So sad for you.'

'As long as I have you, I'll be the happiest man in the world,' he said. 'I love you, Christine.'

He knew she didn't love him, of course. He was no fool. She was dazzled by him, by his looks and charm and money and famous family. Women were programmed by society to want that exact combination, after all. But she wasn't in love with him, and if Tor had still been alive, Angel would have been seriously concerned about convincing her to marry him. Christine had never looked dazzled by Tor; she had looked as if she genuinely liked who he was as a person. Which was exactly what Angel needed to achieve to prevent her from finding out about himself.

It'll only be for a few years, he thought, even as he gave her his very best smile. *Worst-case scenario, if Nicole's plan doesn't work and I really do have to marry this stupid bloody vanilla bitch, it'll only be for a few years. And then I'll push her off a mountain.*

This time, he decided, he wanted his victim conscious as she fell. Rolling an already-unconscious body over the edge of the cliff had been satisfying at the time, but now Angel looked back, it was undeniable that the experience would have been infinitely more pleasant if Tor had been screaming in fear as he realized what was happening to him.

Oh yes, Christine would know exactly what was happening when Angel gave her that shove. After all those years he'd have spent playing the reformed playboy, the damaged billionaire trotting out every cliché in the book for this bitch's benefit, the *least* she could give him in return was the sound of her wailing all the way down to the ground.

Chapter Twenty

London – one month later

Something was wrong. Christine had just finished her last appointment of the day, and even as she said goodbye to the client, a nagging voice in her head was telling her that some aspect of what had just happened had been . . . off. *Wrong.* She couldn't think why; the meeting had been a great success. But ever since, she had been pacing back and forth across her office, wondering what on earth about it could have triggered this strong sense of unease.

She glanced over at the rings lying on her desk, displayed on the black velvet tray on which she had shown them to the potential buyer, a multimillionaire hedge-funder. He had been especially eager to view the unusually set inverted round-cut diamond that had been given to Vivienne by Randon Cliffe; the provenance was hugely important to the client, who wanted to present it to his trophy girlfriend when he proposed to her.

He had viewed others, but clearly his heart was set on the inverted diamond, and Christine had high hopes of negotiating a good price for it. At this level, money didn't matter as much as owning something no one else could have, purchasing bragging rights.

This would be the hedge-funder's second marriage, the old wife discarded for a new version half her age and half her weight who, the hedge-funder had blithely recounted to Christine just now, didn't even know who Vivienne Winter and Randon Cliffe were. She was, however, he had told Christine, a 'dead ringer' for the young Vivienne, and he had been delighted by the photographs Christine had produced, sourced from Vivienne's photo stash, taken for a German magazine, in which Vivienne was holding her hand out to show off the ring, twisting it to make sure the camera caught the unusual setting of the stone.

There had also been some wonderful shots where Vivienne, laughing, pretended to backhand Randon in the face with the ring as he cringed away theatrically, feigning fear. But to Christine's great disappointment, Vivienne had absolutely refused to allow any of those images to be part of the sale. She had actually gone white on seeing the pictures, staring at them in silence for some time. Finally, she had gathered up the photographs, stacked them together and given them to Christine, saying quietly:

'Shred them, please. And if there are negatives, shred them too. They bring back a painful memory.'

Christine had started to protest: the pictures were so fun and playful, she had pointed out, it would be a real shame for them to be lost to posterity. But Vivienne had held up her hand and said: 'This subject is not up for further discussion, Christine,' in a voice as sharp as the *culet* of the diamond.

So that had been that. Christine had obeyed her, feeding the photographs into the shredder with great regret. Still, the remaining ones had been quite enough to make the hedge-funder's eyes light up avariciously. Christine was as sure as she could be that he would ring her up tomorrow with a counter-offer – she had priced the ring and photo rights at eight million pounds – and, after going back and forth for a couple of days, they would come to a mutually satisfactory agreement.

Normally the security guard, who was always present when clients were viewing such expensive jewellery, would have waited while Christine packed away the rings in their numbered cases to be taken back to the basement safe. Instead, she had heard herself asking the guard to get himself a cup of tea from the kitchenette in the main office; clients had to be supervised with the jewels, but she did not. She needed some time to work out why she was feeling like this; time, and space. Hence the pacing; she was hoping that the movement would shake loose the nagging concern from the back of her brain to the front, where it would be easily retrievable.

Was it the ring that was bothering her? Or the photos? No, it wasn't the latter. She examined her reaction to the photographs and couldn't find a single flicker of concern or distress. Whereas as soon as she thought of the ring again, there it was: a distant distress call, like a flare going up far away over a dark ocean from a tiny storm-tossed ship.

So was it the ring that was worrying her? That too was quickly answered. The ring was fine. She knew that with absolute certainty. Christine had an excellent eye, considerably superior to the average gemmologist; she knew how highly she was regarded by her colleagues in the jewellery business. And although the unusual setting of the diamond meant that it was harder to assess how light travelled through it, Christine paused by her desk to look down at the diamond, resting in the black velvet display tray, and could find nothing to trouble her in its lustre and transparency, its near-colourless hue.

Colourless, because almost all diamonds were delicately tinted with shades of yellow or brown that an untrained observer would never detect; truly neutral ones were very rare, and very valuable. Christine was intimately familiar with this one's particular faint hint of yellow. Her eye was so attuned to the diamonds she put up for sale that she could have distinguished them immediately, one after another, as swiftly as they were placed in front of her.

Her gaze moved to the other rings she had shown the hedge-funder, and the warning flare went off again as she looked at the seven-carat purple diamond. It had been another gift from Randon, chosen to echo the violet of Vivienne's eyes; he had paid a few hundred thousand pounds for it thirty years ago, and now it was worth at least twelve million even before the considerations of provenance and attached photo rights. Large green and purple diamonds were so rare that pricing them was known colloquially by jewellers as 'pick a number'. It would have made a classic investment gem, one that was never set, but kept loose in a safe or bank vault – to be sold off, usually, after the owner died and the children started wrangling over the inheritance.

Christine focused more closely on the extraordinary stone. It was emerald-cut; the shallow steps to the wide table at the centre, the flashes of deep light from its planes, were perfect. The colour was not only intense, but markedly even –

Wait. Hang on. The colour is amazingly *even for a stone*

*that was purchased thirty years ago, isn't it? It looks . . .
treated.*

This was not good, not good at all. Precious gems all had
natural imperfections, which were one of the factors in iden-
tifying a particular stone. However, in recent decades a
variety of treatments had become increasingly common.
With the judicious use of heat, you could lighten or darken
the colour of a gemstone, even alter it entirely; you could
improve its clarity and its brightness. To give them a more
consistent colour, emeralds were routinely soaked in oil.

Laboratory tests could detect whether a stone had been
heated, and a ruby or a sapphire, in particular, that had not
would be rare and hence valuable. The most expensive stones,
in general, were untreated. Careful examination would reveal
the imperfections that made them not only unique, but
highly prized to the one per cent of buyers who were serious
connoisseurs; the other ninety nine just liked their stones
big and flawless.

But the widespread use of these treatments had only
happened *after* Vivienne amassed the vast majority of her
jewel collection. Which meant that Christine should not, now,
be staring at the purple diamond ring thinking that the colour
was so consistent, it looked suspiciously as if it had been
treated with coloured oil.

Her heart was racing. The closer she looked at the
diamond, the more her initial view was confirmed. Its colour
was simply too uniform, too perfect for it to be a natural,
untreated gemstone. Christine summoned the memory of
the last time she had seen this ring: two weeks ago, more or

less. She was absolutely sure that the diamond had not looked so suspiciously consistent in shade then.

It was as if someone had dug a lino cutter into her abdomen and carved a hole the size of that seven-carat diamond directly beneath her sternum bone. Slowly, she found herself glancing over at a twelve-carat cushion-cut orange diamond cocktail ring. It was a huge knuckleduster, the massive orange stone surrounded by smaller white half-carat diamonds. With horrible certainty, she realized that her verdict on this was identical. Its colour was so even that any flaws were impossible to spot. And it had not looked so incredibly perfect the last time she had brought it out to show a client.

Christine drew a long, deep breath. Anyone who worked in her field was aware that rings were the easiest item of jewellery to steal. Compact enough to fit in the palm of a hand, they were ideal for the classic jewellery store switch, which involved the potential customer bringing an exact replica of the piece to the viewing so that they could replace the real with the fake. Employees were taught to be particularly alert with the smaller pieces, never to leave the customer alone with them; but someone skilled in sleight of hand could pull off a substitution right in front of a jeweller. Certification and assessment were done before customers viewed the pieces, so it would take a particularly sharp-eyed assistant to notice that the ring they returned to its box didn't sparkle quite the same way as it had when they took it out. CCTV was installed in all jewellery shops, of course, but there was none in Christine's office – no record of her meetings, nothing to play back so that she could try to spot who had swapped the rings.

Christine picked up the orange diamond, surprised to notice that her hand wasn't shaking too badly considering the circumstances. She pulled her DiamondSure machine out of a desk drawer, a recently invented screening device that tested diamonds, distinguishing real ones from synthetics. It was terrifying how sophisticated the process of growing synthetics in a laboratory was now; physically and chemically, they *were* diamonds. Although the coloured ones were easier to make, they were also easier to spot, as their colour saturation was unnaturally even – just what Christine was concerned about with the purple and orange stones.

With colourless diamonds, however, it was impossible to tell the difference without testing equipment. The DiamondSure could only test colourless diamonds from a small percentage of a carat up to a maximum of ten carats. Generally you put a loose diamond on the sample dish with a fibre-optic probe at its base, but the probe could also be released to test mounted diamonds. It was this that Christine did now, moving the probe over one, then another, of the smaller white diamonds.

If someone had done what she suspected, every diamond in this ring would be synthetic. No one would grow a huge orange one and surround it in a setting with genuine smaller stones; there would be no point, as the central one would be the only stone to draw attention. So when both of the white diamonds turned out to be artificial, she knew that the orange diamond must be a fake too – which meant, almost certainly, that the purple one was as well.

It was the worst disaster possible. The reputational damage would be horrendous. If Berkeley could not be trusted to keep extremely valuable items safe on its own premises, it would never be taken seriously as an auction house again. Thefts happened, of course; there were always stories of cover-ups and payoffs and scandals barely averted; but the point was that they *had* been averted. This could be covered up, no doubt. But if she told anyone at Berkeley what had happened, her head would roll.

No one took these jewels out to show but Christine. She was the expert, the point of contact with the clients, the repository of all the detailed knowledge about Vivienne's personal history that added so much extra value. She would be blamed, and that would be only fair, because these jewels were her responsibility.

Christine's desk phone shrilled. She had been sitting in such deathly silence, the sound of her own racing heart-beat the only noise in the room, that she jumped almost out of her skin. Automatically, she reached for it, to hear Angel's dulcet voice cooing from the receiver: 'Darling, are you ready? I'm five minutes away in a cab.'

She had completely lost any sense of time. Angel had been due to pick her up at six thirty, and he was impressively punctual. Her first instinct was to tell him that she couldn't join him that evening, that she needed to stay in the office and run through her records of the client visits she had scheduled recently, to narrow down a list of who had viewed the purple and the orange rings.

But then Christine realized that she didn't need to check her notes. She was living, breathing, sleeping this auction; every detail of it was immediately accessible to her. Those two rings had only been shown together on one occasion, and she knew immediately who had been at that appointment. To her great surprise, the revelation was much less of a shock than she might have anticipated.

'Do you mind driving around the block for a bit if there isn't a place to wait outside?' she said, her voice clear and calm. 'The last meeting ran a little late. I'll be out in a quarter of an hour.'

Summoning the guard, she followed him downstairs and supervised the return of the jewellery to the safe. Then she returned to her office and changed out of her grey Jaeger suit into jeans and a Muubaa sheepskin jacket. Vivienne's gift of aquamarines glinted in her ears and at her throat as Christine picked up her bag, left her office, and glided through the building, looking unusually serene – a serenity that Angel noticed immediately as she climbed into the black cab where he waited. She greeted him with a kiss but refused a glass of champagne; he had brought a bottle plus two flutes. Angel would have been horrified by the idea of drinking champagne out of anything but glass.

He stared at Christine narrowly as he stowed the second glass back in its leather carry case, wondering why she looked so distant, so unusually poised. It had been pleasantly easy to convince her that he was in therapy for his years of abuse at boarding school. He had been subdued, yet attentive, in the time he spent with Christine, while alluding to afternoon appointments with his therapist. In practice these were, more often than not, intense sex sessions with Nicole, and Angel most definitely considered them therapy of a sort. They certainly took the edge off enough to allow him to make gentle love to Christine a few evenings a week – so gentle that he suspected she was getting rather frustrated with the change of pace.

Pure vanilla, all the way. Not even a raspberry swirl every now and then. Christine had wanted this, and she'd got it. As the cab went down Park Lane, heading for Hyde Park Corner, he asked if anything was wrong, but her explanation that she was distracted by all the work she had to get through was completely believable. It was only a matter of weeks until the New Year's Eve auction in Geneva, and as well as the near-constant viewings, Christine was organizing every painstaking detail of the transport of the jewels to their Geneva auction house with Malca-Amit, the specialist high-value cargo service.

'Here we are!' Angel said amiably, as the cab turned into the driveway that led to the south entrance gate of Kensington Palace. 'Look at all the paps still hanging round in the cold weather! Will they ever get tired of trying to get photos of Toby and Missy, I wonder?'

'No,' Christine said with a faint smile as the cab slowed down, the mass of journalists and photographers rushing forward to see who was inside. The gates were swinging open and even as the camera flashes went off, bright in the evening darkness, capturing the passengers inside the cab in case they were important, the vehicle was moving up the central driveway, around the main bulk of the building, past the orangery, heading for Apartment 3 in one of the side wings.

Lights blazed in Apartment 6, the four-story house at the corner of the main wing. It was far enough away from the State Apartments to give Prince Hugo, his wife Chloe and the two little princesses some distance from the camera phones of the tourists who visited Kensington Palace. By seven o'clock, the routine of dinner, bath and bed for the small girls was well underway. Chloe's mother and father were staying for a week, and the atmosphere was cheerful, cosy family chaos, Hugo supervising bathtime with the doting grandparents while Chloe made pasta for dinner. The upper classes mocked Chloe for her middle-class lifestyle, but after his privileged but neglected upbringing, Hugo thoroughly relished every moment of happy domesticity.

Apartment 3 was generally a complete contrast to Apartment 6: Toby's bachelor pad was much more spartan and functional. Its edges were currently softened, however, by the masses of candles and flowers he had bought to celebrate Missy's latest flying visit from Romania, where she was filming a medieval action movie in which she played a Saracen general's daughter who teamed up with a renegade Knight Templar. Pulling out all the stops, Toby had ordered several bouquets from the Pimlico branch of the florist Wild at Heart and a crate of Neom organic candles from Selfridges; almost as soon as Toby opened the front door, Angel started sneezing at the overwhelming scent of a cluster of candles that surrounded a huge bouquet of roses on the hall table.

'Sorry,' Toby said apologetically. 'Bit much, I know. I lit them earlier to make the place smell nice for Missy, instead of the usual Eau de Sweaty Jockstrap, but then the kids came round and Chloe kicked off because she said it wasn't safe to have sprogs over with things burning, so then I blew them all out but it ponged madly because of all the smoke, and Chloe said I did it wrong and you're supposed to snuff them—'

'She's right,' Missy called from the kitchen.

'So then I lit them all again to cover the smell of the

smoke,' Toby explained. 'Missy says I'm an idiot and I should have got non-scented ones if I was going to light so many, but I think it looks romantic with all of them lit, don't you?'

Angel was still sneezing as he and Christine took off their jackets. Ignoring the hall cupboard, Toby chucked them into the spare bedroom as they walked down the corridor, managing to get them to land more or less on the bed.

'Come into the kitchen,' he said. 'Missy's making dinner.'

It was a symbol of how madly in love Toby was with Missy that he beamed cheerfully at the snacks she had laid out on the huge central kitchen island: homemade kale crisps, plus edamame and wasabi hummus with celery and gluten-free crackers to dip in it.

'Hi guys! It's quinoa stir-fry with king prawns and cauli-flower rice for dinner,' Missy said over her shoulder, her face make-up free and shiny with steam from the stove, her cheeks pink. 'It'll be ready in about twenty.'

She was thin enough that Toby's apron nearly wrapped round her twice; when she visited Toby, her assistant sched-uled deliveries from Planet Organic the day of her arrival so that Missy could make sure she had everything she needed for her extremely strict, nutritionist-planned diet. She and Toby preferred to stay in when she was in London, as when-ever they went out the paparazzi attention was relentless. The pattern they had slipped into was to invite Angel and Chris-tine over regularly, the bond forged on the ill-fated charity expedition as strong as ever.

Though it was not mentioned to Christine, there was not a sliver of embarrassment about the three of them having shared a memorable night at base camp. Missy was an actress and Toby a jet-setting prince; although they might have decided that they wanted to be exclusive now, they both came from worlds where, sexually, anything was possible.

Christine greeted Missy and took a seat on a high stool on the far side of the island. Behind Missy's back, Angel pulled an appalled face at the array of healthy snacks.

'So virtuous!' he drawled. 'Don't you find yourself craving Pringles, Tobes?'

Toby rolled his eyes as he unstopped a bottle of champagne.

'I can't have those in the house,' Missy said from the stove. 'They're a trigger food.'

'I've got Guinness – I could whip up a Black Velvet if you fancy one?' Toby was saying to Angel. He handed Christine her usual glass of champagne as Missy continued:

'It's killing me that I can't get toasted crickets from Whole Foods over here! The UK is so behind the curve! In LA they do this great Moroccan spice version, really low in salt and high in protein – Angel, I know you're going to snark on me but honestly, guys, crickets are real low in fat and cholesterol and they're totally environmentally friendly. If you think of them as the shellfish of the air, you'll be a lot cooler about the idea of eating them –'

The security buzzer went, and Toby dashed across the kitchen to answer it.

'Hey? Yeah, cool, thanks,' he said. 'It's Nicole's cab, guys. They're just buzzing her in through the gates.'

'I'll get the door for her,' Angel said, so swiftly that Christine's antennae went up. When the two of them didn't return immediately, she slid off her bar stool, saying she needed the loo. Quietly crossing the living room, she paused at the opening of the hallway corridor. As she had guessed, Angel and Nicole were in the guest bedroom together, and a couple of steps down the hallway brought her close enough to overhear what they were saying.

'My God, it stinks in here! Did someone break a bottle of scent?' Nicole exclaimed.

Angel said: 'It's Toby laying in candles for Missy.'

'Still besotted?'

'More than ever. Pretty sickening, actually. Here, I brought you a glass of fizz.'

'Oh, thanks, darling! Just what I need! I've had a hell of a day – the last meeting in Amsterdam ran really late and then the trains were a mess! Cheers!'

There was a short pause as, presumably, she took a drink of champagne. Then: 'Is she –' Nicole asked, and Angel said quickly:

'Safely back in the kitchen.'

'How's it going?'

'Fine. Absolutely fine.'

'She's still cool?'

'God, yes. Doesn't suspect a thing.'

'And you've been careful, you naughty boy? Have you been managing to keep your hands off her neck?'

'Not even a spank when I fuck her doggy style!' Angel said. 'Not that I've been doing much of that. Missionary position, with me staring lovingly into her eyes and whispering her name, seemed most indicated in the circs.'

'Eww, you'd better make sure you don't freak her out,' Nicole said. There was the sound of a glass being set down on a table, a coat being shrugged off and dropped onto the bed. 'That'd give me the total heebie-jeebies if you did it to me.'

'It's making me want to choke her even more,' Angel said wistfully. 'God, that was fun, Nic! You should have seen her! She started crying, did I tell you? It made my cock hard as a rock. Never gone for the whole crying thing before, but for some reason it really turned me on. I fucked her like a positive *animal*.'

'Lucky her! Well, don't expect me to cry for you, darling!' Nicole giggled. 'I don't know when I last cried – maybe back when Gisele was fucking Herr Hoffman and I was so obsessed with him. Mind you, those were more tears of rage . . .'

'Ah, happy memories! I got Gisele on the rebound. She was so pissed off about you nicking Herr Hoffmann that she'd do simply anything to prove what a good fuck she was . . . God, she was bendy. I owe you for that. So! All good with the you-know-whats?'

'Fantastic!' Nicole said gleefully. 'He'll take them all. He thinks he can recut the huge one and even *add* value to it! Of course, he needs to see them first to confirm, not just photos, but it's great news! He's got a big job on right now but he can take them next week. You can bring them yourself if you don't trust me with them alone.'

'We'll take them together,' Angel said. 'Drop them off, then pick up some filthy whore in the red light district to celebrate.'

'Ooh, lovely! A really trashy one! What fun!'

There was another pause, filled by kissing sounds.

'We should get back,' Angel said, moving towards the door. 'They'll be wondering why we're taking so long.'

By the time he had pushed it open, Christine was round

the corner of the corridor, moving fast across the living room; as Angel and Nicole arrived in the kitchen, Christine was up on her stool, sipping champagne as if she had never left. The huge bouquet on the kitchen island was useful, as it partially blocked Angel from seeing her expression.

She waved a greeting at Nicole, but there was an excellent distraction underway. Toby had now realized that Missy's 'cauliflower rice' was actually cauliflower zapped in a food processor to the texture of fine grains, and then microwaved. He was protesting, while Missy was responding that her form of 'rice' was an excellent low-carb replacement; Angel added fuel to the fire by saying, 'Missy's been threatening to feed us crickets.'

The ensuing theatrical protests from Nicole, and a lively argument between Angel and Toby about the proportion of Guinness to champagne in Black Velvets, meant that no one paid any attention to Christine for a good twenty minutes, which was the bare minimum she needed to process the events of the last hour. Because, back in her office, she had remembered that the week before, Toby – accompanied by Angel – had visited Berkeley to look at selected pieces of Vivienne's jewellery. Having taken Missy to meet Vivienne, Toby wanted to buy his girlfriend something from the film icon's collection, and he had been positively giggly at the idea of looking at rings.

Nathan and Christine had brought out a whole range for Toby to look at, the purple and the orange diamonds among them. It had been a much larger selection than usual, the normal rules relaxed for a royal prince and Vivienne's grandson, and Toby had been like a kid in a sweet shop. When

Angel had suggested that Toby look at the ridiculously huge 114-carat cushion-cut, heart-shaped diamond, currently worn as a pendant, that had been a gift to Vivienne from Randon, Toby had been very enthusiastic.

Enormous as it was, however, this stone was surprisingly disappointing, which was Christine's invariable experience with large cushion-cut diamonds. When the stones were high-colour and high-quality, the effect was to make the diamond look like glass. The cushion-cut lacked the numerous facets of a round brilliant, so the diamond failed to sparkle. The technical term for it was 'dead', and even the unskilled Toby, turning over the stone wonderingly, had commented that it was 'a bit dull'.

The pendant had been set aside almost immediately. Like the orange and purple diamond rings, it was too expensive, too big for Missy's tiny frame, and had only been brought up because no one could refuse Prince Toby if he wanted to see anything his heart might desire – especially not Nathan, who had a major crush on him.

But it wasn't Toby who wanted to see the pendant, Christine thought. *It was Angel who suggested it, because it was heart-shaped. There was much more coming and going at that client visit than I would ever normally allow. We were laughing and chatting and we didn't keep the same eagle eye on the pieces we normally do, we didn't stick to the usual rule that only one piece was being held at a time . . .*

Asked for her professional advice about the diamond, Christine would have unequivocally suggested that the owner consider recutting it to add value. It would be a hard choice, as psychologically, no one wanted to relinquish the possession of a stone larger than a hundred carats. But the resulting diamond would probably be worth more, and besides, a good cutter would produce a few carat and two-carat round brilliants out of the trimmings. No question, a top-quality 96er, plus those extras, would bring more than a 114-carat 'dead' diamond.

Christine was sure that this must be the 'huge one' Nicole had just mentioned, that when Christine returned to the office first thing the next day, she would take out the 114-carat diamond and find that it, too, looked artificial. The Amsterdam cutter – Amsterdam was still, after many centuries, the world centre of diamond-cutting, and plenty of experts were willing to recut gems for higher than normal fees in compensation for their overlooking the lack of provenance – was clearly of the same opinion as Christine, that value might be added to the stone by careful reshaping.

As soon as a gem was recut, there could be no proving what had happened. It was brand, sparkling new. That was the magic of recutting: you created an entirely new gem. Always smaller, usually less valuable, but incapable of being identified as stolen and used as evidence against you.

As Vivienne's grandson, Angel had full access to all the photographs and specifications of her jewellery. It would have been easy for him to pass copies to a contact who had a lab set up to grow synthetic diamonds, making apparently perfect replacements for various large gems, then to have encouraged Toby to set up an appointment at the auction house. With the fake jewels tucked in his pocket, Angel could easily have swapped them over during one of the many moments when everyone in the room was distracted by the presence of a royal prince.

So many pieces were falling into place! Angel's desperation to reconcile with Christine, saying all the right things with such miraculous smoothness, and his equally miraculous transformation. The ease with which he had found a therapist, and the great reports he had given of his treatment . . . the complete change in the way he made love to her, which, now she thought about it, was much too perfect, just like the orange and purple diamonds.

Had he been planning this from the beginning? When he'd realized in Tylösand that Vivienne was considering Christine's auction house for the jewellery sale, had Angel asked Christine out that very evening so that he would have access to visits, the opportunity to swap the gems? No, surely, because as Vivienne's grandson, he could already have done that – or could he? After all, now that she thought about it, Angel had probably never been given free access to the safe before, the opportunity to photograph and substitute pieces.

One thing's definite: every word he said about being in love with me was an absolute lie, she realized. Because when the jewellery was sold at auction, the first thing any sensible buyer would do was to have their purchase authenticated by a third party. Fraudulent stones would immediately be detected. Christine and Berkeley would be blamed, because they had appraised Vivienne's gems before cataloguing them, had certified them as genuine. Their reputations would be ruined. Christine would be unemployable anywhere in her chosen field. It would, effectively, destroy her life.

The strangest thing of all was that, the instant she

understood how badly Angel had betrayed her, Christine had the most extraordinary, ineffable sensation of lightness. She was free.

She had never, she realized, had any true feelings for Angel. She had been flattered by his interest, dazzled by his social status and handsome looks, seduced by his extraordinary sexual abilities. She shuddered: after hearing that snatch of conversation between him and Nicole, the thought of ever having sex with him again made her skin crawl.

After Angel had choked her, she had rejected him, and that had been the first intelligent decision she'd made in a long time. She should have trusted her instincts, should never have taken him back. But his story had been so compelling, so tragic . . .

I was such an idiot! she thought. *I can't believe I fell for the classic line men pull on women when they've behaved badly, the poor-little-boy routine! Well, it worked. I felt too guilty to do anything but take him back!*

It was shocking how easily women could be manipulated this way. She wouldn't have believed she would be susceptible to it. And yet here she was, the girlfriend of a man who had hurt her badly – a man who had choked her repeatedly until she passed out – a man she didn't know at all.

Angel had lied when he said he knew the sexual games he had played at school were wrong. He had enjoyed every minute. And every time he had made love to her since, he had been secretly mocking her stupidity for falling for his sob story, his fake repentance, his pleas for forgiveness.

'I know, right?' said Toby, seeing her flinch and attributing it to the ongoing conversation about eating insects.

'Disgusting! Here, have some more champagne and let's talk about something less revolting . . .'

'Darling, you're very quiet!' Angel said, coming round the corner of the island and giving her a quick hug. Summoning up all the guile she possessed, Christine smiled at him sweetly, hugging him back. She had never imagined that she was capable of acting a part so well.

'I've just got a bit of headache, that's all,' she said. 'I'm sure the champagne will take care of it. I'll have to have an early night, though – back at mine, so I can get a full night's sleep. You don't mind, do you?'

She found herself taking pleasure in adding:

'Of course, after the auction's over, it'll all be different! We should plan a holiday in February. In January, I'll be processing all the paperwork and the post-sale valuations and the shipping, so that'll be almost as crazy as now. But February should be fine, and I'd love to get some sunshine. What about Mexico? I saw some amazing photos of a resort where the king and queen of Herzoslovakia went on their honeymoon – private pools and lovely cabanas, glorious weather, just you and me, very romantic . . .'

If she hadn't been on high alert and unusually acute, it would have been almost impossible for her to notice the flicker of recoil in Angel's eyes, or the smirk that briefly passed across Nicole's face.

'That sounds fantastic!' Angel said, bending to kiss her.

Christine kissed him back, putting a hand on his shoulder, squeezing it fondly. She could do this. She could carry this off. She might not be as experienced at deception as Angel and Nicole, but she was perfectly capable of fooling them.

Of course, that was because they thought that she was nothing but a silly little victim. A dupe whom Angel had targeted from the first, too naive and unsophisticated to, oh, fully appreciate how lucky she was to be choked by him . . .

Toby was refilling her half-full glass; he was the perfect host. This would almost certainly be the last time a prince poured her champagne as she sat in a royal palace, Christine reflected. She should make the most of it. Thanking him with another sweet smile, she sipped her drink and watched Angel and Nicole from below her lowered lashes. She could tell from the way they glanced at each other that they were sure Christine had no suspicions at all about the shitstorm that was about to rain down on her head, courtesy of the two of them.

They'll pay for this, Christine resolved, even as she slid off her stool and followed the rest of them to the big oak table at the far side of the room, where Missy was dishing up her quinoa stir-fry. In a big serving bowl, a gleaming pink paprika-dusted heap of king prawns was piled on top of a mound of cauliflower 'rice', which had been toasted in a pan after being microwaved. Open bottles of Sancerre from the palace cellars were placed at intervals along the table, white wine glasses laid out by the plate settings, and massive silver candelabras glowed at either end, polished that day by one of the palace housekeepers.

Toby and Missy stood at the head of the table, arms around each other's waists, beaming as their guests seated themselves. Not to be outdone, Christine wrapped her arm around Angel's waist for a second, flashing a grin of contentment at

Nicole, who smiled back at her in return, tossing back her enviable mane of dark hair.

And the best part is, they won't see it coming. They think I'm such a total idiot, they won't have any idea that I'm going to screw them back just like they've tried to screw me.

Christine's body sat down at the table, smiling cheerfully, drinking Sancerre and eating the surprisingly tasty food. It took very little part in the banter; but then, no one was expecting her to say much. Angel and Toby were boisterous, Nicole sexy, Missy amused by the upper-class badinage of English males, and Christine thoughtful; that was the pattern of their social engagements.

Which is great, as no one will be at all suspicious that I'm not chattering away, Christine's brain thought, floating free, leaving her body to eat and smile and nod while her intellect worked away, that dedicated, meticulous intellect and drive that had taken her from foster care to huge success in her chosen career.

I was determined to be a gemmologist. I was determined to get the Vivienne Winter sale. And now I've got a new goal. I'm going to save myself, and turn the tables on the two of them.

She raised her glass in a toast, unnoticed by anyone else at the table.

And wow, I'm really going to enjoy taking my revenge . . .

Chapter Twenty-One

London – the next day

A little before midday, Christine let herself into Angel's flat and paused, the door still open, listening with great care and attention to hear if there was any movement inside. The night before, kissing Angel goodbye as he put her into the taxi he had called on his account to take her home – *enjoy these free cabs while you have them, Christine*, she had told herself, *you'll be back to public transport and having to carry flat shoes in your handbag soon enough* – she had asked him what he was up to the next day, if he could maybe manage lunch with her. She had said that she felt bad about leaving early and not spending the night with him; she'd assumed the soppiest expression she could manage, and been quietly amazed to see Angel fall for it, hook, line and sinker.

He really does think I'm a complete idiot, she realized. *But then, I've been behaving like one as far as he's concerned, haven't I?*

If, as Angel declined the idea of lunch regretfully, he had pleaded a therapist's appointment by way of excuse, Christine wouldn't have believed a word of it. The closest Angel had ever been to a therapist, she was quite sure now, was the four-handed massage he regularly got at the spa at the

InterContinental, Park Lane, after his steam temple ritual there. Instead, he had told her that he was booked at noon for a session with his personal trainer. This Christine did believe. Angel took his slim, lean physique very seriously, and paid the man he had nicknamed the Wacky Russian a very large sum to maintain it. The grimace with which Angel had told Christine that it was leg day was further proof he was telling the truth. He always made that face when he told her it was leg day.

She should have, at minimum, a couple of hours alone in his apartment. After Angel worked out, he swam in the pool, visited the sauna and steam rooms; his club at Chelsea Harbour was the height of luxury. And it wasn't one of the days that the housekeeping service came in to clean. Christine had checked that already. Closing the door behind her, she was still on full alert, however. What if Nicole was here? That brief snatch of conversation between her and Angel last night had made it clear they were much closer than they'd led Christine to believe. But Christine had phoned the apartment and rung the doorbell, both with no answer. She was taking every precaution she possibly could.

She let out a long breath. There was no one here but her. Swiftly, she darted across the long expanse of the living room into the lavishly proportioned bedroom, crossing to the walk-in wardrobe opposite the bathroom. She had spent all of yesterday evening and all of this morning thinking of nothing but where the jewels Angel had stolen could be concealed.

Nicole's remarks to Angel last night had made it clear she had not yet taken the stolen gems to Amsterdam. They were still in Angel's possession, which meant they were over-whelmingly likely to be in his apartment. It was possible he had a safe deposit box, but would someone who had stolen his grandmother's jewellery proceed to do something as respectable as rent a box in a bank vault in which to store the stolen property? That seemed unlikely, especially as he would be holding on to the jewels for only a short time.

The lights in the walk-in wardrobe were on motion sensors, clicking on as soon as she entered. Christine started pulling out the shallow built-in walnut drawers. She didn't bother with the underwear drawer, as that was serviced regularly by the cleaners. All of Angel's dirty clothes were posted down the generously sized chute concealed behind a cupboard door in the bathroom, landing in an industrial laundry basket in the basement labelled with his apartment number. The housekeepers sorted it twice weekly, separating hand wash, normal laundry and dry cleaning, ensuring everything was correctly treated and returned to Angel's apartment, neatly placed in the correct drawer or hung in the appropriate section of the wardrobe.

Christine concentrated on ties, belts, cufflinks and watches – the drawers the cleaning staff would have no reason to access. She had great hopes of one silk tie, rolled up and stacked perfectly like its counterparts in a display more typical of a luxury menswear boutique than a private home, but the crum-pled black tissue paper inside its hollow centre did not contain anything. It was there to maintain the shape of the delicate fabric, not conceal a cluster of rings and pendants.

Precious stones were bought as investments partly because they had the highest value to the lowest space requirements.

Easily portable, they were a universal currency. But it meant hiding them was easy, too, and after Christine had gone up the walnut steps that slid from one side of the wardrobe to the other, allowing access to the top cupboards; after she had craned in to check out the back of each one; after she'd searched the side and top zip pockets of Angel's Vuitton luggage, where a pouch of jewels could lie perfectly concealed – she'd often forgotten to empty those pockets out after trips herself, you never noticed anything in them – she still had nothing to show for it. She dropped to her knees and started going through the handmade shoes and boots lined up in pairs on the carpeted floor.

Nothing inside the toes of the shoes. Nothing in the pockets of his heavy winter coats. She had ruled out the bathroom; it was too brightly lit to be a good hiding place. She did try his bedside table drawer, but felt foolish for even looking somewhere so obvious. The regular cleaning service meant there was no point searching under the mattress, down the sides of any upholstered furniture, or beneath sofa cushions.

So, according to the checklist she had in her head, in-formed by a morning spent searching on Google for sneaky hiding place ideas, the next stop was the kitchen. Angel never had much food in the fridge – vodka, lemons, smoked salmon – but there was a huge freezer, and one of the sugges-tions online was to store jewellery in bags of frozen peas, jars of coffee, places thieves would be unlikely to look. As far as Christine knew, Angel had never cooked a day in his life, but there were definitely some items in the kitchen in which the rings and pendant could be concealed.

She was pretty sure she was only looking for those three gems. The first thing she had done on arriving at work was to inspect all the other pieces that had been brought up for Toby's benefit. They would need to be checked, discreetly, by a testing lab; everything to which Angel had had access would have to be verified.

But in Christine's expert opinion, the rest of the jewellery was genuine. Whoever had made the decision about which pieces to substitute – Angel, Nicole, or both of them in tandem – had been tactical. By the standards of this auction, the jewellery they had taken was not premium, no major pieces with a provenance so important they would be under the spotlight. Still, the stones were large enough that, even after being recut, they would have a collective value in the tens of millions. If anyone had asked Christine for a recommendation on what was best to steal from the sale, the rings and the pendant would have been high on her list.

And if she couldn't locate them here, she could pull those items from the sale. God knew what explanation she would give to Vivienne, but that would be the only stumbling block. The absence of three minor items from the auction would cause no negative publicity. They could have been sold privately, or Vivienne could have changed her mind and decided to keep them after all; no one would care. Christine's career and reputation would be safe, as they would not have been if her sharp eye hadn't spotted the fakes.

She was hurrying across the bedroom when she heard a key enter the front door lock, and she froze in her tracks, stopping so abruptly she almost lost her balance.

Voices surged in as the door opened: loud, angry male

voices. This wasn't Angel returning for something he had forgotten. Shouting, scuffling, conflict, feet thudding, the door slamming shut behind the group. Christine ducked behind the open bedroom door, squinting gingerly through the chink; it was all she could do not to gasp in horror at what she saw. One man passed swiftly across the space, then two more, carrying something between them; a fraction later, she realized that it was a body, its legs trailing.

'Drop him,' said a voice.

The body thudded to the living-room carpet. It was Angel. Christine recognized him by the mop of curly blond hair, the blue Helly Hansen warm-up jacket he wore to work out – not by his face, which, as far as she could see, was a pulpy mass of blood. It looked as if he had been punched square on the nose.

'He's making a fucking mess on the carpet,' said one of the men who had dumped him, coming partially into view as he stepped closer to Angel.

Angel was struggling to get up now, hauling himself to his hands and knees, blood spattering down from his broken nose. As had been observed, a red patch was increasingly smearing the white carpet.

'Let him up?' asked the man laconically.

There was the sound of the window-seat cushions yielding as the person in charge sat down there.

'Get a chair,' he said. 'Find a kitchen one, and put him in it.'

The kitchen only had bar stools. Christine could hear, but not see, the third man heading for the open-plan dining area, hoisting up a dining chair and carrying it back to the living room. The man beside Angel reached down with a gloved hand, grabbed the back of his jacket collar and hauled him up like a kitten being picked up by the scruff of his neck, dumping him in the chair.

To pick up a man who weighed twelve stone that easily, with one hand, was an impressive feat of strength. Christine realized not only how much trouble Angel was in, but the danger of being a witness to this. She shot a glance sideways to see whether she could crawl across the room and hide under the bed. She was concealed from view by the half-open door, and the carpet was thick enough to let her move silently, particularly with the noise in the living room as extra cover. But Angel's whole apartment was decorated in too modern a style for her to hide in it successfully. There was no valance over the bed, just a fashionably bare space underneath, where a person lying would be immediately visible. The automatic motion-sensor lights of the walk-in wardrobe meant there were no dark corners into which she could tuck herself.

No, Christine swiftly decided that she was best off staying where she was. Meanwhile, Angel was breathing so stertorously through his mouth that it was audible even through the crack of the door.

'Jesus, fuckwit, tilt your head back!' said one of the henchmen.

'Nah, then the blood goes down the back of your throat,' said the other one. 'Tastes rank.'

'For fuck's sake, get him a towel or something!' ordered the man in charge.

The first henchman could be heard striding over the tiled floor of the kitchen in his heavy boots, banging cupboard doors in his search for a tea towel. He returned, dumping a hand towel in Angel's lap. Angel dabbed gingerly at the blood, trying not to touch the broken cartilage.

'Look, Ange, there's no point pissing around,' said the man on the sofa. 'You owe me. You've got to pay up. And I don't want any more fucking deeds to property in Switzerland that turn out to have some sort of lien or something on 'em for Swiss taxes. Fuck me, I thought the whole *point* of fucking Switzerland was not paying taxes!'

'I didn't know . . .'

Angel's voice was thick and slurry. Christine realized that she couldn't muster up a shred of sympathy for him, however. This was the man who had lied to her repeatedly, choked her, committed a theft for which she would have been blamed. She was positively delighted that someone had punched him in the face and broken his nose. If she hadn't had to stay as quiet as a mouse to keep safe, she would have struggled against the impulse to laugh out loud.

'I don't give a shit, Ange,' the man was saying. 'Whether you did or you didn't know ain't my concern – that's getting my fucking whack. I was already pretty narked at having to sell off a sodding chalet in a foreign country before I even realized you owed fucking property taxes there, plus back interest on 'em as well! Now I'm about a hundred grand short, what with the lawyer and all! It's a bloody nightmare! Massive disrespect on your part! Massive!'

'I'm sorry, George—'

'*I don't give a fuck whether you're sorry,*' George hissed.

Some non-verbal command must have been given, as the man standing beside Angel walked around the chair, lifted one foot, placed it on the seat and tipped it back with considerable force. The chair, and Angel, smashed back onto the floor. Christine could only see the chair legs now, parallel to the carpet. Angel rolled to the side, groaning loudly.

'See? I don't give a fuck,' George said. 'I don't give a *tenth* of a fuck. I just want my *fucking money.*'

Some further instruction must have been issued, because the man who had knocked over the chair now applied the toe of his foot to Angel's stomach. It wasn't a full kick, but the pressure was enough to produce another groan from Angel. He jerked his legs, curling into a ball and moaning. By now Christine was flinching back. She closed her fingers round the handle of the bedroom door, ensuring it didn't move.

And then she thought: *Shit. The jewels! They're worth much, much more than Angel owes to George. What can that chalet in Verbier be worth – a few million at most? But if the jewels are here and Angel tells him where they are, what's to stop George taking the lot?*

'Pick him up and put him on the chair again,' George said, and the men righted the dining chair and heaved Angel's limp body up, one on each side this time. Dead weight was harder to shift. Angel's body sagged forward, and one of the men caught his jacket collar, pulling him straight; each of them pinned him by one shoulder against the back of the chair.

'Fuck me, Ange, you posh boys can't take a beating,' George said, and both of the men sniggered. 'One punch in the face, tip you over, Dunc here gives you a tap with his foot – not even a bloody kick – and you're in pieces. You got to think about this when you borrow money you can't pay back, mate. You got to think about whether you can take what's coming your way. Dunc here's a dab hand with an iron, know what I mean? Don't use no starch, though.'

Angel let out a wail, and Christine's eyes widened in horror. If they pulled out an iron and started beating or burning Angel with it, she would have no choice but to stand here and listen, even if she closed her eyes not to watch. She imagined the smell of burning flesh, the sound of breaking bones, and shivered from head to toe. Sweat beaded on her skin, and she was honest enough to admit that it was as much fear for herself as for Angel, fear of what they would do to a witness if they caught her here . . .

'I've got something,' Angel was saying, his words blurred by the towel. He took it away and said again: 'I've got something I can give you.'

'Not a fucking chalet,' George said very precisely. 'Not a piece of fucking property. I want cash or as good as.'

'As good as,' Angel said, his s's coming out sibilant because his nose was blocked with blood. 'Jewellery. I've got jewellery. S'worth way more than what I owe you.'

Christine was twisting frantically behind the door, trying to slide her hand into her jacket pocket to fish out her mobile phone. Could you text 999? She couldn't ring them; the call would be heard straight away. She had no idea if a text to 999 would go through; she was pretty sure that they could trace the location of a text – or could they? Was that just something she'd seen in a spy film? But if she could silence her phone successfully, which was crucial, it was worth at least trying . . . and it didn't escape her that while she was attempting to contact the police now that Vivienne's jewels were in jeopardy, she hadn't tried to do it while Angel was being beaten up.

She had just enough room to operate the phone, typing in the code that would unlock it, and that, she knew, did not make any sound. She squinted at the screen, desperately trying to remember what happened when she hit the 'Sound' button at the top to silence it. Did the ringer just turn off? Or did it make a noise to show you that it wasn't going to make a noise any more?

'In the safe,' Angel was saying in the living room. 'Jewels in the safe. Above the bed.'

What? I didn't even know he had a safe! Christine thought angrily. *That bastard, pretending I was his girlfriend, convincing me he wanted to marry me but not telling me one bloody thing about his life, keeping so much secret . . .*

'Where is it, and what's the combo?' George barked.

Angel started to speak. As he did so, Christine, hoping that everyone would be concentrating so hard on his words that they wouldn't hear anything else, pressed the 'Sound' button.

To her horror, it buzzed. A single buzz, but definitely loud enough to be audible in the living room. Apparently, her phone did not go straight from 'Sound' to 'Mute', but through 'Vibrate', which was completely ridiculous. Why would Samsung *do* that? If you wanted silence, you wanted it straight away, not with a buzz to let people know where you were!

She held her breath, feeling her ribcage expand, her heart pounding as if it were beating at the hollow of her throat.

Through the crack of the door jamb she saw movement, both the men holding Angel turning to look in the direction of the bedroom.

'What was that?' one of them said. 'Sounded like a phone.'

'You said there was no one else in here!' George said to Angel. 'If you've been pissing me around—'

'No one,' Angel croaked. 'No one here.'

'What the fuck was that then? The boys heard something! Go have a look, Dunc.'

Christine's palms were so sweaty that she was terrified she'd drop the phone. She was sure that if she didn't press the screen again, no other sounds would issue from it – but what if someone rang her? It would buzz! She couldn't believe she hadn't thought of that before. How could she have been so stupid? Why hadn't she just turned off the phone straight away? When she watched horror films with women being stalked and chased, she yelled advice and instructions at the screen – *don't go in the basement! Turn your phone off! Don't just hit him once and run away – keep smashing his head in till you know he can't get up!* But it turned out that when she was plunged into a crisis herself, she could do no better than the panicking woman in the film . . .

Dunc was crossing the living room, coming straight for her. Christine closed her eyes on the basis that if you couldn't see them, they couldn't see you. Her heart was hammering, sweat pooling in the small of her back. With everything she had, she tried to make herself smaller, to squeeze even further back against the wall, so that Dunc wouldn't think to look behind it.

Dunc gave the door a shove as he entered, and Christine

had to press her lips together to avoid letting out a rabbit squeak of total fear. There was enough clearance, however, so that although it bounced into her, it stopped against her face. She stood frozen, her nose pressed to the door, hearing him pause momentarily in the centre of the room, looking around. Then he walked over to the wardrobe, slid the doors open, and, finding nothing, strode back into the bedroom. His bomber jacket rustled as, presumably, he bent down to look under the bed and then straightened up again.

'Where's the safe?' he asked. 'There's no one here.'

Christine sagged with relief.

'Was it that what buzzed?' the other man called.

'Nah, can't've done. What is it, voice-activated? Hang on, though.'

There was a pause, as Dunc thought it through.

'It was coming from the corner, weren't it?' he said. 'Over here, right? Let's have a looksee –'

And his footsteps thudded towards Christine, heavy and inexorable. In three seconds, two, the door would be pulled back; Dunc would be dragging her out. She swore she wouldn't scream, wouldn't cry. Her lips were pressed together again like glue, her eyes still shut. It was stupid, ridiculous, to keep them closed, as if this would save her, as if he somehow wouldn't see her when the bedroom door was wrenched open –

It made such an almighty crash as it opened that despite herself, Christine let out a tiny squeal of shock. The noise was as shattering as if Duncan had ripped the door off its hinges with his bare hands. And the crashing went on and on: splintering wood, shouting, repeated slamming – but

Christine's face would be pulp if this was Duncan ramming the door against her, her ribs smashed, and nothing had touched her, no one was dragging her out –

It took a stupid amount of courage to open her eyes again. Part of her brain was screaming that since nothing was happening to her, she should just stay exactly where she was, exactly *how* she was, with her eyes closed, because clearly some sort of magic was keeping her safe. Wrenching them open was a huge muscular effort; but when she did, miraculously, the door was still in front of her. Dunc hadn't opened it. The crashing and banging and shouting were coming from the living room. And then the sound of glass smashing in the bedroom made her jump out of her skin.

It wasn't just a vase breaking, or a mirror shattering. The entire bedroom window must have been broken with gigantic force: she could hear shards of glass landing on the floor like icicles crashing down. Curiosity won out over safety. Gingerly, Christine craned around the door, and her jaw dropped as she saw a black-clad figure flying across the room, feet first, having presumably kicked in the window. Its hands were wrapped around a rope that it dropped as it landed on its feet in one fluid movement, pulling up the balaclava that had protected its face from broken glass.

Christine would have stayed in the safety of her refuge behind the door, if it weren't for one important fact. The man who had just abseiled down from the roof and into the bedroom was Tor.

Pushing the door away from her, she ran across the bedroom, almost unable to believe her eyes.

'Tor!' she screamed, behaving exactly like the kind of

hysterical female love interest she also despised in films.
'*Tor!*'

'*Christine!*'

Tor swivelled, his jaw dropping, as Christine seemed to
appear from nowhere and hurtle into his arms, hugging him
frantically, her arms barely meeting around his square torso
– the sheer bulk of him, she realized, was padded out by
some sort of Kevlar jacket. She stared up at him in complete
incredulity.

'You're dead!' she heard herself screech. 'You're *dead!*'

Tor's hands closed briefly around her face, cradling her
cheeks, his blue eyes meeting hers in a moment of sheer
happiness. And then so many things happened in such swift
succession that it took her ages, looking back, to sort them
out. Someone hurtled into the bedroom, a man in a bright
blue jacket with a face that was a pulpy mass of red. Angel,
tearing across the room and around the bed. Behind him
came a man chasing him – not George or Dunc or the other
thug – a black-clad figure who lunged at Angel, grabbing
the back of his workout jacket.

There was a struggle. Angel writhed for a moment, his
hands coming up to the front of his body. The zip of the
jacket ripped and the pursuer fell back, clutching the bright
blue jacket in his hands. There was a blur of movement as
Angel dived down the corridor that led to his bathroom. He
slammed the door and clicked shut the lock; the jacket flew
through the air as the man who had been chasing Angel
tossed it aside and shot down the corridor, followed by Tor.
They started kicking the door, repeated smashes of booted

heels against the lock until the wood around it splintered and the door fell open, the two men racing inside.

Christine stood in the middle of the bedroom, both hands pressed to her mouth, once more looking and feeling as useless as a slow-witted supporting character in an action film. Her eyes were as wide as saucers, her chest heaving with panting breath. Through the now-open door to the living room, she could see bodies swarming. Black-clad people with POLICE written in white on the backs and fronts of their jackets had wrestled George and Dunc and the other man to the ground and were putting handcuffs on them. The space seemed entirely full of bodies in movement, disorienting in their speed and swiftness.

The shock of seeing Tor was so absolute that Christine's brain was spinning, trying to work out how he could possibly be alive. True, they hadn't found his body – but they had searched for him for days! He couldn't have survived that long outside in the below-zero temperatures – everyone had agreed on that! It had never been said explicitly, but it had been clear that the search had gone on longer than the authorities truly thought necessary.

How could the Bolivian air force helicopters not have spotted him? Had it all been a setup for some reason? But no, his poor parents – Tor would never have put them through that, surely! Christine remembered their terrible grief at the memorial service.

'He's not here!' Tor yelled from the bathroom. 'He's not here!'

It barely took a moment before Christine realized what must have happened, why Angel had made for the bathroom.

She had thought it was a last desperate attempt at refuge, a rat chased back into its hole; she hadn't realized that the rat had an exit tunnel. She ran down the corridor and into the bathroom, pushed Tor aside, pressed with the heel of her hand on the corner of the knee-height panel to the laundry chute. It was discreetly concealed, with no handle, just a magnetic closure that snapped open when you bumped it. Christine pulled it open, staring down the square black hole. If it hadn't been obvious that Angel had managed to fit down there, she wouldn't have believed it possible.

'He's gone down the laundry chute!' Tor exclaimed as the police officer with him raised one hand to his shoulder, speaking urgently into the radio clipped there, informing the rest of the team what had happened.

'It goes straight down to the basement,' Christine said, imagining Angel shooting down that terrifying chute. It was almost a direct drop, landing in the big laundry basket six floors down. Surely he wouldn't have gone head first? That could kill him on landing if he didn't manage to slow himself down in time . . .

Tor was craning forward, bracing his hands on either side of the tiled wall, his head as far down the chute as he could manage.

'I think he landed,' he said, his voice booming back at them. 'I don't see him in here.'

'I've sent the guys on the ground to the basement,' the policeman said, but another thought had hit Christine. Urgently, she grabbed Tor's arm, pulling him back to the living room, where George, Dunc and the other man were being frogmarched out of the apartment.

'Ask them what the code to the safe is!' she panted to Tor. 'Him! He knows, Angel told him!'

Her arm was stretched out, pointing at George, who was unmistakable: a dapper, svelte man in a pale grey fitted suit, the jacket fastened with one button over a black T-shirt.

'Where the fuck did *you* come from?' George said, staring at Christine with genuine shock.

'She was behind the bedroom door, wasn't she?' Dunc said, jerking his head to the bedroom. 'I was just about to find her when the coppers broke the door down.'

'Fucking Angel. What a bloody liar,' George said with resignation. 'Telling me there was no one else in here. Don't know wlhy I'm surprised. He wouldn't know the truth if he had it tattooed on his arse.'

'Angel's gone down the laundry chute, and we need the code to the safe,' Tor said to the man beside George. 'Because—'

'Angel has stolen goods in the safe,' Christine said; there was no point trying to cover this up. 'They belong to his grandmother. I'm organizing the auction of her jewellery. He stole some of the pieces from the auction house.'

Clearly, everyone here knew who Angel's grandmother was. Equally clearly, no one was at all surprised that Angel was a thief; raised eyebrows, brief nods were the only reaction to this.

'Come on, let's have it,' the policeman said to George, leading him into the bedroom. 'Spit it out.'

'We've got a full search warrant,' Tor said to Christine as they followed. 'We weren't looking for stolen jewellery, though.'

'I don't understand anything,' Christine said feebly. 'I don't understand *anything at all . . .'*

Tor took her hand and squeezed it firmly. 'I will explain everything after this,' he said. 'I promise.'

Another police officer was climbing onto the bed, kneeling up on it, running her hands along the headboard; a wenge wood panel clicked loose and opened, exposing a black safe neatly installed in the recess. George rattled off five numbers, and the police officer tapped them into the electronic key pad. The door swung wide, and a second officer, standing by the side of the bed, photographed the contents in situ before his colleague began to pull them out and lay them on the bed. A big baggie of white powder; a small stack of five-hundred-euro notes banded together with a wrapper; and then, to Christine's huge relief, the enormous purple diamond ring, followed by the orange one and then the pendant. Angel had wrapped each of them in bubble packaging, but the colour of the first two stones shone through clearly.

Her sigh was audible. Tor smiled down at her.

'We can't hand these over to you, miss, obviously,' the officer in charge said. 'Being as they're not your property. They'll have to be returned to Ms Winter directly if it does transpire that they belong to her.'

'That's fine,' Christine said. 'That's totally fine. As long as we have them.'

She heard her voice tremble; she was on the verge of bursting into tears now that everything was all right, more than all right: the jewellery was found, Tor was alive – *Tor was alive!* Her knees started to buckle, and his arm went round her waist. He pulled her to him and hugged her and she buried her head in his jacket and cried and cried at the fact that he was living and breathing and his arms were around her; that somehow, miraculously, he had come back from the dead.

It was frustrating that his jacket was so padded, so big and thick that she couldn't hug him properly; but when she caught her breath, finally, leaning back a little to look up at him, he promptly kissed her, and that made her forget about everything else.

Chapter Twenty-Two

London – a short time later

'Madame?'

Vivienne was sitting in her boudoir, her cat in her lap, stroking it with slow, measured movements of one heavily ringed hand. This room was her inner sanctum, and like all of her boudoirs in her various properties across the world, it was decorated in a deliberately feminine style, designed to make any heterosexual man feel disinclined to step across its threshold. The floor was carpeted in pink, the walls mirrored and hung with pictures, many of them portraits of Vivienne herself. Frills and furbelows, valances and swagged curtains, occasional tables stacked with framed photographs, vases of flowers, trinkets and china boxes; Vivienne had never considered that less was more. One entire mirrored wall was dedicated to Vivienne's own product line, shelves holding her perfumes, nail polish, make-up, body lotions, all trimmed with the strip of faux-fur white leopard bordered with diamanté that was her signature branding.

There was strategy behind this design. By the time Vivienne had been asked to give her name to a line of perfumes she had been over sixty, and adjusting to the fact that she could show less skin than she had once done. Using animal print, she had decided, was an effective way to flirt with sexiness without looking like mutton dressed as lamb. The chaise longue on which she sat was upholstered in white-leopard-printed velvet, as was the chair in front of her make-up mirror. The mirror itself was ringed with lights that enabled her to adjust her make-up for any effect necessary, from full daylight to an evening appearance.

The first thing Vivienne did every morning, even before summoning Gregory with her coffee and croissant, was apply light daytime make-up and don a wig or a turban; no one was allowed to see her bare face or thinning scalp. As she looked over at Gregory, who was hovering nervously in the doorway, her *maquillage* was as perfect as ever. The violet eyes were outlined in Vivienne Plum Velvet pencil, her lips were glossed with her soft pink lipstick, which, as she purred to the camera in her promotional videos, both moisturized and concealed fine lines. Her wig was a dark brown that was nearly black, but not quite: full black was too harsh against the skin for anyone over thirty years old. She wore a soft white cashmere sweater and grey silk lounging palazzo pants, and diamonds glittered in her ears.

'Yes, Gregory?' she said, her tone quite even.

'It's Mr Angel,' said Gregory – and despite his years of working for Vivienne and dealing with all sorts of unexpected emergencies and dramatic crises, many of them involving Angel himself, his entire body seemed contorted with embarrassment. It was as if he was struggling not to utter the words he was dying to say.

Vivienne's carefully made-up features barely moved; her

eyelashes flickered, but the hand stroking the cat continued in its steady rhythm.

'Ah,' she said quietly.

'Grandma! Grandma!'

Angel could be heard tearing across the apartment.

'Madame, I asked him to wait in the salon –' Gregory began, but Vivienne was already nodding at her assistant to absolve him of any blame. She shifted a little, arranging the cushions propped behind her at the back of the chaise longue. She had been sitting here for a while, stroking the sleeping cat, staring ahead of her to the grey London December sky, the rain softly falling on the green grass of Hyde Park, across the double rivers of traffic on Park Lane. Waiting for what she knew was coming.

Whom she knew was coming.

At least she was prepared.

'Grandma!'

Angel pushed past Gregory and burst into the room. His appearance was extraordinary. The blood had clotted on his nose, drying dark and messy. He was still in the tracksuit trousers he had worn to his training session, a form-fitting T-shirt made of sweat-wicking fabric on top, piped with bright fluorescent lines at the armholes and neckline, intended to make the wearer stand out if working out at night. It looked incongruous and flimsy.

He had managed to slow the sheer drop down the laundry chute by jamming his feet against the sides, but that traction hadn't been enough; he had had to use his bare elbows too, and they were bruised and raw. The landing had been clumsy, and he had turned an ankle on the steel bar at the base of the laundry basket. Still, the descent had been so speedy that once he had clawed his way out of the basket and made for the tradesmen's exit of the building, the police officers stationed at the front and back doors and in the parking garage had not been fast enough to reach it.

No one had expected Angel to come running out of that access route. They had been closing in on him as he left his apartment that morning and went down to the parking garage to pick up his Alfa Romeo, intending to drive to Chelsea Harbour. But the police had been forestalled by George and his two heavies, who, having bribed the doorman of the building for information on Angel's schedule, had been waiting by Angel's car. He had fled on seeing them; they had had to catch him, roughing him up in punishment before carting him back to his apartment.

Since Angel's escape down the laundry chute had been so unexpected, the police officers had been too far away to see him dashing out and jumping into a cab. They were currently checking the building's CCTV, but it would be a while before they spotted his grainy figure hailing the taxi, enlarged the licence plate and tracked down its destination.

Angel was in considerable pain from all his injuries. The smashed cartilage of his nose, his bruises, the stress of the day's events, the race to get to Vivienne, felt like the weight of the world on his shoulders. He dropped to his knees in front of the chaise longue. With a tilt of her head, Vivienne conveyed to Gregory that he was to leave the room and close the door.

Visibly perturbed at the prospect of leaving Vivienne alone with Angel in this condition, he hesitated, the first time he had ever questioned an order of hers. But Vivienne's beautiful eyes widened, her head jerked, sharp and imperative, and with great reluctance, Gregory backed away, shutting the door silently.

'Grandma, you have to help me!' Angel said, reaching out to take her hands.

The cat, not liking this intrusion into its cosy territory on Vivienne's lap, stood up, hissed and strolled down the length of the chaise longue, settling by her feet instead.

'You've disturbed Louison,' Vivienne said, her tone neutral. 'She's fourteen years old and needs her rest.'

'My nose is broken!' Angel said, his voice sounding as if he had a heavy cold. 'And you're worrying about your *cat*? Look at me! Aren't you worried? Aren't you going to ask me what happened?'

'Oh, Angel, I know what happened,' Vivienne said gently. 'I know everything. Tor rang me a couple of hours ago, when he was heading off with the police to arrest you. He wanted to warn me in advance. And he and Christine have just called me from your apartment.'

Angel's hands were still outstretched; when Louison left her lap, Vivienne had folded her hands there, making it clear that she would not take his, and now he pulled them back, realizing the full extent of the trouble he was in.

'He's always hated me,' he said swiftly, sitting back on his heels. 'Honestly, Grandma! He was really interested in Christine, and when I started seeing her he was so jealous. You should have seen him at the press launch before the expedition! He was all over her. It was pathetic. I'm not surprised that when he fell down a cliff – because he was showing off, probably – and crawled away, or whatever happened, he decided to blame me, because—'

'Angel. They found my rings in the safe in your flat. The purple diamond Randon bought for me, the orange one Dieter gave me. And the heart-shaped pendant Randon gave me on our tenth anniversary.'

She glanced sideways at the closest occasional table, the framed photographs on which were entirely of her, Randon, or her and Randon together. Until Christine had asked her, Vivienne had forgotten all about the photographs Randon had taken of her, and she of him, all those years ago; it had given her great pleasure to go through the boxes once again, and now that Dieter was gone, she could pull out and frame her favourites without it being disrespectful to him.

She was aware that it had been hard enough for Dieter to live in Randon's shadow – the man universally recognized as the great love of her life, their passion immortalized on screen – without having photographs of him scattered around their various houses, let alone ones that signified such a deep and intimate attachment. Now, however, she could indulge herself as much as she wanted, and one of the main photographs was of her lying on the grey volcanic sands of Lampedusa, an island off the coast of Italy, with the great heart-shaped pendant around her neck, laughing up at the camera. They had hired a yacht to cruise around Sicily and its satellite islands one summer: Pantelleria, with its wonderful dessert wine, Passito; striking little Linosa, with its extinct volcanoes and the pastel-painted houses of its village.

Randon had brought the diamond secretly on board the

yacht, concealed it carefully until the date of the anniversary, and surprised her by dropping it in a glass of Negroni Sbagliato – a version of the classic cocktail with Campari, Martini and prosecco instead of the traditional gin, a lighter drink for summer. It had been prepared by their steward from a huge picnic basket he and the first mate had lugged onto the tender of the yacht and out onto the hot sands of Lampedusa, in a deserted cove where Vivienne and Randon could be completely private.

Yes, Randon had admitted, it was a cliché to put a diamond into a drink; but nobody had ever done it before, he continued blithely, with a diamond that was actually *bigger* than an ice cube.

Vivienne remembered that afternoon so vividly. She loved to bite ice cubes, and Randon knew it. He had watched her gleefully as she worked her way greedily down her drink, not the first of the day – they had drunk two bottles of Gavi dei Gavi at lunch, retired to their stateroom to fuck and then slept the wine off – but the first of the afternoon. Finally, her teeth had closed around the diamond, crunching down on it.

Her eyes had snapped wide, her expression, Randon said, so comical that he regretted for the rest of his life not having his Kodak with him. He had yelled: 'Spit it out!', worried that she would choke on the 114-carat stone; he had been ready to Heimlich her, he told her, but she had obeyed, spitting the stone out into the palm of her hand and staring at it in amazement.

The sheer size of it was astonishing, but it had never been a lustrous, light-filled diamond. When Tor had told her just now about the stones Angel had stolen, she had understood exactly why he had selected them.

Vivienne brought her eyes back from the photograph to Angel's face. His expression was literally unreadable, a blur of dried blood, but his eyes were pleading.

'Ah, your mother's identical expression,' she observed. 'Whenever Pearl did something wrong, whenever she needed to ask me for forgiveness, she would look at me just like that. Wide-eyed, innocent, as if butter wouldn't melt in her mouth. And I fell for it again and again. I gave her everything she wanted. Until, finally, she went too far. She killed some-one, Angel. Do you remember that? I tried to shelter you from it at the time, but you must remember poor Thierry, who did nothing but try to stop Pearl raiding my safe.'

She paused.

'Like mother, like son.'

'I haven't killed anyone!' Angel protested.

'Not for want of trying, Angel,' Vivienne said quietly. 'Tor told me everything. About the cocaine you were smuggling, how he caught you and the two of you fought. You hit him with a rock and pushed him off a cliff. Then you went back to camp and told everyone you'd seen him on the opposite site of the mountain, so they'd search in completely the wrong area.'

'That's rubbish!' Angel did his best to sound thoroughly indignant. 'How dare he say something so outrageous! It's slander! I could sue him for that!'

'Can you explain,' his grandmother asked, 'why they found my rings and my pendant in your apartment?'

'I was just borrowing them,' Angel said swiftly, 'because

I wanted to show them to someone who might want to buy them. Someone very private, who didn't want to go to the auction house. Christine knew all about it. She might deny it, but that's because she wasn't supposed to let them out of her offices, so of course she'll have to cover her back now—'

'Christine was in your apartment searching for them,' Vivienne said.

'No, she was there to take them back!' Angel was warming to this story. 'She just had to pretend that I'd sneaked them out without her knowing, because she could get the sack for doing it – but it was such a great opportunity, this person's fantastically rich—'

'Angel,' his grandmother said quietly. 'I didn't believe your mother all those years ago, when she tried to convince me that Thierry had sexually assaulted her and she'd had to fight him off. And I don't believe you now.'

There was a long silence, during which Angel, despite himself, found his mind filled with the image of Thierry, dead on the floor of Vivienne's Paris bedroom, the Oscar statuette clotted with blood, his mother sobbing and protesting her innocence.

'This is all Tor's fault!' he said sullenly, pushing the memory away. 'He's turned you against me! I don't know *what* happened on that mountain, but his whole story sounds ridiculous. How could he possibly have survived if what he's saying's true? We searched that entire area for five days! What was he doing, just lying there the whole time while the helicopters flew overhead?'

'He thinks he slid down a deep gully in the mountainside,'

Vivienne said. There was a glass of water on the low table beside her, and she picked it up and sipped from it.

'He woke up in a deep snowdrift, all white around him, and he says it was moving,' she continued. 'He was confused, but eventually he worked out that he had landed in a flock of sheep that had taken refuge for the night at the base of the mountain. There was a heavy snowfall all down the mountain slope, which must have slowed him down considerably. And then the sheep broke the rest of his fall. They kept him warm, and of course they were shifting around, making air holes in the snow so they could breathe, which meant that Tor could too. Eventually he managed to get up, but he was still groggy and bruised, obviously, and totally disoriented. He had no idea how much time had passed, but he decided he shouldn't try to head back to camp in case you were lying in wait for him. He had been hit over the head several times before the fall, and he didn't feel he could defend himself.'

She set the water glass back on the table again.

'And also, he was nervous that he might encounter the smuggling team who were bringing you the cocaine,' she went on, her tone still as neutral as if she were narrating the story of a film she had seen recently. 'He was vulnerable, and they were naturally angry with him – he didn't want to risk bumping into them and being attacked. His phone was broken in the fall, so he couldn't use it to call for help. He steered a course away from both the camp and where he thought the mule team would be heading. There was the snow, so he could eat that to keep hydrated, and he had a couple of energy bars in his jacket. Eventually he found a small village, and they gave him some food and took him to the closest town, which was two days' journey away. And when he told the local police what had happened, they took him straight to headquarters in the capital, La Paz – they wouldn't let him contact anyone for days. They wanted to keep it quiet till they could round up the smugglers and trace back the plane the cocaine had been in. Apparently there's so much corruption in the police force they didn't want to risk the information spreading at all. They didn't even tell their own air force. That's why the helicopters were sent – no one but a small group of police officers even knew Tor was still alive.'

'Oh, this is rubbish! He fell off the mountain, hit his head and made up a crazy story so he'd look like a hero instead of a clumsy idiot!' Angel mumbled sullenly. 'Or he gave himself a concussion and actually believed his own nonsense . . .'

'Finally they let him get in touch with the Swedish embassy,' Vivienne concluded. 'And they, the Bolivian authorities and the British ones discussed the situation. By that time the expedition was leaving for the UK, so they decided to ask Tor to lie low and play it out. The British police wanted time to see where you'd been planning to take the cocaine when you got back to London, and roll up as many people in that network as possible. He felt obliged to agree, but he insisted on visiting his family as soon as they'd let him, and he's been lying low there ever since until finally they decided that they were ready to arrest you and your contact. And he also demanded, in return for keeping quiet, that he be there when they made the arrest. Prince Toby pulled some strings, I understand.'

She looked gravely at her grandson.

'The Bolivian authorities have an international arrest warrant for you, Angel. They're going to try you for attempted murder and drug trafficking.'

Angel swallowed hard, staring at the edge of the chaise longue rather than meeting his grandmother's eyes.

'It's all bullshit, of course,' he mumbled. 'It's my word against his.'

'Tor's story is corroborated by someone you bribed at the camp,' Vivienne said. 'One of the local guides.'

'That's what I need!' Angel exclaimed. 'Enough money to bribe people! This guide, whoever he is –'

Fucking João! he thought bitterly. *I gave him more than enough dosh at the time, and now he turns on me? You can't rely on anyone!*

'– must have been leaned on by the Bolivian police,' he continued. 'It's not true! None of this is true! Come on, Grandma – you can't believe this, can you? It's so ludicrous – much too far-fetched to be possible . . .'

But his voice faltered as he raised his gaze once more and saw Vivienne's inexorable expression, her lips set firmly together.

'I just need some help with money,' he said weakly, changing tack. 'If I can pay off the Bolivian police, and this guide who's lying, they won't deport me. They don't have anything on me in the UK. George won't say a word – yes, he's my bookie, I'll admit that, but this whole coke story's complete rubbish. I'll admit I took the rings. I have a gambling problem. I ran up a huge debt with George and he was threatening me. Look what he did to my face!'

He raised a hand to indicate the damage, as if he thought that Vivienne needed help seeing his broken nose. Like his grandmother and his mother, Angel had theatrical instincts.

'I was very wrong to steal the jewellery,' he said contritely. 'I know that. I was just panicking and desperate—'

'You stole from Christine's auction house! You replaced three pieces with fakes! She would have lost her job when they found out!'

Louison, who had been curled up at the base of the chaise longue, found the volume of the voices too high and angry for her now. She stood up and plopped down onto the carpet, slinking underneath the chaise longue to wait there in safety until Vivienne stopped shouting and the atmosphere was calm and cat-friendly once more. Meanwhile, all of Angel's pent-up rage at his plans being so thoroughly frustrated, at bloody Tor coming back to life, at being brutalized in his own apartment and then having to make a humiliating escape down the laundry chute, came welling up in a tide of fury that he was no longer able to keep under control.

'I never wanted to go out with Christine in the first place!' he shouted. 'My God, the nightmare it's been trying to keep that stupid bitch happy! That was all *your* fault – *you* wanted me to go out with her, *you* were the one forcing me to marry her—'

'Because I wanted great-grandchildren,' his grandmother said in a glacial voice. 'And you told me you had stage three testicular cancer.'

With the skill of a great actress, she didn't need to utter another word. She simply let the words lie where they fell, making it crystal clear that she no longer believed Angel's claim of having been sick.

Angel felt strangely light, as if there was a huge hollow inside his thorax. If she didn't believe the cancer story, there wasn't a word he could say in his defence. He would have to switch tack yet again.

'Your reputation,' he managed. 'The publicity. You don't want—'

'Oh, Angel,' Vivienne said quietly. 'Is that all you can say to me? After pretending that you had cancer, and nearly breaking my heart with the thought you would die before I would?'

'This is all your fault, Grandma!' he wailed, the sob in his voice rising. 'You took me away from Mummy, you abandoned me to one nanny after another – I hardly ever saw Mummy or you! How could you expect me to be okay? What did you think was going to happen? You fucked up Mummy and then you fucked me up too – and now she's dead! What do you think's going to happen to me in a Bolivian prison? I could die in there, and then you'd have no one left, no family at all . . . is that really what you want?'

'If it's my fault, Angel, then I'm setting it right now,' Vivienne said. 'I can't let you go on as you are. Maybe this will be the wake-up call that you need. God knows, it's long overdue.'

She meant it. Angel could see that with absolute clarity. There would not be a penny forthcoming from his grandmother to pay for bribes, not even for a lawyer to fight the Bolivian extradition warrant. She was washing her hands of him, prepared to let him rot to death in the jail cell of a third-world country, and all the while she was sitting on a fortune – the jewellery she was auctioning off that should by rights be his, a few pieces of which would solve every one of his problems.

If she died, some of it would come to you, said a small voice at the back of his skull. *If she died right now, there'd be bound to be plenty of money coming your way. Enough to borrow against, to pay lawyers and guarantee bribes, keep you from being shipped to Bolivia and thrown into a hellhole of a jail there . . .*

Angel had not planned for this eventuality. During the frantic cab ride here, desperate and terrified though he had been, he had not allowed himself to entertain the thought that Vivienne might be so intransigent as to refuse to help him. It was inconceivable to imagine that his grandmother, no matter how furious she was, would actually be willing to see him extradited to a country as dangerous as Bolivia. So he had not considered the consequences of that decision, how she might force him to react, because she was driving him to do something unthinkable to save his own skin –

She's old, said the voice in his head. *Yes, she looks amazing for her age, but she's still seventy-three. Becoming frail, delicate. Liable to have a heart attack when her grandson crashes in to see her, covered in blood, and tells her the police are chasing him because he's accused of all sorts of terrible things. Wouldn't that shock an old woman enough so that she dropped down dead?*

It was the only way out, the only way to save himself. And it was her fault, as it always had been. She had pushed him to this. What kind of unnatural grandmother would let her grandson be thrown into a Bolivian jail? How could she possibly look him in the eye, as she was doing now, knowing what would happen to him if she refused to help, and think her conscience was clear?

He would make it quick. He'd be more merciful than she was, condemning him to a slow, horrible fate for God knows how many years in a third-world prison. But she deserved this, she had it coming.

It was her fault. She was making him do this.

Those, in the end, were the words that were ringing in his head as he raised himself on his knees, leaned forward, grabbed one of the leopard velvet pillows from the chaise longue and, gritting his teeth, shoved it into his grandmother's face and held it there as she struggled beneath his weight.

Go fast, he thought, his heart racing. *Die fast. Have a heart attack – go fast – you're seventy-three, how long can you hold on, for fuck's sake?*

She was writhing, but her hands weren't coming up to pull at his, as he was expecting and dreading. Those fingers, those bony fingers with the rings on them, digging into his, pulling at them; how awful would that be? It would haunt him forever, even though he was completely sure that this was the fate she had earned by neglecting him and driving his mother to drugs and refusing to help him when he needed it so dreadfully—

The bullet slammed into his right shoulder. He registered shock, his body jerking back at the impact, one hand letting go of the pillow and raising to the point of impact, feeling the hole, the blood starting to pump out of it. And then Vivienne shot him again, at much the same angle, and the sheer pain of his shattered shoulder knocked him out. He fell backwards, the pillow, still grasped in his other hand, falling on his chest.

Gasping for breath, Vivienne lowered the pearl-handled derringer. She had loaded it and tucked it away underneath a pillow to one side of the curving back of the chaise longue after Tor had rung her, twenty minutes ago, knowing that Angel, on the run, had very few places left to go. She had kept the gun after the run of *The Letter* had finished; Randon had insisted upon it.

'Just in case,' he had said. 'You never know, darling – with all these jewels I'm lavishing on you, someone might try to grab some. I like to feel you could defend yourself. But please don't shoot me in a fit of temper, will you? You're more than capable of it!'

Randon hadn't known what she was truly capable of, Vivienne thought. No one had, until today; not even her. But when she had opened the safe in her boudoir, taken out the derringer, and placed it beside her, she had known that she would be prepared to defend herself if it were necessary.

The door burst open; Gregory raced into the room.

'Madame!' he exclaimed in horror, staring from Vivienne to Angel's prone body, and then back to Vivienne again, and the gun she was holding in her lap. 'Oh Madame, I should never have left you alone with him!'

'It's over now, Gregory,' she said softly. 'Ring for an ambulance. And call my publicist, please.'

Vivienne glanced at her once-beloved grandson, at the ruin of his handsome face, the blond curls that were so like his mother's, whom Vivienne had also once loved so much.

But not enough. Clearly, not enough.

'Help me up, Gregory,' she said, clicking the safety back on the derringer, then holding a hand up for assistance in coming to her feet. 'I can't possibly stay in the room with him. I shall wait in the salon. With a large brandy.'

Holding the gun by her side, she looked down at Angel.

'You had better turn him onto his side first,' she added. 'The one that's undamaged. Otherwise he might choke to death.'

Gregory, shuddering at the sight of Angel, did as she instructed. Then he placed an arm around her back for balance as they walked slowly from the boudoir.

Louison slunk out from under the chaise longue. But she did not follow her mistress, nor did she jump back onto the piece of furniture and curl up once more in the cushions that were warm from Vivienne's body. Instead she padded over to Angel's body, sat down beside it and hooked out one white paw, dabbing with curiosity at the blood that was slowly oozing from the bullet wounds onto the pink carpet.

Chapter Twenty-Three

Geneva – New Year's Eve

'Three hundred million dollars!' Christine exclaimed in delight. 'Well, nearly – two hundred and eighty-seven million dollars! That's nearly two hundred million pounds! More than double what the Elizabeth Taylor auction made. Vivienne will be over the moon – you know how badly she wanted to beat her!'

'I'm happy we have good news for Vivienne,' said Tor, and he and Christine, for a moment, exchanged a glance that had nothing at all to do with the triumph of the jewellery auction.

Around them, the roar and bustle was so loud that Christine had been almost shrieking to make herself heard. Hundreds of overexcited guests, released from the solemnity of an auction at which they had watched records being broken, seen one legendary jewel after another, and rubbed shoulders with royalty, film actors, A-list musicians and reality TV stars, were hitting the champagne and screaming in ecstasy at one another.

They were celebrating not only their purchases but the fact that they had been present at one of the most sought-after, exclusive events of the year. The Berkeley publicists had been so besieged by demands for tickets to the auction of Vivienne Winter's jewels that they had decided to move the location from their own auction house to the ballroom of the five-star Bel Lac hotel on the Quai du Mont Blanc, requiring a stratospheric surge in the security budget. Armed guards were stationed at regular intervals around the room and on the lakefront terrace outside, which had been cordoned off from access both to hotel guests and auction attendees. Until the jewellery was safely transported back to the safes in Berkeley's offices, a few streets away, the stunning panorama of Lake Geneva and the snow-covered slopes of Mont Blanc by night could be viewed only through the glass French windows of the ballroom.

Tor's allusion to Angel's shooting by his grandmother was rare; he and Christine did not talk too much about that shocking day. Angel had been taken to hospital, where they had patched up his shoulder as best they could, but the nerve damage was so extensive that he had lost most of the use of his right arm. Given this circumstance, Vivienne had reluc tantly arranged a deal with the Bolivian authorities, who had dropped the extradition attempt in return for a large dona- tion to a high-ranking official's favourite 'charity'. She could not face the prospect of her grandson, now partially disabled and physically unable to defend himself, spending decades in prison there.

The situation with the British authorities had been vastly helped by the fact that Angel, when he came round to full consciousness, had suffered a complete mental breakdown. He was psychotic, raving, threats of violence against his grandmother, Christine and Tor flowing non-stop from him;

there had been no question that he needed to be sectioned. Spoilt for his whole life, indulged in every whim, used to getting everything he wanted by virtue of his money, charm and beauty, he had awoken to find himself in a place where all of those advantages had been ripped away.

With his right shoulder wrecked and his arm partially useless, Angel no longer had the effortless physical ease he had always relished. A drugs screen had revealed the amount of legal and illegal substances he had been taking and the hospital had put him on a strict regime of non-opiate pain-killers, which were failing to do the job. Having never been taught self-control, patience or stoicism as a child, Angel experienced this deprivation as a total outrage, and his furious, foul-mouthed protests against the hospital treatment regime had only confirmed the diagnosis that he was a danger to himself and others.

With her extensive contacts and stable of high-priced lawyers, it had not been difficult for Vivienne to have Angel declared unfit for trial and arrange for him to be taken care of in a private mental facility that, for a very large fee, special-ized in the kind of difficult cases that required both sensitivity and discretion. Ironically, like the Chateau Sainte-Beuve, it was a last-chance saloon for the spoilt children of celebrities and aristocrats, a holding cell into which the scions of the rich and famous were dumped when they could no longer be allowed to roam free.

Angel's theft of the gems had been hushed up, his injury explained as an unfortunate accident while he had been checking his grandmother's gun for her to ensure that, all those years after she had fired it in *The Letter*, it was still in working order. All gossip about the truth of the tumultuous events of that day had been ruthlessly suppressed. It had been thoroughly impressed upon the police officers who knew about the attempt to arrest Angel, plus their backup team, that any leaks to the newspapers would be traced back and punished with extreme harshness. George and his two thugs had been arrested for a variety of offences, including distribution of illegal narcotics, running illegal betting syndicates and match-fixing, and Angel's testimony had not been necessary to press any of those charges; his name would not be mentioned at their trial.

There was no statute of limitations for attempted murder in Britain. If Angel were released from the facility, he could be prosecuted for trying to kill Vivienne. This, at least, was what he would be told - although, with the theft having been covered up, along with the fact that Vivienne had fired at him in self-defence, it would be a difficult case to bring. Angel, however, would not be informed of this. His doctors would hold the threat over his head while attempting to gradually engage him in the therapy he so clearly needed, once the drug withdrawal and psychotic symptoms abated. It would, they had told Vivienne, be a lengthy process. She had raised not the slightest objection to this, despite the fact that it was costing her a small fortune. The facility was extremely secure. For a considerable amount of time, Angel would be going nowhere.

Vivienne had rung Christine the day after the dramatic events that had culminated in her shooting of her grandson. With great dignity, she had apologized to Christine for Angel's theft of the jewels, assured her that the sale would be continuing as planned with Christine at the helm, and promised her that Angel was safely contained where he could not hurt anyone; not even himself.

Naturally, this had been a huge relief to Christine. And then, when she had arrived in Geneva to set up the auction and tackle the complicated logistics of using the ballroom of the Bel Lac Hotel, Vivienne had invited Christine for tea at the Montreux villa, where she had taken up residence immediately after Angel's committal. She was putting the Park Lane apartment on the market. As she had watched Angel's body being carried on a stretcher through the hallway, she had known that she would never be able to enter her boudoir again. Gregory had organized overnight bags, and they had slept in the Grosvenor House Hotel that night; it was practically next door. They had flown to Switzerland the day afterwards, while the best moving company in the country started the long, carefully supervised process of packing up Vivienne's possessions.

Over Earl Grey and Fortnum's shortbread at the villa, Vivienne had given Christine a beautiful pearl and diamond necklace, presenting it as an apology for everything that had happened with Angel. Christine had made an attempt to refuse the gift, but it had been impossible to say no to Vivienne. Besides, the necklace had been perfectly chosen. Christine was wearing it at the auction, and it made her simple black dress look as if it had cost ten times its actual price.

Vivienne had also dealt with the subject of Tor during that visit. Without quite admitting that she had told Christine that Tor was a married womanizer, Vivienne had indicated that she felt, in retrospect, that she might have misled Christine about him. She had been misinformed about his character by ill-wishers, she said, and was retracting all the negative comments she had made. She had then indicated that she would take no offence if Christine and Tor found themselves becoming close after Angel's disappearance. This had been a huge relief to Christine, as it was exactly what had already happened.

'I need to go and tell Vivienne the fantastic news,' Christine said now, fizzing with triumph. 'Wow, this is so amazing! We went over the estimated value on every single piece!'

Vivienne had not been present in the ballroom during the auction. She would have been overrun, swamped with fans and admirers wanting to pay homage; it might even have distracted attention from the business of bidding for her jewellery, with people gawping at her rather than raising their paddles. Besides, in the wake of Angel's disappearance from the social scene and the lurid rumours surrounding it, Vivienne had withdrawn from any public appearances, not wanting to fan the flames of publicity.

Instead, they had worked out a compromise that would allow her to enjoy the excitement of the sale at close quarters, sequestering her in a private sitting room a few doors down from the ballroom. She had watched the proceedings on a video link organized by the hotel. Christine was due to head there to congratulate her on the success of the auction, and prepare her for meetings with some of the winning bidders.

'Oh hey, Christine,' someone drawled above her, and she looked up to see Lil' Biscuit, diamonds gleaming in his ears and at his neck, wearing a superbly cut cobalt suit.

'Hi!' Christine had never resolved the issue of what to call Lil' Biscuit. She gushed instead, avoiding using any name in return. 'Hasn't it been such an amazing experience! I'm so glad you and Silantra could be here. I wish we could have convinced you to bid, but of course you've secured your fabulous pieces already . . .'

'Well, that's just what I wanted to discuss with you,' Lil' Biscuit said in his deep boom of a voice, and Christine panicked for a split second, before reminding herself firmly that his contracts were iron-clad and notarized. There was no way he could pull back from his agreements to purchase any of the various necklaces, parures and tiaras he had bought for Silantra.

'Uh . . .' she began, but Biscuit was already continuing:

'So you pulled in two hundred and eighty-seven mil,' he observed. 'Nice, but three hundred mil would be an even better number, wouldn't it? Good and round.'

'Of course,' Christine said, her brain whirling. 'That would be *fantas*—'

'So here's what I'm thinking,' he interrupted. 'It was a real pleasure for us to meet Ms Winter in London, and that was the deal – we wouldn't pay that much money not to meet her in person, right? But Silantra and I have a good friend who couldn't be there, and it'd be super-cool if he could get to take some photos with her, now we have the chance.'

He gestured to the man by his side, who was even more strapping than Lil' Biscuit, in a very different style: he looked like a mixture of Scottish and German genes, pumped up by American protein and a great deal of weightlifting.

'Gray Macfarland,' the man said, proffering an enormous

hand and enveloping Christine's in his. It made her feel like a five-year-old meeting a giant. 'The pleasure's all mine.'

'What I was thinking,' Biscuit continued, 'is that we agree to negotiate on something extra to purchase from Ms Winter's collection. Something special enough to cost thirteen mil. You get to say you made three hundred mil, Silantra and I get our extra piece, and Gray gets to meet Ms Winter.'

'I'm her biggest fan!' Gray said. 'I'm sure everyone says that to you, but I really am! And also Randon Cliffe's! God, what a handsome man.'

He looked hopeful.

'I was thinking – is there anything that Randon might have worn? I would just *love* that. A watch? Cufflinks? I wouldn't care at all if the style was dated. Just to own something that was once his, that Vivienne Winter had kept . . . wow, that would be *amazing*!'

'I can't promise anything,' Christine said, thinking quickly; any items Vivienne possessed that had belonged to Randon Cliffe had not been part of the sale. She had no idea whether they existed – or whether Vivienne might be prepared to part with them if they did. 'But even if there isn't something of Randon's, I'm sure we can work out something suitable for a man to wear.'

Vivienne still owned a great deal of jewellery that she had told Christine she would never wear again – items they had decided not to list in order to avoid the auction becoming unduly repetitive. Brooches and tennis bracelets, in particular; the former were much less fashionable than they had been, the latter simply not that distinctive or interesting. There was plenty of raw material to work with.

'Nowadays there's a big trend to reset pieces of ladies' jewellery into cufflinks or shirt studs, for instance,' she continued. 'It often happens with family jewels, when they're willed to a male heir who wants to wear them himself. I'm positive that we could come up with some pieces that were gifted to Vivienne by Randon Cliffe that we could repurpose to be worn by you, Mr Macfarland. Then you'd have the link between Vivienne and Randon that you're after.'

'Gray, please! And wow, that would be just wonderful!' Lil' Biscuit's 'good friend' exclaimed with a beaming smile.

Suddenly, a vivid image popped into Christine's mind. It was of Vivienne's photograph of Randon's erect penis with the long strand of pearls wrapped around it, the strand that had sold tonight for nearly a million pounds, though without the photograph rights attached; much as Vivienne had been amused to see that picture, she had not given her consent for it to be made public.

Looking from Lil' Biscuit to Gray, however, Christine realized wistfully how much she could have negotiated from these clients in a private sale for the pearl necklace together with that photograph and a very strict confidentiality agreement never to have it reproduced. No question at all, these two men would have paid an absolute fortune, and they were clearly very used to keeping secrets. Gray might never have worn that pearl necklace in public, but she was sure that he and Lil' Biscuit would find plenty of uses for it in private.

Reluctantly, she pushed aside speculations of how much extra she could have made from this very particular sale. She could charge a great deal for whatever she did sell to them.

As with the Elizabeth Taylor auction, the costume jewellery pieces in particular had tonight raised sums way beyond anything they would normally have fetched. A charm bracelet given to Vivienne on the set of *Nefertiti* – just a silver chain hung with different Italian-themed trinkets as a memento of her stay in Rome, possibly a gift from a producer but so trivial by Vivienne's standards that no one could even remember – had gone for eight thousand pounds, rather than the five hundred at which Christine had set the reserve.

She glanced at Lil' Biscuit. 'Of course, our valuation will be influenced by the price inflation we've seen at the auction,' she pointed out. 'Clearly, buyers are putting even more of a premium on Vivienne's pieces than we realized.'

Lil' Biscuit inclined his head towards her, a silent appreciation of her bargaining skills, acknowledging that she had just told him that what he would be buying for that thirteen million dollars would, considering the book value of the gems in question, seem distinctly overpriced.

'And we can meet her now?' Gray asked with unrestrained enthusiasm. 'This is so exciting!' He was clasping his hands together. 'Wow, I can't believe I'm going to meet Vivienne Winter! James, I'm so excited!'

Lil' Biscuit shot him a glance in which 'Cool it!' and 'Honey, you're so sweet' were equally mingled.

'Okay, we have a deal,' Lil' Biscuit said. 'As long as Gray can take photos with her.'

'Same rules as before – no selfies, but we have a photographer,' Christine said. 'We'll be happy to provide you with several images once Vivienne has approved them.' *And had them retouched and Photoshopped to her specifications, of course.*

As Christine and Lil' Biscuit negotiated, Silantra had slinked over to Tor's side. This was the only possible verb one could use to describe the way she moved in her chosen outfit. Auction guests, still in shock at her appearance, goggled at her unashamedly; Silantra, as always, maintained enough Botox and fillers in her face to look as serene and aloof as her body's rampantly sculpted curves were highly sexualized.

'Hey,' she said to Tor. 'Uh, cool that you're alive.'

'I think so! I certainly prefer it to the other option.'

Tor grinned at her, keeping his eyes firmly on her face. By now, he had had plenty of time to process the presence of a woman covered in what looked like sheer netting, thickly sewn with diamanté, worn over a 1950s-style silver bandeau bikini; but even so, the sight of her abundant cleavage would distract anyone who had a pulse.

'That whole shit that happened to you was *crazy*,' Silantra drawled. 'Like something out of a soap opera! You know, getting knocked on your head and forgetting who you are for a whole, like, *month*. And the local peasants finding you and nursing you back to life.'

Once it had become necessary, for Vivienne's sake, to conceal what Angel had done, this had been the cover story to explain Tor going missing for so long. It was, as Silantra correctly observed, far-fetched, but no one had been able to come up with anything better. She wasn't insinuating that it wasn't true, however; as the most famous reality star in the world, she was expressing appreciation for a truly spectacular real-life plot point.

'In a soap, though,' Silantra was saying, 'there would be this gorgeous girl looking after you, and you'd fall in love with her. But then you'd have a wife back home, and when you remembered her, you'd forget the other one. I saw an old black and white film like that. It was, like, really romantic but sad at the same time.'

'No gorgeous Bolivians looked after me, sadly,' Tor said cheerfully. 'That was a missed opportunity.' He glanced fondly at Christine. 'But I have a lovely lady now.'

'Yeah, that happened fast!' Silantra observed. 'Christine was, like, with Angel last time we were here!'

'After Angel had his breakdown, we comforted each other,' Tor said smoothly. 'These last weeks have just been crazy – you can imagine. Christine's been through so much.'

'Oh yeah, totally! How *is* Angel?'

'Still having his rest cure,' Tor said. 'They think he's got delayed PTSD from all the stress of searching for me. It was really tough on everyone, but Angel apparently pushed himself so hard that he collapsed. When he heard I'd survived after all, it brought it all back and he went into shock.'

He surveyed Silantra with an amiable, bland expression. 'Poor guy,' he added.

'Yeah, that's sad,' Silantra agreed. 'Hey, hopefully he'll be better soon.'

Tor nodded, the expression on his face not altering a whit.

'I was actually sort of wondering,' Silantra said faux-casually, getting to the point of what she had approached Tor to ask, 'if you were in touch with Nicole at all? You know, Angel's friend? I was trying to call her, uh, to see if she's doing okay, 'cause they were pretty close, but her number isn't working any more, and I just get bounceback from her email.'

'I'm sorry, no,' Tor said blankly. 'No idea.'

It was clear to Silantra that he was telling the truth. 'Oh,' she said, deflated. 'D'you think Christine might know?'

'You can ask her, but I'm sure she doesn't,' Tor said, shaking his head. 'Nicole was Angel's friend. Christine wouldn't have any idea where she's got to.'

Silantra, who had found Nicole one of the most talented and inventive sexual partners she had ever encountered, was still pouting in disappointment as Christine gathered the little group together and headed out of the ballroom down the lavishly appointed corridor, tapping on the door marked 'Salon du Lac'. It was a typical five-star, Grand-Hotel-style sitting room, with white and gilt panelled walls, matching side tables laden with vases filled with hothouse flowers, deep-pile carpets and oversized chintz armchairs.

The furniture had been arranged so that Vivienne, settled on a huge sofa, was the centre and focus of the room. A photographer was setting up for the post-auction publicity shots, while the huge TV screen on which she had watched the proceedings was being wheeled off to one side.

Dripping in diamonds, a white fox fur draped round her throat, Vivienne resembled nothing so much as a queen on a throne; crossing the room to pay homage to her definitely felt like approaching royalty. In a matched pair of armchairs on either side of her were her two closest friends in Switzerland, Eugene and Franco, a gay couple who lived in a villa further down towards the lake, and whom she had invited to keep her company during the auction. They had all been drinking champagne cocktails, and Eugene and Franco looked a little tipsy. Their eyes were bright, and Franco's toupee was a little askew. Vivienne reached out swiftly to adjust it.

'Oh, wow, Ms Winter, you must be the most beautiful woman in the world! This is a dream come true for me!' Gray exclaimed, winning an immediate, dazzling smile from Vivienne, who extended her hands and purred:

'Well, what a darling young man! We love him already, don't we, boys? Call me Vivienne, sweetie.'

Striding across the room, Gray practically dropped to his knees in his eagerness to take her hands. Christine effected the introductions, explaining that Lil' Biscuit was prepared to make a purchase that would bring the total auction sum to a round three hundred million dollars. Vivienne, now positively cooing with delight, lavished thanks and compliments on Biscuit, Silantra and Gray, the latter looking as if he were about to cry with happiness at being so close to his idol.

Christine gave the photographer his instructions and stood back as Lil' Biscuit and Gray took seats on the sofa, flanking Vivienne, while Silantra stood behind the trio, beaming a smile, showing off both her magnificent teeth and her magnificent bosom. As the photographs were being taken, Toby and Missy entered the room, clinging to each other with shy, conspiratorial smiles. Toby had placed a bid, through a proxy, on a comparatively small Burmese ruby ring of Vivienne's as an engagement present for Missy, and it had succeeded. Missy had just been told the news.

She was going to wear the ring on a chain around her neck for a year, during which they would keep the engagement secret to determine whether Missy could cope with the tensions of being both a film star and a royal bride. Serious discussions would ensue between the palace and Missy's team to see if this could be made to work. What kind of restrictions would have to be imposed on Missy's career choices for the palace to accept her as Toby's fiancée? Would she be prepared to go along with their dictates and consider her status as a possible member of the royal family to be at least as important as her job?

No one sensible or practical would have placed money on Toby and Missy actually managing to make the engagement work, let alone the marriage; but at that moment the sight of their blissful faces, their arms around each other, their identical dazed expressions of happiness, was so adorable that it would have been downright cruel to do anything but offer congratulations and best wishes.

Eugene and Franco, sipping their latest round of cocktails, watched Toby and Missy, as well as the group around Vivienne, in sheer gossip ecstasy. They could be relied upon for absolute discretion. The couple had known Vivienne and Dieter for many years and never breathed a word to anyone about the stories Vivienne had told them, the celebrities they had seen get drunk or take drugs and behave scandalously at her parties; Vivienne trusted them implicitly.

In fact, as the group was rearranging itself for a different setup, Vivienne winked at both her dear friends, signalling that she was very much looking forward to dissecting this whole hugely juicy scene the next day. It was the ritual on New Year's Day for her to join Eugene and Franco for a lavish brunch they hosted. For years, it had been her and Dieter heading down the hill in their chauffeured Rolls, but now it was just Vivienne, sitting in state in the back of the enormous car, arriving to a spread of Beluga caviar with sour cream on blinis, tiny Alpine strawberries grown at great expense in Eugene and Franco's greenhouse, cherries pickled by their Slavic housekeeper, and little *budini di riso*, sweet custard rice tarts driven up from the best bakery in Lugano on the morning of New Year's Eve.

Eugene and Franco had picked Vivienne up that evening and brought her to the auction in their own Rolls, and when she was visibly tiring after the series of visitors to the Salon du Lac had lavished her with congratulations on how wonderfully the auction had gone, they escorted her out again. It was a triumphal procession, Vivienne leaning on Tor's arm and smiling from side to side at the hotel guests and auction participants who flooded out into the hotel's reception to see her. The crowds fell to each side on her slow approach like the parting of the Red Sea, fans calling: 'We love you, Vivienne!' and breaking into applause.

She waved to them graciously, the liveried doormen springing to open both sets of doors for her, the lavender Rolls waiting at the bottom of the steps.

'Thank you, dear,' she said to Tor as he handed her into the car. 'I'm very happy for you. She's a nice girl.'

'She is,' Tor said, his smile beaming. 'She is a very nice girl indeed.'

He pressed Vivienne's hand as he released it. There was nothing he could say about Angel. How did you condole with a woman who had been forced to shoot her own grandson in self-defence, especially when that grandson had previously tried to murder you?

Tor knew that Vivienne had lied to Christine about him in order to give Angel more of a chance with her. While he did not understand why it had been so important for Vivienne to push Christine into Angel's arms, he was not surprised that Vivienne, as always, had put her own interests first. Tor had applied his usual logical approach to the situation, recognized that he couldn't change a selfish old woman who had somehow become part of his extended family, and forgiven her.

He knew, besides, that Vivienne had talked to Christine, taking back the stories she had told about him and giving, as it were, her blessing to Christine and Tor as a couple. That was more than enough for him. The past was the past, as far as Tor was concerned.

Unexpectedly, Vivienne reached out to hug him, causing him to crane awkwardly into the back seat of the car.

'And you're a good boy, Tor,' she said softly. 'I'm very glad you're still here with us.'

He hugged her and then stepped back, offering a hand as stability for Franco and Eugene as they climbed in too, both elderly men relishing the opportunity to wink and flirt with big, good-looking Tor. He shut the door, the Rolls pulled away, and Christine came to his side to wave Vivienne off. Behind them, the windows of the hotel were filled with faces pressed unashamedly to the glass, watching the legendary Vivienne Winter make a magnificent exit.

'And now you can relax,' Tor said to Christine, wrapping an arm around her.

She huffed out an ironic giggle.

'Tor, it may be New Year's Day tomorrow, but I have

back-to-back meetings with people collecting their pieces before they fly out of the country! And then, on the second, I've literally got to start organizing transports all over the world. I told you, I've got a solid month of work ahead of me . . . oh, and I should go to Vivienne's tomorrow, if I can, and put together a list of things Lil' Biscuit would want that I can get away with charging thirteen million for! I'd love to get that extra money as soon as possible so that I can claim the three hundred million on the press release.'

She paused.

'Wow, listen to me! I honestly can't believe I've pulled this off – *three hundred million!* This has been the most insane year of my life. I genuinely feel as if I'm going to wake up tomorrow and realize it's all been a dream.'

Despite her list of everything she had still to do, she relaxed back into the curve of Tor's arm. It was very cold outside; snow had been predicted for that evening, and there was that sharp snap in the air, a sting in the nostrils with every inhalation, that suggested it was on its way. The sky had been white all day, and barely any stars could be seen over the lake. But the two of them lingered even after the tail lights of the Rolls had vanished down the Quai du Mont Blanc, relishing a moment together.

The last week had been so jammed with work that Christine had only stopped to eat, wash and sleep. Tor had flown in that day to spend New Year's Eve with her, and she could only hope that she would get the jewels back to the Berkeley safe and locked away, the organization of the post-sale business wound down, before the stroke of midnight.

'You're freezing!' Tor eventually exclaimed. 'We should go

in.' He pulled her in front of him and started rubbing her bare arms vigorously to warm her up.

'Let's stay just another minute. It's bracing,' Christine said, taking a long deep breath of icy air, feeling it chill her lungs. 'I need this after being inside all day.'

'We'll come back in the spring,' Tor said. 'Right in front of where we're standing is a huge fountain. Actually, it's crazier than that – it's not really a fountain, just an enormous spray of water called the *Jet d'Eau*. It's so big you can see it from the sky when you fly over the city. It's been too windy to turn it on while you've been here – no one wants people on the Quai du Mont Blanc to get soaked as they walk along the promenade. But when they light it up, it's stunning. Very romantic. We'll come back and stand right here, just like this, and watch it with all the time in the world, because you won't have to rush back and do a million things . . .'

Christine had coped with the shock of Angel's betrayal, to a large degree, by pushing it to the back of her mind; she was so consumed by the demands of the auction that it had been the only way to survive. When it was all over – which would take at least a few more weeks – she was planning to take a holiday, go back to the Hotel Tylösand. This time she could soak in the spa, walk on the beach, fully relax. It would be like restarting her life after the insanity that had been her time with Angel; pressing a reset button, climbing out of the rabbit hole she had fallen down the first time she saw him in the spa and was star-struck by his beauty.

She did not feel damaged by what had happened with Angel. Shocked, disoriented, hugely relieved it was over; but not damaged. It was as if she had been loaded on to a rollercoaster ride that had whirled her around, taken her to dizzying heights, then dropped her from them with terrifying speed, spun her so fast and furiously that she had completely lost any sense of orientation. Finally, though, it had brought her back to the start: no bones broken, but needing plenty of time to catch her breath, settle back down, let her bruises fade, feel the ground once more stable beneath her feet.

Christine's plan was to tell Tor that she wanted a few days at Tylösand by herself. They hadn't yet had sex: when you came off a ride that crazy, you were totally shaken up, your legs wobbly, your whole body reeling. You didn't get on another one straight away, but you clung to something steady while you got your bearings. Tor was not only steady but fully prepared to wait, the opposite of Angel: exactly what she needed. She would go to Tylösand, immerse herself in beauty and tranquillity, be by herself with nothing to do but relax for long enough to get used to it . . . and then, when she was ready, she would want to see Tor.

Hopefully when I ring him and ask him to come, he'll be around! she thought ironically. *It'll be my bad luck if he's training for an expedition, or filming himself heli-skiing down a mountain in America . . .*

If he could come, he would. If not, it would be her turn to wait, as he was now patiently waiting for her. And that would be okay too.

'I can't wait to come back here with you,' she told him.

Tor tilted his head back, looking up at the sky.

'Snow's coming,' he observed. 'The lake will be beautiful tomorrow.'

Christine reached up to kiss him lightly.

'Will you come for a walk with me during the day?' she said. 'I'll sneak out for an hour or so to get some fresh air.'

'I can think of nothing I would rather do on New Year's Day than take a walk by Lake Geneva with you by my side,' he said gravely, wrapping his arm around her. 'I wonder if I can hire a wetsuit to make another dramatic entrance to impress you? God knows if there's any bank to the lake, though! I might end up crawling out of it on my belly like a seal, which wouldn't be quite so impressive . . .'

Christine was giggling at this image as they turned to go back inside. And, cold as she was by now, she felt a warm rush of happiness as she realized that, on the whole of her mad rollercoaster ride strapped in next to Angel, he had never once made her laugh the way Tor did.

Chapter Twenty-Four

Rio de Janeiro – New Year's Eve

'They're calling it the sale of the century!' the TV presenter announced with fulsome American enthusiasm. 'It's a truly historic event, as you can tell just by the A-list celebrities who are gathered here in Switzerland to celebrate the "Life in Jewels" of Vivienne Winter . . .'

Lounging in a hammock on the balcony of her hotel suite, sipping a caipirinha, Nicole watched the results of the auction being reported on the tablet propped on her lap. The sun had set a while ago and the last deep golden rays were still fading from the sky, streaking the glorious expanse of sea, but Nicole's attention was entirely on the screen. CNN and the BBC were both covering the jewellery sale with great enthusiasm, compensating for the absence of Vivienne in the auction room by showing clips of her at premieres wearing the most famous of her jewellery, Randon by her side.

The cameras panned eagerly over the invitees whose faces were instantly recognizable to the public: Prince Toby, Missy, Lil' Biscuit, Silantra, Gray, the singer Catalina and her new husband. Behind Catalina was seated the Countess of Rutland, wearing one of Vivienne's tiaras in her magnificently arranged rose-gold hair; she was accompanied by her good friend Lady Margaret McArdle, the Earl having remained at their stately home to look after their twin daughters.

Nicole's eyes widened when the reporter, nearly breathless with excitement, announced the sum that had been raised. Three hundred million! It was more than anyone had expected.

'Well, I did my bit to help! You're welcome,' she murmured, raising her glass at the screen.

It was eight thirty in the evening, and she needed to start getting ready. She had been invited to an exclusive New Year's Eve party in the rooftop suite of a visiting Venezuelan businessman she had met by the hotel pool earlier in the week. But she lingered, watching Christine on the screen being interviewed about the success of the sale. A dowdy little thing, who really should have got her hair and make-up professionally done if she was going to be on TV.

Nicole's mouth twisted as she surveyed Christine, noticing her beautiful necklace – pearls and diamonds, set in gold filigree. Christine couldn't possibly have afforded that herself; it must have been a gift from Vivienne. The little bitch had come out of this very well! Angel was locked away in some upmarket loony bin for posh people, Vivienne had never got that great-grandchild she was so desperate for, and yet here was Christine, smelling of roses, draped in jewellery Vivienne had given her. With Tor standing behind her, no less.

How on earth had Tor survived Angel's pushing him off that mountain? The story about him being rescued, comatose, by heroic Bolivian peasants, and only recovering his memory after a month, was ridiculous, but the media seemed to have eaten it up with great excitement. Tor's quiet reluctance to be interviewed at length about his ordeal had made him even more of a hero in the eyes of the world. One journalist was pushing a microphone into his face now and asking eager questions about his miraculous survival, which Tor was fending off politely, explaining that he was here to support his godmother and didn't want to draw attention away from the incredible amount of money her auction had made for charity.

Nicole had no idea what had actually gone down in London. All she knew was that Angel had dropped completely off the radar. It had been a frightening time, as she rang his phone over and over again, eventually getting the recorded information that his mailbox was full and could take no more messages. Sensing that something had gone badly wrong, she had packed up and left the apartment she had been renting, checking into a hotel under an assumed name.

The following day, she had taken the risk of going to his apartment building and bribing the doorman to find out what he knew. The information that Angel had been the subject of a police raid, that three men had been taken out from his apartment in handcuffs and that glaziers were up in the penthouse at that moment, replacing the glass that had been smashed in by (as the doorman had been told by an excited policeman) an SAS guy abseiling down from the roof and breaking dramatically into the apartment, had been more than enough for Nicole. She had not gone this long without an arrest to her name by taking unnecessary risks.

Immediately she had decided against using her keys to sneak into Angel's apartment and access his safe. For all she knew, they had posted an officer there or set up cameras to see if anyone would try to do exactly that. Instead she had returned to her hotel, packed up and taken a Eurostar to Paris, and thence a plane to Rio de Janeiro – travelling with a fake passport, of course.

Thankfully it was Angel, and Angel alone, who was on the hook for the theft of the rings and the pendant. Nicole, as was her wont, had been careful to avoid leaving her finger-prints on anything, literally or metaphorically. None of the gem cutters she had spoken to in Amsterdam would say a word to the authorities. She thoroughly regretted not having taken the diamonds with her to the Netherlands, but Angel had insisted on holding on to the real ones for as long as possible, wanting to wait until, hopefully, more people had viewed the fakes at Berkeley.

His reasoning had been self-protective. If several clients had looked at the diamonds and not spotted that they were substitutes – because Nicole had been assured that only the most expert, proficient gemmologist would be able to tell the difference between real and fake – Christine would have a longer list of possible suspects, and Angel would not be in the frame. He could sympathize with his girlfriend without her having any doubts about his involvement. Whereas if she noticed the fakes soon after Toby and Angel had looked at them, and told Angel about them, he would have the real ones on hand and could at least attempt to switch them back.

Still, even though it was Angel in whose possession the diamonds had presumably been found, it was definitely wisest for Nicole to leave London as soon as possible. She had to assume that if Christine and the police had discovered the jewellery substitution, they might also have connected

Nicole in some way to the fakes. She had no idea for how long Angel had been under observation, whether his phone or apartment had been bugged. The only safe course was to slip away discreetly. Once she had left the country, she was fairly confident that no one would bother to pursue her.

Nicole had told Angel that the finder's fee from Silantra and Lil' Biscuit would be payable when the auction was over, but she had lied. The contracts were signed; as soon as they had become the legal owners of the jewels, the money had been wired to her account at the bank in the Turks and Caicos, adding to the considerable balance she had previously maintained there.

So she had no money worries, which was always pleasant, and Brazil was as friendly and welcoming as ever. She made an appointment with one of its best plastic surgeons, an international celebrity with his own private island off the coast of Rio, where his most exclusive clients were invited to recuperate. Nicole had decided that it was time for some tweaks to her appearance. She had always wanted a rounder bottom than her flat Asian one, curves that she could flaunt in a thong on Ipanema beach. Her ideal posterior, in fact, was Silantra's, as was many women's, but Nicole knew her smaller frame would look ridiculous with those cosmetically exaggerated cushions.

More importantly, she also needed to alter her features. It was a shame: she was very fond of her natural face. But she had a sex tape to sell of herself and Silantra together during their rendezvous in Paris, and she absolutely could not afford to be identifiable as the woman not just romping naked with the reality star, but giggling with amusement as she encouraged Silantra to speculate on what her husband was getting up to, halfway across the world, with his boyfriend. The part where Silantra, donning her favourite strap-on, told Nicole that she was going to give it to her up the ass, make Nicole her bitch just like Gray did with Lil' Biscuit, was worth a fortune. Nicole had invested a lot of money in the spy camera built into that heavy leather tote bag she had carried to Paris, but it had definitely paid off.

Still, once Lil' Biscuit found out that Nicole, after taking a huge finder's fee, had betrayed him and Silantra so badly, his wrath would be mighty, and Nicole had no intention of living in seclusion for the rest of her life. She wanted to party in LA and New York, in Miami and Tokyo and Antibes, without constantly looking over her shoulder for him or one of his minions ready to wreak revenge. And in order to be sure she could do that, she needed to be unidentifiable.

Her plan was to offer the video directly to Biscuit and Silantra. She had briefly considered selling it to an online website, but discarded the idea, because if the tape became public, Lil' Biscuit would undoubtedly hunt her down like a dog. The rap scene was not a safe place for women who kissed and told. Rumours still swirled about another mogul married to a very famous singer; his secret girlfriend had allegedly threatened to go to the tabloids with all sorts of gossip about their setup, only to die shortly afterwards in mysterious circumstances.

Going public was, therefore, not an option. Certainly, blackmailing Lil' Biscuit and Silantra would make them extremely angry, but they would pay her an extortionately large sum of money as long as she signed a cast-iron confidentiality agreement that would both bankrupt her and send her to prison if she ever sold the video to anyone else. Stabbing them in the back, on the other hand – by selling it to TMZ or a porn site – *that* would be grounds for the same fate as the secret girlfriend had suffered.

So Nicole's eyes would become more angled. The surgeon was intrigued by her request to deepen the epicanthic fold, as clients invariably wanted it reduced, not exaggerated. That in itself would be enough to make her much less recognizable; no one would suspect that someone with Chinese heritage would undergo surgery to emphasize it, since the prevailing fashion in Asia was to make oneself look more Western, not less so. Her chin would become more defined, her cheeks less full. Subtle alterations, but ones that would change her face sufficiently so that, if she had the bad luck to bump into Silantra or Lil' Biscuit, post-surgery, she would not be recognizable as the Nicole who had had vigorous sex with Silantra and then sold them the evidence.

It truly had been excellent sex, Nicole thought rather wistfully. But opportunities for a large score were finite, while those for sexual pleasure were, in her experience, positively infinite. Look at this evening: the charming and handsome Venezuelan businessman had been eager to assure her of the many other attractive guests who would be attending. There was a hot tub on his roof terrace, the cocktails would flow, and other substances, the businessman had assured her, would be readily available; the perfect way to spend New Year's Eve. Nicole was fresh from a thorough waxing by the hotel's beautician. All she had to do was rub gold-flecked oil into every crevice of her body, don her tiny Eres bikini, slip on a silk Agent Provocateur cover-up and glide upstairs, ready to watch the midnight firework display as she created some explosions of her own.

She missed Angel. God knew what he was going through in the upmarket mental facility in which Vivienne had incarcerated him. But, Nicole reflected, finishing her caipirinha, she had seen Angel arrive at the Chateau Sainte-Beuve a comparatively naive fourteen-year-old, only to take to the regime there more eagerly than any student before or since. She would certainly not put it past him, after a while, to have the medical staff of the loony bin eating out of his hand, willing to certify him as fully recovered in return for being initiated into the very specific and delicious games that Angel knew so well how to play.

Regretfully, she reached round to rub her bottom, which no longer bore any marks from Angel's various activities. She did hope, for his sake, that he was managing to convince someone to spank him every so often. She was crossing her fingers that tonight she might find a sexual partner whose tastes were more chilli than vanilla . . .

Christine and Tor were on screen together now, clinking glasses with the director of Berkeley Geneva and the chief executive of Vivienne's charity foundation. The image switched to a shot of Vivienne, draped in diamonds and white sable, being escorted through the lavishly appointed corridor of the Geneva hotel, crowds lining the passageway, applauding her and calling her name as she graciously smiled from side to side, her bearing even more regal than ever.

I really hope they're not letting Angel watch the television in that hospital Vivienne's put him in, Nicole reflected. *Because if he sees this, he'll pick up anything in his room that isn't nailed down and throw it right at the screen.*

Chapter Twenty-Five

Montreux – New Year's Eve

As Nicole readied herself for that evening's party, back in Switzerland the three occupants of the back seat of the lavender Rolls were happily drifting off to sleep, lulled by the smooth motion. Worn out by the excitement of that evening, they had all closed their eyes as soon as the car had pulled away, quite understanding that they were merely postponing their delightful gossip until the next day, over brunch. It was an hour's drive back to Montreux, on the far side of Lake Geneva, and Vivienne, Eugene and Franco were fast asleep as the Rolls swept through Lausanne, not waking as the great car reached the town of Montreux and began to climb into the hills above it.

Fifteen minutes later, the car came to a halt on Vivienne's driveway, and Gregory, seated beside the chauffeur, opened the panel behind him. The sound of soft snoring was the only sound that greeted him. He gave several loud taps on the glass, hearing the occupants shuffle and stir themselves; then a couple more taps, just to make sure they were all awake. He got out of the car, his movements unhurried, giving them time to collect themselves, stretching his arms and rolling his neck, eventually opening the door for Vivienne.

'We're home, Madame,' he said, glancing briefly, tactfully, inside the now-illuminated interior of the Rolls. Vivienne was letting out a yawn as she adjusted her wig – Franco was doing much the same with his toupee – and composed her expression to full alertness. The three passengers kissed each other, and Eugene offered, as one or other of the elderly men always did when saying goodbye on New Year's Eve:

'Darling, you're very welcome to come to us tonight, you know. The guest suite's ready and waiting for you, and Gregory can bring you anything you need from here.'

And Vivienne smiled and gave the accustomed response:

'You're so sweet, darling. But no, thank you, I prefer to sleep in my own bed and wake up in my own house. I'll see you for brunch at noon.'

'The *budini di riso* came up from Lugano today!' Franco piped up. 'So delicious, I'm tempted to have one before bed tonight . . .'

'You should, my love,' Vivienne said, taking the hand that Gregory had extended inside the car to give her enough help to pull herself out. 'Treat yourself. We're not going to be around for ever, are we?'

'Good night, *carissima*!' Eugene said.

'*So* much to talk about tomorrow!' Franco added happily.

A retainer less established than Gregory, less familiar with Vivienne's ways, might have expected Vivienne to go straight to bed after such a busy day. But tonight was New Year's Eve, and this was a very particular anniversary for Vivienne. It was the night that Randon had died, flying his Cessna while insanely drunk, heading across the Channel in a doomed attempt to see her by midnight.

491

Days previously, their second divorce had been finalized. They had both agreed, utterly exhausted, that they had nothing left to give; they had spent the previous two years tearing away at each other. When they were apart on film sets, they had thrown themselves into well-publicized affairs in an attempt to torment one another; when they were together, they had spent their evenings drinking their way through San Lorenzo's wine cellar before staggering out, screeching at each other in the middle of Knightsbridge as they made their way tipsily back to Brompton Square, nearly causing a series of late-night bus and taxi crashes.

But none of that, in the end, had made Randon and Vivienne decide to divorce again. It was the realization that the revenge affairs had followed the same pattern; the words they were yelling had been spoken hundreds of times before. Even the drunken lurches across Knightsbridge, horns blaring, brakes squealing, drivers sticking their heads out to curse at them and then yelling in amazement when they realized who they were – even those had happened so many times that suddenly, one evening, as Randon banged on the front door of the Brompton Square house, shouting at Vivienne, who had made it home first, to undo the double bolt and let him in, he stopped abruptly in the middle of a string of curses, sank to the doorstep and closed his eyes. And Vivienne, slumped in an armchair in the living room, didn't realize for several minutes that he had stopped yelling, because her ears were ringing so loudly with the echoes of her own shouts back at him.

When she eventually got up and opened the door, finding him collapsed on the entry step, half snoring, she looked down and said simply: 'We're on a terrible merry-go-round, Randon, my sweet. It's time to get off.'

'I was thinking "ancient rep circuit",' he said, looking up at her. 'Like being trapped in hell, forced to act in the same awful play night after night with no way out.'

'We're clichés,' she said, as he heaved himself to his feet. 'I think I saw camera flashes tonight, but we're not the draw we once were.'

'My God, no! In the old days we'd have been followed home by a positive cloud of paps!'

Randon was on his feet, swaying, his eyes blurred with alcohol, his jaw sagging. Propping himself against the door-jamb, he extended one hand to Vivienne.

'We had a great run, didn't we?' he said. 'Best play ever, when it was good. Our own *Private Lives*. But yes, it's over now, Viv, my darling.'

He stuck his hand out; it shook visibly as he extended it.

'"Since there's no help, come let us kiss and part,"' he said, quoting a famous sonnet as he took her hand, planted a kiss on it and let it fall. Turning, he walked unsteadily away down the black and white-tiled walkway, back to the Brompton Road. And Vivienne watched him go without saying a word to bring him back.

It was quintessential Randon to choose a dramatic exit rather than come inside the house and sleep it off in a spare bedroom. He told her later that he had trudged through Knightsbridge to Piccadilly, staggered into the Ritz, demanded the best suite available and passed out there for two days, refusing to let the cleaners enter, sustaining himself entirely on the contents of the minibar.

The divorce, however, had been easy enough. They had no fight left in them, and their lawyers' attempts to stir them up in order to generate more billable hours had fizzled and failed. Having divorced once before, their property had been divided up already, their assets portioned. They had each left the second marriage with exactly what they had brought into it. When the decree nisi came through, Vivienne was in Nice with a lover and Randon in Devon on his estate there, where he had apple orchards and made lethally strong cider and apple brandy every year.

Two empty bottles of the brandy were found on his kitchen table the next day, evidence of how much he had put away before he rang Vivienne at nine o'clock on New Year's Eve and announced that he would be landing in Nice in a couple of hours. He was clearly in no condition to fly a plane. Vivienne, sobbing, had implored him not to do it; she had called the local police station to tell them what he was planning, rung friends in the UK and begged them to ring 999. But Randon's mansion was twenty miles from the closest village. By the time a police car reached it, the Cessna had already taken off from his private airstrip.

He had gone off the radar twenty minutes after leaving the English coast behind, and in his transmissions to air traffic control he had been slurring his words so badly that it was hard to make many of them out. In answer to their increasingly horrified instructions, all he had done was to repeat, over and over again, the same words:

'I'm going to see Vivienne. I have to see Vivienne . . .'

Those recorded transmissions had been played endlessly in the years after his death, torture for Vivienne; every time she heard them, in a snatch of a television programme or radio broadcast, they brought back all the horror of the few hours that had followed, the worst of Vivienne's life. Her great fear, of course, was that Randon would crash his plane and kill others as well as himself; and even when, after a while, she realized that he must surely have cleared the British coastline, there was still the possibility that he would manage to cross the Channel, make landfall in France and wreak havoc there.

She stayed up all night and most of the next day, waiting to hear of a Cessna wrecked in some remote area, a witness who had seen a plane go down over a mountain range. Eventually she passed out with exhaustion. When she awoke, the lack of news meant, as everyone knew, that Randon's plane must be at the bottom of the sea.

Although they had seemed as alike as two peas in a pod, Randon and Vivienne had turned out to be radically different. He was stuck in his pattern of wild living, had continued to drink like a fish after their break-up, while Vivienne found that whenever they were separated, her alcohol consumption became much more moderate. A naturally addictive person-ality, Randon had added Vivienne to the list of things he could not do without. Vivienne had eventually outgrown the relationship, but he had not. With a clear, cold eye, Vivienne had assessed her situation and realized that as long as she stayed with Randon, she would be trapped in chaos with him.

So she had moved on, spending that fatal New Year's Eve with a lover, not a bottle of brandy. Vivienne was aware that Randon had made that last, drunken flight out of desperation, because he knew that for her, the break-up was final this time. He had never meant to kill himself, she was sure of that. But the recklessness that made him so dangerously attractive, his love for the impulsive, dramatic gesture, had been fatally exacerbated by a sense that this time, he had nothing left to lose.

New Year's Eve had never, since then, been a date of celebration for Vivienne. She could only see it as an end, never a beginning. As she entered her villa, Gregory knew not to help her off with her furs. Instead, he moved ahead of her to open one of the French windows that led onto the terrace, with its magnificent view of Montreux and Lake Geneva below. Normally, Vivienne would have kicked off her shoes on entering the house, but tonight, still swaddled in her sables, she followed Gregory across the huge living room, stepping outside as he poured her a Calvados in a snifter glass and brought it out to where she stood on the terrace.

Vivienne did not drink it, however. Taking the glass with a nod of thanks, she set it on the wide stone balcony and stood, elbows propped on the balcony, as Gregory retired to the kitchen to foam milk for her bedtime drink, to which he would add a few drops of amaretto. Below her shone the bright white headlights of cars descending the hill road to join the midnight party in Montreux, their red tail lights flashing in and out of the curves like traces of fire. Villas set into the hillside gleamed softly, their windows curtained against the cold night air.

There were very few stars tonight. She had never stood here with Randon, but they had both been night owls, had often gazed at the midnight sky together. He knew most of the constellations, and after pointing them out to her with an air of triumph, he was prone to quote Keats:

> 'And when I see upon the night's starred face
> Huge cloudy symbols of a high romance
> And think that I may never live to trace
> Their shadows, with the magic hand of chance . . .'

But Randon never continued the sonnet to its finish. Beautiful as its last couplet was, its words were quite opposed to how Vivienne and Randon had chosen to live their lives.

> '. . . I stand alone and think
> Till love and fame to nothingness do sink.'

To the two of them, love and fame were everything; and not all kinds of love, either. They had loved each other and themselves with equal intensity. For Vivienne, the love of a mother for her daughter, or a grandmother for her grandson, had been lesser things. Randon and she had never been more than children themselves, she knew – selfish, spoilt children who had never grown up, reaching for their objects of passion, ignoring anything that stood in their way.

At her age, Vivienne was brutally honest with herself about who she was and the choices she had made. She had pushed Pearl aside for Randon, and she had never looked after Angel the way she should have done. She remembered a line from that film she had shot decades ago, *In Love and War*, playing the Spanish peasant girl, with Randon as the heroic British rifleman: 'Take what you want, and pay for it, says God.' It was a Spanish proverb; she had delivered that line over his dying body, tears pouring from her magnificent eyes. Even in her unconvincing accent, she had reduced audiences around the world to tears.

It was exactly what she and Randon had done: taken what they wanted, and paid the price. Looking back, she could acknowledge that Pearl and Angel had been part of that price.

But only to a degree. They were adults. They had made their own choices, and in their turn had chosen the consequences. It was so painful, still, to remember Angel as a little boy, that adorable child, so beautiful, so innocent, forced by Pearl that terrible day in Paris to hide the jewels that she had stolen . . . Thierry's body on the floor, blood pouring from his smashed face . . . and then Angel himself lying in her boudoir, his face broken and bloody in a horrible echo of Thierry. Oh, those cries of Angel's when Baxter led him from the room all those years ago, when Vivienne had forced Pearl to give her custody of him, his little heart breaking at being separated from his mother . . .

Had Angel been doomed from that moment? Vivienne had asked herself that question many times. After that scene – after seeing his mother murder a man to cover up her own crime – would Angel ever have had a chance to be normal? Even if Vivienne had spent more time with him, would that have helped? After all, what did she, a film star from childhood, know about being normal? She had failed, signally, with Pearl. For Angel, she had tried to find the best nannies and schools that money could buy, and that hadn't worked either.

Vivienne had been a great lover, but a terrible mother and grandmother. That was the truth, and Vivienne faced the truth squarely. She had chosen her two great loves, fame and romance, over her daughter and her grandson, and she would almost certainly make the same decisions if she had it to do over again.

Vivienne knew that she wasn't crying. And yet her face felt damp, she realized; damp and icy cold.

She looked up to the black sky. The long-forecast snow was here, falling so softly that she hadn't noticed it at first. It was time to finish the ritual. Time to go inside to her cosy bed, her warm, foamy milk and her memories. She never took a sleeping pill on New Year's Eve. She liked to lie in bed, tucked up and snug, indulging herself in a rhapsody of wonderful memories of Randon in his heyday, when he had been at the height of his beauty. The glory they had lived together, the sheer, overwhelming delight of being the king and queen of the world for those wonderful years . . .

Ah well, nothing lasted forever. Snow was falling into the glass of Calvados; if she left it much longer, it would dilute, and Randon would have hated that. Vivienne raised the glass, icy now and frosted with snow, and poured the brandy in a long, slow trail of tawny liquid over the edge of the balcony.

Gregory, who had been with her for years, was familiar with her New Year's Eve ritual. He would never disturb her, just as Dieter, too, had been tactful enough to leave her alone for as long as she needed. But Gregory was concerned at Vivienne staying out for long in the cold midnight air, and by now the snow was falling fast. He allowed himself the faintest tap on the open French window, the tiniest creak as it moved on its hinges, an infinitesimal signal that it was time for her to come in.

He was quite right. It was freezing, and it was very late. Pulling her sables closer around her, Vivienne turned back to the house. Gregory was waiting to help her over the threshold and take the furs; Vivienne made her way to the lift that would carry her up to her room, the bedtime drink waiting for her on her bedside table in its insulated mug, the silk pyjamas folded for her on the coverlet, the cashmere bedjacket, and Louison curled up by the pillows, purring softly.

Gregory began to pull the heavy velvet curtains closed, moving more slowly than usual. It had been a long day for him, too, and he was tired. Outside, the snow was falling more and more heavily, settling in a thick layer, muffling everything in a pall of white until, in only a few minutes, the brandy that Vivienne had poured out in memory of the love of her life was no longer visible.

Acknowledgements

Huge thanks to:

The amazing team at Pan Macmillan, who continue to be the most fantastic publishers – smart, loyal and brilliant. My editor Wayne Brookes is not only superb but a hilarious correspondent! I will miss the lovely and efficient Louise Buckley and Eloise Wood, but the charming Alex Saunders is already tasked with giving me information about how to do my hair for future events . . . Kate Green is a great publicist and Jeremy Trevathan a wonderful and very amusing publisher! Stuart Dwyer does a terrific job with my UK sales and I'm so grateful to James Annal for his fantastic cover designs.

Dan Evans at Plan 9, who does such a superb job with my website and business cards; you should all use him for yours.

Matt B, my reading twin, as always, for all his help, support and loans of Eleanor Burford/Philippa Carr/Jean Plaidy/Kathleen Kellow/Anna Percival/Elbur Ford books!

Sarah Weinman, who fell over while walking and reading *Mile High* and subsequently raved about it so much a publisher promptly emailed me to ask about US rights!

The team of Facebookers who suggested names of 'Songs to Push People off the Mountain to': Dawn Turnbull for 'Free Falling', Tony Wood for 'Slip Sliding Away', Alison Gaylin for 'Push It', Franco Milazzo for 'He'll Be Coming Down the Mountain', Sally Quilford for 'Come Fly With Me', Nikki Bywater for 'Skyfall', and Britin Haller for 'Wind Beneath My Wings'.

Lee Clatworthy for suggesting 'libertine' as a perfect, non-sexist way to describe Grace Kelly's wild ways with men!

The gorgeous team of McKenna Jordan and John Kwiatkowski and everyone at Murder by the Book, for bringing my smut to Texas.

I couldn't have written this book without the Rebecca Chance fanfriends on Facebook and Twitter cheering me up with delightful banter! My thanks goes to Angela Collings, Dawn Hamblett, Tim Hughes, Lauren O'Brien, Jason Ellis, Tony Wood, Melanie Hearse, Jen Sheehan, Helen Smith, Ilana Bergsagel, Katherine Everett, Julian Corkle, Robin Greene, Diane Jolly, Adam Pietrowski, John Soper, Gary Jordan, Louise Bell, Lisa Respers France, Stella Duffy, Shelley Silas, Rowan Coleman, Serena Mackesy, Tim Daly, Joy T. Chance, Lori Smith Jennaway, Alex Marwood, Sallie Dorsett, Alice Taylor, Joanne Wade, Marjorie Tucker, Teresa Wilson, Ashley James Cardwell, Margery Flax, Clinton Reed, Valerie Laws, Kelly Butterworth, Kirsty Maclennan, Amanda Marie Fulton, Marie Causey, Shana Mehtaab, Tracy Hanson, Beverley Ann Hopper, Nancy Pace Koffman, Katrina Smith, Helen Lusher, Russ Fry, Gavin Robinson, Laura Ford, Mary Mulkeen, Eileen McAninly, Pamela Cardone, Barb McNaughton, Shannon Mitchell, Claire Chiswell, Paula Louise Standen, Dawn Turnbull, Fiona Morris,

Michelle Heneghan and Bryan Quertermous, Derek Jones and Colin Butts, the very exclusive (i.e. tiny) club of my straight male readers. Plus, of course, Paul Burston and the loyal Polari crew – Alex Hopkins, Ange Chan, Sian Pepper, Enda Guinan, Belinda Davies, John Southgate, Paul Brown, James Watts, Ian Sinclair Romanis and Jon Clarke. And the handful of beloved relatives brave enough to read my books – Dalia Hartman Bergsagel, Ilana Bergsagel, Sandy Makarwicz and Jean Polito. If I've left anyone out, please do send me a message and I will correct it in the next book!

As always – thanks to the Board.

And love to the FLs of FB, who are all diamonds with a few killers mixed in!

extracts reading groups
competitions books new
discounts extracts extracts
competitions discounts
books new extracts
events books discounts events
extracts new reading groups
new titles reading groups
interviews
books events extracts extracts
discounts events books
new books events interviews new books extracts
events new events

discounts extracts discounts books
www.panmacmillan.com
extracts events reading groups
competitions books extracts new